THE
WATCHER

Kate Medina has always been fascinated by the 'whys' of human behaviour, an interest that drove her to study Psychology at university and later to start a crime series featuring clinical psychologist Dr Jessie Flynn. She has an MA in Creative Writing from Bath Spa University and her debut novel *White Crocodile* received widespread critical acclaim, as did *Fire Damage*, *Scared to Death* and *Two Little Girls*, the first three books in the Jessie Flynn series.

Before turning to writing full time, Kate spent five years in the Territorial Army and has lectured at the London Business School and the London School of Economics. She lives in London with her husband and three children.

 Facebook.com/KateMedinaAuthor
 @KateTMedina

Also by Kate Medina

The Jessie Flynn series
Fire Damage
Scared to Death
Two Little Girls

Standalone novels
White Crocodile

KATE MEDINA

THE WATCHER

HarperCollinsPublishers

HarperCollins*Publishers* Ltd
1 London Bridge Street
London SE1 9GF

www.harpercollins.co.uk

First published by HarperCollins*Publishers* 2020

1

A catalogue record for this book
is available from the British Library

ISBN: 978-0-00-821405-0 (HB)
ISBN: 978-0-00-821406-7 (TPB)

This novel is entirely a work of fiction.
The names, characters and incidents portrayed in it are
the work of the author's imagination. Any resemblance to
actual persons, living or dead, events or localities is
entirely coincidental.

Typeset in Sabon LT Std by
Palimpsest Book Production Limited, Falkirk, Stirlingshire

Printed and bound in Great Britain by
CPI Group (UK) Ltd, Croydon, CR0 4YY

For Bettina and Sean

1

One Year Ago

The jetty was made of weather-beaten wooden slats, yawning gaps between each, and with every step he took Robbie could focus on nothing but the grey-black water heaving twenty metres beneath him. He shuddered and his stomach clenched tight. His mind sought out the last time his father had brought him here, so many years ago that the memory was as distant as the horizon. A family open day at the lifeboat station – he must have been only five or six. It had been midsummer, he remembered, bright sunshine and a faint breeze frothing the tops of the swelling waves. The rusty steel handrails of the jetty had been festooned with blue and red balloons, leading the small children along its rickety fifty-metre-length to the lifeboat shed at its end, drawing their eyes away from the drop to the sea.

But Robbie hadn't been distracted by the balloons.

The very second that he had stepped onto the jetty his attention had been snatched by the chasm below. A jumbled mosaic of brown, yellow and white beach pebbles below him at first, then slippery, seaweed-smothered stones, then that heaving, swirling sea. He had been fixated by that sea – so far beneath – the only thing to stop him falling into its swallowing depths, the bleached wooden stats that flexed and groaned with each timid step he took.

He hadn't even known then, about the boy. Or about the boy's dog.

Even so, he had felt the nastiness of this place. Sensed it.

And now he did know about the boy and about the boy's dog. He knew everything.

One, two, three, four. Don't stand on the cracks in the pavement. Don't stand on the cracks between the planks. The yawning, wide gaps that will suck you down and swallow you whole.

'Robbie.'

His gaze snapped up. Though his father tried to hide his feelings, had learnt to hide them well, Robbie had learnt to read them better and the look of distress in his father's eyes as he'd looked back and caught him stepping awkwardly, sideways, crab-like, from plank to plank, was toddler-book easy to interpret.

You're fourteen not four. His father didn't say it. Couldn't risk it. Couldn't risk upsetting him.

'Are you OK, Robbie?' That empathetic, singsong voice that Robbie had grown to hate.

He nodded, didn't speak. He spoke rarely, only when he had absolutely no choice, when shrugs, eye rolls and hand movements failed to communicate what needed to be said.

His father smiled, an awkward smile that didn't attempt to touch his eyes. He turned and continued his determinedly hearty walk along the jetty toward the lifeboat shed, his yellow cagoule billowing as it filled with autumn wind, making him look like a giant, animated canary. Robbie followed, head down, his gaze focused on the planks, on the grey-blue deadliness far below.

The lifeboat was huge and red, its bow extending from the open doors of the lifeboat shed, towering above them.

'I always wanted to join,' Allan said, running his hand along the boat's hull. 'To do something great like that.'

Why didn't you? Robbie thought. *Because of me?*

He didn't say that either. Instead, he turned and looked to the horizon where the undulating grey line of sea meeting sky was punctured by the dark grey hulk of a ship. A container ship? A cruise ship? A navy vessel? How far out was it? Kilometres out to sea – too far to identify.

Was the boy out there too? Had he travelled that far by now?

Had his skin and bones?

2

Claudine Fuller twisted the key in the lock, reaching up to flip open the top bolt, ducking down to unlatch the bottom.

'Out you go, Lupo.'

The dog looked up at her, its azure-blue eyes catching the kitchen ceiling lights, making them look almost translucent, depthless. She could dive into those eyes, lose herself in them. She often felt as if Lupo could see right into her soul, as if he *understood*. And now she felt as if she could see right into his. She was sure, sometimes, that he was a wolf, a heroic, storybook wolf. *White Fang*. She had wanted to call him White Fang, from the adventure story by Jack London that she had adored when she was a teenager, but Hugo had thought that it was a ridiculous name. Hugo didn't read, despite the scores of leather-bound hardbacks creaking the shelves of his study. To her knowledge the only thing that touched those books was the end of Junita's feather duster. Claudine wasn't permitted in Hugo's study. It had never been an explicit command, but the implicit edict was clear. When he was at work or socializing without her, the room was locked; when he was at home, he was perennially in there, 'working', though she suspected that much of Hugo's so-called work involved arranging extra-curricular activities he didn't want her to know about.

The feel of Lupo's cold, wet nose tucking into her palm brought her back to the present.

'Sorry, boy,' she murmured, pushing open the kitchen door and stepping onto the York stone patio to watch him streak across the dark lawn and launch himself into the woods.

A flash of white – gone.

Another flash, a second later – gone.

He could disappear for half an hour, roaming through the woods that encircled their house and garden, part of their fifty-acre property, but so thick that the sunlight struggled to penetrate the trees' dense canopy even during the day. Timid by nature, Claudine rarely ventured beyond the edge of the fastidiously clipped lawn, beyond what she knew. *An exotic bird in a gilded cage.* She had always been that way. *My beautiful, delicate, dependent girl*, her father had used to call her when he was alive. She envied those independent women who had the guts to study hard, go to university, build their own impressive careers, chase their dreams. But she just wasn't constructed that way. Her dream had always only ever been to marry someone like her father, a strong man who would look after her. *Control me.* She pushed the thought from her mind. And so, she had married Hugo, charmed by his self-confidence, his relentless self-belief. Now, fifteen years married, she saw it for what it was: an unswerving conviction that most others were quite simply beneath him. He had married her because she was beautiful and docile and because she had needed him. Hugo loved to be needed.

Claudine shivered. A stiff breeze was swaying the tops of

the trees, creaking branches and stirring leaves into a furious stew. Though she would never dare to admit it to Hugo, she had always hated this extravagant house, hated the isolation, the loneliness. Hugo didn't like her to work. He said that it reflected badly on him, made it seem as if he couldn't support his wife. Hugo and his mates adored to tease each other about money, wealth. At a dinner party a couple of weeks ago, when someone had asked him which mortgage provider he recommended, he'd announced – 'I'm not that end of the market, mate' – and had then laughed uproariously at the man's expense and his own genius wit. The poor man had only been trying to tap his knowledge of the property market, but Hugo had taken it as an opportunity to stamp on his ego. Just for fun, of course. *No hard feelings.* Even though twenty of West Sussex's finest had been clustered around the dinner table, their ears flapping like Dumbo's.

I hate this house. But most of all, I hate those woods.

Hugo loved them of course, loved the kudos of inviting his bloated property industry friends over to shoot pheasant in the autumn. Claudine would find birds in the garden gasping for air, their chests peppered with shot, or twisting in pathetic circles on the lawn, their wings mangled. But it was the look in their eyes that always cut her deepest, the look of futile hopelessness. Whoever thought animals weren't sentient beings were idiots. She used to try to rescue them, drive them to the wild bird sanctuary in Sidlesham, but it was ten kilometres of narrow country lanes and, by the time she'd got there, most of the poor things had died of shock. The shooting season was well underway now, but she hid indoors, the radio turned to blaring; let the poor birds spend their last sorry moments alone.

Another flash of white.

Lupo.

She stared hard into the soupy darkness.

Lupo?

But the white shape wasn't moving, wasn't a streak. Why was he standing still? What was he looking at? Usually he just *tore*.

As she squinted hard into the black gaps between the trees, she realized that it couldn't be Lupo. It was the wrong shape, too big, too tall. *Unless.* Unless, he was standing on his hind legs, looking up into the trees, stalking a squirrel perhaps. He didn't usually, he was a sled dog not a hunter . . .

'Lupo,' she called. Still the shape remained motionless. 'Lupo.'

Could he hear her? The wind was strong, blowing away from her, carrying her scent and surely her voice. But the trees were swirling, their branches creaking, and she'd never had a strong voice.

'Lupo?'

The harder she stared, the more the dark trunks and black gaps between blended and the white shape shifted until it was gone, and she was no longer sure what she had seen.

Shivering again, nothing to do with the chill wind this time, Claudine stepped back inside the kitchen and pulled the door quickly shut, ducking to flip the bottom lock into place, standing on tiptoes to slide the top lock home.

What on earth had that been? That odd, immovable white shape in the woods? A ghost?

No, of course, not. Even she didn't believe in ghosts. *My beautiful, delicate, dependent girl.* She needed to toughen up, be braver, take control of her imagination, her thoughts, rather than letting them control her.

But where was Lupo? He should be back by now.

3

'Karma? I'm surveying fucking karma and from where I'm sitting it looks great.'

Claudine heard Hugo's voice booming around the glass atrium that housed their swimming pool as she moved through the changing area. He perennially sounded as if he was addressing a crowd through a loudhailer.

'Don't call me again.'

She stepped quietly onto the honed granite tiles that surrounded the swimming pool in jet black. The water, tiled beneath its surface in pale blue-grey granite punctured by scores of tiny, sunken lights, sparkled like the Caribbean Sea on a brilliant midsummer's day; the temperature in the pool house, too, equator hot. Hugo, reclining on one of the oak steamer chairs, his chest and stomach gaping from a loosely tied white towelling robe, lowered his mobile from his ear.

'Who were you talking to, darling?' Claudine queried in a low voice.

'No one you need to worry about, baby.' His eyes roved

from her toes back up to her face. 'You know that I don't like you dressing in jeans.'

'I'm only hanging around the house, Hugo. I'm not seeing anyone today—'

'Me, Claudine. You're seeing me.'

She gave a pensive, scolded schoolchild nod. 'Lupo hasn't come back. I let him out about forty-five minutes ago. He disappeared into the woods and he hasn't come back.'

Hugo made no move to stand. 'There'll be a few dead pheasants out there that the gun dogs failed to find.' He smirked. 'I'd imagine he's chowing down on fresh kill.'

Claudine dipped her gaze. Hugo knew how much she loved animals, hated killing.

'I can't even hear him barking,' she said, despising the plaintive tone that crept into her voice whenever she spoke with him, hating the way that Hugo made her feel. *My beautiful, delicate, dependent girl.* 'I can usually hear him barking when he runs through the woods, the odd bark, at least.'

Hugo lifted his shoulders disinterestedly.

'Would you go out and look for him, please, Hugo?'

Hugo spread his hands, indicating his supine form. Claudine's eyes glanced over the paunchy spread of his gut, feeling bile rise at the thought of how it slapped against her thighs at night, when he climbed on top of her and spread her legs.

'No, Claudine, I won't,' she heard him say. 'I'm not about to start crawling around in the woods looking for that sodding dog in my dressing gown. And stop treating him like a surrogate child. He's a hulking great wolf, not a bloody baby.'

Claudine winced, not only at Hugo's tone. *Not a bloody*

9

baby. They hadn't been able to conceive. She hadn't known until they were married that Hugo was sterile; evidently, he hadn't thought it relevant. She had suggested a sperm donor, but of course he wouldn't hear of it, wouldn't entertain the thought of bringing up another man's child.

'I thought I saw something outside,' she murmured, her mind's eye finding the image of that strange, pale figure. 'In the woods.'

The ring of Hugo's mobile bookended her sentence. 'I need to get this, Claudine. Leave me, will you. It's a business call.'

Claudine gave a tiny nod. What business associate would be calling Hugo at a quarter-to-ten at night? She was pretty sure some of Hugo's business calls were as legitimate as much of the time he spent 'working late'.

Pulling the door to the swimming pool complex closed behind her, Claudine crossed the basement hallway, catching sight of her hunched, folded reflection in the darkened glass doors of the wine cellar, inwardly cringing at the outward manifestation of her timidity. She stopped suddenly.

A noise?

Not the boom of Hugo's voice, but something else, lighter, irregular. She tilted her head to listen.

Nothing for a moment, then there it was again, that same light, uneven noise.

The external door from the basement hallway opened out onto a sunken patio area that led, via a short flight of curved York stone steps, to the lawn. They rarely used the door or the sunken patio beyond it, shaded and dank as it was even in summer, preferring instead to access the garden from the kitchen or sitting room doors upstairs.

But there the noise was again, louder now, impossible to

ignore, coming from beyond that seldom used door. And with a huge sense of relief, Claudine realized that it was the sound of scratching. Nails – claws – on wood. Unmistakable now that she had stepped over, was pressing her ear to the solid wood.

Lupo. He *had* come back. Her beautiful soulful wolf was home.

It occurred to her briefly as she reached for the key that it was odd Lupo had returned to this door when she'd let him out of the kitchen. When she always let him out of, and he always returned to, the kitchen. But as her fingers closed around the chill copper, she pushed the niggle of uncertainty from her mind. *My beautiful, delicate, dependent girl.* Her hunched, submissive reflection in the wine cellar doors had brought her up short, given her a two-thou-sand-volt shock. She hadn't realized how unsparingly her mental state had manifested itself in her physical bearing. Her reflection had been ridiculous, that of a beaten, cowed, bovine creature. She couldn't continue as she was, letting life cow her, Hugo, control her, bully her. She had to force herself to be stronger. She would never be happy if she didn't. Lupo must have heard or scented her as she walked past the door. *White Fang. My wolf.* Wolves could scent game carried on the wind from over three kilometres away – she'd read that somewhere. Or perhaps he had seen her through the swimming pool's glass atrium, talking to Hugo. It was like a goldfish bowl, the swimming pool. Anyone standing outside on the dark lawn or hiding in the trees could look in and watch them, watch their every move, while remaining entirely invisible themselves. The thought had always disturbed her and she didn't like to use the swimming pool at night, certainly not alone. But that would

11

change now. She would make that change. Be stronger, braver.

As she twisted the key in the lock, an involuntary shiver ran down her spine, a lingering sense of that odd white shape out in the woods. Lupo. But it had been Lupo, hadn't it?

There it was again, the scratching, shaking her out of her reverie. And now that she was standing right by the door, she could hear sniffing coming from the crack beneath it. The tension drained from her.

A blast of cold air hit her full in the face, bringing tears to her eyes as she pulled the door open wide. White, filling her clouded vision. Something huge and white.

But not Lupo. *Not Lupo.*

A face.

She saw that now.

A face.

A mask.

Pale eyes beneath the mask, that pierced straight through her.

Fear, terror, was instantly acid sharp in her mouth. Her head exploded with pain, then only blackness.

4

A couple of weeks ago, Eunice Hargreaves had watched one of those nature documentaries on the Discovery Channel that she did so enjoy and, as she pulled back her bedroom curtain and peered out onto the deserted A234, she felt as if she had been teleported from the confines of her cottage bedroom and deposited high on a snowy peak in the Canadian Rockies.

The wolf was standing quite still, looking up at her, its attention no doubt caught by the movement of her curtains as she'd parted them. It was huge and powerful and pure, pure white, with depthless azure-blue eyes that caught the moonlight and reflected it back at her. Transported to the wilderness of that documentary, her aching joints and the ache in her heart for darling Derek that kept her up at night were momentarily forgotten and she was a young girl again, awed by the beauty and majesty of this animal.

Caught up in her imagination, it took her a long moment to realize why the wolf wasn't moving, wasn't running. Her rheumy gaze found the length of rope that tethered its ice-blue collar to the lamp post outside her front gate. Electric light then, not the moon, reflecting in the dog's eyes, and Eunice was back in Walderton, blue ropes bulging through the diaphanous skin of her hands with the effort of gripping tightly to the window frame to stop her frail body from toppling. Back to the grim reality of her life, the all-encompassing loneliness she had felt since her husband died last year, punctured only by weekly visits to a charity lunch club in Chichester, the odd, fleeting, duty pop-in from a neighbour.

Dropping the curtain, she hobbled to the bedside table. Who should she call? 999? But, no, a huge wolf-dog tied to a lamp post in the middle of the night wasn't a desperate emergency, though how on earth was one supposed to find the number for the local police station – if there even was one any more with the government cutting every public service to the quick? And there was another number, wasn't there, a not-quite-emergency police number? 112? Or was that for America? She and Derek had spent their fortieth wedding anniversary in New York and they had been robbed at knifepoint in Central Park. The police had responded ever so quickly, though they'd been quite brash when they arrived, but she really couldn't remember if Derek had dialled 111 or 112 and if that then meant that the English, not-quite-emergency number was 112 or 111 . . .

I'll try both, she decided, pragmatically. *Quite simple really.*

5

The house was huge, mock-Tudor, or perhaps genuine Tudor, given its size and position, on the brow of a hill at the top of a gently sloping fifty-metre-long gravelled drive that cut off from Blackheath Lane on the outskirts of the village of Walderton. Detective Inspector Bobby 'Marilyn' Simmons had driven through the village itself on the way here from his home in Chichester, and though it was knocking three in the morning, the gibbous moon's cool light had illuminated a poster-child English village, chocolate-box quaint with its whitewashed, flower-basket-bedecked pub, crooked, tiled houses with leadlight windows and a neat, triangular village green on which cricket would doubtless be played and Pimm's drunk in the summer. All very beautiful and yet even Dr Ghoshal's morgue held more appeal for Marilyn. The mere thought of living in a Marplesque village such as this one, where everyone made it their express business to know everyone else's, brought him out in hives.

Crunching his ancient Z3 to a stop on the sweep of gravel drive in front of the house, Marilyn cut the engine. Tilting his head back, he let his eyes drift closed for a brief moment and tried to focus his mind on the blank pink insides of his eyelids. He didn't yet know what he would encounter behind the ornate facade of this grand house, but from DC Darren Cara's panicked voice on the radio, it wasn't going to be rose-garden pretty. Snapping his eyes open, he pushed open the driver's door and climbed out. Though he had managed barely three hours' sleep, he felt fine, good even, he'd venture to say. His puritanical new approach to life seemed, unfortunately, to be serving him well.

He was far from the first attendee at the crime scene. Piccadilly Circus would doubtless be quieter at three in the morning. Six members of Burrows' CSI team were clustered around the forensics van, getting suited and booted on the gravel drive. Beyond them, DC Cara was pacing across the expansive, pillared and porticoed porch, his baggy forensic overshoes inflating and deflating in time with each stressed step, as if linked to miniature pairs of bellows. Marilyn was pretty sure it wasn't only the bleaching effect of the moon's cold light that had boil-washed the colour from his face.

'What have we got, Cara?'

'Murder, Guv.'

Marilyn drily raised an eyebrow. 'I got that far myself, thank you, Detective Constable.'

Cara didn't smile, not even a flicker to massage his superior officer's ego. 'Double murder. A married couple, early forties. The man is called Hugo Fuller and his wife is Claudine. She was found floating face down in the swimming pool and he was tied to a lounger and stabbed, through the, uh—' He stopped speaking to clear his throat.

'Through the . . .?'

'Uh, through . . . through the eye.' Despite the throat-clearing, his voice was a parched croak. 'Both eyes actually.'

'Lovely.' Marilyn suppressed the ghost of a twenty-five-years-on-the-job, seen-it-all, cynical smile. Cara had transferred from Traffic to Surrey and Sussex Major Crimes just over a year ago, and though they had dealt with a few sexual assaults, a couple of adult murders and a particularly traumatic child murder during that time, Cara hadn't seen any of the bodies in situ, at the crime scenes. He was now undergoing Major Crimes' equivalent of a baptism, though to be fair to the kid, this one sounded like baptism by fire.

'Who found them?' Marilyn asked.

'One of Surrey and Sussex's dog teams. They were called out to retrieve a husky that was tied to a lamp post in the middle of Walderton. Some old lady was woken by it barking. The dog had a tag on its collar. There was no answer at the door, but the dog team said that they saw a light on around the side of the house. The garden wraps around the house, there's no fence dividing the front from the back, and the lawn slopes down from this floor on the brow of the hill, to the basement level at the back.' He raised a gloved hand and flapped it behind him, indicating where a gravel path cut off the sweep of gravel drive and curved around the right side of the house, out of sight. 'They followed the path, down the hill, to the indoor swimming pool. The lights were on inside and the walls are all glass.'

'Do we have any information on the couple?'

'Yes, sir. Hugo Fuller runs . . . *ran* a property business. Buying freeholds and living off the ground rent, something like that. It's very lucrative.'

Marilyn surveyed the enormous Arts and Crafts facade. 'Clearly.'

'And his wife supports a few local animal charities.'

'You're well informed, Cara.'

'They're high profile in the local area. I've read about them a few times, Guv.'

'Read about them? In what?'

'*Sussex Life.*'

Marilyn pulled a face. '*Sussex Life?*'

'It's good to be plugged in,' Cara said, with a note of defensiveness. 'Learn about the area I'm working in, the people. I didn't grow up around here.' It was an unnecessary statement. Cara's accent was pure London, his heritage multi-racial: Barbadian father and white-Irish mother. It didn't take a genius to work out that he hadn't grown up in this bastion of lily-white Englishness. 'You might have seen pictures of the Fullers in the *Sussex Society* pages,' he continued. 'They're in there all the time at one function or another.'

Marilyn rolled his eyes. 'Do I look like someone who reads the society pages? *Any* society pages?'

DC Cara looked at his boss. Nicknamed Marilyn, after Marilyn Manson – a moniker his colleagues had bestowed on him the first day he joined the force and that had dogged him ever since – because of his disconcerting, one azure-blue, one brown, mismatched eyes and his penchant for dressing head to toe in black, he did not, in any way, look like someone who read the society pages.

'No, Guv,' muttered Cara, suitably admonished.

6

Marilyn followed Cara into the hallway, stepping gingerly onto polished cream marble, ice-rink slippery under his forensic overshoes. The whole ground floor of his Georgian terraced house could have fitted snugly into the Fullers' hallway. A gargantuan gold-framed mirror occupied the lion's share of the wall dead ahead, making midgets of Marilyn and Cara even as they walked towards it. They passed the door to a playing-field-sized sitting room to their left, all gold damask sofas and thick white shag-pile rugs; a dark study space to their right, bedecked with heavy oak bookshelves lined with pristine leather-bound hardbacks, none of which looked as if they had ever been touched let alone read; a walnut kitchen next, bifold doors beyond the island opening out onto what Marilyn assumed was the garden, although it was too dark to tell. A wide cream marble staircase, adorned with an intricately sculpted gold banister, curved away to the upper floors and a chandelier that wouldn't have looked out of place in a banqueting hall in Buckingham Palace hung from the ceiling above, throwing shards of tinkling light around the pale vanilla walls. The decor bellowed from the rooftops: *Footballers' Wives*. The Fullers were clearly over-burdened with wealth, but not much taste.

On doctor's orders, Marilyn had been teetotal for the past twenty-nine days – *Not that I'm counting every single, painful bloody minute* – and as he followed Cara carefully across the hall floor, approaching his own Lilliputian reflection in the Fullers' mirror, he had to acknowledge that it was doing him good. He looked, if not quite ten years younger, certainly a solid few months – and at his age, forty-nine now, three months away from his fiftieth and dreading the relentless downward slide that he was sure his next birthday would herald, he'd take those. He'd take a week, a day, a few minutes. Seconds. It had got to him, that impending birthday. Hanging over him like the ageist sword of Damocles.

'As I said before, the garden slopes downstairs, front to back,' Cara said, as he stopped at the top of a set of cream marble stairs that descended to a basement level. 'There's a wine cellar, gym, sauna and swimming pool on the level below this one, but it's not underground.'

The hallway at the bottom of the stairs was a quarter the size of the main hallway, with a matching cream marble floor and pale vanilla walls, and lit by a mini-me chandelier. Racks of wine bottles were visible through dark double glass doors to their left – the wine cellar, Marilyn supposed, de rigueur in this kind of residence – a gym straight ahead, equipped with more torture equipment than Marilyn had ever felt the need to use in his life, and a frosted-glass doorway to the right, which Cara pushed through, holding it open behind him.

The changing room area they entered was operating-theatre bright from rows of recessed spots, two more clear

20

glass doors to their left revealing a sauna and steam room. An open archway dead ahead led to the swimming pool, their dual figures reflected, Lilliputian once again, in the wall of black glass beyond the placid blue rectangle of water.

Cara stopped just this side of the archway and held out an arm. 'Hugo Fuller is to your left, Guv. Claudine Fuller in the pool, also to your left. Neither of them have been touched or moved.' He pressed himself against the wall, giving Marilyn space to go first; not, Marilyn suspected, out of deference. Cara had clearly had more than his fill at the first viewing, and as Marilyn stepped through the archway, into the foliage-lined Caribbean-warm glass orangery that housed the twenty-five-metre swimming pool, and saw the horror show that was Hugo Fuller, he appreciated exactly why.

Jesus Christ.

The man was reclining on a wooden steamer chair, facing the pool, the wall of glass and the dark garden beyond. Facing. Staring. Sightless. His eye sockets were filled with, what – *mush*, was the word that instantly popped into Marilyn's mind, *pure mush* – his face a mask of coagulating burgundy blood. Blood coated his bare chest, had soaked the lapels of the white towelling robe swathing his corpulent frame and pooled sloppily into his lap. But it wasn't his eye sockets, horrendous as they were, that hitched the breath in Marilyn's throat. It was the scratches, gouges more accurately, deep vertical gouges that ran from his hairline down his face, through his eye sockets – had they done that to his eyes? – before furrowing down his cheeks to his chin. He looked as if he had been savaged by a wild beast. Marilyn swallowed, forcing down the rising bile, as subtly as he could.

'So that's Mr Fuller,' he said, in the absence of anything else popping into his brain. 'What about the wife?'

He turned, grateful for the opportunity to look away, his gaze fixing with relief on Mrs Fuller. Claudine, Cara had said. She was fully dressed still in dark jeans and a black long-sleeved shirt, raw silk, expensive – ruined now, Marilyn thought ridiculously – floating face down in the swimming pool, her blonde hair fanning out in pale, seaweed tendrils around her head, a meaty patch on the back of her head where, despite the water, the blonde tendrils were matted with blood. Dead, without question, unless she was a champion breath-holder. Cause of death? Marilyn didn't want, or need, to speculate. That wasn't his job.

He turned at the sound of ponderous footsteps – his lead CSI, Tony Burrows, looking tired, his moon face puffy with recently vanquished sleep.

'Burrows, good morning. Welcome.'

'Even sparrows are not farting at this ungodly hour, Marilyn.'

'Perils of the job, Tony.'

'Indeed.' Stifling a yawn with the back of one latex-gloved hand, his gaze moved past Marilyn's left shoulder to find Claudine Fuller. 'Poor woman.'

Marilyn nodded. 'Leave the bodies where they are. I want Dr Flynn to see the scene as we found it. This isn't normal.'

Burrows grimaced. 'Can any murder really be classed as normal?'

'You'd be surprised.'

'Unfortunately, it's a long time since anything about human nature surprised me.'

Marilyn shook his head and stepped aside, so that Burrows could view the horror that was Hugo Fuller. 'No, this, Tony, *this* is something else altogether.'

7

Jessie felt as if she was swimming upwards through black treacle. She surfaced, her ears tuning to the nagging sound of her mobile's ring, her eyes flickering open, shut, sticking shut. She forced them open again, her brain lagging way behind, lost in that treacle of dense, muggy, hungover sleep. The room was pitch-black, no telltale leak of light from below the curtains. Twisting sideways, she fumbled her mobile from the bedside table.

'Marilyn.'

'You're needed, Dr Flynn.'

'What time is it?'

'Ask me no questions and I'll tell you no lies.'

'Oh God, that early.'

'For a double murder, even I get up in the middle of the night.'

Double murder. 'What?'

'I'll tell you when you get here. As soon as you can. I'll text you the address.'

Silence on the end of the line; the only sound, Callan

snoring softly beside her. Odd that the telephone hadn't woken him. Usually he was bolt upright at any noise courtesy of the antennae that came with his job as a military policeman. Always on call, even when he was fast asleep. And he had driven them to dinner last night, so he didn't even have 'hangover' as an excuse like she did. She gave him a soft kiss on the shoulder, feeling the warmth of his skin against her lips, sucking in his scent for a brief, calming moment before twisting away, wincing at the chill air that wrapped around her as she climbed quietly out of bed.

It was at times like this that she questioned her own sanity at ever having got involved with Surrey and Sussex Major Crimes and Detective Inspector Bobby 'Marilyn' Simmons. Though, to be fair, it hadn't been a well-deliberated choice, far more the employment equivalent of boiling a frog. A couple of the cases she had worked on while a clinical psychologist with the Defence Psychology Service had overlapped with civilian cases that Marilyn had been working on, and she had ended up helping him, proving herself far more adept at understanding criminals' psychology than she had ever expected to be.

The second of those cases, last November, had been the one which had abruptly ended her army career. She glanced down at the scar that ran across her left palm from the knife attack, still raised and ugly, but faded to a deep brown, no longer the furious purple that had goaded her for so many months. And though her fingers would never be dexterous, her repaired extensor tendons were functioning now, more or less, and her hand no longer felt like the grotesque hand of a mannequin. Her dismissal from the army had pretty much coincided with Surrey and Sussex Major Crimes' last criminal psychologist, Dr Butter, retiring,

24

and the rest, as they say, was history. It filled a gap for both her and Marilyn and, like the scar on her hand, her hankering for her old job was fading, the only connection she now had with the military the man currently asleep in her bed.

The ping of a text arriving shook her back to the present. *Double murder.* Shit, she needed to switch her brain on and get moving.

In the dark, she fumbled some clothes from the cupboard and took them into the bathroom where she splashed warm water on her face, cleaned her teeth, and shucked on jeans and a navy V-neck jumper, the latter fraying at the sleeves where she'd chewed it in a misguided attempt to stop chewing her nails. *Never mind,* she didn't imagine that Marilyn's invitation required a designer ensemble.

Downstairs, she pulled on her trainers and reached to the key rack for her Mini keys, finding an empty space. Callan's car was in the garage for its annual service, and he'd borrowed her Mini yesterday. He had learnt to line his shoes on the shoe rack, almost as precisely as she lined up her own, even though she knew that if it was his own house, he'd kick them off in a muddy heap on the doormat. The shoes he managed, to assuage her OCD; the keys were a bridge too far. Shoving her hand in his coat pocket, her fingers closed around a folded envelope which she pulled out so that she could reach back in for the keys tucked beneath it.

The thick white hallmarked envelope sprang open in her hand revealing the crest of the Ministry of Defence Hospital Unit, Frimley Park Hospital. Callan had told her that his only contact with his neurologist was now six-monthly check-ups and he'd last been a couple of months ago. His brain, the bullet, all fine – he'd told her – so why the letter?

Her gaze flicked to the stairs: no sound, the landing in darkness. She could read the letter, shove it back and he'd be none the wiser.

Her fingers itched as she felt the rough edge of the torn envelope. He hadn't been honest with her, so she had a right to read it, didn't she? But then an image rose in her mind, watching her mother standing in the dark hallway of her family home, glancing furtively over her shoulder to check that she was alone – as she had just done – then searching her father's coat pockets, the two outside, the one inside, finding nothing, sagging, physically sagging with thwarted frustration, ducking down and rifling through his briefcase, more frustration, more repressed, suppressed fury. Watching again, months later, as her mother frantically, blatantly, right in front of her, searched his pockets and briefcase again, knowing in her heart that her husband was having an affair, being stonewalled, told she was delusional, unhinged.

Her mother had been right of course. Jessie's father had been sneaking around behind her back for more than two years by the time she had found irrevocable proof, stoking his affair with Diane while his wife cared for their desperately sick eight-year-old son. Living with suspicion had destroyed the remaining soft parts of her that hadn't already been destroyed by her son's illness. And seeing her mother, Jessie had promised herself that she would never live that way herself. But here she was, standing in a darkened hallway, Callan asleep upstairs, being suspicious, furtive. She couldn't read his letter in secret, had to ask him about it. Her own intense obsession with privacy wouldn't let her invade Callan's, because she would be furious with him if he invaded hers. Stuffing the envelope back in a vague semblance of the way she had found it, she grabbed the

26

keys, snatched her navy puffa from the coat rack and pulled open the door.

As soon as you can, Marilyn had said. What the hell was she going to face when she got there?

8

'Can I go in alone?'

'Alone?'

Jessie clocked the undercurrent of hurt in Marilyn's tone and suppressed a smile. 'You can accompany me, if you don't speak. If one of your senses is occupied, by noise—' A pause, the ghost of another smile. 'Chatter, the other senses don't work properly. And I need to focus so that I can—'

'Get a sense?' Marilyn cut in.

She met his gaze and grinned. 'No flies on you, DI Simmons.'

Marilyn rolled his eyes. He was becoming acclimatized to her foibles, her need to immerse herself in the scene alone, or, at a minimum, in silence, *to get a sense*. In truth, he operated pretty much the same way himself, alone, in silence, trusting his intuition, usually just DS Sarah Workman, his quiet, dependable, supportive crutch, omnipresent. The last case he and Jessie had worked on together, only six short weeks ago – six weeks that felt a lifetime of disturbed sleep and self-recrimination long – she had operated the same way, frustrating him at times by how self-contained she was. The child murder – *double* child murder – had battered his emotions like no other case he had worked on in his twenty-five years with Surrey and Sussex Major Crimes, had dumped his confidence, his self-belief, in the garbage can. He had screwed up unforgivably, blamed himself, rightly in his opinion, for the death of that second child; a little girl he was sure could have been saved if he hadn't missed the hole, that gaping black sinkhole, in his logic. Her death, that sinkhole, was the reason for his new-found teetotalism. He had felt compelled to offer his resignation, which had been turned down, his exemplary record deemed to have more than made up for that one mistake, however unforgivable a mistake he considered it to have been. But he had been grateful, as he was a walking cliché: the detective inspector with no life outside his job; he would have been rudderless without it.

'Ready?' Jessie asked.

She had hurriedly climbed into the forensic overalls and overshoes that one of Tony Burrows' CSI team had handed her. Now she pulled her waist-length black hair into a messy bun, securing it with the band she habitually wore around her wrist for just such occasions and tucked the bun and stray strands into the overall's elasticated hood.

Marilyn nodded. 'I'm steeling myself for round two.' He glanced behind him at Cara, who still looked paler than the Fullers' shiny Dulux Pure Brilliant White painted front door. 'DC Cara?'

'Yes, sir.'

Marilyn ignored the waver in Cara's voice, was happy to give the kid a break. He didn't have a strong stomach himself at the best of times and was surprised, given the horror show awaiting them downstairs, that his own voice wasn't wavering.

'Listen and learn, Cara,' he said, laying a hand on Jessie's shoulder. 'Listen and learn from the maestro.'

Jessie rolled her eyes. 'Could you be any more patronizing?' she cast quietly over her shoulder as she turned and crossed the pillared porch, Marilyn a step behind her, Cara following a few paces behind him.

'Patronization is the glue in any successful hierarchy,' he muttered back, with a wink. 'When he's an aged DI himself, I expect him to adopt the same condescending attitude, keep the minions from getting above their station.'

'To me, I meant, DI Simmons, not to him.'

'You can handle it, Dr Flynn,' he muttered, as he followed her over the threshold, into the Sussex house of horrors. 'Oh, and just for the record, I don't chatter.'

9

The house was a monument to opulence, an Aladdin's cave of gilded gold everywhere – staircase, mirror frames, bowls and statuettes – that caught the light cast from the elephantine chandelier's myriad dangling crystals and threw it around in diamond spangles. *Should have brought my sunglasses.*

'Walk down the length of the hall and take the stairs, dead ahead, to the level below,' Marilyn called out.

Jessie moved gingerly down the hallway as instructed – the combination of overshoes and polished marble life-and-death slippery – past a determinedly masculine study lined with leather-bound volumes (*for show*, she found herself thinking), a lavishly decorated sitting room, gold photographs adorning a marble mantelpiece (most featuring a stunning white dog with ice-blue eyes, no children visible), then finally a massive kitchen doubtless designed and constructed by some high-end designer she'd never heard of and had no interest in ever hearing of.

A draught at the bottom of the stairs she'd descended from the hallway to the level below pulled her attention to

31

a door that gaped open, revealing a sunken patio area that segued, via a flight of wide curved stone steps, to the manicured lawn above. Woods hemmed the lawn on all sides, thick and dark, unpenetrated by the deep orange rays of the dawn light. The corpulent form of Tony Burrows, Marilyn's lead CSI, clad in a white forensic onesie overall identical to the one she was wearing, just a good few sizes larger, squatted on the patio.

'We believe that he approached the house through the woods,' Marilyn said, as they stepped outside.

'He?'

'Burrows found a couple of muddy footprints on the patio. Men's. They're not Mr Fuller's.'

'What size are they?'

'I'll have that in a moment,' Burrows called out. 'But they're definitely men's, unless it was a "she" in clown shoes.'

'Isn't that possible?' Jessie asked.

'Yes, it's possible,' Burrows conceded.

'The state of the victims, particularly Mr Fuller, concurs with it being a "he",' Marilyn cut in. 'From a strength perspective.'

Unless it's a female body-builder wearing clown shoes. Jessie didn't say it. Marilyn would take her through his first-cut reasoning now, as they surveyed the crime scene, and she would discuss it with him, challenge him. But she had worked with him enough times to know that he would never reach a conclusion without microscopically examining every angle and the nth degree multiple times first. There would be plenty of time to air her more outlandish ideas.

'And he entered the house via this door?' Jessie asked Burrows.

'Yes. There are a couple of other faint footprints on the

marble.' He indicated two yellow numbered cones. 'And there's blood on the floor over there and a patch on the skirting.'

'There's no damage to the door,' Jessie said. 'It wasn't forced.'

'No,' Marilyn confirmed. 'It was unlocked and opened from the inside.'

'That suggests that either they knew the man, were expecting him, or—' she broke off. 'Though why then approach through the woods?'

'So as not to be seen,' Cara ventured. 'Even if they were expecting him, if he wanted to kill them, he wouldn't want to be seen by anyone else as he came to the house.'

'There almost certainly wouldn't have been anyone to see him anyway,' Jessie said. 'It was night-time, dark. The drive opens onto a narrow country lane that doesn't appear to go anywhere much. The nearest neighbours are, where?'

'Those on the outskirts of the village of Walderton, over a kilometre away by road, about five hundred metres as the crow flies.' Cara pointed. 'That way, straight through the woods. The dog was found tied to a lamp post in the middle of the village at a quarter-past-one this morning.'

'Who found him?'

'An old lady. She said that she was woken by the sound of a dog barking persistently and got out of bed to investigate.'

Jessie nodded, gazing out across the flat expanse of lawn, frosty with dew, which reflected the dawn light, making the grass look as if it was scattered with orange diamonds, to the dense, dark wall of trees. No diamonds there, no light, no sparkle. Though she loved solitude, had chosen to live in a cottage down a quiet country lane precisely to avoid unwanted human contact, she also loved the fact that her cottage was small, cosy, just a lounge and kitchen downstairs, two bedrooms and a bathroom upstairs. If she was feeling nervous, if a case she'd worked on had lodged itself in her brain, she could search from top to bottom in sixty seconds, prove to herself that a serial killer hadn't crammed himself into her laundry basket ready to rise and strike like a snake charmer's adder when she was brushing her teeth. Despite her initial intention of living in splendid isolation, she also now loved Ahmose's fatherly presence next door, loved his presence and loved him, her adopted parent, more even than her natural parents or certainly more than her father. The magnitude of this house, of its grandiose seclusion, made her shiver. She couldn't imagine swimming in that pool, a goldfish in a bowl watched by – who? Anyone who had a mind to hike through those dense trees. It was the stuff of nightmares. Had Claudine Fuller felt secure here? Though the autumn sun was now rising above the treeline, those dense woods remained unpenetrated by its glow.

'The dog was removed for a reason,' she said.

'Unless it ran away and someone found it and tied it to the lamp post,' Cara ventured.

'Had it been seen in the village before?'

Cara shook his head. 'The dog teams said that the woman who called it in had never seen it before and it's a small village and she's nosy – their words not mine.'

'We'll question everyone in the village,' Marilyn said. 'Obviously. About the dog and about any suspicious people, movements, et cetera, they might have noticed in the past week or two.'

Jessie nodded. 'And that's the closest village?'

'Yes,' Cara said. 'It's the only one within two kilometres of the house.'

34

Jessie shuddered. *Splendid isolation.* 'Then I think we can assume the dog doesn't typically run away.'

'I wouldn't bloody run away if I lived here,' Marilyn muttered.

'The woman . . . Mrs Fuller, was patron of a number of animal charities,' Cara said in a resolutely professional tone. 'I think she would have provided the dog, Lupo, he's called with a good home. Cared for him, loved him.'

Marilyn winked at Jessie, then spoke in a similarly professional tone. 'So, can we assume that our perpetrator removed the dog so that it couldn't guard? Couldn't warn the owners of an intruder?'

'Perhaps,' Jessie said. 'But, if someone, a stranger, can just take the dog and tie it to a lamp post, I'd say that it wasn't a great guard dog in the first place. What breed is it?'

'A Siberian husky,' Cara said. 'They're not great guard dogs evidently, as it's not in their nature to be aggressive to people.'

Jessie nodded. Stepping over to the door through which the Fullers' killer had entered, she squatted down.

'Don't touch.' Burrows' voice boomed in the eerie silence. 'Following instructions from Lord-God-on-High to leave everything inside the house as it was until you arrived, I am still to process the door, both inside and out.'

Jessie placed her hands on her thighs, as much to balance herself in the crouch as to stop herself from involuntarily reaching out and fouling up Burrows' crime scene. Though she was wearing gloves, she knew that he still viewed her as an amateur when it came to moving responsibly around crime scenes, and he was right to do so.

'There are faint vertical marks on the paintwork near the bottom of the door,' she addressed the comment to Marilyn – Lord-God-on-High – who was hovering over her.

'From the dog?' he asked.

Without answering, she reached out, fingers bent into claws.

'DON'T TOUCH.' From behind her. *Burrows*.

'I'm not touching, I'm miming.' Her gaze grazed from the bottom to the top of the white-gloss-painted door, tracking from left to right as it rose, searching every square centimetre. She looked across and met Marilyn's questioning look. 'There's no glass in the door and no spyhole. And there are no other scratches on the door, not even minor ones, no wear and tear. It's—' She paused. 'It's as you would expect for a door that belongs to this house – pristine.' She looked back to the base of the door. 'Apart from the bottom.'

The scratches in the paintwork were too far apart, surely, for a dog's compact claws. So – what then?

'What's your theory, Jessie?' Marilyn asked, lowering himself gingerly into a crouch next to her, with audible clicks from both knees and a heartfelt 'ouf'.

She didn't answer. Was thinking, visualizing.

Not claws. So – fingernails?

The image made her deeply uneasy. The image of someone – a man – someone with big feet, squatting by the door raking his fingernails down the paintwork. But that image, disturbing as it was, didn't quite fit either. Could fingernails really cleave these marks in paint? They were too weak, weren't they, to tear paint from wood? They'd just glance off, leave dull streaks on the paint's surface, or bend and break.

A tight, claustrophobic feeling in her chest – *So what on earth did make these marks . . .?*

She looked across, met Marilyn's searching, disconcerting mismatched gaze. 'I'm sorry, but I don't have a theory. Not yet, anyway.'

10

Callan opened his eyes and lay still, staring up at the ceiling. He had been half-aware that Jessie had left, but it had been pitch-black then and he must have crashed straight back to sleep. Now, the dull grey light of morning was seeping through the curtains and his body clock was telling him that it was time to get up for work, even though it was a Sunday. If Jessie had been here, he would have slept in, found something more interesting to do than sleeping, but there was no point in staying in bed alone.

Tossing back the duvet, he stood, too quickly. His head spun and he fumbled his hand onto the bedside table to steady himself, knocking the bedside light to the floor in the process. *Fuck.* Feeling dizzy and disorientated, he sat back down on the edge of the bed and dropped his head to his hands, closed his eyes and stared hard into the insides of his eyelids, seeking to find the quiet place that he went to when he was trying to stave off an epileptic fit. His neurologist had referred him to a counsellor.

Lots of people find it helpful.

He'd resisted; it wasn't his thing.

Just try it. Go once and then decide whether you want to continue.

So, he had. Once.

Where are you most happy? she had asked him.

Making love with my girlfriend. He didn't say it, reckoned that the birdlike woman, with the pearl-pink lipstick and neat greying-blonde bob would not have appreciated the aside. She had reminded him of his mum – someone's mum at least.

Running, up on the Downs, he'd said instead.

Imagine it. Close your eyes and take yourself there.

He closed his eyes and felt as if he was coiled in barbed wire and that it was tightening around him with every word the woman said.

Which part of the run do you like best?

I have a favourite route I take.

Describe it to me.

I run to a place called Foley Hill. There's a track that cuts through the trees.

What are the trees like?

Thick. A mix. It's autumn now so the leaves are turning.

Describe the colours to me.

Look out the window, he retorted, in his mind. *Yellow, orange, red, brown*, he said.

Lovely. It sounds lovely. And the path. What's that like?

It's steep. Near the top I almost have to scrabble up using my hands. It's slippery now as the ground is carpeted with leaves.

Go on.

Despite his cynicism, the barbed wire was uncoiling, the tension draining, and he could see Foley Hill in his mind's eye. More than that – he could feel it, smell the leaf mulch, feel the chill of the autumn air cooling the sweat on his skin.

Nearer to the top of the hill, the trees thin out and the summit is bare, he volunteered. *On a clear day, I can see all the way to the south coast.*

Is there a bench? Can you sit?

No, I stand. He always stood, panting, his heart beating like a jackhammer, gulping in the cold air.

Good, that's good. When you feel an epileptic fit coming on, close your eyes and go up to Foley Hill. Imagine that it's a stunning autumn day, like the one you describe, sunny but chilly . . .

He still wasn't sure that he believed in all that shit, but he had been so desperate then, a week ago, when his neurologist had told him the news, that he'd have tried anything. He had just wished, at the time, she'd stop talking so that he could fully concentrate on taking himself to Foley Hill, but now that she wasn't here, that quiet woman who was somebody's mum, he couldn't go there at all. Dropping his hands, he opened his eyes. Usually it was stress or tiredness that kicked off his fits. Now, he felt neither, and still he could sense an attack coming on. He slumped back flat on the bed and jammed his eyes shut again, willing his muscles to relax and his mind to transport him to Foley Hill. Maybe he was just lacking in imagination, because all he could feel was the claustrophobic stuffiness of the central heating, and all he could see was the inside of his neurologist's office. The MRI scan of his brain, sitting on the desk between them like a ticking bomb.

Your epilepsy is getting worse because the bullet is shifting. It's causing more trauma, more swelling.

Why? Why is it shifting?

A shrug. It hadn't been the reaction he'd expected. Something more professional would have been good.

Because you don't sit still.

I can't spend my life sitting still.

Another shrug. *There you go.*

And in response to Callan's crossed arms, crossed legs – defensive body language Jessie would say, and she'd be right.

When we agreed not to remove the bullet originally, two years ago, we took a calculated risk. If you were a couch potato that risk would probably have paid off. It had a decent chance of paying off anyway.

And now?

His neurologist had spun the MRI scan of his brain around on the desktop. His brain looked like a cauliflower cleaved in two, the bullet a dark grey conical shape above the white glob of his left eye.

Whenever brain swelling occurs, it increases the intracranial pressure inside the skull. This pressure can prevent blood from flowing to your brain, which deprives it of the oxygen it needs to function. This swelling can also block other fluids from leaving your brain, making the swelling even worse. Damage or death of brain cells may result. The bullet is causing localized swelling and my advice is that it should be removed.

You said, two years ago, that the operation was too risky.

Then, yes.

And now?

It's no less risky.

Callan lay on the bed, staring up at Jessie's bright white ceiling, waiting for the fit to come. Stress, tiredness. Stress.

It's no less risky. His brain was fogging as if the room was filling with smoke, his muscles contracting, limbs twitching, starting to flail. He could feel them – a part of him, but not – beyond his conscious control. He caught his shin on the edge of the bedside table, something crashed to the ground, the lamp, for the second time in two minutes – Jessie would kill him – and that was the last thing he remembered.

Gradually the fit subsided. He lay still, panting and sweating, feeling chilled right through to the marrow of his bones. His heart was beating the way it did when he sprinted to the top of Foley Hill, clawing his way up the last steep fifty metres with his hands. But he wasn't at Foley Hill. He was lying on the bedroom floor in a pool of vomit, shivering uncontrollably, feeling like a drug addict coming down off a hit. Curling up into a ball, he cradled his head in his hands. *Fuck.* His fits were getting worse, more frequent, more violent. It was only a matter of time before one happened at work, or when he was driving, or in front of Jessie. He was lying to everyone, his boss, his colleagues, his mother. Jessie. Himself. He needed to make a decision.

Ten minutes later, downstairs in a T-shirt and tracksuit bottoms, he felt in his coat pocket for his house keys, found them tucked underneath the letter from his neurologist sent as a follow-up after last week's appointment, summarizing their discussion, laying out his options. As he held the envelope in his fingers, he thought back to yesterday afternoon, borrowing Jessie's Mini, leaving the keys mangled with his house keys, in his pocket. Her Mini keys were gone, his house keys remained.

Flicking open the envelope's flap, he withdrew the letter. He didn't need to read it, had read it enough times in the past twenty-four hours to have memorized every word. Had

Jessie read it? They had lived together for nearly a year now and he reckoned that she wouldn't have done, that she had too much integrity, respected privacy, hers and his, too highly. He hoped that he was right. When he had decided which of Dr Bose's rock-and-a-hard-place, operate-or-leave options to take, he wanted to tell her himself. Ripping the letter in two, he shoved it in the kitchen bin, underneath the food cartons from the take-away curry they'd had after the pub last night.

Back in the sitting room, he pulled his running shoes off the shoe rack by the front door.

Because you don't sit still.

He looked at the sofa. No – it wasn't him. He'd have to take his chance with not sitting still.

Slamming the door behind him, he walked to the end of the path and started running as soon as his feet hit the tarmac. He'd go up to Foley Hill again – go there for real, instead of trying to force his imagination to take him there. He just hoped to God that Jessie hadn't read that damn letter.

11

'We think that the woman, the wife, Claudine Fuller, was hit over the head with something heavy, then dragged into the swimming pool area. Dragged by a foot or a leg.' Marilyn indicated the thin snail's trail of dried blood, visible only as a dull line against the glistening black marble floor. 'We haven't fished her out of the swimming pool yet, as I wanted you to see her in situ, but you can see that she has blunt instrument trauma to the right temple and another to the back of the head, probably as she turned to run. The man, Hugo Fuller, was incapacitated with a stun gun, then bound to the chair with rope.'

Jessie and Cara followed Marilyn into a white-tiled changing area, brightly illuminated by scores of tiny, recessed ceiling spots. Through a curved doorway, Jessie saw a thick vertical slice of azure swimming pool, the dark legs of someone – Mrs Fuller, Claudine, doubtless – floating face down on its surface, the lawn and gardens beyond the swimming pool glistening under the cold, bright autumnal sun, the grass diamonds gone now, the woods though, still unpenetrated by light.

'I asked Burrows to leave the crime scene untouched until you'd seen it. It was clear that Claudine Fuller was dead when we arrived. It was clear to the dog teams, an hour before we arrived, that the poor woman was dead.'

Jessie nodded. 'Thanks for that, but I think you're putting a little too much faith in my abilities, Marilyn.'

'You saved my career, Dr Flynn,' he muttered, so that only she heard.

She shrugged off the compliment. Although she would never admit it to Marilyn, she already felt out of her depth with this nasty double murder. His expectation was weighing on her; and Cara's expectation as a young, keen newbie – *Listen and learn, DC Cara* – was equally weighty. She had solved the last case that she and Marilyn had worked on together, the high-profile murder of two ten-year-old girls, but she believed she'd been lucky, caught a break and saved him. *Luck, not genius.*

'Her hands and feet are tied,' Cara said, unnecessarily, as they stepped through the arched doorway onto the black-tiled surround of the swimming pool, honed thankfully rather than polished. She didn't fancy skidding on her Tesco's plastic bag overshoes and ending up in the pool with Mrs F.

Jessie nodded. 'She wouldn't have been able to swim,' she murmured, equally unnecessarily.

They regarded Claudine's floating form in solemn silence for a few moments, Jessie's eyes finding the bloody mess at the back of her head.

'Seen enough?' Marilyn asked.

She nodded.

Knocking a fist against the glass wall of the swimming pool, he motioned to Burrows who was standing on the patio talking to two of his CSI team. 'All yours,' he mouthed, pointing to Mrs Fuller.

He moved further along the edge of the swimming pool, Jessie and DC Cara tracking dutifully behind.

'Now to the horror show that is Mr Hugo Fuller.' Stepping sideways, Marilyn extended his arm, as if he was a magician revealing the result of a particularly tricky act. Jessie almost expected him to burst forth with a 'Ta da'. Her eyes lingered on his extended fingers, saving herself momentarily; they flicked to the supine form of Hugo Fuller.

Jesus Christ. She gagged, couldn't help herself. Swallowing back the rush of hot acid bile that coursed up her throat and filled her mouth, she took a couple of heaving breaths. 'Jesus Christ.'

Marilyn nodded. 'My thoughts exactly. Hugo Fuller was stun gunned to subdue him and then tied to the chair.' His voice was determinedly matter-of-fact as he extended his arm again to indicate two small elliptical burn marks on Fuller's corpulent chest.

'Does a stun gun render the victim unconscious or paralysed after operation?' Jessie asked, her tongue working around the acid coating her mouth.

'It depends on the voltage, but basically a stun gun causes complete disruption of the muscular and electrical system of the body for the time that it's activated, causing total and painful paralysis. Once the cycle is complete the effect of the stun gun ends.'

'But there must be significant after-effects. It must knock the breath from you, mentally, if not actually physically paralyse you for a decent length of time after it is deactivated, particularly if you're not expecting it.' She indicated Fuller's mobile, which was lying in a pool of blood on the floor beneath the lounge chair. 'If you're chillaxing by the pool in your towelling robe, chatting on your mobile.'

'Yes, you're right. It is safe to assume that the after-effect of the stun gun would have disabled Hugo Fuller long enough for the perpetrator to tie him to the lounge chair so that he could then murder him.' He looked to Cara. 'As soon as we're finished here, find out which company Fuller's mobile is registered with and find out who he was speaking with this evening.'

'Yes, Guv.'

'What was the actual cause of death?' Jessie asked.

'We'll need Dr Ghoshal to confirm, but both Burrows and I believe that a penetrative injury through the eye was the most likely cause of death.'

'And the scratches down his face?'

Marilyn shrugged. 'To cause pain? Torture him?'

Jessie gave a non-committal nod. The whole scene – not just the brutal, gut-wrenching horror of it – was bothering her. It didn't feel right.

'The brain is able to perform critical functions despite serious local damage, whether caused by a penetrating trauma or another trauma,' she continued. 'Such as a stroke, or an operation by a neurosurgeon. I remember a case I studied, where a man was doing a bit of DIY at home in the evening, while having a few drinks, and lost control of the nail gun—'

Cara grimaced and went a shade paler, if that were even possible.

'A six-inch nail went straight through his left eye and penetrated his frontal lobe.' Jessie gave Cara what she hoped was a reassuring smile. 'He was fine.'

She looked over and met Marilyn's gaze, knew what they

46

were both thinking. *And Callan.* A Taliban bullet lodged in his temporal lobe and still operating as normal. But for how long?

'Yuh . . . uh . . .' She fought to regain her train of thought, an image of that envelope from Callan's neurologist rising in her mind. 'To kill via the brain requires causing a significant enough injury to cause widespread swelling or major intracranial bleeding, which depending on the exact kind of bleeding can cause compression of the brain, spasm of the arteries, or both, leading to tissue death and ultimately brain death. A single knife, nail or stick of wood in the eye that penetrates the brain, provided that it doesn't hit a major artery, and isn't waved around, would probably not kill a healthy person outright. Though obviously, given the range of outcomes, it's not the most sensible idea—'

She sensed Marilyn looking hard at her. 'If I'm not mistaken, you're chattering, Dr Flynn.'

Lifting her shoulders, she flashed him an apologetic smile. Why was she *so* nervous? The scene, obviously, the grotesque, abattoir horror of it. But Callan, more, she realized. Contemplating Hugo Fuller's injuries had taken her right back to Callan, to this morning, to that letter.

'Sorry, you're right, I'll stop.' A pause. 'Rambling, that is.'

'And – so,' Marilyn asked.

'Cause of death?'

He nodded.

'The eyes – both, I'd say. But then there must be some significance to that. It's a grim way to kill someone, even for the killer.' She flapped a hand in Hugo Fuller's direction. 'It would have been so much easier just to stab him through the heart, particularly as his chest was exposed.' She looked from Fuller – reclining in that lounge chair, his eye sockets caves of blood, blood and aqueous fluid streaked down his face and chest, those wild animal gouges to his face – to his wife, Mrs Fuller, Claudine. Dead, yes, but in a more humane way, if murder could ever be termed humane. 'I know that you're a betting man, Marilyn.'

'Not any more.'

'Huh?'

'I'm giving clean living a go.'

Jessie rolled her eyes. 'Is that a blink-and-you'd-miss-it kind of a go?' She caught his gaze and realized, from his look, that he was entirely serious. 'Oh, I'll put a lid on the facetious comments then.'

'You do that, Dr Flynn. And the bet?'

'That she was alive and sentient when she was put into the pool. He might have knocked her unconscious, stunned her or whatever, at the back door to incapacitate her while he dealt with the husband, but I'd bet that he then waited until she came around before he dropped her in the pool.'

'Because it's unnecessary?' Marilyn murmured.

'Yes.'

'What?' Cara cut in. 'What's unnecessary?'

Jessie broke eye contact with Marilyn and swung her gaze to meet Cara's questioning look. 'Tying Hugo Fuller up. If he wanted to kill them both by the most expedient method, he would have done the wife in the hallway, once she'd let him in, and then come in here and stun gunned and killed the husband. Or just killed the husband. Hit him over the head with something, or stabbed him in the heart. Unless . . . unless the perpetrator wanted him to watch his wife dying.'

She looked back to Hugo Fuller, *chillaxing*, trying to

suppress the heave in her stomach at the sight of him, the sharp taste of bile bubbling up her throat. He looked like a medieval torture victim. Her gaze moved from Fuller to Cara who, despite his natural skin colour, looked paler than she did midwinter. Apparition pale. Ghoul pale. She knew exactly how he felt.

'I'm struggling with it too,' she said in a voice pitched low enough that Marilyn wouldn't hear. 'Though I presume that it gets easier with experience.' She flashed him a quick smile. *Presume . . . hope . . . pray.* The Fullers, the azure water sparkling with its dozens of submerged lights, the tropical heat of the pool house, was making her feel as if she was a castaway on a midsummer's ocean, two of her ship-mates dead, rotting beside her.

'I think you may find that whatever was used to take out Fuller's eyes didn't reach his brain,' she continued, refocusing back on Marilyn. '*Deliberately*, didn't reach his brain, or not at first anyway.'

'He was alive for that?' Cara murmured.

She nodded. 'It says to me anger, real fury. And hatred too. Intense hatred. His eyes are—' she broke off, sucking in a breath to fight another stomach heave. Burrows would have a cardiac if she vomited in the middle of his crime scene.

'Mush?' Marilyn said.

She nodded. *Mush.*

'It's to do with seeing . . . watching. The killer made the husband watch his wife die and then took his eyes out. Deliberately took his eyes out. And he was alive,' she finished, her voice strangled. 'I'd bet a lot that he was alive throughout.'

'And the scratches?'

49

'Made by the same implement that carved those scratches into the door, I'd say.' She paused. 'And I think that they . . . this might have something to do with dogs.'

Marilyn raised an incredulous eyebrow. 'Dogs?'

12

Callan knew that he should slow down, but adrenalin and endorphins were coursing through his veins making him feel impossibly alive, healthy, whole again. A rare feeling, intoxicating in its intensity. He crested the hill, virtually scrabbling on his hands and knees the last few metres were so steep, his heart punching against his ribs, lungs screaming for oxygen. Head thrown back, he stood, sucking in the freezing, liquid air, but still his lungs heaved and sucked like a punctured pair of bellows and the pounding in his heart had moved to his head. Pounding, throbbing. He straightened, too quickly, must have done, because he staggered dizzily, his flailing hands finding the trunk of a tree, clasping the solid wood, leaning against it now, his tongue out, panting like a dog. Closing his eyes, he sought out the quiet place in his mind that he'd told that mumsy therapist about, that he went to when he felt an epileptic fit coming on.

Good, that's good. When you feel an epileptic fit coming on, close your eyes and go up to Foley Hill. It's a stunning autumn day, like the one you describe, sunny but chilly . . .

But he was here already, bodily, standing on the top of that hill he'd described, feeling the chill wind curl around him, willing the dizziness, the drum-thump in his head to recede, and he couldn't go there in his mind also. Hands grappling at the tree trunk, he slid to his knees, the rough bark sandpapering the ends of his grasping fingers. The ground slammed up to meet him and then he was gone, only faintly aware of what his body was doing, writhing, jerking, his limbs flailing, feet pedalling in the damp leaf mulch. Through frosted glass he saw the shifting mosaic of branches and leaves above him, bright patches of chill blue sky, and something else too. Something pale.

A face?

Someone?

Was someone here, watching him? He tried to call out, but his body wasn't his own, his brain was fog, and his tongue was rubber-useless in his mouth.

Slowly the fit receded and he lay on the damp carpet of orange-brown leaves, shaking and sweating, his skull nursing a brain that had been cleaved in two with an axe.

Twisting onto his front, he vomited once, twice. Pushing himself onto his hands and knees, he hauled himself to standing with his grazed fingers, leaning against the trunk of a tree for support. His vision refocusing, he looked around. He had had the strong sense that someone else had been up here with him, still had a lingering feeling that he wasn't alone. But he could hear nothing, see no one, just the blank trunks of trees, the motionless carpet of orange-brown leaves masking their roots, not even the scamper of a squirrel or the chirp of a bird to carve up the dead silence.

Fuck. His epilepsy was getting worse, much worse. Usually it was stress and tiredness that kicked off fits, but he had slept well the past few days and his job hadn't been stressful for some time. And yet here he was, covered in leaf mulch and vomit, his head pounding as if a road drill was going to work on his skull. He needed to tell Jessie, couldn't keep pretending that everything was all right. He owed her time to prepare herself for the operation because now, standing here, post two fits in the past hour, he knew that he didn't have a choice but to let them operate.

13

If she glanced sideways, tilted her head just a fraction, she'd see the lifeless form of Hugo Fuller through the glass wall of the swimming pool complex, still strapped supine to that lounger. Dr Ghoshal, the pathologist, was there now, his beanpole frame doubled over Fuller, the look on his face pure query. No disgust there. No horror.

And the look on Fuller's?

Jamming her eyes shut, Jessie tilted her face skywards and took a few deep breaths, sucking the chill morning air deep into her lungs. Her chest was so tight with tension that she felt as if the air was barely reaching the back of her tongue. She had never seen anything like the sight of that body. Of that face. Of those cavernous black eye sockets.

Her gaze moved from Fuller's supine form to the base of the door that led from the sunken patio, where she was now standing, inside, to the door through which Claudine Fuller had let in death. It hadn't been fingernails that had done that to Fuller's face, his eyes, just as it hadn't been fingernails that had made these marks on this door.

It hadn't been fingernails.

Had it been claws?

Strong, sharp claws.

But not a dog's – surely?

Ducking her gaze to the patio, Jessie shut out the sound of Marilyn next to her, tapping the leather-soled toe of one navy suede Chelsea boot impatiently against the York stone. Though he operated in the same way that she did, needing space to 'get a sense', his natural lack of patience made him chafe against that desire in others.

Could it have been a dog? A huge dog – bigger even than a huge male Siberian husky? Raking and – what – whining? Sniffing? For Claudine, the animal lover.

An involuntary shudder ran through her. Someone walking over her grave.

She stood, wrapping her arms tight around her torso.

'It's—' A sudden vibration in her pocket, the third she'd felt in the past few minutes. She couldn't answer it now. Pulling her mobile half out of her pocket, she glanced down at the screen. Three missed calls from Callan. 'Sorry, Marilyn, just give me a second.' She fired off a quick text – **at the crimescene xx** – and slid the phone back into her pocket. She'd call him back as soon as she could.

'It's what? Premeditated?' Marilyn said. 'Clearly.'

She shook her head. 'Creepy, I was going to say. Really fucking creepy.'

Marilyn gave a grim half-smile. 'That's not a very professional term, Dr Flynn.'

'No—' A pause. 'I think—' She broke off again. How to verbalize her thoughts? 'Look, Marilyn, I know that this is going to sound mad . . .'

Marilyn smiled. 'I'd be disappointed in you if it didn't.'

Jessie bit her lip. 'Madder, maybe, than even you give me credit for.'

'Go on.'

'I think that . . . I think that our perpetrator pretended to be the dog returning, pretended to be Lupo, and scratched at the door.'

Marilyn raised a cynical eyebrow.

'For the wife. She loves dogs. So perhaps . . . probably, actually, probably after Lupo had been gone for some time, she started to get worried. And then she heard the scratching. Scratching and sniffing under the door, perhaps, like dogs do. She wouldn't have given it a second thought, would have just yanked the door open, and—' Unwrapping her arms from around her torso, she spread her hands.

Marilyn shook his head. She hadn't convinced him. From the look on his face, she hadn't even got close. 'There's no way that fingernails made those marks in the door's paintwork,' he said.

'No, you're right, they didn't. Couldn't have done.'

'And – so?'

'And – so—' she broke off with a shrug. 'You've heard of Freddie Krueger. Edward Scissorhands.'

'*Edward Scissorhands* was a comedy. Wasn't it?'

'I never watched it. I only saw the posters. And *Nightmare on Elm Street* definitely wasn't a comedy.'

'It would probably look like a comedy now, with those forty-year-old special effects.'

Jessie gave a crooked smile.

Marilyn sighed. 'What the hell are you saying, Jessie? That Freddie Krueger caught the dog, tied it to a lamp post outside some old biddy's house and then hiked back through half a kilometre of trees to scratch at the Fullers' back door?'

Jessie lifted her shoulders again. *Yes, that's pretty much the long and the short of what I'm saying.*

Marilyn mashed his fingers into his eye sockets. He felt as if someone had plucked his eyes out, ground them in a bowl of salt and jammed them back in his head. But at least he still possessed eyes.

'Jesus Christ.' Dropping his hands, he met her gaze. 'What? I recognize that look. What now? What are you thinking now, Miss Psychic-Psychologist-Psychobabble?'

'Hugo Fuller's eyes. The marks on his face.'

'His eyes were gouged out with a knife.'

'Were they?'

Marilyn tilted his head questioningly. 'Weren't they?'

Jessie shook her head, slowly. 'No, I think they were clawed out. You could see. The marks on his forehead, the marks on his cheeks. It wasn't a knife.'

'So how did he die? Claws couldn't penetrate his brain.' But even as Marilyn said it, Jessie could sense his lack of conviction. She didn't pull him up on it, just looked back down at the door, the marks.

'They're similar, aren't they, Marilyn,' she said finally. 'The gouges down Fuller's face and the marks on this door. So similar as to be probably caused by the same thing. The same tool. The same—' She broke off with another shrug. It was all she seemed to be able to do this morning – shrug.

The same hand. The same claw.

She didn't say it – because it didn't need to be said.

Marilyn remained silent for a long moment. 'God help us,' he said finally, with a gargantuan sigh. '*God help us.*'

14

'As I said, I'm Hugo's stepmother,' Valerie Fuller said coldly. 'Not his actual mother. So, you had that wrong.' She was leaning against the door frame, arms folded, hugging a chunky-knit argyle cardigan tight across her ample chest. She had already pulled the front door three-quarters closed behind her, to keep the heat inside her neat barn conversion, Detective Sergeant Workman assumed. She hadn't invited Workman to step inside, showed no indication that she was going to. 'Thank you for taking the time to come over and tell me about his death in person, though a phone call would have sufficed,' she added.

DS Workman had drawn or, more accurately, been handed the short straw, Marilyn being still occupied at the Fullers' crime scene with Jessie Flynn, DC Cara and Burrows' CSI team. She was beginning to regret her label as the team's 'tea and sympathy' woman. However, it was abundantly clear that Valerie Fuller required no sympathy and that she could, doubtless, very efficiently make her own cup of tea.

'It's against regulation to break the news of relatives'

deaths over the telephone. It has to be in person, face to face,' Workman explained.

The Surrey and Sussex Major Crimes family liaison officer, who Workman had just asked to wait in the car, had expected to stay with Valerie Fuller for a day or two, helping her to work through her grief. *Not necessary*, she had been told, in no uncertain terms. Mrs Valerie Fuller seemed ambivalent about her stepson's brutal demise.

Workman nodded. 'Stepmother,' she echoed. 'I will ensure that is changed in our records.'

She flipped the collar of her navy woollen overcoat up around her neck and lifted her shoulders, sinking into the warm wool. The barn conversion was nestled at the end of a narrow valley between two hills, the valley creating a wind tunnel with its apex at the doorstep on which she was standing. Mrs Fuller seemed oblivious to her discomfort – or, if she had noticed, she gave no indication that she cared.

'How old was Hugo when you married his father?' Workman asked.

'Five.'

'And his mother?'

'She died when he was two and a half.'

'That's sad.'

'Yes, I suppose.' Her tone was offhand, patently lacking in concern. 'But he wasn't a very nice boy,' she added, suddenly, unexpectedly.

'You mean, he became a not very nice boy because of his mother's death?'

Valerie brushed a stand of blonde hair from her forehead. 'No, that's not what I meant. Hugo wasn't ever a nice boy. He was wrong from the start. I knew him before his mother died, you see. I was his father's secretary, so I knew the family. Not well, but enough. Even when Hugo was little, a toddler, an age when every child should just be adorable, there was something hugely unappealing about him.'

'In what way?'

A careless shrug. 'In every way. His personality, his demeanour, the way he interacted with others, animals and people. Everything.' She gave a dismissive little laugh. 'You know how some people are just born wrong. Hugo was one of those.'

Workman resisted the urge to object, but she wasn't here to debate. She was here to break some terrible news – which she had done – and to gain some information, as quickly as possible, given that she had already lost all feeling in her ears. But to her, saying that someone was 'just born wrong' denied the presence of any nuance in the nature–nurture debate. Was anyone really just born wrong? And to say that a child hadn't been affected by his mother's death revealed, to her mind, an absence of humanity. She felt sorry for the toddler Hugo, the young Hugo who must have mourned his mother's loss and sensed his stepmother's hostility.

'Did you have any of your own children?' Workman asked.

'I had two girls with Hugo's father. Kitty and Florence.'

'How old are they?'

'Kitty is thirty-four and Florence thirty-two.'

'So, six and eight years younger than Hugo.'

'About that, yes.'

'Do they keep in touch with Hugo?'

'No.'

'Why not?'

Valerie Fuller rolled her eyes, a small but pointed

movement. 'I've already told you, surely. Hugo was a little shit. My girls never liked him. Anyway, he went away to boarding school when he was eleven, so they didn't see much of him when they were growing up. They were never close.'

'Eleven?' Workman asked.

'Yes, and to be quite frank it wasn't soon enough.'

'Where did he go?'

'Fettes College. Hugo's father went to Fettes College, his father before that and God knows how many Fuller boys before that. I don't come from boarding-school stock. I was Godfrey's secretary, so I was distinctly lower-middle-class in relation to him. I had to work hard to be an appropriate Mrs Fuller, to fit into his world. I was what one would term as a trophy wife. I was twenty-five years Godfrey's junior.'

'When did Godfrey pass on, if you don't mind me asking?'

'Nearly twelve years ago, now.'

'Do you still miss him?'

A fleeting thawing of her expression. 'Yes, I do. We had a good marriage, all in all.'

'Did he have a good relationship with Hugo?'

Valerie Fuller's expression iced over once again. 'Godfrey adored Hugo. He was terribly proud of his son, of who he had become. Hugo was rich, as you know.' Another dismissive wave of her hand. 'That nasty little business of his was very lucrative.'

'Nasty business?'

Valerie nodded. 'Hugo set up and ran a property business, buying up freeholds and increasing the ground rent many times over, exploiting people living in cheap leasehold accommodation. There's no law against it, so the poor sods had to pay or lose the roof over their heads.'

Workman nodded. She knew little of Hugo Fuller's background or business interests, though all those details would be thoroughly fleshed in over the course of what would, hopefully, be a quick investigation. It would benefit no one to have a murderer of the like of who had killed Hugo and Claudine Fuller so viciously on the loose.

'Do you think his murder could have had something to do with his business?' she asked.

'I have no idea who would have murdered Hugo and Claudine, though I can't imagine that anyone Hugo dealt with on a professional basis – I'm using that word in a very tongue-in-cheek fashion, by the way – would have viewed him with fondness.'

'And his business was successful?'

'From a monetary perspective, absolutely. Though, of course, Hugo should have been successful. He was brought up with every advantage, plenty of money, the best education, and his father doted on him. Godfrey gave him money to help him set up the business.'

'It was a good investment, by the sound of it.'

Valerie bristled. 'There were a number of failures before that. Hugo wasn't clever, but he *was* cunning and entirely lacking in morals. The business he ended up in was the business that suited him perfectly.'

'What about Claudine Fuller?'

'What about her?' Valerie asked, in a tone that suggested Workman's question had been genuinely odd.

'Did you have much of a relationship with her? Did you like her?'

Valerie lifted her shoulders. 'I met her for the first time at Hugo's engagement party and then again at their wedding. They married two or three years before Godfrey died.'

62

'And?'

'And she seemed far too sweet a girl to have got tied up with Hugo, though it shouldn't have surprised me that he chose someone he could dominate.'

'And you haven't seen much of her since?'

Valerie shook her head. 'We saw them for dinner once, shortly before Godfrey died, and I saw them both at Godfrey's funeral. That's it. I was happy to sever contact with Hugo once Godfrey passed on. I have . . . had no love for Hugo and I doubt that he had much for me.'

Workman nodded. 'Do your daughters still live locally?' she asked.

'No. Kitty lives in North Devon. She's married to a local GP and has two young boys. Florence is in London, working in publishing. She's living the single life.'

Workman nodded. 'This may sound like an unnecessary question, but I do need to ask what you were doing last night between the hours of ten p.m. and one a.m. this morning.'

Valerie smirked. 'You're not really sizing me up as Hugo's murderer, are you?'

Workman met her smirk with an apologetic lift of her shoulders. 'I'm sorry, but I do need an answer.'

'I was having dinner and playing bridge with some friends in Bosham. I arrived at seven-thirty p.m., give or take a few minutes, and left at around midnight. I'll give you their number.' She ducked inside for a minute and returned proffering a sheet of cream notepaper with the names Dan and Margaret White written on it and a local phone number scribbled beneath. 'And I didn't nip over to my stepson's house to butcher him and his wife on the way home.'

Workman returned her cynical half-smile with a hollow one of her own.

'No, I'm pretty sure that you didn't.' She held up the piece of paper. 'Thank you for this and, once again, please do accept my condolences for the death of your stepson and his wife.'

15

Darkness had fallen by the time Jessie dragged her exhausted body and brain from the Fullers' crime scene and drove home, the twin cones of her Mini's headlights picking out silent country lane after silent country lane, no one seeming to be out and about on this chilly autumn Sunday evening. She was slightly ashamed to admit that she had glanced quickly through her rear passenger window to check that the back seat and footwells were empty, before opening her driver's door, climbing in and locking it immediately behind her. Ridiculous, she knew. As if anyone who could do her damage would be small enough to squeeze into a space that struggled to house a supermarket bag full of shopping. But still, she'd felt tense and jittery walking down the Fullers' gravel drive on her own, back to her car, those horrific murders and the disturbing nature of the crime scene having already wormed their way deep into her psyche.

She parked outside her cottage as the clock nudged nine p.m. The lights were off downstairs, but a pale rectangular light shone through the lounge window – Callan must be sitting on the sofa, working on his computer. But when she opened the front door, she saw his computer lock screen, the badge of the military police floating on a snowscape, and an immobile Callan-sized shape, flat out on the sofa. Grabbing her knitted argyle throw from the chair, she draped it gently over him. His face, in the semi-darkness, was pale as the gritty wheat throw, and though he didn't stir, his eyes were flickering from side to side underneath his lids. Dead asleep, but his mind agitated nonetheless.

What are you thinking about, Callan? The contents of that letter?

She had forgotten to return his phone calls and now, sensing it was better not to wake him, she couldn't ask. Her gaze found his coat, hanging on the rack. Would the envelope still be in its pocket? Though she felt a strong pull to tiptoe over and check, she knew that she wouldn't. She was obsessive about privacy. When she had lived with her father and his new wife Diane, in their narrow terrace in Fulham, she had understood that every day when she went to school Diane would be in her room, looking through her stuff, invading her privacy, just because she *could*. Diane always left something out of kilter, so that Jessie would know. And then at Hartmoor Mental Hospital, eyes had watched her through the sliver of reinforced glass in the door that trapped her, against her will, in that tiny prison room. Nothing private; nothing sacred, not body or mind.

She trailed her fingertips across Callan's forehead, her heart swelling with love. His skin felt cold, but clammy with fevered sweat. Pulling the throw further up, she tucked it in around his shoulders. Still, he didn't stir. Ducking down, she pressed her lips to his forehead, then headed upstairs to bed.

16

She was jerked into consciousness, suddenly and sharply, by a noise that she'd used to cringe and block her ears against when she was at school. Fingernails scraping down a chalkboard. Frowning, she rolled over, hooking an arm and leg over Callan, tucking her face into the warm, concave space between his neck and shoulder. He stirred, but didn't wake. When had he come upstairs and got into bed? She didn't know; hadn't woken.

The noise came again, louder this time, and even though she moulded herself to Callan's solid, safe bulk and yanked the duvet over her head, she could still hear it.

Scrape. Scrape. Scrape.

Razor-sharp nails clawing down board, or wood, making her teeth grit and goosebumps rise on her skin. Rolling away from Callan, she slid out from under the duvet. Her bedroom was cold – not the normal night-time cold of radiators gone to sleep, but ice-box cold, depths-of-midwinter cold, the type of cold that burrowed through to the very core of your bones. She pulled her dressing gown from the back of the bedroom door and shrugged it on, wrapping the tie tight around her waist, hauling the collar up around her neck. It was jet black outside, she saw from the bedroom window, the moon a bold splash of white gold high in the sky, casting no light on the fields below.

Scrape. Scrape. Scrape.

The noise was coming from downstairs. A ridiculous image of Miss Coffs, her GCSE maths teacher, rose in her mind, skinny and impossibly posh in her tweed suit, with her coiffed Margaret Thatcher hair, standing in her tiny sitting room, dragging one carnation-pink-polished nail down a line of quadratic equations. The thought made Jessie cringe and smile in equal measure.

It was cold on the landing as well, as if every window in the cottage had been left open, letting the outside flood in. And now that she was walking down the stairs, she could hear another sound too, that of lapping water. Had she left the kitchen tap on?

As she stepped from the bottom stair into the sitting room, she sank ankle-deep into ice-cold water. She yelped, hopping from foot to foot until the cold had numbed her skin and she felt it no more.

Scrape. Scrape. Scrape.

No Miss Coffs in her lounge, but still the sound of her carnation-pink nails. She sloshed across the lounge. At the kitchen window loomed a huge, pale shape, its hand raised as if to snatch her attention. Not a hand though, she realized with sudden horror, but a paw, a massive, pale wolf's paw, razor-sharp claws bared.

Scrape. Scrape. Scrape.

She swallowed.

My mind is playing tricks. A dream – it has to be.

She could barely breathe. She wanted to scream, to run back upstairs to Callan, to hide under the duvet and press herself against his safe, warm bulk, but she couldn't move, not a muscle.

Wake up. Control your body.

Instead, she watched helplessly as her hand stretched out and grasped the key in the lock, her fingers working to their own tune, turning, swinging open the door, letting in . . . letting *it* in.

The chill night air sliced through her skin. A freezing breeze ruffled her hair and flapped the hem of her dressing gown around her knees. The silence was absolute and she could smell something primeval, musty. She wondered if there was a place one reached where it was impossible to feel more afraid, and if there was, she was there, breathless with terror, trapped and helpless inside her own body.

One step at a time, her foreign legs bore her outside, eyes casting around for that huge, pale creature she had seen through the window.

Where had it gone?

Behind me? She spun. No, nothing, just the kitchen door gaping open, an empty expanse of pale ceramic tiles shiny with damp, water leaking over the threshold and pooling around her bare feet.

A noise. A whimper.

She twisted back to the dark garden. And saw him. Not the pale monster, but Lupo, sitting in the centre of the lawn. Deep gashes ran down his face and his eyes were gone, but there was something in those depthless black sockets that pleaded with her, begged her to let him in, save him.

'Jessie, what the hell are you doing?'

She leapt and spun again.

69

Callan was standing on the doorstep. He looked hard, and solid and safe, and all she wanted to do was to hurl herself against him, but her body still wouldn't cooperate, so she remained where she was in the middle of the freezing lawn, shaking and shivering.

'Jessie!'

'Lupo,' she called.

'What?'

'I thought I saw Lupo in the garden. The Fullers' dog. Lupo.'

'You were sleepwalking.'

She shook her head. Had she been? 'No, I was awake. I felt awake.'

'Come in now. It's freezing.'

She met his gaze dully and nodded. She felt as if she was floating underwater, everything muffled by dense liquid, her movements slow and ponderous. Should she tell him about the . . . the what? The animal? The wolf? That huge pale figure at the kitchen door? *No* – she knew that she wouldn't. He'd think that she was crazy. Perhaps she was crazy.

'What time is it?' she murmured, instead.

'Just past midnight.'

'Not late. I thought it was three or four, that I'd been asleep for hours.'

He shook his head, held out his hand. 'Come inside, gorgeous. Come back to bed.'

Jessie nodded. She let herself be led meekly inside, stood while Callan locked the kitchen door behind her, felt his strong arm slip around her shoulders and guide her upstairs. But still that image of a broken, bloodied Lupo filled her mind.

17

'Hugo Fuller had decidedly questionable morals, by the sound of it, but that doesn't mean that he and his good lady wife deserved to die.' Marilyn cleared his throat, a grating sandpaper rasp in the silent room. 'Far from it. Very far from it. Now, any questions for me before we hear from our resident clinical psychologist, Dr Jessie Flynn?' His gaze tracked along the rows of assembled faces, before alighting, settling, on Jessie's. He raised his arm, gesturing to the gaping space beside him at the front of the room. 'The floor is all yours, Dr Flynn.'

Resident clinical psychologist, Dr Jessie Flynn.

She couldn't remember the last time Marilyn had referred to her formally, except in jest. Pushing herself reluctantly to her feet, grabbing her notebook, just something to hold to calm the shake in her hands, though it contained no notes related to the case, she rose and skirted around the chairs to join Marilyn at the front of the incident room. Twenty cynically expectant faces stared back at her, a sea of crossed arms and legs echoing the facial expressions, none of it confidence-boosting. Jessie's gaze flicked quickly to the huge whiteboards paving the walls, where the fledgling investigation played out in crime-scene photographs; schematics of the Fullers' house and the woods hemming it; maps of the local area already marked with likely approach routes to the house and escape routes from it – multiple approach and escape routes, needles-in-haystacks multiple, courtesy of the house's grandiose isolation; as well as flipchart sheets, each filled top to bottom with 'to-do lists'. *Just the beginning.* The first few broad-brush strokes that would be painstakingly fleshed out, coloured in with many hundreds of hours of mainly terminally tedious grunt work.

Unless.

Unless they caught a break.

Her job, to catch them that break. She wasn't sure that she was up to it.

'OK, uh, thanks for coming in,' she said. Her voice wavered and she was angry at herself for it.

'They didn't have choice,' Marilyn cut in. 'It's called work and they get paid to be here.'

Jessie joined the ripple of laughter with a muted smile. Marilyn had sensed her unease, she realized, and the joke had been his way of lightening the atmosphere after the deadening video walkthrough of the Fullers' house. The sight of the couple's ravaged bodies – Hugo Fuller's in particular – had been almost as horror movie on the screen as it had been in real life, and Marilyn was perhaps trying to demonstrate that they were all on her side, or the same side at least. But his casual aside served only to knock her off her stride. She had been all set to begin, keyed up, focused.

She flicked open her notebook and glanced unseeing down

at the randomly opened page, buying herself time. Why on earth did she feel so nervous? Because she'd done nothing but one-on-ones with individual patients for years? Her job, getting into the mind of one person, not selling her ideas to twenty. Or because, although she had helped Marilyn on two previous investigations, this was the first time that she had been wheeled out as an expert from the get-go? Surveying the faces in front of her, most of whom had been on the force for years, she felt like a one-eyed man called in to guide the fully sighted through Daedalus' labyrinth.

'OK, so, uh, it's personal,' she began. 'I believe that it's personal, that the killer has some personal connection to the Fullers, most likely to Hugo Fuller.'

A man's voice, calling out from the back of the room. She didn't see whose. 'Why most likely to Hugo Fuller?'

'Because I think that he was the intended target. The autopsy will confirm or refute, but I think that his wife was killed first, tied up and drowned in the swimming pool, while he was made to watch. So, while she clearly suffered, he suffered more.'

Another man's voice. 'What if he didn't like his wife?'

A burst of harsh laughter, too loud, graveyard humour to paper over the canyon-sized cracks of tension and unease in the room.

'It's irrelevant,' she said when it had died down, her smile fading too, readopting the mask of professionalism to paper over her equally canyon-sized confidence cracks. 'Even if Fuller didn't like his wife, by killing her first, the murderer was deliberately drawing out the torture for him. For any human being, however cold or lacking in morals, seeing another human being killed, someone you have lived with and potentially loved at some point, would be incredibly traumatic. And also, he would have known what was coming, known that he was next.'

'Isn't it possible that the killer tied Fuller up to keep him subdued while he did the wife and that it was nothing to do with watching or drawing out torture?' the same man challenged – a middle-aged, dark-haired, jowly man who Jessie didn't recognize. 'There was most likely only one killer, wasn't there, DI Simmons, and Fuller was a big man.'

Jessie looked across at Marilyn, waiting for him to answer.

'The forensic evidence we have, limited to footprints so far, suggests that there was only one killer,' Marilyn said. 'A man. Other forensic evidence collected at the scene has been sent to the labs and is being expedited, so that may yet prove us wrong, but, yes, we are ninety-nine per cent sure that this crime was perpetrated by one man.'

'Right,' the man at the back continued. 'There was one killer and two victims and so he probably couldn't have handled both at once. And, as I already said, Fuller was a big man.'

'If he had just wanted to kill both of them by the most expedient method, he would have killed Claudine Fuller in the downstairs hallway, when she opened the door to him,' Jessie said, adding for clarification: 'To the dog . . . to what she thought was the dog. Then he would have come into the swimming pool and killed Fuller. Fuller was lying on a lounger facing away from the patio where the intruder entered. The only light onto the patio was the dim reflected light from the swimming pool's conservatory. There is a solid door and a changing room between the hallway and the swimming pool area and the swimming pool has noise – the sound of the air-conditioning system, the pool filter, the bubble of the Jacuzzi. It's unlikely that Hugo would have heard his wife being killed, so he still would have been surprised. I believe that the set-up was deliberate and that the murderer wanted Hugo Fuller to watch.'

'So you're saying that Hugo Fuller knew the killer?' DC Cara asked.

'Not necessarily. Fuller may have known his killer personally or he may never have actually met him. But yes, I would say, without doubt, that something Fuller did, either to this man, or to someone he loved, was a driver for the murders.'

'Why?' asked Sergeant Arthur Lawford, the exhibits officer, frowning. He was a veteran of forty years, had started in Major Crimes when Marilyn was in short trousers (though Jessie had trouble imagining Marilyn in anything apart from his battered black leather biker jacket and faded black jeans, or one of his identikit, drainpipe-legged, black suits), and Lawford was happy to languish at sergeant level, had no desire to be a star player. She met Lawford's insipid blue gaze.

'The murders, particularly that of Fuller, were exceptionally violent, but not in a way that demonstrates impulsive aggression or lack of control. To my mind, the crime scene demonstrated a very planned and calculated level of aggression, of nastiness for want of a better word, that to me says personal. The killer wanted Hugo Fuller to suffer, not just physically but also, and more importantly perhaps, psychologically. For the whole time the perpetrator was tying up and killing Claudine Fuller, Hugo would have known . . . known what was coming and he almost certainly would have known why, worked out why. Or been told why, if he couldn't work it out himself.'

Jessie's mind filled with an image, the swimming pool, the heat, a big man tied to a wooden lounger, struggling hard, knowing that it was futile, that he couldn't free himself, then offering the killer inducements, anything he wanted, anything, just to *stop*. And when he realized that the killer couldn't be bought, crying, howling, begging.

'Tears,' she murmured.

'What?' Marilyn asked.

'Tears,' she repeated, lifting a hand to indicate the photographs tacked to the board behind her, but not turning to look herself. She'd had her fill of Hugo Fuller's injuries this morning, in addition to another painful shot in the arm when she'd let her eyes graze around the walls while she'd been finding her confidence at the beginning of this meeting. She didn't need a third dose. 'I'll bet that there are tears mixed with the blood on Fuller's face. He would have struggled and fought, to start with, maybe been angry, abusive. Then he would have tried to bribe the killer, boasted about his wealth, offered the killer anything, *anything*, to stop. But then, as the horror show playing out in front of him progressed, he would have realized that he was fucked, and he would have cried. Cried and begged . . .'

She tailed off, her gaze tracking around the faces, taking in the changing expressions as they digested the information she had just shared. Though most of them had worked for Surrey and Sussex Major Crimes for a number of years, she doubted many had worked on a case this determinedly gruesome. They had seen the crime-scene video, but most had probably already compartmentalized it, pushed the gory details to the backs of their minds. She could see, from the looks on people's faces, that her words had forced an uncomfortable clarity.

'Business?' a voice croaked from the back of the room. 'Could the personal be related to his business?'

Jessie nodded. 'Yes, it could be related to his business, because his business was effectively personal. It affected people's lives, the roof over their and their families' heads.' She glanced at Marilyn to see if he had anything to add.

'His business was basically screwing poor people,' Marilyn added. 'He bought up freeholds on cheap properties, mainly blocks of flats and terraced houses in poor areas, and then raised the ground rent by a few thousand per cent. So, where people were previously paying negligible sums for their ground rent, they were suddenly forced to pay hundreds or thousands of pounds a year. If they couldn't pay, their property was repossessed and they and their families were kicked out.'

'Shouldn't that be illegal?' Cara asked.

Marilyn lifted his coat-hanger shoulders. 'If everything that was morally repugnant was made illegal we'd all be working 24/7 rather than just 18/7, so count your lucky stars that it isn't.'

'It may not be to do with his work,' Jessie cut in. 'There may be another reason entirely.'

'Like what?'

She resisted the urge to shrug. *God knows.* 'Look into his background. If he screws people professionally . . . meta-phorically professionally,' she added hurriedly. 'He could be screwing people all over the place. Metaphorically . . .' *Think of a different word.* But she couldn't. She felt as if her brain was floating around, untethered, in that swimming pool with Claudine, at the back door with her as she opened it to . . .

Scratching.

Sniffing.

Edward Scissorhands?

Freddie Krueger?

'Metaphorically and, uh . . .' She spread her hands and smiled. 'Literally.'

'It was a messy crime scene. Can we assume that the killer is disorganized?'

'No, absolutely not. I'd say exactly the opposite. It was messy because it was vicious, but actually, the murders were well thought out, well planned and well executed. There was one killer, two victims, so he had to plan well to ensure that he overpowered both Hugo and his wife, so that he could then enact the theatre he'd planned – the "show" – for Hugo Fuller.'

'What about the dog?' Marilyn asked.

Jessie glanced over to the picture of Lupo, looking pure wolf, pure *White Fang*, on the board. She had loved *White Fang* when she'd been a teenager, had wanted to be there, in the Yukon territory, in charge of a dog team. The ultimate in escapism. She had loved any book that had allowed her to escape from the broken edifice of her teenage life, had devoured hundreds in the year she'd been incarcerated in Hartmoor Psychiatric Hospital. She wondered quickly whether Claudine Fuller had wanted to escape as a teenager too, whether she had wanted to escape as an adult, as a wife. 'He took the dog and tied it to a lamp post in the village deliberately.'

'The dog wasn't found until one-thirty a.m.,' Marilyn said. 'But the pathologist, Dr Ghoshal, estimates that Hugo and his wife were killed between ten p.m. and midnight. Again, he will confirm after the autopsies which are scheduled for tomorrow.'

'The dog is very noticeable and the village is small.'

'Miss Marple, eat your heart out,' Marilyn muttered, almost under his breath.

'So, it is logical to assume that the murderer took the dog and tied him up somewhere else,' Jessie continued. 'Somewhere he wouldn't be found, perhaps in the woods surrounding the Fullers' property, and then he moved him to the village after the murders. Otherwise, I think he would have been seen earlier. Again, that shows planning, thought. He brought along a lead to tie Lupo up. It's not the actions of a disorganized killer.'

'And it's not the actions of a random nutter,' Marilyn finished. 'Even though many of you may have been thinking Langley Green, while viewing that video walkthrough of the crime scene.'

At the mention of Langley Green – the inpatient mental health clinic in Crawley – a couple of the civilian workers sucked in audible breaths. Marilyn didn't want that, didn't want them boxing up the killer as a deranged psychopath in reaction to the nature of the crime. He didn't want people picturing him as a creature with red eyes, horns and a forked tail, someone you'd be able to identify just by catching his eye in a crowded room, immediately recognize the insanity lodged in the brain behind the gaze. He wanted them sensible, focused and, most importantly, open-minded. 'I will reiterate. Neither Dr Flynn or I believe that these murders were the work of a random nutter, so erase that thought from your minds.'

A sudden, high-pitched screech from the street outside, a child in pain or terror. Jessie flinched. Another screech. *No, not a child. Foxes, either fighting or mating.* It was the kind of sound that could scrape fingernails down your soul, particularly after what she'd seen in that house yesterday and after her dream. Outside the grimy windows, a dull autumn day was pushing away the last vestiges of darkness, but she could still see the ghost of her own animated reflection, the faint reflected backs of the heads belonging to the faces in front of her making her look as if she was viewing a phantom theatre performance through opaque glass.

DS Workman raised her hand, polite as always. 'Has this person killed before?'

This time Jessie did shrug. 'I don't know, is the honest answer. But I would say that he has definitely fantasized about the killing of Hugo and Claudine Fuller. Visualized it. It's incredibly—' she broke off, struggling to put into words what she was thinking. 'It's a very "stage-set" killing, very theatrical. And, as I said before, I believe that it's to do with watching.'

She sensed Marilyn's head swivel, his eyes focus on her. 'Can you elaborate on the watching?'

She nodded. 'He made Hugo Fuller watch his wife being killed and then he took Fuller's eyes out. Deliberately took his eyes out, *before* he killed him. So, I would say that whatever personal reason drives the killer, watching is key.'

Silence in the room. The absolute, stilled silence of a stunned audience, a collective holding in of breath. Not even the ambient noise usually associated with a room full of people: the scuff of feet on worn carpet, the crossing and uncrossing of restless legs, the rustle of clothing.

'Is he likely to kill again?' DC Cara's voice, breaking the deadening silence, pulling her mind back into the room.

Though Jessie had dreaded this meeting, she had most dreaded this question, the one question that she felt entirely unqualified to answer. Even less qualified than the others that had come before. She shook her head, a shake that morphed into a half-nod, to stillness.

'I believe that he will only kill again if he has another

80

personal axe to grind. Probably the same axe to grind that he had with Hugo Fuller, whatever that axe is.'

'Motivation,' Marilyn muttered. 'The classic – motivation. It always comes down to motivation. We need to find out what the killer's motivation is. And quickly.' The arc of his raised arm indicated the mosaic of photographs tacked to the whiteboards. 'Because I, for one, don't want to attend another crime scene that looks like this.' He laid a light hand on Jessie's shoulder. 'Thank you, Dr Flynn, for that very thorough briefing.'

With a fleeting smile and an overwhelming sense of relief, Jessie returned to her seat at the back of the room.

'And now DS Workman will give us a summary of what she learnt from Hugo Fuller's mother yesterday evening,' Marilyn said.

'Stepmother,' Workman corrected, rising to her feet. 'And it's not much, I'm afraid.'

18

Jessie heard the efficient clack-clack of Detective Sergeant Sarah Workman's sensible, low-heeled navy courts on lino tiles, closing the gap between them. She was tempted to break into a full-on Usain-Bolt-hundred-metre sprint, put as much distance as she could between herself and whatever task Workman intended to rope her into, but instead, she arranged her expression into a semblance of professionalism, turned and waited for Workman to catch her up.

'Can I have a quick word, Jessie?'

'Sure.'

'Thank you.' Workman dusted an invisible piece of dirt from the sleeve of her navy suit jacket with fidgety fingers. She seemed uncharacteristically nervous, jittery. Jessie had only ever experienced the professional face of DS Workman, the woman who was Marilyn's unfailingly supportive crutch, his walking, talking Rolodex, his diary, his details woman, his inexhaustible memory. The steadfast Workman who remained centred even when the walls surrounding them were plastered with images of eviscerated corpses, of the worst examples of what human nature could inflict on others.

'Here or somewhere private?' Jessie asked, sensing that whatever Workman wanted to talk about didn't relate to the case.

'Good morning, ladies.'

Is it? 'Morning,' Jessie replied, shifting back against the wall to let Arthur Lawford and another man from the incident room meeting, who she hadn't been introduced to, walk past.

'Private. Do you mind?' Workman replied, when the men had disappeared through the swing doors at the far end of the corridor.

'No, of course not.'

'I wanted to ask you a favour,' Workman said, as the door to the ladies' toilet shut behind them.

Jessie, backed up against the row of sinks, nodded. 'Ask away.'

'It's a big favour and it has nothing to do with work. I know that I shouldn't ask, given how much you've got on with the case, but I can't think of anyone else to turn to.'

With the thought of taking more on, Jessie felt a sudden, sharp burst from the electric suit – stress, tension manifesting itself in her old nemesis that she had fought so hard to control. She had no room, in the mess that was the Fullers' murders, to perform favours, any favours.

'Anything,' she said, ignoring the suit. 'Really, anything.'

Workman smoothed a fidgety hand over her low-maintenance bob. 'There's a boy I know. Well, more a young man, really, I suppose. He's fifteen. I met him at Age UK charity. We both volunteer at a lunch club there on Sundays, serving food to the old folk, washing up, that kind of thing.

83

It's for people who live alone, to give them company and a decent meal once a week. There's a minibus that drives around ferrying them back and forth.'

Jessie nodded encouragingly, though she felt anything but.

'He has a . . .' Workman touched her fingertips to her mouth '. . . a severe cleft palate. It was repaired when he was a baby, but he was left with significant facial deformity and a bad lisp. He has been bullied virtually since birth.' A flickering, nervous smile. 'Relentlessly bullied.'

Relentlessly bullied.

Jessie tightened her grasp on the steadying edge of the sink behind her back as the electric suit hissed, not for him, but for herself, for her past.

'He needs help.'

'What about the NHS?'

'He's had everything that the NHS will provide. Mental health among teens is at crisis point and the NHS can't cope. There aren't the resources.'

Jessie nodded. She knew about the limits of the NHS mental health provision all too well herself from her own days working as an NHS psychologist before she had left and joined the Defence Psychology Service.

'The bullying continued the whole time that Robbie was being treated by the NHS psychologist. Allan, his father, said that it was as if the help that Robbie was getting was being undone as soon as he'd received it.' Workman raised a flat hand, above her head, as if measuring the height of an invisible child. 'That he could never get any traction, never get to a state where he felt positive enough about himself to stand up to the bullies. He hadn't had any coun- selling for eighteen months and he's gone downhill fast since it finished – become hugely more anxious, terrified about going to school, agoraphobic, and his self-esteem is destroyed. And he's depressed, clinically depressed. Allan feels that Robbie is slipping away from him, slipping somewhere he may never be able to come back from.'

Jessie nodded, her mind's eye finding the images of those celluloid corpses papering the walls of the incident room.

Slipping somewhere he may never come back from.

They both knew what Workman was talking about; it didn't need to be said.

Jamie.

Suicide.

The electric suit hissed and snapped, worse than it had been in weeks, thoughts of her little brother Jamie always a bright red cape to her electric suit's bull.

'Robbie asked you for help?' she managed.

'Oh, God no, he's far too proud for that. His father did. He's a single parent, mother walked out years ago from what I can gather, and he has struggled to bring Robbie up. They can't afford to move from the area, though the boy has moved schools twice. But with kids linking up on social media, bullied children just can't get away. It follows them. Robbie's a fabulous boy – Allan has done a great job – but he can't do anything about the bullying. He's a fixer by nature, I think, and he can't fix this, though he has tried, really tried, for years. He couldn't stop the bullying and he can't mend what it has done to his son.'

'How long have you known them?' Jessie asked.

'I met Allan first. He was arrested for assault, four or five years ago now. He pushed some shitty kid at Robbie's school, a cocky, sporty kid called Niall Scuffil, and Niall's mum called the police. Niall had broken Robbie's arm a couple of months before, jumped on him when he was walking

85

home from school. A few other kids were watching, egging him on. Boys and girls.' Her voice caught on the word 'girls' and she pursed her lips, as if she had a bitter taste in her mouth.

If Workman was expecting girls to be above bullying, she would be – clearly had been – sorely disappointed. Jessie knew that well enough from her own teenage experiences that girls could be vile and, from what she heard, many girls now were worse. Tougher, over-sexualized, grown up too soon with all the internal psychological tensions that created.

'I was the arresting officer. I went around to speak to Niall's mother, gave her a piece of my mind. She withdrew the charges, but with very poor grace.'

'And nothing happened to Niall?'

'It was Robbie's word against eight others. Though Allan said that Robbie was so ground down by then, he didn't even complain. He just took it.'

'Dragging himself through the days probably takes all his energy,' Jessie said. 'Just surviving.' She knew that well enough herself from her own teenage experiences and hers hadn't been nearly as bad as Robbie's, from the little Workman had told her.

She grasped the edge of the sink behind her, relishing the feel of the cold porcelain against her skin. She felt nauseous – sick and intensely hot. The tiredness, she reasoned, her sleepwalking episode of last night disrupting what little shut-eye she'd had. Nothing to do with the electric suit scorching her skin, brand-hot with the memories.

'I can see him later today. After the Fullers' autopsy.' The words rushed out of her before her logical mind could intercept them.

'Are you sure?' Workman tilted her head, gaze searching Jessie's face.

'Yes, I'm sure,' she said, forcing a smile that she hoped didn't look as fake as it felt. If she didn't do it today, tomorrow might easily become 'tomorrow never comes' and, from what Workman told her, never wasn't an option for Robbie Parker.

19

'Remind me again why you want me to attend the Fullers' autopsy,' Jessie asked Marilyn, as they walked side by side down the basement corridor that led to Dr Ghoshal's autopsy suite.

Jessie didn't know if it was the product of the disturbed sleep or her imagination, overactive in anticipation of what was to come, but the neon-white strip-lit corridor felt freezing cold, as if they were advancing along a horizontal ice shaft. She rubbed at the goosebumps on her forearms.

'I asked you to attend because this is the first case you will have worked on from beginning to end with Major Crimes and I want you to experience every aspect of a murder investigation,' Marilyn said, glancing across at her. He raised an eyebrow. 'And because you might make a useful contribution.'

'What, like filling Dr Ghoshal's spotless stainless-steel sink with half-digested bacon sandwich, perhaps?'

Marilyn smiled. 'You're making me feel hungry.'

'Oh God, yuk.'

'My fridge was empty, so I only managed a couple of well-past-their-sell-by-date Weetabix.' He clapped a hand on her shoulder. 'You will thank me for this afterwards.'

'How did you arrive at that dubious conclusion?'

'Because I know that you're the kind of woman who likes a challenge.'

Jessie rolled her eyes. 'Don't you dare try to dress this one up as doing me good.'

'You'll see.' Marilyn opened the door they had reached and they entered a small room with metal lockers on one side, a fitted bench on the other. A changing room? Or an unprepossessing antechamber into hell, Jessie caught herself thinking.

'Ready?'

'You can't possibly expect an affirmative to that question.'

Suppressing a smile, Marilyn rapped his knuckles twice on the door opposite the one through which they had entered and pushed it open without waiting for an answer. Taking a steadying breath, Jessie followed, stepping into a low-ceilinged white-tiled room, beige vinyl covering the floor and running a quarter metre up the walls, ubiquitous in hospitals and clearly morgues. There were interrogation-chamber-bright lights, a row of metal doors that looked like the entrances to industrial-sized fridges (and probably were) set into the far wall, and three people dressed in green scrubs and clinical face masks occupying the space. Jessie had watched as many crime box-sets as most people, flicking channels late at night and ending up on *Silent Witness* for want of anything better to watch (though to be fair it did make for great late-night viewing) and the autopsy suite she had stepped into was nothing like the high-tech room that the cast operated in, with its plate-glass viewing gallery and space-age decor.

Dr Ghoshal's coolly appraising brown eyes met hers over his clinical face mask. 'Welcome, Dr Flynn. Is this your first autopsy?'

Jessie nodded. 'Can't you tell from the colour of my skin, which perfectly matches the colour of your tiles?' *And the colour of the corpses on your dissecting table* – she didn't say it. She had met Dr Ghoshal only a few times, though had gathered pretty much instantaneously that cracking feeble jokes about the contents of his autopsy suite would be strictly *verboten*.

'I will make the experience as pleasant as I possibly can then, Dr Flynn.'

'Thank you.'

Marilyn had admitted, on the walk down the corridor, that the last of Dr Ghoshal's autopsies he had attended, that of ten-year-old Jodie Trigg, he had excused himself and exited only a few short minutes after he'd entered. He said that he just couldn't stomach watching that little girl being hacked to pieces, however clinically and dispassionately. He couldn't recall his excuse, though he knew that Dr Ghoshal would have seen right through it as if through sparkling clean window glass. The weakness of his stomach and of his resolve hadn't been only because of Jodie's diminutive age, but also because he blamed himself wholly for her presence on the dissecting table in the first place. If they'd been quicker, made fewer mistakes in the investigation, she would have lived.

'It's the first time I've ever walked out of an autopsy in my twenty-five-year career in the force,' he had said, with a slightly embarrassed shrug.

Glancing over at Marilyn now, Jessie saw that his expression was stone, his gaze focused unwaveringly on Hugo

Fuller. He looked as if he would very comfortably be able to see this one through. She wished that she could claim the same. She still hadn't looked directly at either body, had just glimpsed them through the comforting opaqueness of her peripheral vision.

'Let's start with Mr Fuller, shall we,' Dr Ghoshal said.

From the corner of her eye, Jessie saw Marilyn step forward to take up a sentry position by Hugo Fuller's feet. She forced herself to look at Fuller directly for the first time, at his face, at the pale, naked slackness of his body. Her gaze skipped beyond him, to Claudine. Despite the severity of Fuller's injuries, the ravaged pits of his eyes, the gouges carving his face, he was easier to look at than his wife. Her corpse was so alabaster pale that Jessie could almost have convinced her brain that Claudine was carved of marble, not made of flesh and bone. But the expression on her face, in death, held a depth of sadness that was heartbreaking. What had Claudine been thinking about when she died? Had she been thinking about the loss of her own life? For some reason, perhaps just a fanciful one, Jessie thought not. Her mind found the photographs lining the mantelpiece – the only photographs – in that depressing mausoleum of a house, of Lupo, Claudine's baby left behind, no one to care for him or to love him. Had that been her final thought? Jessie was sure that if she had been Claudine, it would have been hers.

Her gaze moved back to Hugo Fuller and she stepped forward as Dr Ghoshal had instructed, taking up a position by Marilyn's side. Perhaps it was because she knew him to be a shit, suspected him to be responsible for both his own and his wife's murders, that she didn't feel as upset as she had expected to.

'Shall I begin?' Dr Ghoshal asked.

'Yes,' Jessie answered, with only a tiny waver in her voice.

The noise of Dr Ghoshal's scalpel slicing through Hugo Fuller's skin was, to Jessie, lions tearing a zebra's flesh from its bones. The sound of him methodically carving off the top of Hugo Fuller's skull with the circular reciprocating saw, the sear of a diamond blade through steel, even the low, monotonous hum he was making – 'his concentration hum', Marilyn had warned her – like a hive of furious bees. Her stomach felt as if it was filled with bubbling acid that threatened to surge up her throat. She cast her gaze around the white-tiled autopsy suite, until it alighted on a stainless-steel sink behind and to her right. *Five strides, a couple of seconds.*

'How did he die?' Marilyn's voice pulled her back.

'Devastating trauma to the brain,' Dr Ghoshal said.

'Through one eye?'

'A single stab wound to the brain can be survivable, DI Simmons,' he replied, in his perennially prosaic tone.

The man with the nail gun, Jessie thought. And, far more importantly, *Callan*. She still didn't know the contents of that letter from his neurologist, still regretted letting her obsession with privacy trump her curiosity.

'Two stab wounds, however,' Ghoshal continued. 'More challenging. And once the instrument was in Mr Fuller's brain, it was moved around – waggled, for want of a better word. Your man was determined to kill.'

'What instrument was used?'

'A knife or skewer perhaps, narrow, thin-bladed, not serrated, driven through each eye socket, into the brain.'

'Eye socket?' Marilyn asked. 'You mean eyeball? Through his eyeballs?'

Dr Ghoshal's eyes rose fractionally ceiling-wards, enough for both Marilyn and Jessie to clock the movement. 'Eye sockets, DI Simmons,' he repeated. 'The contusions to Mr Fuller's face, the mutilation to his eyeballs, occurred ante-mortem. I wouldn't imagine that there was much of his eyeballs left when he was finally put out of his misery with the thin-bladed instrument driven into his brain.'

Marilyn nodded. Jessie took a breath. The bubbling acid was rising up her throat. She gulped, trying unsuccessfully to swallow it down. It would be too humiliating to vomit now. She focused her gaze on the stainless-steel fridge doors across the room, on the three of them in reflection: Dr Ghoshal, a runner bean in his green scrubs, Marilyn, a thin black crow in his suit, she as apparition pale as Fuller's corpse, even when reflected in steel.

'Both the mutilation to his eyes and the contusions down his face were caused by the same instrument, I would say,' Dr Ghoshal continued. 'And I'm sure that you won't be surprised to hear that they would have caused very considerable pain.'

'Torture?' Marilyn asked.

Dr Ghoshal lifted his narrow shoulders. 'It would most certainly have been torture for Mr Fuller, though whether torture was the primary motivation is not for me to ascertain.' His coolly appraising gaze moved from Marilyn to Jessie. 'What is your theory on the contusions to Mr Fuller's face and the ante-mortem trauma to his eyeballs, Dr Flynn?'

Jessie forced herself to hold Ghoshal's gaze, tough given its searching intensity. Was he testing her? Probably.

'I think that they had two purposes. Firstly, to torture him, cause extreme suffering before his death. But I also believe that they had meaning both for the murderer and for the victim.'

Dr Ghoshal raised an eyebrow. 'Meaning?'

She nodded, with far more certainty than she felt. 'My theory . . .' she broke off, glancing over at Marilyn, checking in. His face was poker – she was on her own facing Ghoshal. 'My theory is that the murders are personal and that they are to do with watching.'

'Watching? Watching what?' Ghoshal asked.

'I don't know. But I do believe Fuller would have known exactly why he was being tortured and why the killer was employing the methods he employed.'

'Were the contusions done with the thin bladed instrument that was used to kill him?' Marilyn asked.

Dr Ghoshal shook his head. 'It's clear from the pattern of the contusions, which are spaced identically apart from each other, top to bottom, and from their consistent depth, that they were done at the same time, not individually.'

'With what?'

'Some type of large, sharp, fork-like instrument, I would suggest,' Ghoshal said, after a moment. 'Or—' he broke off, raising a gloved hand, fingers bent into a claw. He rotated his hand, spreading fingers, moving them closer together. It was the first time since they had entered the room that Jessie had seen him look anything other than entirely unhesitating.

'Fingernails?' Marilyn ventured.

Ghoshal shook his head. 'Human fingernails would be too weak to cause trauma this extensive.'

'An animal?' Jessie asked. 'A dog?'

Dr Ghoshal didn't answer for a moment. 'It would have to be a huge dog to inflict contusions this far apart. Also, I don't believe that a typical dog's claws would be sharp enough or have enough force to create this depth of trauma.' He picked up a metal ruler from the tin tray, held it to Fuller's face. 'The distance between each contusion is two point eight centimetres. That's a very big dog. A very big, very strong, very vicious dog.'

'But a dog could have done it?' Jessie pressed. 'A big dog, as you say? A wolf-dog?'

'Perhaps,' Ghoshal said finally, his coolly cynical gaze rising to meet Jessie's. 'It's possible. Not probable, not probable at all, but I suppose that it is possible.'

20

Jane Jones, Hugo Fuller's secretary, lived in north Chichester, on an estate of modern red-brick terraced houses, all bordered by privet-hedge-trimmed front drives and neat, handkerchief-sized back gardens. Workman had telephoned the offices of Winner Fuller earlier and been told that Hugo Fuller hadn't turned up for work today, though that wasn't unusual evidently, as he often had meetings out of the office.

She had also been told that Jane Jones, Fuller's secretary, was working from home today as she was waiting in for a furniture delivery. The man on the phone had sounded young and 'cat's away, mice will play' delighted that neither the boss nor his wing-lady were in evidence today; he clearly hadn't connected news reports of a couple brutally murdered in their Sussex country house with Hugo Fuller. Marilyn had, so far, managed to hold back the names of the victims from the journalists who had already picked up on the murders, though he doubted that luck would last until the evening news.

'Jane Jones drives the same car as you,' Marilyn said to

Workman, indicating the navy-blue 2016-registration Ford Fiesta parked on the tarmac drive. 'Same make, same colour, same age!'

'And if Dr Flynn was here she would doubtless draw some conclusions about our shared psychology from that coincidence,' Workman said with a smile.

Marilyn raised an eyebrow. 'And she'd be right to. You know that we policemen—'

'Persons,' Workman interrupted.

Both eyebrows raised, accompanied by a roll of his eyes. 'Police*persons* don't believe in coincidences.'

A white, oval ceramic plaque painted with a sprig of bluebells proclaimed that this was number fourteen. Raising his hand, Marilyn knocked on the lilac-painted front door. It was answered with brisk efficiency, within seconds, by a woman of a similar age to Workman, mid-forties, dressed in a pair of slim-legged navy trousers and a white crew-neck jumper. Her medium-brown hair was short, cut into as an efficient style as the manner of her door opening – much like Workman's own hair and door opening. There was, indeed, something very 'kindred spirit' about Hugo Fuller's secretary; the man had had commendable taste, in secretaries at least, Workman surmised, avoiding the amused glance Marilyn shot her as he held up his warrant card.

'Detective Inspector Simmons, Surrey and Sussex Major Crimes. And this is my colleague, Detective Sergeant Sarah Workman.'

Jane Jones eyeballed them both dispassionately from the doorway. 'How can I help you, Detective Inspector Simmons?'

'Could we come in for a moment, please?'

'If you must.' She stood back and ushered them into a small, neat sitting room at the front of the house, containing a simple beige leather three-piece suite and a smoked-glass coffee table, the window overlooking the Ford Fiesta and shared patch of grass beyond. Marilyn spoke when they were all seated.

'I'm sorry to tell you that your boss, Hugo Fuller, was murdered last night.'

If either of them had expected her to expire with shock, they were disappointed. Jane Jones took the news as if Marilyn had informed her that her supermarket delivery was missing a couple of essential items.

'You don't look surprised,' Marilyn said. 'Or particularly upset.'

Jones lifted her shoulders. 'Mr Fuller was my boss, not my husband, my brother or son. And I'm sure that it won't have escaped your notice, even this early in any investigation you might be conducting, that he wasn't the nicest man.'

'So, you think he had it coming?'

'No, I wouldn't say that. I *didn't* say that. I mean, really, does anyone have it coming?'

Marilyn didn't answer, though if he had his response would have been in the affirmative. Though he put equal effort into every murder he dealt with, give or take, he couldn't say that he was equally surprised when some people became victims. Certain individuals lived in a world where their getting their comeuppance was only a matter of time.

'Was he murdered at home?'

'Yes.'

She suppressed a shudder. 'I never liked that house.'

'You've been there?'

'A couple of times to collect things for work. We didn't socialize, if that's what you mean.'

'What didn't you like about it?'

'The isolation mainly. And though it was grand, they didn't have great taste; or I suppose I should say, *he* didn't have great taste. It was all his taste of course.'

'Of course?'

Jones arched an eyebrow. 'Hugo quite unequivocally wore the trousers.'

'In what way?'

'In every way, Detective Inspector Simmons. Work, home, marriage, taste, you name it. I don't think that Claudine got a look in, poor love. How is she, by the way? Is she holding up OK?'

'I'm afraid that Claudine Fuller was also murdered.'

Jones' hand flew to her mouth. For the first time since they had entered her home, she looked shocked and genuinely sorry. 'Oh, God, no. You didn't say.'

'I'm sorry,' Marilyn said. 'I should have mentioned that at the beginning. It was a double murder. They were found dead in the early hours of this morning, in the swimming pool complex attached to their house.'

'I'm so sorry. Poor poor Claudine. I hope it wasn't too dreadful for—' She broke off. 'What a stupid thing to say. Of course it must have been dreadful.' She met Marilyn's gaze. 'Do you have any idea who killed them?'

He shook his head. 'We're at a very early stage in the investigation, Mrs—'

'Miss.'

'Miss Jones, and we don't have any leads at the moment. We were hoping that you could help us with that.'

She nodded. 'Of course. Whatever you need.'

'Thank you.' Marilyn leant forward, steepling his fingers. 'Can you tell us about Hugo Fuller's business?'

'His business was buying up ground rents to leasehold

properties. The revenue came from the tenants' ground rent payments.'

'We've done a little research, Miss Jones. He didn't have a great reputation for being a fair and generous landlord.'

Jane Jones' mouth tightened. 'It's business, Detective Inspector Simmons.'

'But there's business and there's business, isn't there Miss Jones?'

'That's very cryptic.'

'Hugo Fuller's business was buying up freeholds and ramping up the ground rent by hundreds or thousands of per cent, wasn't it? And if families couldn't pay, they were kicked out of their properties, made homeless.'

'No one is truly homeless in this country, Detective Inspector. The council has a legal responsibility to house everyone.'

'Didn't you have any moral objection to what you were doing – working for a business like that, a man like that?' Workman cut in.

Jones shrugged. 'He paid my salary on time and he was a decent boss.'

Workman raised an eyebrow. 'Decent?'

'He was never nasty to me, if that's what you're asking. And he never pretended to be anything he wasn't.' She smiled, a cynical, slightly bitter smile. 'He was a "does what it says on the tin" kind of man.'

'What about the people he was screwing?' Marilyn asked. 'I can't imagine that they shared your view regarding Hugo Fuller's decency.'

A raised eyebrow, accompanying another cynical smile. 'Do you mean metaphorically or physically screwing, Detective Inspector?'

21

Bethwine Close was a somnolent cul-de-sac of ten, small, two-storey detached chalet-style houses bordering farmland on the southern edge of Chichester, all of which Jessie imagined would be occupied by retirees. All but one. Climbing out of her Mini, she stood for a moment, letting the breeze funnelling off the fields swirl around her, chilling her skin, temporarily lifting some of the weariness the past thirty-six hours had coated her in.

She could hear the hum of cars on the A27 a few hundred metres to the north, which from this distance sounded like the flow of water in a nearby stream, and the odd rustle – from an animal? – cutting across the latent hum. Apart from that, there was no other sound: the glow of television screens was visible from behind closed curtains in a couple of the bungalows, but no accompanying voices from televisions or occupants, no shouts or sudden shrieks of laughter. It was an odd place for a family to live and Jessie wondered if Allan Parker had chosen this mute backwater entirely deliberately, an attempt to shelter Robbie from the cruelties of other children – at home at least – by surrounding him with adults.

The Parkers' house was at the end of the close, behind a waist-high brick wall, which bordered a small, lawned front garden. A concrete path led to a front door, the top half glazed with leaf-print-patterned glass; a concrete drive to Jessie's left was occupied by a silver Ford Focus. She stood on the doorstep for a few more moments, not yet having summoned enough energy to knock, knowing the intensity of engagement required behind it. The enervated feeling the breeze had momentarily lifted had settled back, shroud-like, the moment she'd stepped through the Parkers' front gate. Raising a hand to briefly smother a huge yawn, she pressed her finger on the bell.

The door was answered, almost before she'd lowered her hand, by a slight, middle-aged man with wispy, mouse-coloured hair combed carefully across a patch of pink skin on the top of his head, shiny as a peeled egg. Pale blue eyes popped from behind wire-rimmed glasses.

'Hello, you must be Dr Flynn. I'm Allan Parker, Robbie's dad.' The hand that shot out and enveloped Jessie's squeezed with a strength which belied the slightness of his build. 'Thank you so *so* much for coming. I can't tell you how grateful I am – how grateful we both are. Sarah told you, of course, how much Robbie needs your help.'

He virtually doubled in half as he backed away, still clutching Jessie's hand, drawing her inside the hot little hallway. He brought to her mind an obsequiously welcoming courtier from the trashy period drama she'd watched on Friday, the night before all hell had broken loose with the Fullers' murders, rain hammering at the windows, Callan working late. Workman had said that Jessie was Robbie's

102

last hope and clearly his father felt that acutely. It was a position she'd rather not be in, with the pressure of the murder case.

'It's my pleasure, Mr Parker,' she said, looking at the top of his inclined head – at the pink skin through the swirl of mouse hair.

'You found it OK?' He released her hand and pushed the door closed, shutting off the last remnants of breeze. 'We're a bit off the beaten track out here. It's terribly unsociable of us, but we like quiet.' His narrow lips curled into a smile so unnatural it looked cut out from a joke book and pasted on.

'I have satnav,' Jessie said, with a brief, unconvincing smile of her own.

There were no family photos in the cramped hallway, only a large, wall-mounted black and white photograph of what looked to be a lifeboat shed on the end of a long, wooden jetty jutting out into the sea, black water and pale polka-dotted shingle beach in the background. The photograph seemed out of place – too modern, too art house – for the house and its occupant.

'Is that the lifeboat station in Selsey?' she asked, as much to break the expectantly laden silence as anything else.

'Got it in one,' Parker said and his voice was too animated for the subject matter, too cheerily booming for the cramped hallway. 'I found it at a gallery in Chichester.'

'Do you volunteer for the lifeboats?'

He shook his head, the joke-book smile fading from his face. 'I always wanted to, but I never found the time. It's been hard finding the time to do anything much,' he mouthed, jabbing a long, pale index finger at the ceiling. 'Since Robbie's mother left.'

In the potted history Workman had imparted, Jessie remembered the mention of an absent mother. 'When did she leave, if you don't mind me asking?'

The raised hand flapped in an ineffectual motion on the end of his arm and his gaze wandered away, somewhere over Jessie's head. 'Oh, God, so many years ago that she's just a dim and distant memory. Robbie was only nine months old.'

'It must be tough bringing up a child alone,' she murmured, thoughts of her own teenage life, her parents' car-crash parenting rising in her mind. She pushed them away before they took hold.

'I like it,' he said, in a quiet voice.

And for a moment, she thought that he meant bringing up a child alone. *Odd.*

'It's a great thing, isn't it? People risking their lives to help others.'

'Oh, right, yes, it is,' Jessie said, her eyes re-finding the picture.

'I've always been very drawn to the lifeboat station. I used to take Robbie there sometimes when he was little.'

He smiled again, this one limp around the edges with suppressed sadness. Jessie figured that it was probably his normal smile – the smile that had become 'normal' over years of disappointment and hardship.

'There's a nice pub close to the lifeboat station and we'd pop in for fish and chips. I'd prop the Robster up on the bar stool and he'd chat to all the old timers, the boatmen. They've seen it all, those old boys. They don't judge. I liked being around them – we both did. We haven't been for a while though. Robbie stopped wanting to go.'

Another sad, distant smile and a jerky shake of his head,

the movement as if to dislodge a foreign object wedged in his brain. It reminded Jessie of Callan after he'd had an epileptic fit, when his mind was on the bullet lodged in his brain, the unconscious action of trying to eject it.

'Sorry, I'm rambling. Here, let me take your coat.'

Jessie shrugged off her puffa jacket and handed it to him.

'Robbie is upstairs in his room. Are you happy to chat to him there, or do you want to chat in the lounge? I'll make myself scarce if you prefer the lounge.'

'Probably the lounge,' Jessie said. 'As he doesn't yet know me, his room is too familiar. It might make him feel as if I'm intruding on his territory.'

Parker nodded. 'I'll pop up and get him. Do you want a tea or coffee?'

'No, thank you.'

'Lemonade, Coke, water?'

Jessie shook her head. 'Nothing, thank you.'

Another of those effortful pasted-on smiles and then Allan suddenly closed the distance between them with one stride, hooking a pale hand over each of Jessie's shoulders.

'Thank you,' he said, squeezing with a strength that Jessie found as surprising, as unnerving, as his handshake.

She resisted an intense urge to wrench herself from his grasp. Though she recognized that his touch was driven by gratitude, it felt wholly, creepily inappropriate. Forcing a barely there smile of her own, she stepped purposefully sideways, pretending to study the photograph of the lifeboat station. *Robbie stopped wanting to go.*

'Thank you for doing this,' she heard Allan say from behind her. 'Sarah Workman told me how busy you are and I really appreciate it. And Robbie, whatever he says or does, he appreciates it too. Beyond anything. *Really* beyond anything.'

105

22

'Shall we begin with the metaphorical, then move on to the physical?' Marilyn suggested, unfazed. In his twenty-five years with Surrey and Sussex police, he'd seen it all; a habitually philandering married man didn't scratch the surface.

Jones gave a clipped, efficient nod – slightly disappointed, Workman sensed, not to have generated at least a modicum of shock in either of her guests. 'What do you want know?'

'You didn't have any moral objection to the type of work Hugo was involved in?'

'It wasn't illegal.'

'It *was* immoral, though.'

Jones shrugged, her gaze steely. 'We weren't selling drugs, trafficking humans or selling knives to teenagers to stab each other with, unlike Tesco and Asda, and I don't suppose you've been over there questioning their morality.' Her gaze moved to Workman. 'So, morality is a bit elastic, isn't it? Big companies and rich people get away with not concerning themselves unduly with morals and it's only people like me, the solid, lower- and middle-class workers who are supposed to care. Well, I'm sorry, but I don't have the luxury of being able to care. I'm a single mother with a teenage daughter to look after and bills to pay. I'm nice to my neighbours, I don't kick dogs or pull the wings off butterflies and I give to charity when I can afford to. I do my bit. It's a little bit, but it *is* still something.'

Marilyn nodded. It was one of the first times Workman had seen him lost for words. She suppressed a smile. Despite her and Jones' surface kindred-spiritness, with their shared car choice and manner of door opening, she had been turned off by the woman's sharp manner, had been struggling to like Jane Jones. But her opinion was turning full circle. Just as Jones' boss, Hugo Fuller, had been a 'does what it says on the tin' kind of man, she was a 'does what it says on the tin' kind of woman, and Workman had always admired straight talking. Jones needed a secure job to pay the bills and give her daughter a decent life and no one could reasonably hold that against her.

'Do you think any of the company's clients harboured bad feelings towards Hugo Fuller?' she asked.

'I'd be surprised if any of them didn't.'

'Enough to murder him?'

'If you dance with the devil . . .' Jones paused. 'Most of the people we dealt with were decent, hard-working people who were just doing their best, but a minority weren't. And people can get aggressive when it comes to protecting the roof over their family's head. Hugo definitely wasn't popular among his clients, if I can put it like that.'

They were back to the parental feelings again – how far parents would go to protect their children. Most people considered a roof over their head to be a basic right and Hugo Fuller had been enriching himself by denying people that right.

'Do you remember if any clients became particularly aggressive in the past year or so?' Marilyn asked.

'There were always angry emails and phone calls, some that went further than others.'

'Further?'

'We had a couple turn up to the office this year. One in January and one a month or so ago. Both men. The last one was covered in tatts.' Her mouth twisted, as she ran her hands down both arms. 'They were everywhere. I do find tattoos quite repulsive.'

Marilyn gave a non-committal nod. Workman wondered if he had a secret tattoo. She could imagine the teenage Marilyn ticking every box that could feasibly be described as rebellion.

'How did Mr Fuller deal with the men?' he asked.

'He called the police and had them arrested. Hugo wasn't brave.' That cynical smile again. 'I can give you their names.'

'We'll have them on record, if they were arrested.'

She nodded. 'I remember Hugo ranting about the disgusting state of the British justice system, so I assume that neither of them were charged. Hugo kept all the threatening emails and recordings of the telephone calls. I can email them to you. It's all stored on iCloud so I can access them from my home computer.'

Marilyn pulled a business card from his pocket and passed it to Jones. 'My email address is on there.'

'Do you think I'm at risk?' Jones asked, laying the business card on the smoked-glass coffee table.

'How visible were you to the clients?'

'Not very. I was employed to organize Hugo, not to liaise with the clients.'

'Who else is employed by the business?'

'There are six other employees, all young, all cheap, and the turnover is pretty high – youngsters don't stick around long these days. Hugo was the figurehead. His ego wouldn't let him be anything else. He liked the limelight and it was very much his business.'

'Can you give me a list of their names and contact details?'

'Yes, of course. I'll print you a list before you leave and also email them to you.'

'Thank you,' Marilyn said. 'Even if the murders are linked to Fuller's business, I'd be surprised if any other employees are targeted, though obviously I can't guarantee that. However, if you feel under threat at all at any time, call 999. Colleagues of mine will visit Winner Fuller's other employees to inform them of Hugo's death, ask them to be vigilant and see if they can add anything more to what you've told us.' He paused. 'Now, how about we move on to the physical.'

Jane Jones rose from the sofa. 'Give me a minute.' She left the room, returning a minute later with an innocuous-looking black mobile phone, which she held out to Marilyn. 'Hugo's,' she said simply.

'What did he use it for?'

She raised an eyebrow. 'What do you think he used it for?'

'The physical?' Marilyn said, holding out an evidence bag. 'A little black phone – the electronic version of a little black book. How unoriginal.'

Jones shrugged. 'Originality wasn't one of Hugo's strong points.'

Workman thought of poor Claudine, floating face down in the swimming pool. Had she known? Probably. If Hugo was as much of a 'does what it says on the tin' kind of man as Jones said he was, he probably wouldn't have bothered to cover his tracks too thoroughly.

'Why did he give it to you?'

'As a nod to showing some consideration for his wife, I suppose. He kept it on him during the day and asked me to look after it for evenings and weekends.'

'And you were fine with that?'

She raised an eyebrow. 'I thought we'd had the morality discussion. Well-paid, secure jobs with decent hours are hard to find. And if I needed to leave early or take the odd morning or afternoon off to go to an event at my daughter's school, Hugo was fine with that.'

'Do you think Claudine knew about her husband's extra-curricular activities?'

'She found out about a couple, a few years back. That's when he asked me to look after his phone evenings and weekends.'

'Did you take messages?'

She shook her head. 'I never answered it. I wasn't his pimp – or theirs.'

'Do you think Claudine knew that he was continuing having relationships outside his marriage?'

'I'd be surprised if she didn't.'

'Ronseal?' Marilyn said.

Jones met his gaze and gave another of those cynical smiles. It was obviously her stock smile when discussing Hugo; often required, unfailingly delivered.

'Do you have the names or any of the details of any of the women he had had, or was having affairs with?'

110

Jones shook her head. 'As I said before. I wasn't his pimp or theirs.'

'Were there many?'

'I think he always had a couple on the go. I used to hear him laughing about them with Adrian Foster, the accounts guy. Adrian's fiancée unequivocally wears the trousers, and I doubt that Adrian would be allowed to squeak without asking her first, so he enjoyed living vicariously through Hugo. And Hugo absolutely loved an audience, so they were both happy.'

Marilyn nodded. 'Do you think Hugo upset any of the women?'

'I don't doubt that he did. Call me old-fashioned, but I think it's hard for women to have a sexual relationship with someone without getting emotionally involved to some extent, even if they start out with the intention of not doing so. But I can't imagine that Hugo would have misled any of them, made any of them promises he had no intention of keeping.' She smiled. 'There's that song, isn't there – something about not being able to promise you golden rings, but promising you everything for tonight. That would have been Hugo's approach, and if any of the women got upset, I'm sure that he would have been generous with parting gifts. He wasn't poor, as I'm sure you've worked out.'

'Hugo Fuller received two telephone calls on the night he was murdered – very shortly before he was murdered – both from an unregistered mobile phone that hasn't been used or activated since that evening. The first call lasted for just over two minutes and the second for twenty seconds. Do you have any idea who could have made those calls to Fuller?'

Jones shook her head. 'No idea, I'm afraid.'

The street lights on Jane Jones' estate had flicked on to replace the sinking sun.

'That was a depressing discussion,' Marilyn said, as they walked back down her drive, to his Z3 parked on the road-side.

Workman shrugged. 'That's life, sir. Down, dirty and not very exciting.'

'I think I prefer murder and mayhem. At least there's life in that, if you get my meaning.' He smiled a cynical half-smile that Jane Jones would be proud of.

Workman nodded. She did get his meaning. Hugo had been the posh end of low-level filth and she felt as if, even having only talked about him, she could do with hopping in the shower and scrubbing herself clean.

23

The only things that Workman had told Jessie about Robbie, beyond the fact that his mother had walked out when he was a baby, and that he had been badly bullied since starting school, was that he had been born with a cleft lip and palate. Tessier Type 4: severe, bilateral, a deep cleft on both sides of his mouth. Baby Robbie's had been one of the worst the surgeons had seen and though they had repaired it as best as they could, he had been left with facial disfigurement and a speech impediment.

The doctors thought he wouldn't make it because of the high chance of infection, Workman had told her.

He was electively mute until he was nine years old, because the other kids teased him so badly about the sound of his voice. He still only speaks when he has to. She'd given a sad smile then. *To me. He speaks to me though, when we're doing the washing-up at the community centre.*

Fuck, Jessie had found herself thinking. *This is all I need, with the murders . . . and Callan. I'm sure something's up with Callan.*

113

And now? How did she feel now?

Looking at Robbie, the way he walked, sidled, actually, into the sitting room, *his* sitting room, in *his* home, shoulders sunk, spine rounded, eyes glued to the hard-wearing beige carpet, a heavy dark fringe shielding his face, Jessie felt intense sadness and the uncomfortable sense of being catapulted back fifteen years, to her own miserable, marginalized post-Hartmoor Psychiatric Hospital teenage existence. Most bullies were lazy and stupid, picked on easy targets. It didn't remotely surprise her that Robbie had been – was being – bullied.

Relentlessly bullied, Workman had said. *Relentlessly.*

Jessie extended her hand; it took Robbie a moment, from under the concealing darkness of his fringe, to notice. A pale hand emerged from the ragged sleeve of the oversized, iron-grey sweatshirt that swathed him to his thighs.

'Hi, Robbie. I'm Sarah Workman's . . .' she was about to say *colleague*, but she stopped herself. *Too impersonal.* 'Friend.'

'The psychologist,' he murmured, barely audible.

'Yes. The psychologist.' She smiled. Not, she figured, that any facial expression she might make would penetrate that fringe. 'Let's sit down, shall we.'

She waited while he selected the chair with its back to the sliding glass doors that opened onto the back garden and folded himself into it. When he was hunched octogenarian-like in the seat, Jessie realized what had driven that choice. The straight, high back of the chair blocked the light the setting sun cast through the patio doors, throwing shadow over his face, blending what little of his features his fringe failed to hide.

There was an identical traditional, straight-backed

reading chair on the opposite side of the fireplace, facing Robbie's, and a low, squishy sofa, shoved up against the facing wall. Settling herself in the chair, she shuffled it subtly sideways so that it was at an elliptical angle to Robbie's, facing him, but not directly, combatively so. Folding her hands in her lap, crossing her legs, right over left, she mirrored his introverted sitting position. Tapping into a patient's subconscious to create rapport by aping their body language was an age-old trick and she always used it. This session would be hard enough without turning her nose up at the easy wins, however pop-psychology people thought they were.

She had no notes on Robbie, nothing to refer to . . . only the few brief lines that Workman had sketched in her mind.

He was hospitalized with stab wounds in his legs from a craft knife at the age of nine. A furious, angry shake of her head. *Who knew that art lessons could be so dangerous?*

. . . the outline, stick figure of a boy . . .

One boy, Niall, the pack leader, broke Robbie's ankle when he was ten, playing football. It was dismissed as an accidentally awkward tackle.

. . . drawn in charcoal on grey paper . . .

They broke his arm when he was walking home from school when he was twelve. The kids from his year who 'witnessed it' said he tripped over the kerb and fell. Eight voices against one, so they were believed. An incredulous look on her face. *Girls, there were girls in the group too.*

. . . no light, no colour in the sketch . . .

He has tried to commit suicide twice. The first time when he was twelve. The last time, nine months ago.

Jessie hadn't asked – *How?* Hadn't wanted to know.

115

Suicide, a boy attempting suicide, was far too close to home for her, too raw.

Jamie.

Her eight-year-old brother, hanging from a curtain rail by his school tie, his beautiful face bloated and purple.

Robbie.

Jamie.

Robbie.

Jamie.

'Would you like a drink before we start, Robbie?' Her voice croaked around the lump wedged firmly in her throat.

Looking out from underneath his fringe, for the first time since he had entered the sitting room, Robbie met Jessie's gaze. His eyes were a pale green, soft, beautiful and so so unusual. She held his gaze and smiled, didn't let her eyes rove down to his mouth. He would have spent his whole life coping with people staring at him as if he was an exhibit from a Victorian freak show: pointing, whispering, cringing, sniggering, the whole gamut of heartless human emotions.

And pitying him too.

He would doubtless have experienced pity. Endless pity. And it would have hurt far more than the rest. Pity always hurt the most. The last thing he needed was to be faced with an adult, his only hope, Workman had said – *Please, for me, please see him. You're his only hope* – feeling sorry for him, pitying him.

Robbie shook his head. 'No, I don't want a drink, thank you.' His robotic voice still barely there.

Despite enunciating each word independently, an island to itself, his severe lisp made him hard to understand. Jessie would need to listen closely, couldn't afford to have to ask

116

him to repeat; he would have had more than enough of that too in his short life.

Two deep scars ran upwards from his top lip, one to the base of his nose, half of which was missing, the other half misshapen with stitched scar tissue. The second deep scar ran to the base of his right eye, the lower lid bumpy and raw. His face wasn't easy, comfortable, to look at.

'I'm aware that you didn't request to see me, Robbie. That your father spoke with Sarah Workman and asked if she could help.'

'It is fine. Sarah told me about you. Thank you for agreeing to help me.'

She smiled, suppressing a shiver, not sure if it was the chill air in the room, several degrees cooler than the small, hot hallway, or the intense presence of the boy sitting opposite. She had been unnerved when she was standing at the front of the incident room this morning, selling her ideas to twenty people, but usually she was comfortable alone, with just one patient. Why wasn't she now? The fact that talking to him felt like being transported back fifteen years, looking at her own teenage self hunched in a chair, excluded, isolated, teased, tormented, her self-esteem shattered? Robbie had experienced the full smorgasbord of cruelty that children could inflict on each other. If only she could slip into his shoes now, with the benefit of hindsight and maturity, of having clawed her way, bruised and bloodied, to a good place in life, go back and deal with the bullies for him.

She pictured herself trailing her former best friends before her year's incarceration at Hartmoor Psychiatric Hospital down the school corridor to lunch, the four linked arm in arm, the corridor too narrow for five abreast. Laughing and joking, too loud, contrived, she realized now, phoney clubby jollity to intensify her feelings of exclusion and isolation. Choosing a table for four despite there being countless free that seated six. *Sorry, Jessie, there's no room for you.*

It had escalated, of course. Bullying without consequences always did. Exclusion had morphed to insults, to physical attacks.

Your hair is disgusting. Don't you ever wash it?

You're embarrassing to be seen with. Ask your mum to buy you some decent clothes.

Your lips are so thin, no boys will ever want to kiss you. You're so stupid.

So endlessly, endlessly stupid, so she had stopped putting her hand up in class.

She was told about parties, but not invited to them; it was no fun not inviting her if she didn't know about them. She was followed into the toilets and attacked, her hair torn from her head in clumps, head banged against the tiles. But there were no bruises, so it never happened.

Her mother reported them numerous times, was told that it was four girls' words against Jessie's and, given her psychiatric problems, it was understandable that she overreacted.

We'll ask the girls to be extra nice.

Unless you're offering lobotomies with your history lessons, these girls don't know how to be nice.

That's what Jessie would have said now.

And back then?

She just took it. Her mum was drowning in pain from Jamie's suicide and Jessie had already caused enough trouble, so she didn't mention the bullying again.

The electric suit hissing across her skin snapped her back to the present, to Allan and Robbie Parker's lifeless sitting room, hotly oppressive suddenly, the beige walls shrink-wrapped as tight around her as the walls of the box-prison she'd lived in at Hartmoor, a quizzical expression on Robbie's ruined face. How long had she been caught in her own thoughts?

'I'm sorry. My mind just . . .' *Wandered.* She couldn't say it, not to this boy who had spent his whole life being tormented or ignored. *I'm a professional, here to help you, and I can't even focus on you.*

'It's fine,' he murmured, watching her intently.

'Do you mind if I open the patio doors?' Jessie asked. 'I'm working on a murder case and I haven't had much sleep. I could do with a blast of fresh air to wake me up.'

'I saw a mention of the murders on the Internet,' he said, standing. As Robbie slid open the door, cool autumn air swelled into the room, curling around Jessie.

A movement in the garden caught Jessie's eye, a tabby cat dropping lithely down onto the lawn from the neighbours' fence and disappearing into the twilight at the bottom of the garden. When she looked back to Robbie she saw that he had removed his iron-grey sweatshirt and slung it over his shoulders. But instead of the empty sleeves hanging down his chest, as would have been normal, he had draped them carefully over his bare arms from shoulder to wrist. His fingers, curled into claws, clutched the ragged end of each sleeve. Her gaze moved from his arms – the sweatshirt's flat, iron-grey arms – to his face. He was watching her from the concealing darkness of his fringe. He gave a tentative, shy smile before his gaze flitted away.

'I'm hot too,' he murmured. 'Even with the door open.'

'You can open it more,' Jessie said.

He shook his head. 'I am fine now.'

119

Fine.

That ubiquitous word that said nothing, meant nothing, hid a multitude of sins. What was he thinking? She had no idea, not yet. And though he had spoken little, she recognized the awkward intensity of someone for whom social interaction was a huge and unnatural effort.

'You know Sarah Workman from the Age UK charity,' she began. Sarah Workman, with her sensible navy shift dresses, matching courts, low-maintenance bob and low-maintenance attitude, had to be a safe-as-houses opening conversational gambit.

He nodded. 'I volunteer at their Chichester Sunday lunch club, serving food, washing up.' Each word clearly enunciated in that lisping, robotic voice. Such an easy target, and nasty kids did so love an easy target. 'I didn't realize Sarah was police for ages. She seemed too—' He broke off with a slightly embarrassed shrug.

'Normal?'

He smiled as best he could. 'Square.' A pause. 'You won't tell her.'

Jessie smiled back. 'No, of course not. Everything we discuss is confidential. You have my absolute word on that.'

'What about my father?'

'You can tell him what we've discussed, but I won't.'

'But I am only fifteen. Isn't that below the age of—' he broke off, fumbling for an appropriate word.

Consent? He probably wouldn't need to worry about that in the context of its normal meaning.

'Psychological consent?'

He nodded.

'It is, but your dad has given permission for me to see you alone and to keep our discussions confidential.'

Robbie seemed to be thinking, ruminating over her words. 'I don't mind if he knows.'

Jessie shrugged. 'It's up to you, but I won't tell him anything. It's important you know that everything you tell me will remain within these four walls. And I'm not easily shocked. I've seen a lot, heard a lot.' *Too much, probably for one person, in my own life and in others.*

Robbie gave a thoughtful nod. 'Do you work with the police? Is that how you know Sarah?'

'Yes, I've worked on a couple of murder cases with Sarah and her boss, DI Bobby Simmons.'

'Marilyn?'

Jessie smiled. 'You've heard about Marilyn?'

'Sarah talks about him. We do a lot of washing-up together. She seems to live for her job.'

'They both do and they're very good at them.' Jessie kept the comment short, neutral. She had no right to talk about Sarah Workman or Marilyn, beyond light banalities.

'She told me that she works so hard and does charity work to keep herself busy as she was unable to have children,' Robbie said. 'She seemed very sad about it.'

'Infertility can be devastating. It can, understandably, take over people's lives, and it's tough to admit that there are no more options.'

'Do you have children?'

A sharp twinge in Jessie's chest; she shook her head. 'No.'

'Will you?'

'I'd like to, but not yet.' A brief, half-hearted smile. 'I need to convince someone to have them with me first.'

'You won't have a problem. Not like me. No one will want to have children with me.'

121

'That's not—'

'Don't say, "That's not true." Saying stuff that is untrue only makes things worse.'

Biting her lip, Jessie nodded. What the hell had she been thinking? What the hell was wrong with her today?

'You're right and I'm sorry. I should know better than to come out with meaningless platitudes.'

She *did* know better, but her brain was all over the place, none of those places good or helpful. A portion was trapped in that hot swimming pool complex with Hugo and Claudine Fuller; another portion in the incident room, surrounded by photographs of Fuller's face, the black pits of his eye sockets, her mind floundering for clarity; another portion stuck fifteen years ago, with her own psychologically bleeding teenage self.

'My mother wished she'd never had children.' His voice pulled her back. 'Never had me, at least.'

Jessie met his gaze. *I'm sure that's not true.* She wasn't going to risk another meaningless platitude.

'Sarah told me you live with your father,' she said, instead.

He nodded. 'My mother left when I was a baby. She was horrified that she had given birth to a . . . a monster.' No emotion in that lisping, mechanical voice. It was as if he'd announced he was popping to the shops or nipping around to a friend's house. *Friends.* Something most children took for granted.

'Is that what your father told you?' she asked gently.

'Once.'

'Once?'

'He told me that my mother was a whore who had run off with another man.' Still no expression in his voice, just the flicker of a muscle underneath his good eye.

122

'People say stupid things that they don't mean, that they regret, when they're angry.'

'He did regret saying it, but he meant it when he said it.'

'Had she run off with another man?'

He nodded. 'A man with no children.'

'Relationships are hard. Marriage is hard.' She knew that herself and she'd only been in a relationship for five minutes, had never been married, didn't know if a lifelong commitment, even to Callan, would suit her. Suit her or suit him. 'You shouldn't blame your mother. And your father certainly shouldn't, not in front of you. He was angry – and anger is an intense emotion that drives people to speak and act irrationally.'

Robbie nodded, though not in a way that indicated agreement; more a cynical tilt of his head. 'Dad told me that she had another child, a normal child. He didn't get to run away. He was stuck with me.'

'It's nothing to do with you,' Jessie snapped, with more force than she had meant, but what he had told her made her furious. *Anger is an intense emotion.* The poor kid had enough to deal with without being told that his mother was a whore in one breath, being blamed for her absence in the next. 'What happened to your parents' marriage was nothing to do with you. Relationships are difficult.'

'Their relationship wasn't difficult until I came along.'

'Did your father say that too?'

Robbie shook his head. 'I worked that one out for myself. They were together and happy for ten years before I arrived.'

His gaze broke from hers, moved off around the room, jerkily, as if looking for something to fix on.

'How old were you when your father said that? About the monster?'

'Eight or nine. Old enough not to care.'

Jessie knew that wasn't true. Being told that your mother left because she'd given birth to a monster. Christ, that would cut any child to the bone. Any adult, too.

'It didn't affect me. I never knew her.' Expression in his voice this time – insistence – a well-practised denial. But Jessie sensed the waver underneath, almost, but not quite, imperceptible.

Abandonment always affected children and Robbie's had been one of the worst; blamed by his father for driving his mother away because of the physical defect he was born with, could do nothing to change.

'Were you being bullied by then?'

He nodded and shrugged, affirmation and studied ambivalence. The shrug, the ambivalence, well practised. 'I have been bullied for as long as I can remember.'

With the shrug the sweatshirt's sleeves bagged, even though his fingers were clenched tight around its cuffs, and Jessie's gaze snapped to the crazy criss-cross of gashes on his forearms. So much, so many, that she couldn't for a second compute, comprehend. She had seen self-harm before, knew its stamp, had been expecting the lines, the knife marks, the razor-blade slashes, though not this madness of intense violence. And so recent. She had never seen such extreme self-harm, and the rawness and ferocity shocked her.

Some bullied children turned their trauma inwards, into self-hatred, self-harm; others outward into aggression. Girls tended towards self-harm, cutting, bulimia, anorexia; boys aggression, violence. She wasn't surprised that Robbie's trauma had morphed into self-hatred. He seemed too gentle for violence – or perhaps just too far gone, too repressed, totally and utterly ground down.

I have been bullied for as long as I can remember.

Workman had known, clearly known, how desperately Robbie needed help.

'I saw my mother once.' His quiet voice pulled her back.

'When?'

'A few years ago, when I was ten or eleven.'

'And you recognized her?'

'My dad keeps a lot of photos. He doesn't know that I know about them, but I look at them sometimes.'

'Where did you see her?'

'In Portsmouth, one Saturday. I was waiting for Dad outside a shop and I saw her.'

'Did she see you?'

A barely there shake of his head.

'Why not?' Though Jessie was pretty sure that she already knew the answer to the question.

'I hid.' His voice, like the shake, also barely there.

'Do you think she would have recognized you? She hasn't seen you for many many years.'

He gestured listlessly to his face, and again the sleeve of the jumper bagged, revealing the carnage of his forearm. He lowered his arm and his fingers moved, as if playing piano keys, as he worked the sleeve back into place. Watching him fiddle with the cuff of the iron-grey woollen camou-flage-cum-comfort-blanket, Jessie realized how little Sarah Workman had told her about him, his history, how little she had asked. They were both so focused on the murder cases that until half an hour ago, when Robbie had walked into the room and Jessie had relaxed into the role that was her forte, this, *he*, had felt like an unwelcome intrusion. But now she was glad to have the opportunity to do some good. She felt as if she was having no impact on the murder investigation, that her inexperience with criminal cases was being cast in unremittingly sharp relief.

'Do you think she wouldn't have recognized me?' he asked, meeting her gaze.

'You're not the only teenager on the planet who has a cleft palate. Far from it.'

'I'm one of the only ones with a cleft palate this bad.'

He was right and she wasn't about to contradict him, make that 'platitudes' mistake again.

'Have you ever had friends?' she ventured. There was nothing to be gained from beating about the bush.

He shook his head.

'Do you have any pets?'

Another shake. 'My dad is allergic to cats and, because we're both out during the day, we couldn't have a dog.'

'You enjoy working at the lunch club?'

He gave a pensive half-nod. 'Old people need company, don't they? Lots of them are lonely.'

The way he said the word 'lonely' cleaved a canyon through Jessie's heart. She nodded. 'Yes, lots of them *are* lonely.'

He looked up from under his fringe and met her gaze. 'I met Mrs Fuller,' he murmured.

'Claudine?'

He nodded. 'She was nice. Kind.'

'When did you meet her?'

'She came to the lunch club once. She wanted to make a donation, I think. A big one.'

Jessie thought of that huge, isolated, gilded mausoleum of a house. *Makes sense.*

'Do you believe in capital punishment?' he asked suddenly.

'No.'

'Why not? Isn't it fair that if someone takes a life, they should lose theirs?'

'At first glance, perhaps it's fair.'

'So why don't you believe in it?' he pressed.

'Because I believe that society needs to set a good example. A society that condones capital punishment tacitly condones killing and that attitude brutalizes everything. You can't punish someone for killing by killing.'

Another pensive nod, though if he had been being more honest with her, the nod would have been a firm shake of his head. She knew that he would have endlessly fantasized about killing the bullies, administering slow and painful deaths. She had fantasized the same at his age, fed off those fantasies to keep herself from drowning in depression and self-hatred.

'I was bullied too,' Jessie said. 'When I was a teenager.'

'You?' Incredulity in that robotic voice. 'But you're . . .' He faltered, his gaze dipping, cheeks flushing. 'Beautiful.'

Beautiful and horribly damaged. She didn't say it.

'My brother died . . . committed suicide when I was four-teen.'

'I'm sorry.'

She waved her hand vaguely in the air. 'It's complicated, but I ended up burning my father and stepmother's house down and so I was sent away for a year – incarcerated, I suppose, is a better word, in a mental hospital. When I came back my friends didn't want to know me.' She faltered. 'Actually, worse than that, they deliberately wanted to hurt me. I didn't understand why.'

'Because it's fun,' he said simply.

'Yes. If you're nasty, bullying *is* fun.' She paused. 'Doubtless you've been told that bullies are trying to make themselves feel better by making someone else feel bad.'

He nodded. 'It must be standard teacher response.'

Jessie smiled cynically. She had been told that the girls who bullied her must be desperately unhappy to want to cause someone else such pain. But she hadn't given a shit if they were unhappy then, and she didn't give a shit now. Unhappiness didn't excuse nastiness.

'There are absolutely no excuses for bullying, no justification under any circumstances. Children who bully are nasty, plain and simple, and they always choose easy targets, because they're cowards.'

Jessie noticed Robbie's fingers whitening as he tightened his grip on the cuffs of his sweatshirt; her mind's eye sought out the devastation of his forearms.

'I'm an easy target,' he murmured.

Jessie nodded. She didn't normally reveal anything of herself to patients, but it had felt right to do so with Robbie. She knew how terribly isolated he felt, had felt, doubtless for the whole of his life. She also knew that he would be looking ahead into a life that held no hope and she had wanted to give him some. Recognized how desperately he needed hope.

'You are an easy target, as I was, and you need to stop being an easy target, as I did.'

Jaw muscles clenched under his skin. She had jammed her finger hard on a nerve. Deliberately.

'It's different for me. My face . . . I can't.'

'That might have been true when you were younger, but it isn't now.'

No verbal response, the cues to how he was feeling physical: in the avoidance of eye contact, the tension in his jaw, the whiteness of his fingertips.

'You're not that child who needs to take this shit any

128

more,' she continued. 'It's because of mental conditioning, delivered and received over many many years, that you are still sucking it up. Fight back.'

What the hell am I saying? She knew she shouldn't be talking like this, that the professional veneer had slipped long ago, but she couldn't help herself. The electric suit was hissing and snapping, cauldron-hot, despite the cold breeze funnelling through the open patio doors.

'You're giving the bullies free entertainment. Why should you be their fun for free?'

Robbie's head was dipped, his expression shrouded by his fringe.

'Robbie . . .' she said.

He didn't answer.

'Bullies operate in packs to give them collective strength because they're cowards. Get one alone. Teach him a lesson that he won't forget and all the others will hear about it, learn from it. That boy, the one who broke your ankle on the football pitch, what was his name?'

His continued silence was a red rag to the electric suit.

'Cut the head off the snake and the body dies,' she pressed. 'You don't need to accept this shit any more. You don't need to keep giving them that free show.'

A shrill ring. Robbie looked up and met Jessie's gaze for a fraction of a second, before hers found her mobile – Marilyn – then the clock on the wall. It was a quarter-past-nine. She had been here for well over an hour, hadn't realized.

'It's Marilyn,' she said, to Robbie, pressing the answer button. 'Hold for just a second, DI Simmons.' She never called Marilyn that; it was purely because Robbie was listening. 'Really, it will just be a second.' She looked up. 'I'm sorry, Robbie. I need to take this.'

'Marilyn calls.'

'Unfortunately, Marilyn does call. Another session?' she asked, rising from the chair. 'Later this week? I'll text you when I have a better idea of my diary.'

'Are you sure that you have the time?'

No, I don't. 'Yes, of course I have time.'

'Thank you.'

'The head of the snake,' she repeated, as she pulled open the door. 'Bullies are snakes. Take off the head and the body dies.'

24

Somewhere a child was screaming. Denise Lewin fought upwards towards the sound through thick, downy layers of sleep. She jerked awake to a cool, dark room, Simon snoring softly beside her, her pulse through the roof, skin sticky with perspiration.

'*Muuuuummmyyyyyyy!*'

'Leo. Coming, darling.' Sleepily, she slid out of bed and padded across the landing. 'Mummy's coming.'

He was sitting up in bed, his back ramrod straight, his teddy bear, Baloo, clamped to his chest, staring out through the bedroom window into the garden. Tears were pouring down his face. The moon was bright, a gibbous moon – the thought came randomly to her – bathing the lawn and shrubbery, the silvery weeping willow in the centre of the lawn that rustled and swayed on windy nights in an ethereally pale glow. Why had Simon left the curtains open? She never did that, she knew that Leo scared easily. Leaning down, she wrapped an arm around his shoulders, flicked the bedroom light on with the other hand.

'Nooooo,' he screeched. 'See me.' He jammed his face into the bear's stomach. 'See me.'

'There's nothing out there, darling. No one can see into your room.' But she flicked the light off anyway, plunging them back into darkness. Leo lowered Baloo from his face; his tear-stained eyes were wide and fearful. Rising, she went to the window. The garden was silent, deserted and motionless apart from the weeping willow, which was swaying, just gently, its sagging, silvery fronds shifting to and fro.

'Look, it's only that silly old weeping willow. That was what scared you.'

Leo shook his head determinedly. 'Nooo. Ghostie.'

Denise pulled the curtains closed, stuffing the edge of the right carefully behind the edge of the left, so that there wasn't even a knife width's gap between them.

'It's Mummy and Daddy's fault. We shouldn't have left the curtains open.' Perching on the edge of Leo's bed, she reached for his hands. They were burning hot, clammy with sweat. 'You're boiling, sweetheart, and drenched. It's too hot in here. Let me open the window, just a tiny bit.'

'*Nooooo!*' Leo jerked away from her, snatching up Baloo and pressing him to his face again. 'Noooo. Ghostie, wash.'

'Wash?'

Leo nodded frantically. 'Wash. Wash.'

'Oh, *watch*,' Denise said, finally cottoning on. 'No, sweetbean, of course there isn't a ghost outside watching you.'

'What the hell's going on?' Simon, standing in the doorway, stifled a yawn with the back of his hand.

'Sorry, darling, I didn't mean to wake you.' She stroked Leo's hair. 'Go back to sleep, sweetheart. Daddy's got his important work to go to in the morning and you've got nursery.'

132

His tiny mouth fixed into an intractable line, Leo shook his head. 'Ghostie.'

Denise stood. 'He thinks he saw someone, some*thing*, in the garden, watching him,' she hissed into Simon's ear. 'It's just the weeping willow. It's breezy and the moon is so bright tonight that the willow looks almost luminous. You shouldn't have left the curtains open.'

Simon bent and ruffled his son's hair. 'Shall I go and check that the garden is empty, bean?'

Walking to the window, he pulled back the curtains and pressed his face to the glass. He shifted left and right, stood on tiptoes, squatted down, making a show of searching every corner of the garden. 'Mummy's right,' he said, turning back to Leo. 'It was just that silly old weeping willow. It looks like a ghost, doesn't it?' Simon held out his hand to his son. 'Hop out of bed and come and look.'

Baloo clutched tight in his bloodless fingers, Leo shrank back against his pillow and shook his head vehemently. 'Ghostie,' he insisted.

'OK. Let me grab a torch and go and have a look around the garden. Will that make you happy?'

After a long moment, Leo gave a tiny nod. Denise sat, squished against him, arm wrapped around his trembling body, while Simon tramped downstairs. A couple of minutes later they heard a door slam and a disc of light appeared in the garden, Simon's shadowy form behind it, his dressing gown flapping around his ankles. He walked down the length of the garden to the back corner where the broken fence opened out onto the woods, into the other corner, back up the far side, into the centre to search around the weeping willow. He stopped and Denise noticed him hesitate, focus the torch light on a patch of lawn in front of the tree.

'No ghosts out there, bean,' Simon said, in a jolly singsong voice, appearing in Leo's bedroom door a few minutes later.

But Denise didn't like his expression. Something was wrong. 'Simon?'

'Like Mummy said, it was just that silly weeping willow.' Walking to the window, Simon reached his hand through the curtains and Denise noticed him shake the lock, checking that it was fast. Then he pressed the curtains tightly together as she had done.

'We'll leave your door open and the hall light is on. Mummy and I are just across the landing. Now there is nothing to worry about. Go to sleep.' He kissed Leo's head and then tucked the duvet around him and Baloo.

'Has the gardener been?' he asked Denise, when they were back in their own bed.

'No, I haven't had him in for well over a month. You said it was getting too expensive, what with the cleaner and everything else.'

Simon nodded slowly.

'What? What is it, Simon? What did you see in the garden?'

'Nothing.'

'Don't lie to me.'

'I'm not—'

'I *know* you. I can tell when you're lying, and I saw you peering at something on the ground by the willow. What was it? What did you see?'

'Nothing important.'

'Well, it must have been something.'

He gave a patient sigh. 'It was just footprints.'

'Footprints?'

'Yes, *footprints*, Denise,' he mimicked in a squeaky, high-pitched voice.

134

She ignored his mocking tone. 'Whose? Mine?'

'A man's.'

'*A man's?*'

'Keep your voice down. I don't want to frighten Leo again.'

'Hold on a bloody minute. You're frightening *me* now.'

'It was footprints, for God's sake, Denise. Not Freddy bloody Krueger.'

'But you haven't been in the garden for ages, so they couldn't have been yours.' Her voice rose. 'You certainly haven't been since it rained three days ago and before that it was dry for at least two weeks.'

'Stop getting hysterical,' Simon snapped.

'Don't patronize me.' Denise twisted around to face him, furious now. Fury fuelled by fear. '*Don't* patronize me. I'm asking questions, *logical* questions, not getting hysterical. That's such a bloody stupid man thing to say.'

Simon raised his hands. 'OK, OK, sorry. But you *are* overthinking it. The back fence is broken. Loads of dog walkers use the woods. A dog probably ran in here and the owner came in to get it.' Lowering his hands, he jabbed her gently in the side with one finger.

She slapped his hand away. 'Don't you poke me.'

'I'll poke my wife if I want to poke my wife,' he said, poking her again, harder, then sliding his arm around her shoulders and pulling her to him.

She resisted for a few moments before sagging against him with a heavy sigh. 'Please take this seriously, Simon.'

'I am taking it seriously, Denise. Really, I am. But you must be able to see that it's a storm in a teacup. For Christ's sake, only last week you marched into the house complaining that some dog had shat on your delias.'

'Dahlias,' she corrected, with a reluctant half-smile.

'Dahlias, delias, whatever.' Simon stroked his hand down her arm.

'But—'

'But what?'

Curling her knees up to her chest, she shrugged, feeling stupid. 'The murders.'

'Come on, Denise, they were a random one-off. Those people were stinking rich and that Hugo bloke was a complete scumbag.'

'I thought you said that you didn't know him.'

'I don't know him, but I've heard about him and I've read about him. His business was buying up cheap freeholds and then ramping the ground rent up a thousand per cent. He was ruining people's lives, poor people's lives, while he lived like a king. No wonder someone whacked him.'

'Whacked him.' Denise nudged him playfully. 'Who are you? Al Capone?'

Simon grinned and nudged her back. 'Do you really think a murderer is going to bother standing in the middle of our bloody garden staring up at the window of a three-year-old? Really?' He widened his eyes and opened his mouth in a mock scream. 'Perhaps there's a serial killer sitting in our bedroom cupboard right now, waiting for us to switch the light out so that he can leap out and—' The flat hand on her arm turned into a claw and his nails dug into her skin. 'Whack us.'

'Stop it, you idiot.' Shrugging off his arm, she lay down and pulled the duvet to her chest.

'There's nothing to worry about, Denise. Now can we please go to sleep.' Reaching over to the bedside light, he switched it off, then shuffled over and slid an arm around her stomach. 'Or maybe, now that we're awake—'

'No.'

'I'm going away on business tomorrow morning for three long, miserable, lonely days.' The hand on her stomach slid lower.

Denise knocked it away. 'Not on your life, work trip or not. It's three in the morning and I'm snatching a few more hours before the brat wakes up for the day.' She gave him a quick kiss on the forehead, then rolled away from him. 'Nighty nighty, lover boy.'

25

With first light, the search teams were back on the job, spreading further out around the Fullers' house, forcing their way through tangled undergrowth and dank woodland that the feeble autumn sun refused to penetrate, maps clutched in sweaty hands, despairing at the size of the search area and the needle-in-a-haystack nature of their task. The location and terrain was torment, with the denseness and what felt like unnatural quiet of the woods and the whispered rumours going around of killer wolf-dogs, and they kept an eye on each other, more nervous than usual.

Other teams were 'on the knock', trudging up and down front paths and driveways in Walderton village – where Lupo had been found tied to the lamp post – and the other villages that bordered the woods and fields surrounding the Fullers' land. They were asking if anyone had seen a suspicious character in the vicinity on Saturday night or any nights before that, heard anything suspicious, anything out of the ordinary or of note, anything at all. They had garnered, as was typical when many interviewees were older people, a list of fantastical sightings: of dodgy telephone repair men who were quite clearly anything but, of delivery drivers purely in the village to case the joint, of shadowy figures flitting between buildings at dusk, of odd noises in the deep of the night.

At the press conference that morning, Marilyn had asked the assembled journalists and TV reporters to respect the Fullers' relatives' grief – he didn't mention there were no relatives apart from Hugo's stepmother Valerie Fuller, who was very far from grief-stricken – and keep reporting to a minimum, though he held out little hope that they would accede to his request. A brutal murder was gold dust when it came to circulation and viewing figures, though at least he had, so far, managed to keep a lid on the more specific and horrific details. The last thing he and his teams needed was hysteria overtaking this sleepy corner of West Sussex, or worse, another loon fancying himself as a copy-cat.

And even Paws for Thought, the little local dog charity that had taken in the Fullers' dog Lupo, had called asking for Surrey and Sussex Major Crimes to send a policeman to stand outside their front door and ward off journalists and ghoulish sightseers. Marilyn had passed that call on to Workman, having absolutely no interest in getting into a debate with a crazy dog lady about the effect too much stranger attention would have on an already deeply trau-matized Siberian husky. The mind boggled.

'Is this your first "knock"?' Cara asked, looking across, but not quite meeting Jessie's gaze.

She nodded. 'DI Simmons thought I'd benefit from a few hours' experience at the sharp end, as he puts it.'

'I'm not sure that trudging from house to house in small

Sussex villages interviewing bored housewives and retirees qualifies as the sharp end. Detective Sergeant Workman and I already spent the morning telephoning every one of Hugo Fuller's clients who might possibly have held a grudge against him and turned up nothing useful, and I was hoping for something more exciting this afternoon,' Cara said, rolling his eyes.

Jessie raised an eyebrow in exchange. 'Keep an open mind. We may yet hit the jackpot, young Darren.'

'I'll try, aged Dr Flynn.'

'Jessie,' she countered. 'Call me Jessie. Or aged Jessie, if you prefer.'

Despite the gruelling barbarity, stress and sleeplessness of the past couple of days, she was enjoying these few hours spent with DC Darren Cara on the knock. Wandering from house to house in the mellow afternoon sun – the clouds had cleared mid-morning to reveal the first warm autumn day in weeks – it was easy to feel relaxed, as if they were canvassing opinion for a neighbourhood survey or collecting for a local charity. In his early twenties, Cara was a good six or seven years younger than she was, but she had already worked out, from the flitting, flirty eye contact that never stuck and the amusing quips he perennially slipped into their conversation, that he was keen on her. If it hadn't been for Callan and the age gap, she would have been quite keen on him too. He was handsome, fit, more city worker than policeman with his well-cut grey suit and well-trimmed jet-black hair, square jaw and intense, dark brown eyes. He was hot, and he was sweet, though she knew he'd be horrified to hear her refer to him by the second of those two adjectives.

'Ready?' He flashed her another disarming smile as he

raised his hand to knock on the sage-green front door of a neat, detached red-brick house, down a quiet, leafy lane on the north-western edge of the village of Stoughton. The back gardens of the houses on this, the north side of the street, were bordered by countryside, fields and woods, the same countryside and woods that segued, a couple of kilometres away, to the Fullers' grounds and house. Marilyn was spreading his net wide, and DCI Janet Backastowe, fearsome head honcho of Surrey and Sussex Major Crimes, still smarting from the car crash that had been the 'Two Little Girls' investigation, had thrown him an embarrassment of resources.

'Ready as I'll ever be. Go for it, Darren.'

A blonde-haired woman, mid-thirties, answered Cara's knock.

'Good morning.' Her tone was a tentative question. She raised a sudsy yellow Marigold-gloved hand to swipe at her fringe, an unconscious tic that she snagged just before the glove made contact. Dropping her hand, she wiped the suds into her floral, Cath Kidston apron. She was very pretty, Jessie thought, in a wholesome way. She could imagine her modelling clothes for Boden. A little blond-haired boy, aged three or four, was hiding behind her legs, one hand clamped to her left kneecap. Jessie saw a flash of blue-and-white-striped sailor T-shirt, navy trousers and one bare foot. She could imagine him modelling clothes for Boden kids. The picture-perfect Boden family.

'Good morning,' Cara said.

He'd dug out his warrant card before he'd raised his hand to knock, bitter experience reminding him that, despite the suit, the appearance of a well-built, multi-racial, twenty-something man, knocking on front doors on a weekday

141

morning in rural Sussex, might arouse mistrust. It shouldn't be that way, but too often it was, though Jessie had already worked out that he was too down-to-earth to let it bother him, that he enjoyed his job too much to care.

'I'm Detective Constable Darren Cara from Surrey and Sussex Major Crimes, and this is my colleague, Dr Jessie Flynn.'

The woman's eyebrows rose into her choppy blonde fringe. 'Doctor?'

'I'm a psychologist,' Jessie said. 'Working with the police.'

'Oh.' She giggled. 'I hope you haven't come to analyse me. I'd hate to think what you'd find.'

Not much, Jessie thought, immediately regretting the unnecessarily bitchy observation. She knew nothing about the woman beyond that she was a mother – *Envy, twisting my bitter heart out of shape* – and probably a housewife. She forced a smile, one that she hoped looked genuine.

'Don't worry, I'm only here to observe. I've just started working with the police and evidently going on the knock, as it's called, is part of the baptism.'

'Is it about that poor couple's, uh—' She broke off, glancing down at her son. 'About that couple in the paper?' She had very large, silvery-blue eyes that widened as she spoke. Jessie glanced at Cara and imagined that he might be thinking about diving into them.

'Yes,' Cara said.

'Oh, you'd better come in then. I'm Denise Lewin and this is my little boy, Leo. Kick the door closed behind you. Leo and I were just doing some tidying up.' She stepped backwards, walking as if through thick mud, her arms spread wide, a high-stepping comedy walk, dragging her son with her. 'You'll have to let go of my leg, bean, or we'll both end up flat on our backs on the hall floor and embarrass ourselves in front of these nice police people.' Bending at the waist, she unpeeled her son's fingers from her leg. His hand immediately flew to grip the sudsy Marigold-glove. 'Just give me a moment to switch the television on for Leo.'

Jessie and Cara waited in the hallway while Denise settled her son on the sofa and found a cartoon for him to watch.

'Would you like a cup of tea?' she asked, leading them into a spotless and airy farmhouse-style kitchen, an oak table seating six set in front of glass double doors. The doors opened out onto the garden, framing a pale silver weeping willow, halfway between sapling and tree, which occupied a space in the centre of the lawn. Jessie's gaze strayed from the willow to the broken-down garden fence and the trees beyond it clustered thick and dark, as far as the eye could see.

'Grab a seat,' Denise said.

'Is your husband here?' Cara asked

'No, it's just me and Leo, I'm afraid. Simon left this morning for a three-day business trip to Wiltshire, so we're on our own until Thursday evening. I can speak for him though. We were at home together on Saturday night.'

Unpeeling the Marigold glove from her hand, she dropped it next to the sink and flicked the kettle on.

'It's horrible, isn't it?' she said, as she set down a full teapot, a jug of milk and three cups, a couple of minutes later. 'Really horrible. The local news didn't say much, just that they'd been found dead in their house on Sunday morning. Do we need to be concerned?'

'We don't believe that the killer will strike again, but there's no harm in being vigilant,' Cara said. 'Obviously lock doors and windows at night.'

At his words, an image of a blonde woman reaching to unlock the door to her dog rose in Jessie's mind. The Fullers had locked their doors and windows and it hadn't saved them. The killer – *her killer*, she needed to think of him as *her* killer, crawl deep into his mind, live with him in hers, if she was ever going to be able to understand him and be of any help to the investigation – was smarter than that. Locked doors wouldn't stop him. Her gaze tracked around the kitchen, looking for a dog basket, dog bowls. There weren't any. They were safe, here, from that trick at least.

'I heard a helicopter buzzing around all day Sunday.' Denise's voice pulled her back. 'Simon said it was just people being ferried to Goodwood, but I knew that something was wrong. I looked out of the window, saw the numbers under its belly.' She patted her own trim stomach. 'It was clearly a police helicopter and hopefully us taxpayers aren't paying to ferry rich people to Goodwood horse races in police helicopters!'

A look of concern pushed the fleeting smile from her face. Denise was an open book, Jessie thought, emotions and thoughts ticker-taping across her face almost as they would on the face of a child.

'It was so low, hovering just above the treetops, and so close to our house at times, that I thought it would either get swallowed by the trees or burst in through our sitting room window. We watched *Apocalypse Now* a couple of weeks ago, as Simon is *such* a war nut, and it reminded me of that film, of the American army helicopters hovering low over the paddy fields, machine-gunning all those poor people.'

Cara nodded. 'Did you know the Fullers?' he asked. 'Had you ever met them?'

'I saw them in the summer at a village fete. Walderton village, just up the road. But apart from that, the Fullers and us don't . . . didn't quite move in the same social circles.' She pointed a finger at the ceiling. 'They were up there somewhere and we're just . . . *normal*, I suppose. Just normal, middle-class, if I can dare to use that term, people.'

Cara smiled and nodded again.

'But I think that my husband . . .' she tailed off, another look of concern capturing her expression, silencing her voice.

'What?' Cara pressed.

She shook her head and laughed. 'No, nothing. Simon says that I talk too much. You're always wittering on, he says.'

Simon was right – Denise did like to talk. However, she was probably lonely, stuck in the house all day with a small child, Jessie reasoned. And though she sympathized, the slow pace and meandering chat were beginning to irritate her. She doubted that Cara had had much experience with bored housewives, and he was struggling to focus the conversation on what they were here to achieve. She had a ton to do, they both did, and she couldn't imagine that Denise, lovely though she was, would add anything constructive to the picture they needed to build of this killer, of what had happened out there, in that isolated house across the woods, three nights ago. Laying her hands flat on the table, she cleared her throat.

'Did you see or hear anything suspicious on Saturday evening, Mrs Lewin?' she asked. 'We estimate that the murder happened between ten p.m. and one a.m.'

Denise tucked her top teeth over her bottom lip and, after a brief pause, shook her head.

'Nothing?' Jessie pressed.

Another shake. But there was something about her expression . . .

'I'm not a hundred per cent sure about my geography,' Jessie continued. 'But isn't the Fullers' house just on the other side of those woods?'

'Well, not *just*,' Denise replied. 'It's probably two or three kilometres away. Well, two maybe, so no, not *just*.' There was an edge to her voice, an edge, Jessie sensed, that was driven by nerves, fear, even. Alone in the house all day with only a small child for company, a small child to protect. It could set the imagination running riot and Jessie had the impression that Denise's defences against wild-running imaginations were minimal.

'But the woods are the same as those that border the Fullers' property?' she pressed. They were here for a purpose, to gather crucial information; they couldn't afford to be oversensitive to people's feelings, even childlike Denise's.

Denise bit her lip again and nodded, her gaze slipping to the double doors, fixing on the woods beyond. 'They own most of the woods evidently,' she murmured. 'But there are public footpaths cutting through them. There's one that runs just the other side of our garden fence. It's used by dog walkers mainly. The woods are thick and I don't think many dog walkers can be bothered to fight their way through it, so they stick to the paths. And obviously there's shooting in the autumn and winter, so there are notices up.'

Jessie nodded. She sat back and withdrew her hands from the table, sending Cara a body language signal that she hoped he understood: that she knew this was his show and he was the lead player. He was as perceptive as she had expected him to be.

'How about in the few days preceding the Fullers'

146

murder?' he asked. 'Did you see anyone suspicious hanging around, either out in the woods or in the neighbourhood?'

Again, Denise shook her head.

'A man you haven't seen before? A car that you haven't seen before? One that doesn't belong to one of your neighbours? Any odd or unexpected activity?'

'No. I'm sorry.'

Jessie was watching her closely, her changes of expression. Something was troubling her – something more than imagined fears.

'Mrs Lewin—'

Her silvery-blue gaze moved to meet Jessie's. Moved, but didn't quite meet, focusing somewhere around Jessie's left ear.

'Is something bothering you, Mrs Lewin?'

She smiled, a vague, distracted smile. 'Can you see into my mind, Doctor?'

'If I could see into people's minds we wouldn't be here asking you questions. We'd have the Fullers' murderer in custody by now,' Jessie replied flatly.

Denise half-nodded. 'Yes, of course—'

'Mrs Lewin. I can tell that something is bothering you. Please tell us what it is.'

Silence for a long moment and then, 'It's just that—'

'Just that what?' Jessie prompted.

Her gaze found Jessie's fully now. 'I'm sorry, I've forgotten your name, Doctor.'

'Flynn. Jessica Flynn. But please call me Jessie.'

'I'm pretty sure that you'll think I'm mad if I tell you.'

Whatever Denise had going on in that head of hers wouldn't even scratch the surface of some of the loonies – totally unprofessional term, but hey, she was only thinking it, not saying it – that Jessie had met in her years as a psychologist. Wouldn't scratch the surface of her own tormented mind.

'Really, I won't think you're mad. Please just feel free to tell us anything.'

'OK, well, it's just that last . . . last night, Leo woke up screaming. He said that he'd seen something in the garden. A ghostie, he kept saying.' She smiled apologetically. 'I questioned and questioned him, we both did actually, but he didn't say any more than that. He's only three so it can be hard getting sense out of him.'

Cara leant forward, steepling his fingers. Encouraging body language – Jessie suppressed a smile.

'Did *you* see anything in the garden?' he asked.

Denise shook her head. 'His scream woke me up. I was half-asleep when I went into his bedroom. Simon . . . my husband, had left the curtains open and it was a bit breezy.' She glanced over her shoulder to the double doors to the garden. 'I never leave the curtains open as Leo has an active imagination, so I was cross when I saw them open, cross with Simon.' She gestured over her shoulder, without turning. 'There's that weeping willow in the middle of the garden and it was moving in the wind. The moon was bright last night and it made the willow look almost luminous . . . luminously white. I'm sure that was what Leo saw.'

Her perfect white incisors dug into her bottom lip again.

'Did you see anything?' Jessie asked. 'Anything apart from the willow?'

She shook her head.

'Are you sure? I really won't think that you're mad. Neither of us will. Anything, any tiny detail, can be really helpful.'

Denise shook her head again, a vague, non-committal

148

shake that turned into a half-nod. 'Just, uh, just . . . there were some footprints,' she murmured.

'Footprints?' Cara asked.

'Yes. A man's, Simon thought they were.'

'Where?'

'In front of the weeping willow. Simon went out in his pyjamas and dressing gown with a torch to search the garden to make Leo feel better, and then I saw him stop and have a good look at the ground in front of the willow. The grass is a bit sparse and often damp there as the tree shades it from the sun, and when he came back in he told me that he'd seen a couple of footprints.' She glanced over her shoulder again, at the garden. 'But it's really nothing to be frightened about. The fence is broken, as you can see, and dogs do run in here. As Simon pointed out, I found dog poo on my dahlias last week and *we* don't have a dog.'

'So, your husband thought it was someone trying to catch their dog?' Cara asked.

'Yes.'

At the mention of dogs, Jessie felt something in her chest tighten.

'Can we see the footprints?' she asked.

Denise's eyes widened in surprise. 'Why do you want to see them?'

'Purely because we're here and we might as well,' Jessie answered. 'It's nothing more than that.' She eyeballed Cara across the table, willing him not to contradict her, alarm Denise.

'It's just routine,' Cara said, picking up on her cue, rising from the table. 'My boss is a stickler for detail and he'd kill me if he thought I'd left even one tiny stone unturned.' He smiled. 'Would you show us, please.'

They waited, listening to the shriek of cartoon characters having an animated fight in the sitting room, while Denise unlocked the kitchen door, then followed her out into a large garden. It was a hundred foot long and fifty wide, south-facing, Jessie could see from the angle of the sun, flowering borders along three sides, four or five slats missing from the fence in the back right-hand corner, a couple of others hanging crookedly from the horizontal support. The weeping willow was young, a baby still, barely fifteen feet tall, but a dominating presence in the middle of the lawn all the same, its shadow gobbling their feet, their legs, torsos, as they approached it.

'We're in a conservation area so we weren't allowed to cut it down,' Denise said. 'It's a pain because of the shade, but we loved the house and the fact that the garden backs onto fields and woods and isn't overlooked, and everything's a compromise, isn't it?' She stopped a few feet short of the willow and waved her hand vaguely. 'I didn't come out myself, so I didn't see exactly where the footprints were, but I think about here.'

Cara and Jessie stepped forward, their feet squelching in unison. The grass was sparse, as Denise had said, dejected-looking tufts struggling up from damp red-brown earth.

'It's damp,' Denise added unnecessarily. 'We're clay here, so it doesn't drain well.'

Cara nodded. 'It rained heavily this morning. I woke early.'

Didn't sleep more like, Jessie thought. She hadn't either. Who could have done after what they'd seen at the Fullers'?

They circled the area in front of the willow, studying the ground. There was nothing to see beyond a couple of semi-circular indents that could have been made by the heels of shoes. Or the hooves of a pony. Or pretty much anything.

Jessie looked up, met Denise's silvery-blue gaze. 'What did *you* think?' she asked.

'Think?'

'About the footprints? You said that your husband, Simon, thought it was a dog walker. Did you agree?'

Denise shrugged. 'Well it couldn't possibly have been a ghostie, could it, as a ghost wouldn't leave footprints. And as Simon pointed out, who on earth is going to be bothered hanging around in our garden at two a.m. when they could be tucked up in bed? I mean, we're just . . . well, we're just normal. Boring. Nothing to see here!' Her perfect white teeth flashed, as she made jazz hands. 'No, it was clearly just a dog walker. As I said before, lots of them use the public footpath. Serves us right for not fixing the fence.' She dropped her hands. 'My poor dahlias. I'm not sure that they'll ever forgive me.'

26

'Thank you for staying open late for me,' Jessie said.

'No problem,' Cherry Goodwin replied. 'We don't close until six anyway, so it's only an extra hour and I've got more paperwork than I can begin to get through. I've hardly had a free moment all day, what with the press and other ghoulish gloaters trying to get a look at Lupo. That's what you're working on, isn't it? The murder of Lupo's owners?'

'Yes,' Jessie said simply. She didn't want to talk about the case; couldn't talk about it.

Though she had enjoyed the hours she'd spent with Darren Cara on the knock today, their efforts had been fruitless: no one they'd talked to, with the possible exception of Denise Lewin and her son's 'ghostie', had seen or heard anything useful in relation to the Fullers' murders, but everyone had been agog nevertheless, spilling over with questions that she and Cara had politely but firmly declined to answer.

Late afternoon, she'd found herself back in the incident room, alone and surrounded by images from the Fullers' crime scene, viewing, thinking, making no concrete progress, but always circling back to the same theories: that the Fullers' murders were personal and to do with watching. Watching and dogs. The photos on the incident room wall that had snagged her attention time and again were the close-ups of the scratches at the base of the door through which Claudine Fuller had let in death. And the scratches – gouges, more accurately – down Hugo Fuller's face. Not fingernails. Not a dog's claws either – not a normal dog at least, or so Dr Ghoshal had said. So, what then? She still had no idea.

There was an oil on canvas displayed above the Paws for Thought reception desk, a little black and white, Jack-Russell-type dog, drawn with thick strokes of paint. It was beautifully done, the peaks and troughs of oil paint giving the scene – a stony beach and the dog at the centre of it – life. It was the type of painting that Jessie would have itched to pick chunks off with her fingernail when she was a kid. The little dog was hiding underneath an upturned fishing boat, its head resting on its paws, tilted slightly to one side, as if its attention had been caught by something. But its eyes were dull. If dogs could feel sadness, that little dog was deeply sad.

'That's the first dog that I rescued,' Cherry said, following Jessie's gaze. 'God, twenty-five years ago now, it must have been. I took him home and kept him as my pet. Then, a few months later, one of my friends found two puppies that some moron had dumped in a bin bag in a layby. She couldn't keep them as she lives in a flat, so I got numbers two and three.' She grinned. 'It was a slippery slope after that. I registered for charitable status, started raising money, and hey presto, Paws for Thought was born.'

'Where did you find him?'

'Up in Selsey, cowering under a fishing boat. I'd taken my nephew to the lifeboat station. He was only five or six then. I'm going to his wedding in a fortnight's time. It was November, bloody freezing, and the poor little dog was soaking wet. He was half-dead when I found him.'

Now that Cherry had told her the beach was Selsey, Jessie could recognize it from the faint, grey line of the lifeboat pier, stretching out into the water in the top left-hand corner of the painting. She had only been up there once, this summer with Callan, to buy some lobsters from the fishing sheds for a treat dinner one Saturday. They hadn't walked down the lifeboat pier, but she had thought at the time how spindly it looked, the kind of pier a kid would construct from broken matchsticks, and how she wouldn't have liked to sprint down it in a howling gale to launch a lifeboat into a raging sea. Jessie turned back to the reception desk. Cherry was jabbing at the computer.

'You never found the dog's owner?' she asked.

Cherry's gaze remained focused on the screen, her brow creased. 'No. He didn't have a collar or any identification. I told the police and put up notices on lamp posts around the beach, but no one ever came forward. It was odd because he seemed pretty well cared for, healthy and well fed, and he was gentle and loving, as if he had been loved, but at the same time he had lots of old injuries.' She balled her fists. 'Both his front paws were misshapen, like clubs. They'd clearly been broken at some point. And one of his ears was half-missing, not bitten off by another dog, but a straight cut, as if it had been severed with a knife. He whimpered when I picked him up. I think that someone had given him a few good kicks in the ribs. He was such a sweetie. It makes me sick that people can treat animals like that.' A whirr and the printer on the reception desk sprung into life. Sitting back, Cherry dragged orange-painted nails through her choppy, hot-orange pixie cut. 'I'm printing out some instructions. You said that you'd never had a dog before.'

'No, I never have.'

And why was she now? Because her heart that had already lost two big chunks – one, her brother, years ago, the second, secret, much more recent – had space in it to love. But mainly, she knew, because of those photographs in the Fullers' house, her knowledge of how Claudine had suffered enough without her beloved Lupo being stuck in a dogs' home for years or going to a home where he wouldn't be properly loved and cared for.

Coming out from behind the desk, Cherry handed Jessie a small pack of paper. 'You don't need to read them now. I'll tell you everything you need to know, so they're just for reference, in case you forget. The top sheet also has all the centre's contact details, in case you have any questions or a problem with Lupo. We'll take him back, obviously, if you do.'

Her gaze moved from Jessie's to the picture above the desk. 'I called him Selsey, for obvious reasons. I heard rumours that he belonged to a teenage boy. A couple of people said that they'd seen him walking around with the dog. I made some enquiries, found out where he lived and went around there. It was miserable.' She frowned. 'God, I remember it so clearly. The mum was nuts. She was wearing a short-sleeved man's T-shirt and there were needle tracks all down her arms. The front garden was like a junkyard, full of broken bits of shit and empty vodka bottles. She basically told me to fuck off and went back inside. "Fuck

155

off, he's gone, ain't he. Dumped us like his shitty fucking dad." There was a girl, his sister I assume, about twelve or thirteen. She stayed on the doorstep, looking at me. She didn't seem to be the full package, if you know what I mean, but at least she smiled. I felt desperately sorry for her too, stuck in that dreadful home.'

Raising a hand, she ran it over the curled-up figure of the little dog. 'Sorry, that sounded terrible, didn't it? I'm not judgemental. I just remember leaving that house feeling utterly shit about life. I went back to the police and asked about the boy and they said that his school had registered him as a missing person. They thought that the kid had run away. Run away and dumped his dog.'

Jessie raised an eyebrow. 'Just gone?'

Cherry shrugged. 'You know, having seen where he lived, I really wouldn't have blamed the kid.'

'Did the police do anything?'

She shook her head. 'I don't think so. He was weeks away from being sixteen, the police said. A crazy number of children go missing in the UK every year, though you're police, so of course you know.'

'Actually, I don't,' Jessie said. 'How many go missing?'

'One hundred and forty thousand and half of those are between the ages of twelve and seventeen. I read it – I can't remember where now.'

'That's a huge number. They can't all stay missing.'

'No, obviously, a lot return at some point, but a lot don't. And it is a huge number, but that's the point, isn't it? We all lead our cosy little lives thinking that nothing bad happens out there but actually that's rubbish. Fundamentally, the world is a nasty place. Some kids feel the need to run away because their lives are so shit and others get taken, trafficked or whatever. Like all those thousands of girls in those grooming cases throughout the country, that everyone ignored for years and years. Who the hell would have thought that could happen in our so-called civilized society? I thought that the world was cosy too, until I found that little dog and started the rescue charity and now I know better. I've seen it all.'

Not quite all, thought Jessie, an unwelcome, unbidden image of the Fullers rising in her mind.

'I mean, all those children – where do they go?' Cherry paused.

Jessie lifted her shoulders, but didn't answer. Even though she'd had no idea how many children went missing every year, she did know, from the last case she'd worked on, how easy it was for them to disappear – to make others disappear – particularly the marginalized in society.

'We're not great at looking after the vulnerable in this country. Animals, children, old people, they all get thrown to the wolves,' Cherry said, her gaze finding the picture. 'Even though he died years ago now, I still miss him. I really do.' She put a hand on Jessie's arm. 'Anyway, enough of my reminiscing. Shall we go and see Lupo?'

27

Denise sighed. She hated it when Simon was away. Hated his absence at any time, particularly when darkness descended, but now, what with that murder on Saturday night only a couple of kilometres through the woods, and the visit from the detective and his psychologist colleague this afternoon, she was even more nervous. She just needed to make sure that her anxiety didn't transmit itself to Leo. He was a sensitive child at the best of times and another screaming fit in the middle of the night would push her over the edge, send her doolally.

There's no harm in being vigilant and obviously lock doors and windows at night, that cute, multi-racial young detective had told her. She *had* quite fancied him. If the topic they'd been discussing hadn't been quite so hideous, she would have really enjoyed their chat. And she would, obviously, lock all the doors and windows. She had absolutely no intention of *inviting* people into her house. If they wanted to get in, they would have to break in. Smash a window. Kick a door down. And she'd hear and be straight on the phone to the police and they'd be around in an instant, sirens blazing.

Why am I even thinking these ridiculous thoughts?

Their house, their lives, their whole existence was so different from the Fullers' as to almost be on another planet. Most people envied those with money, but really, who on earth wanted to live in such isolation? She'd seen that woman – Candice, Clarise, whatever her name was – at the August bank holiday weekend dog show. She'd been there handing out the prizes and Leo had won the prize for the best fancy dress aged ten and under. Denise had spent two whole days making him a Peter Rabbit outfit and he had looked wonderful. He'd deserved to win and she was delighted when he had, as those village fairs could be so *un*fair. She had warmed to the woman, Candice, Clarise. No – Claudine – that was it.

Denise thought Claudine Fuller had looked terribly sad when she'd given Leo the prize. She had stopped to chat for a moment, just pleasantries, but Denise had felt a strong sense that Claudine was aching for some normal human contact, warmth, friendship. She'd mentioned to Simon, how sad she thought Claudine Fuller had looked. Sad behind the eyes, despite the dazzling smile that she had fixed to her face as if with quick-dry concrete. A rictus smile, Denise caught herself thinking at the time. But Simon had been annoyed with her, annoyed with her comment, with her having the audacity to comment on Claudine Fuller at all.

'You're fixated by the woman,' he had snapped. 'By her wealth.'

It had been a ridiculous thing to say. She'd chatted to Claudine for barely five minutes and only because she was trying to be pleasant. She'd bitten down on a nasty retort, because she knew that Simon was going through a tough time at work. Even so, there had been no need to snap at her like that, not on a family day out.

Poor woman. Claudine *had* seemed nice. She hadn't had any children herself, and Denise had felt sorry for her, standing there in her stiff pastel-pink skirt suit and matching low-heeled courts, a silver-tipped pastel-pink leather bow on each toe – a ridiculous outfit really for a village fun day. It had set her apart from everyone else, and perhaps that was what she had intended. Or perhaps that was what her husband had intended for her. He was there too, in his mustard-coloured moleskin trousers, a tweed jacket and matching tweed cap, standing apart from everyone else, including his wife, in a very 'Lord of the Manor' kind of way. The only thing missing from his attire a double-barrelled shotgun and cartridge belt. His wife had kept glancing over at him – *checking in* – Denise had thought at the time, with a strong sense that he was the one in control, pulling the strings, his beautiful wife only a perfect pastel-pink-suited puppet.

Emptying the dregs of her tea into the sink, Denise glanced at her watch. Six p.m. Still forty-five minutes until Leo's bedtime. She could hear the *Scooby-Doo* theme tune echoing from the sitting room, where Leo, post-bath, was watching television.

Zoinks.

Creepers.

You meddling kids.

And her and Leo's favourite: *Ruh-roh, Raggy.* Scooby-Doo's characteristic signal to Shaggy that the monster was close by.

She knew all the catchphrases, had watched it so many

times, holding Leo's hand and giggling with him, jamming a cushion playfully over his eyes when he'd been frightened, that she could recite them in her sleep.

There's no harm in being vigilant and obviously lock doors and windows at night. She'd do that now, with Leo occupied by *Scooby.*

The kitchen windows were all fitted with window locks – no need to check those.

And the double doors to the garden? She was sure they were locked too, but no harm in checking anyway. The garden beyond the glass was pitch-black, only the gibbous moon high in the sky, half-obscured by clouds that appeared, from where she was standing, to whip across its curve, masking, unmasking, masking again. It was windy again and the weeping willow was dancing. It *did* look ghostly. No wonder poor Leo had been frightened by it.

The kitchen doors were locked – she shook them just to check – the key nestling in the lock where Simon insisted it stayed so that they could escape in case of fire. She would have preferred to leave it in a drawer, but his family's house had burnt to the ground when he was eight and he still remembered his father having to fling a chair through one of the kitchen windows so that they could escape, as the key to the back door had been stowed in a drawer, and the front door locked and double locked.

You have no idea what a fire is like until you're caught in one. You can't breathe, you can't see and you are totally disorientated. The key stays in the lock where we can find it if we need to.

Fine. She had been fine with that. But now? Claudine Fuller, in her pastel-pink suit, filled her mind's eye. It *had* been sadness sitting right behind the poor woman's eyes.

Denise had been right, whatever Simon said. Claudine had been sad and now she was dead, drowned in that splendid swimming pool attached to that splendid, terribly isolated house, a life, a world so different from the one Denise occupied. And right now, standing in her cosy kitchen, *Scooby-Doo* echoing from the sitting room, of that she was glad.

Turning away from the garden, she busied herself in the kitchen for a few more minutes, washing up her teacup, wiping the crumbs from the kitchen table into her cupped hand and dropping them into the bin, giving the floor a cursory sweep. She could murder a glass of wine, but wouldn't allow herself one, not when she was home alone. Well, perhaps a small one, but only later, when Leo was asleep. The fridge, that cold bottle of Chardonnay that she and Simon had cracked open last night, was calling to her. *God, if it wasn't for Leo, I'd be an alcoholic by now.*

Crossing the hallway, she walked into the sitting room, skirting quietly around the back of the sofa so as not to disturb Leo's viewing. There were double doors to the garden in here too, matching those in the kitchen. She twisted the handle: locked. Of course they were. She and Simon liked to leave them all open in the summer, let the outside billow into the house, but since chilly autumn weather had arrived a few weeks ago, they hadn't opened them.

With a piercing scream, she leapt back from the doors.

Her next thought, barely coherent: *Leo, my baby. I must protect my baby.*

Then: *Oh God. God, God, God.*

28

Jessie watched Cherry twist the sign on the front door from 'Open' to 'Closed' and lock the door. She turned back to Jessie. 'I didn't use to lock it when I went out back to see the dogs, but I've had a visitor, so I'm more careful now.'

'A visitor? Someone breaking in?'

'No, not breaking in. Heavens, I don't even know why I'm bothering to lock the door as they just seem to be able to get in anyway.'

Jessie met her gaze with a raised eyebrow. 'What do you mean?'

'Someone or something has been getting into Paws for Thought at night.'

'Every night?'

'No, I don't think so. Just sometimes.'

'You don't sound that sure.'

'I'm not sure . . .' Cherry tailed off with a shrug.

Jessie thought of the Fullers, of someone, some*thing*, tricking its way into their house. She looked past Cherry to the double doors, to the faint shape of her Mini outside. The tiny car park was lit only by the rectangle of light cast from the glass door to reception, most of it in darkness. She was pleased now that she'd have Lupo to accompany her when she left this evening. She'd wait for Cherry to lock up too, wait until she'd got into her car.

'How do you know that someone's been coming in at night then?' she asked.

'I found a muddy footprint on the doormat.'

Jessie frowned. The whole thing sounded mad. 'When?'

'About a month ago.'

Jessie turned back to the door. The doormat was red, carpet-style, surrounded by a black rubber border. It looked like the type of doormat that would be sold under the moniker 'grabs dirt'. There was a scattering of faint foot-prints on it now, hers included, the most recent, still shiny with damp from the pothole she'd sunk into while feeling her way blindly across the car park.

'What kind of shoe print was it?'

Cherry looked confused. 'What do you mean?'

'A man's? Woman's? Smooth-soled, a trainer, a rugged work-boot type?'

Cherry widened her eyes and shrugged. 'I don't know. I didn't even think about it at the time. We were open by then and I just saw a huge muddy print on my doormat.'

'Huge?'

'I don't know. It was just a muddy print.'

'But not a woman's shoe?' Jessie moved back to the doormat, and planted her boot next to the print she had made when she'd entered.

'No, not a woman's shoe, or not a dainty woman's shoe anyway.' Cherry sighed. 'I just like things to be tidy. I think it's important, don't you think? Particularly for an animal charity. I think people come in here expecting us to be dirty and chaotic, and I want them to leave with entirely the opposite impression. I want them to know that they can adopt an animal from us without it being riddled in fleas or infested with mange.'

Jessie nodded. The reception area was spotless. Nothing here to rile her OCD, goad the electric suit into life.

'When I saw the print, I just grabbed the Hoover from the cupboard and whizzed it over the doormat. It was only a bit later that I realized how odd it was that the print had been there at all, because I Hoover every night. It didn't occur to me at the time as I was in such a rush, but clearly it shouldn't have been there.'

'Is there anything else that makes you think someone is breaking in at night?'

'They're not breaking in.' Cherry sounded tense. She was clearly more disturbed by this visitor than she was admitting. 'They're letting themselves in.'

'With a key?'

Cherry shrugged. 'I don't know. I assume that, or they're picking the lock.'

'What is the lock like?'

'It's a Yale lock. Nothing fancy.' She paused, catching the look on Jessie's face. 'Do you think I should be worried?'

Jessie answered with a non-sequitur. 'What security do you have?' She did a three-sixty of the reception area. 'Is that camera real?'

'No, it's a dummy. We're only a small local charity and pretty backwater. I didn't want to spend the money for a real one and I've never needed to.'

'Before now.'

Cherry lifted her shoulders and gave a reluctant nod at the same time. 'Yeah, I suppose so.'

'Get a real one. You can get them online for a pittance.'

'Yes, but then I have to pay someone to connect it up, and that won't come cheap. We're hand to mouth here and I want to spend every penny we have on the dogs. We don't have anything to steal and we've never had any problems. It's not like we house the Crown Jewels.' A defensive tone was rising in her voice and Jessie let it drop. Putting Cherry's back up over her security arrangements wouldn't help anyone, and she wasn't here for that anyway.

'You can get a stand-alone camera off the Internet really cheaply,' she said, as a final parting shot. 'Like a Teddy Cam.'

'Huh?'

'A Teddy Cam. It's just a nickname. It's a camera hidden in a stuffed toy, so that you can set it on the mantelpiece and have it watch your nanny, or whoever you want to watch. Or you can just get a small, very discreet wireless camera to prop on the top of the desk, or a light fitting, or stick on the wall. An intruder wouldn't even notice it.'

'Aren't they just a green light for creepy snoopers?'

'Yes, if you have a mind to be a creepy snooper. However, they're also a green light for you to have CCTV cheaply.' She paused. Cherry didn't strike her as someone who was in the slightest bit au fait with modern technology, and she still looked unconvinced. 'Have you told the police about your visitor?'

Cherry nodded. 'They sent a community liaison officer around after I called the first time, the day after I found that print on the doormat, but he didn't do anything. I think he thought I was nuts to be honest. To be fair to him, it's not the most convincing story, is it? That someone breaks into a dog rescue centre to lie in a dog's basket for a few hours.'

'To do *what*?'

'To lie in a basket.' Cherry looked embarrassed. 'Didn't I say?'

Jessie shook her head, incredulous. 'No, you didn't say.'

Cherry pressed her fingertips to her forehead. 'I'm sorry. I'm just so busy, my brain doesn't seem to work half the time. That's one of the reasons that I haven't got around to sorting out a camera. I work as a freelance bookkeeper too, to pay the bills. I'm kind of maxed out. Sorry.'

'It's fine. Don't worry.' Jessie wanted Cherry to get back to the point. 'Tell me about the basket.'

Cherry sighed. 'After that first time, when I found that footprint on the doorstep, I had a good look around. Actually, I didn't immediately, because, as I said, it didn't occur to me that a footprint was strange. But while I was sitting down having lunch and I had a moment to think, I realized that the footprint shouldn't have been there. I was sure that something must be missing, but I couldn't find anything. None of the dogs had been taken, none of them hurt. All the computing equipment was still here, nothing taken from the desk or the kitchen. The dogs' food supplies were undisturbed.'

'But?' Jessie pressed. She wanted Cherry to get to the point.

'I keep one of the cages empty as much as I can, in case any emergency abuse cases come in. It's the last cage on the right, at the back of the kennel room. I'll show you when we go through to see Lupo. I looked in there last, and that's when I noticed that the basket had an imprint in it.'

'An imprint? Of what? A human?'

Cherry shrugged. 'Of something big. A big dog, like a German shepherd.' She paused. 'Or, yes, a human.'

'Are you telling me that you think someone has been breaking in here to sleep in a dog's bed?'

'I suppose so . . . I am, yeah.' She paused. 'And they also play with the toys.'

29

Denise sucked in a desperate breath, a free-diver surfacing from a hundred feet below, her heart jammed gaggingly thick in her mouth.

She could see what it was now. What it was that had made her almost expire with utter terror. No monstrous form in the garden eyeballing her through the glass, but only the reflection from the television, brighter than usual as the night was so pitch-black. The *Scooby-Doo* monster, frozen for a second on screen, a huge, pale, malevolent, masked monster.

Ruh-roh, Raggy.

Gone now, the Mystery Machine chugging across the glass in its place. If she hadn't still been so tense that she could barely catch breath, she would have laughed out loud with relief.

She turned. Leo's frightened little face stared at her from the sofa, his mouth popped into a horrified, startled 'O'. He looked as if he was about to cry. He looked as she felt.

'Oh, God, I'm so sorry darling.' Hand pressed to her

chest, to try to force her breath to calm, she sat down next to him on the sofa. 'Mummy's fine, bean.'

Wrapping her arms around him, she pulled him onto her knee and hugged him tight. The jumbled look of fear and concern on his little face made her feel as if the wad in her throat would pop right out of her mouth on a gush of tears. Her beautiful, sensitive little boy.

Pressing her lips to the top of his head, she murmured, 'I love you so much, bean.' She didn't even realize that she was crying until the dampness on his duck's-fluff hair wet her cheek. 'I love you so much. So so much and whatever happens, I will always, *always* look after you.' She smeared the tears into her sleeve and forced a smile. 'Ruh-roh, my little Raggy-boy.'

He smiled back, a lopsided, not-really-sure smile. 'Ruh-roh, Mummy.'

30

They exited the reception area, into a second, much larger room, ten metres wide and twenty or so long, concrete-floored, built-in cages lining either wall, a walkway in between. As soon as Cherry cracked open the door from the reception area, a tide of barking rose: a few excited yaps at first and then more, louder, deeper; a cat's chorus, if it hadn't been dogs, as if barking was contagious, which Jessie reasoned it probably was. By the time Cherry had closed the door behind them, locking them together in the kennel room, there was a line of excited dogs jumping against their cage doors. At the far end of the walkway, beyond the double rows of cages, was a glass door that led into a grassy, high-walled outside space.

'Lupo is at the far end,' Cherry shouted above the noise. 'Don't put your fingers through any of the cages. They're all friendly, but some are a mite too friendly and it's feeding time soon.'

The barking rose and then fell, like some 'normal distribution' of dog noise as Jessie and Cherry walked down the walkway, past a motley assortment of mutts of all shapes and sizes.

Cherry stopped at the second-to-last cage on the right-hand side. 'Here's Lupo,' she said.

Jessie's eyes widened. She hadn't expected him to be so big. In fact, she hadn't known what she'd been expecting – stupidly hadn't thought beyond Claudine Fuller's sad, bedraggled body, beyond those photos of Lupo, her baby, everywhere in that cold mausoleum of a house, beyond the sad horror of her dream. *God*, along with Callan he'd fill the whole of her tiny sitting room. Two Gullivers in Lilliput, one human and one canine.

Cherry must have picked up on her hesitation. 'He's lovely, very gentle. Really, no trouble at all.' She paused. 'We need the cage.'

Jessie nodded in a way she hoped looked more unequivocally firm than it felt. 'I'm taking him, of course. I just—'

'Didn't expect him to be so big?'

'Yes.'

Eunice Hargreaves, the old lady who had seen him tied to the lamp post, had described him as a wolf – a wild wolf roaming free in the Canadian Rockies – and here and now Jessie could see why. He didn't belong in a concrete cage. He probably didn't belong in a tiny workman's cottage in the Surrey Hills, but at least she had a decent garden and her cottage was surrounded by countryside. Callan ran most mornings before work, so he could take his doppelganger Gulliver with him, and she could walk him too. Once this case was over. Once she got back to her normal life again, or at least until Marilyn came knocking again. Once . . . once . . . once. The case had hardly begun and she so desperately wanted it to end.

172

'Is that the empty cage you were talking about?' Jessie asked, tilting her head. 'The one you found the imprint in?'

'Yes.'

'Can I see?'

'Sure, but there's nothing to see.'

'What about the bed, the imprint?'

'I shook the bed out, put it back as it should be. I like things to be tidy.'

Oh God. What about evidence?

'What about—' she broke off. This wasn't about a murder. It wasn't even about theft or vandalism. Whoever was visiting hadn't broken in, they had a key or had picked the front door lock. They came quietly, left as quietly and did – what? – in between? Lay down in a dog's bed? Played with dog toys? She glanced over at Cherry with her mad shock of hot-orange hair, thick black eyeliner and orange lipstick. Jessie wasn't surprised that the community liaison officer hadn't believed her. Jessie was struggling to believe her.

'And the toys?'

'I can't get the teeth marks out of them, obviously, but I wash them.'

Stepping sideways, leaving Lupo – the only dog who hadn't leapt against his door when they walked past – sitting in his basket looking as forlorn as that poor little Jack Russell in the oil painting in the reception area, Jessie unlatched the door of the empty cage. It was a spotless space that she would have been delighted to call her own: not a speck of dirt on the concrete floor, the dog bed, a large circular disc of royal-blue fleece, clean and thickly padded, two stainless-steel dog bowls, both empty and sparkling clean, and a selection of toys laid out next to the

173

bowls. Ducking down, Jessie pressed her hand into the fleece bed. It sprang back at her, without leaving a dent.

'Can I lie on it?'

Cherry looked doubtful. 'I thought that you said you weren't police.'

'I'm not. But I do work with them. I'm a—' What? What was she? Marilyn wished that she was Surrey and Sussex Major Crimes' resident psychic, but at the moment she felt like excess baggage, dead wood. 'I'm a clinical psychologist and I work with the police to help them get into the mind of killers.'

Cherry looked doubly doubtful. 'So, you could help me understand why some whacko keeps breaking into my facility and hanging out in one of the dogs' cages?'

Jessie didn't even nod to that question. Crouching, she twisted sideways and planted her backside in the centre of the large disc of padded fleece. It felt springy and comfortable. Twisting on her side, she curled up in a ball, resting her head on her arms. She was too embarrassed to catch Cherry's eye.

'It's comfortable,' she said, purely to make conversation.

It *was* comfortable. She lay for what felt like three hours, though was probably less than a minute, withering under Cherry's cynical gaze, and then pushed herself to her feet and looked down at the disc of royal-blue fleece.

'There's no imprint, no indication that I was ever there, so whoever comes obviously stays for a decent amount of time and squashes the stuffing flat. What is it stuffed with, by the way?'

Cherry's shrug was frustrated. 'I don't know.'

Ducking back down, Jessie picked up the rubber bone and inspected it. There were faint marks, like two dashes – incisors – and a dent either side of the dashes – canines.

174

'They're faint,' Cherry said by way of explanation.

Jessie rotated the bone in her hands. There were more tooth marks on the toy, as if it had been chewed multiple times. The same on the small rubber ball.

'How many times do you think this . . . this, uh . . . you've been visited?'

'I don't know,' Cherry said. 'I only discovered that we were being visited because of the muddy footprint and that was a month ago.'

'And the imprint and the teeth marks?'

'I only saw those when I had a good look around because of the footprint. I have a couple of staff members, who get the cages ready for occupants. But, as I said, this cage is kept empty and clean. We have no cause to go in there unless we have an abuse case being admitted. And we're always in a rush here. We have space for twenty dogs and that's a lot of animals to look after, and they're always coming and going, so there's the home visits to organize and carry out, and the paperwork, endless paperwork. There's only ever two of us working here, so we're stretched.' She sounded defensive.

'How many teeth marks were there on the bone when you checked, after you found the muddy footprint?'

Cherry's brow wrinkled, with concern. 'Oh God, I hadn't thought . . .'

'Were there a few?'

She nodded.

'So they could have been visiting for months and you wouldn't have noticed?'

Cherry shuddered. 'Oh God, do you honestly think that might be the case? That's a horrible thought.'

'This isn't *The Hound of the Baskervilles*,' Jessie said, forcing a smile.

'Isn't it?'

'If it was, you'd be dead by now.' She had meant it as a joke, to lighten the atmosphere that suddenly felt lead heavy, but as soon as the words had left her mouth, she realized how ridiculous a statement it had been. This charity was Cherry's life's passion, the dogs her babies. The thought that someone or something was letting themselves in at night must be horrifying. And now Jessie had planted the seed that the person might be dangerous.

'My boyfriend is a military policeman. This is totally outside his jurisdiction as it's not military, but I can ask him to come around and have a look. Maybe give you some advice about security.'

Cherry nodded gratefully. 'I don't want to be any trouble.'

'It wouldn't be,' Jessie said. 'I'm sure he'd be fine about it.'

Would Callan be fine about it? He didn't seem to be busy at work at the moment, so he'd have time, and how hard could sourcing and installing a couple of cheap CCTV cameras be?

'That would be great. Thank you so much.'

'I'll call you when I've spoken to him.' She held up the bone. 'Could I take the bone?'

Cherry looked even more doubtful.

'I'll return it.'

'What do you want it for?'

'Just for, uh—' she broke off. *For evidence* – she didn't say it. The words sounded ridiculous, even to her own ears. Evidence of what?

'Sure. If you want to,' she said. 'Do you think that we should be worried? For the dogs or ourselves?'

Jessie shook her head. 'No.' But even as she said it, she

really wasn't sure. She had met some crazies in her life, but this was new to her. 'Shall we get Lupo?' she asked, changing the subject. She had nothing else to add on the shelter's night visitor and she needed to get going. They had a killer to find. She would speak to Callan though, ask him to come and take a look. If she mentioned it to Marilyn, he'd laugh her out of the place: *You're supposed to be finding the nut jobs, not turning into one.*

31

'What the hell is that?' Callan asked, when Jessie stepped into the living room, towing Lupo on a lead, behind her.

'It's an animal commonly known as a dog,' Jessie replied. 'Or Canis Lupus Familiaris if you want to get technical.'

'Whose is he?'

'He's ours.'

Callan didn't smile. 'What?'

He looked tired, his amber eyes washed out and bloodshot, black rings underneath them, as pronounced as hers when she'd swum with mascara. She hadn't picked a great moment to bring a wolf-dog into the house. But was there ever a great moment? And she hadn't had much choice around the timing.

'He's ours,' she repeated. 'I've, uh . . . we've adopted him.'

'What?'

Jessie hunched her shoulders. 'Stop saying "What?". It's making me nervous.'

'How about "What the fuck?" Is that any better?'

'Nope.' She stroked Lupo's head. 'He needed a home.'

'Lots of dogs need homes. I didn't think we were currently

in the market to offer creatures homes. We both work full time. And we've . . .' His eyes dropping from hers to study the carpet. 'I've got a few things on my mind at the moment.' Unconsciously, his hand rose to his head. His conscious brain engaged as his fingers brushed his temple and he turned the movement into a drag of his fingers though his blond crew cut.

'I know that it's not ideal, but—' she broke off, her mind's eye finding those gold-framed images of Lupo on Claudine Fuller's mantelpiece. The huge, soulful black and white photograph on canvas that she'd also spied in the kitchen. 'He needed a home.'

'Where did you get him from? And can you take him back?'

'He was the Fullers' dog.'

'Who the hell are the . . .' he began. 'The murdered couple?'

Jessie nodded.

'Can't a dog shelter take him?'

'A dog shelter did take him.'

'And – so?'

'I just—' she broke off. How to explain it, so she didn't sound mad. 'The woman, Claudine, loved him. Lupo was Claudine's baby and she's not here to look after him any more. I went to their autopsy yesterday and saw her. She looked so sad.'

The look on Callan's face was pure incredulity. 'She's dead.'

'I know she's dead, but she still looked so sad. It was as if she was thinking about Lupo while she was being killed, knowing that she was leaving her baby behind with no one to look after him.'

'You're nuts. And no.'

She clearly hadn't managed to explain herself without sounding mad.

'Please.'

'I love your soft side, even if you do a great job of hiding it most of the time, but we're not the right home for any dog, let alone a dog like that. Do you understand how much exercise he'll need? How much mental stimulation? He's not a Chihuahua.'

'Our next-door neighbour had two Chihuahuas when I was growing up and they were aggressive little fuckers. They're the land piranhas of the dog world. They used to squeeze under the neighbour's gate and take chunks out of my ankles when I was walking home from school.'

Callan smiled despite himself. 'A Pomeranian then.'

'I'm not a small-dog person. We're not small-dog people.'

'We're not any dog people.'

Tilting her head, she cartoon-grinned. 'But we could be. I like walking. You run every day and you can take him with you.'

'One reason I run is to have time alone, get away from people.'

'I hate to point out the obvious, but he's not a person.'

'*Things*. Get away from things. Be on my own.'

Jessie put her arm around Lupo and lifted his paw, in a 'hiya' wave. 'I'll be good company,' she said, in a squeaky voice. 'And I won't annoy you at all. You'll hardly notice I'm there. And you might get to quite like running with a big, hairy wolf-dog like me.'

Callan rolled his eyes, suppressing a smile. 'Still no.'

Jessie sensed a chink in his armour, dived for it. 'You like him really. I know you do.'

'I really don't.'

Another paw-wave. Lupo stood statue still beside her, despite her clutching his paw. 'He's like you, Callan. Cool, calm, collected, a still-waters-run-deep kinda guy. He's your doppelgänger. How could you reject him, you cruel, cruel man?'

'He'll give you a bite in a minute, if he's got any sense.'

Jessie lowered Lupo's paw to the ground, slowly, gently, casting exaggerated looks at him. 'Phew. I got away with it!'

The ghost of another smile. 'For fuck's sake, Jessie Flynn. Why the hell did I ever get tied up with you?'

She grinned. 'Because you love me. And because I keep you on your toes by doing all sorts of unexpected things like bringing huge, hairy wolf-dogs into the house.'

'It's not going to do your . . .' he tailed off, the subject still sensitive, despite all the progress she'd made. Despite what he had going on in his head – the bullet, the mystery letter that couldn't be anything but bad – all far more important than her stupid psychological problems.

'OCD? It's not going to do my OCD much good,' she finished.

'Right.'

'I'll be fine. He's white. He matches.'

'Huskies blow their hair twice a year.'

'Blow their hair?'

'Shed. All of it. Twice a year. There'll be hair everywhere.'

'Why do you think Hoovers were invented?'

Callan sighed. 'For the record, I think it's a terrible idea—'

Jumping up, Jessie flung her arms around his neck and kissed him. 'Thank you, thank you thank you.' Pulling back, she met his gaze, biting her lip. 'And now that you've agreed to give a needy dog a home, there's just another teeny-tiny good deed that I need you to do.'

32

Once Jessie had unpacked the bowls and food that she'd bought for Lupo from Paws for Thought and given him dinner, she fetched Callan a cold bottle of beer from the fridge, poured herself a glass of Sauvignon, and settled down on the sofa next to him, tucking her bare feet under his legs, taking his hand. Despite the beer and the cosying, his expression remained one of pure cynicism.

'Cherry Goodwin, the woman who runs Paws for Thought, thinks that someone has been breaking in,' she began.

'Breaking in to do what?'

'To do nothing, though that sounds ridiculous now that I'm saying it out loud.'

Callan frowned. 'They must have a purpose. People don't break into places for no reason.'

'You'd think not – but in this case, that doesn't appear to be true.'

'Tell me what she said – exactly what she said.'

'She told me that she's sure someone has been visiting Paws for Thought at night.'

'Breaking in or visiting? They're very different.'

'There's no sign of a break-in, so I suppose it's more like visiting. Uninvited visiting.'

'So how does he or she get access?'

'Cherry doesn't know, but she assumes that he or she has a key or can pick locks.'

'Is it every night?'

Jessie shook her head. 'Again, she doesn't really know, but she doubts that it's every night. Probably more like once or twice a week. There's a cage at the far end of the compound that she tries to keep free so that she has somewhere to put emergency abuse cases. It's furnished, if that's the right word, with a basket, dog toys, bowls, et cetera.'

He nodded. 'And . . .'

'And she's found, on quite a few occasions, evidence that something . . . someone I suppose, has been in the cage.'

'How does she know?'

'Because she found an imprint in the basket.'

'An imprint? Of what?'

'Something big. Bigger than a dog, or at least bigger than most dogs. She thinks that it was a human.'

Callan raised an eyebrow. 'Jesus.'

'And she found teeth marks on the toys in the cage.'

'Human teeth marks?'

'Yes.'

He laughed. 'Jesus Christ, there are some proper weirdos out there.'

'Don't laugh,' she said, slapping his leg.

'I'm not laughing.'

'You are laughing, and it's not funny.'

His amused gaze met hers. 'It's a bit funny, to be fair.'

'It's really not funny, Callan. It's incredibly disturbing. I told Cherry to call the police, but she's already had a community liaison officer around and he wasn't helpful, and there's never been anything stolen, any damage or any harm done to any of the dogs.' She reached for his hand, entwined her fingers with his.

'What?' he asked, a blend of amusement and suspicion in his voice.

'Will you go and have a chat with her?'

'To what end?'

'To reassure her. You're the policeman-cum-dog-whisperer now, after all. You're the perfect man for the job.'

'I'm a military policeman-cum-very-reluctant-dog-owner and Paws for Thought is civilian jurisdiction.'

'Your visit need not be on an official basis. Just go as a . . .' She was going to say, *friend*, but given that she'd only met Cherry once, and Callan had never met her, friend was a stretch. 'You won't need to do any actual policing.'

'Does she feel under threat?'

'She said not, but I'm not sure she was telling the truth. I'd feel under threat if I was her.'

Callan nodded without enthusiasm. 'OK, I'll have a look around and give her some advice about security.'

'Can you also fit a couple of cheap security cameras?' She tilted her head and smiled beseechingly. 'Argos in Chichester opens at eight a.m. You can go before work.'

'For fuck's sake.'

'Please. I promised her I'd ask you and I don't want to let her down.'

He grimaced. 'I'll go tomorrow morning. For another beer and a kiss.'

'Cheap at the price.' Tilting forward, she planted a soft

184

kiss on his cheek, feeling the rough stubble grating her lips, then slid off the sofa, stepped over Lupo who had settled himself at Callan's feet, and padded into the kitchen.

33

The cold air and silence hit Sophie like a physical shock after the dense heat of Sheiks. She had already been sick in the nightclub's toilets, hadn't made it to the bowl in time and had coated her calves and feet with vomit. The cubicle had rocked and swayed as she struggled to wipe herself down with toilet paper and she had slipped in the vomit, having to snatch at the toilet seat for support, covering her hand in urine. The thought that she didn't even know whose urine it was had sobered her up just enough to realize that she'd gone too far, needed to go home. Now. Right now.

Lucy was long gone. Sophie had been dancing with a boy she'd fancied for ages and hadn't wanted to leave, said she'd make her own way home. Sometime later the boy had disappeared and she'd found herself alone. She was aware that she was swaying, as she tottered down the road in search of a taxi, but however hard she focused on the narrow stone slabs that edged the pavement, she couldn't plant her feet in a straight line.

'I'm pissed,' she said, out loud, clutching onto a lamp post to steady herself. 'So fucking pissed.'

'Need a minicab, love?'

She hadn't noticed the car in the dimly lit street, but now she turned and saw that it was a small, dark-coloured hatchback and that she must have stumbled straight past it. She nodded to the man who was holding the passenger door open. She still felt sick, was aware that she must stink of vomit and urine, and the adrenalin of the evening was draining from her limbs. She was cold and tired and she could already feel the muggy fingers of a hangover cloying at her brain. She wanted to step into a Tardis and be magically transported to her bed, sleep until lunchtime tomorrow, wake up to the smell of roast lamb wafting up the stairs.

As she stepped towards the car, her stiletto heel snagged between two paving stones and she staggered. A strong arm snaked around her.

'Woah, love. Steady there.'

As his face oscillated in front of her, she formed the impression of a man around her dad's age, dark hair, black-framed glasses, the rims so thick they reminded her of joke-shop glasses people used to disguise themselves in bad comedies, chapped lips that were smiling. Smiling and speaking.

'Where to, love?'

'Twenty-one Marine Drive, Birdham,' she managed.

He gripped her arm to steady her, while she slithered awkwardly sideways in her tiny skirt. It occurred to her, momentarily as he shut the passenger door, that it was odd he'd ushered her into the front seat. She would have preferred to get into the back, like she usually did in taxis, so that she could stare out of the window and not have to chat.

But now that she was settled in the warmth and comfort, she couldn't bring herself to care. It was a car, a lift home, and taxis were like hen's teeth on a Wednesday half-term night in Bognor. It felt so good to ease her feet from the silver stilettos. They had looked so glam with her thigh-length black dress when she'd left home, but they were now clenching her toes in a vice. Anyway, the man was nice – kind and considerate. None of the boys she'd been out with had ever opened a car door for her, or waited until she was settled before closing it, and all of them would have had a good ogle at her knickers, when her skirt had ridden up as she'd climbed in the car. He had just looked off down the road politely.

'You out alone?' he asked, pulling out into the traffic.

She shook her head. 'I was with a friend, but she left earlier.'

'Some kind of friend to leave you on your own, when you're drunk.'

He had a local accent, Sophie thought, soft and quiet. Tilting her head back against the headrest, she closed her eyes and shook her head.

'She wanted to go and I wanted to stay. Anyway, I can look after myself.'

'Sure you can,' he said.

The scent of pine from the air freshener dangling from the rear-view mirror couldn't quite mask the sharp tang of his body odour. The smell made Sophie feel even sicker, and she leant away from him, resting her head against the chill window, the cool glass salve to her thumping head.

'I'll lock the door, so that it doesn't open by itself with you leaning against it,' he said, and she heard locks click shut.

Whatever, she thought, focusing on an air vent in the grimy dashboard, to try to stop her brain from slopping around inside her skull. The man had a nasty-looking cut on his forearm, she saw, as he moved again, to flick the windscreen wipers on. It had started to rain, fat drops that snapped and popped against the windscreen. She hadn't noticed the gash on his arm when he'd ushered her into the car. Hadn't noticed anything much.

'How did you get that?' she asked.

'What?'

'The cut. It looks nasty.'

He glanced down at his arm. 'Oh, uh, DIY,' he muttered, shucking the sleeve of his jumper down to cover it. 'I was putting up some shelves.' He smiled across at her, showing a line of straight, white teeth. 'What's your name?'

'Sophie. What's yours?'

'Charles,' he said, after a moment's hesitation.

She smiled. 'Like the prince.'

'Yeah. Like the prince.'

'I like Meghan.'

'Do you?'

Sophie nodded. 'Well, I don't actually like her much, I'd just like to be her.'

'Why's that then?'

'Because I quite fancy Prince Harry.'

'Don't all young women fancy Prince Harry.'

He turned off the main road suddenly, into a narrow, tree-lined street, and darkness closed in around them. Sophie could see only a strip of cracked tarmac, picked out by the narrow column of the headlights, and the packed trunks of trees, crowding the tarmac on either side.

'This isn't the way,' she said.

189

'Sure it is. I've been driving a cab for years and I know every road. It's a short cut.'

Was it? Her mind, still hazy, refused to focus. She didn't have a driving licence anyway and spent every car journey with her mum or dad looking at her mobile phone. How well did she know the roads? Not well at all, she realized. She had no idea where they were. There were millions of narrow, tree-lined country lanes like this around Chichester.

'Can't we stick with the main road?'

He shook his head. 'We've gone this way now and I'm not turning back.' He glanced across. 'Trust me, OK, love.'

The car bounced and groaned, going too fast for such a narrow lane, Sophie thought, as her stomach heaved. The man's eyes were fixed on the tarmac and he was gripping the steering wheel hard. Sophie thought of that cut on his arm again. It had been deep and there had been other, fainter marks, surrounding it. They looked like scratches, from twigs. Or fingernails.

Another bounce, and her stomach heaved again. But it wasn't only sickness she felt now, but also a gnawing fear in the pit of her stomach, banishing the alcoholic fog from her mind. The car hadn't had anything on the outside to show that it was a minicab, had it? And inside? Her eyes grazed across the dirty dashboard, to the windscreen, to the torn paper pine tree air freshener swinging from the rear-view mirror, blurred now by her tears. God, she'd been so stupid, climbing blithely into a stranger's car, without knowing anything about him. Slowly, surreptitiously, she reached her hand from her lap to the door handle, along it, fingers feeling for the lock.

'It's central locking,' he said, smiling across at her. 'The controls are here on my door.'

She hadn't realized that he'd been watching her.

'I want to get out,' she said suddenly.

'I can't let you out here, love.'

'Please. Please just stop and let me out.' Her voice was rising, a raw edge of fear that made him visibly wince.

'Sorry, I couldn't have that on my conscience, letting a young girl out of my car in the middle of the woods at night. What if something happened to you? I don't want to be reading about you in the paper tomorrow morning.'

At his words, the picture she'd seen in the paper of the Fullers, the newspaper headlines that her dad had pored over for the past two days, rose in her mind. Her dad had been obsessed with the article, with seeking out news of the murders on the television. He had barely talked of anything else, but when her mum had asked him why he was so interested in people he didn't even know, he'd got angry. *I just want to keep my family safe, that's all*, he'd said. And now, here she was, trapped in a car with a man she didn't know. *A mad man. The killer.*

Pressing herself against the passenger door, as far away from the man as she could possibly get, Sophie jammed her eyes shut, biting down on a sob. She couldn't fall apart, had to think. What the hell was she going to do? *God, I've been so so stupid.*

The seatbelt tightened across her chest and she realized suddenly that the car had stopped. Terror snapped her eyes open.

'Marine Drive, love. Which house is yours?'

34

Denise Lewin bolted upright in bed.

'Leo?'

Her heart was racing, a thousand beats a second, and her forehead was beaded with sweat.

Leo?

She listened. No noise from Leo's room on the opposite side of the wall, behind her headboard, or from anywhere else inside the house that she could hear. Absolutely no sound. Nothing at all.

But what had woken her so suddenly?

There must have been something.

Fumbling for the bedside light, she snapped it on, bathing herself in a disc of bright yellow. Feeling horribly exposed, she switched it off again. She had slipped the carving knife from the knife block as she left the kitchen this evening, slid it back in and grabbed the whole knife block – the bread knife, fish knife, gutting knife, the lot – carted it upstairs and plonked it on her bedside table. Now, the light turned off, she stretched out a hand, wrapped her fingers around the cold aluminium handle of the carving knife and drew it silently out of the block.

A noise, a crash?

It must have been something to bolt her from sleep so suddenly. But now, there was just that absolute silence. The absolute, deadened silence of deep night-time. Sliding out of bed, the knife clutched in both hands in front of her, Denise tiptoed to the bedroom door. The landing light was on – Leo insisted on it – and usually she was glad of the light, but now, as she walked across the landing, she felt merely vulnerable. A target.

But for who or what?

Her heart was knocking in her chest, her blood rushing like a burst fire hydrant in her ears. Her shoulders were tensed and she barely dared to breathe, waiting . . . waiting for what, though? For the ghostie of Leo's imagination to leap out and engulf her? For that monster from *Scooby-Doo* that had so terrified her when she'd seen its reflection in the lounge doors?

Ruh-roh, Raggy.

I'm mad. I'm going totally doolally crazy.

She reached Leo's ajar bedroom door, safe.

But of course I'm safe. This is my house and the doors are all locked.

Unwrapping the fingers of her left hand from the knife, she reached out. As the door swung open, it took her eyes a moment to adjust to the darkness, for the block shapes inside Leo's bedroom to morph into his chest of drawers, his toy trunk, his cabin bed. And Leo. Eyes closed, blond hair messed, eyelashes fluttering on his apple cheeks as he dreamt, looking so innocent, so heartbreakingly adorable that she wanted to snatch him up and gobble him whole.

God, she loved him so much it actually hurt. A physical ache in the pit of her stomach.

Baloo, his teddy bear, was on the floor where he must have tumbled when Leo had relaxed his grip as he drifted to sleep. Tiptoeing across the room, Denise ducked down and picked Baloo up, tucked him carefully under Leo's podgy arm. Her boy really was still so little, just a baby. She glanced towards the curtains. Tight closed, not even a hair's breadth of a gap between them; she'd never make the same silly mistake that Simon had.

The barbed-wire ball of tension inside her uncoiled as she breathed out. Nothing here, nothing to worry about.

Backing onto the landing, she pulled Leo's door partly closed and walked back to her own bedroom, smothering a yawn into the sleeve of her pyjamas. She felt ridiculous now, creeping around her own house clutching a carving knife like some deranged horror movie harridan. She'd never tell Simon. He'd honestly think that she had completely lost it.

Sliding the carving knife back into the block, she climbed back into bed, all thoughts of ghosties and *Scooby-Doo* monsters fading from her mind now. There was nothing to worry about. It was their home, the doors and windows were all locked, and they were safe.

35

Though it was knocking two a.m. and she'd promised to be home by midnight, Sophie thought her luck might be in as she stood on the pavement, sheltered by next-door's magnolia, and rummaged in her handbag for her door keys. Her heart was still beating like a jackhammer from the taxi ride, though her head was clear for the same reason, the alcoholic fug erased by the terror. It *had* been a taxi after all, must have been, despite the fact that it hadn't sported recognizable markings. The man – Charles – had deposited her home, safe, though the intense fear she'd felt while she'd been trapped in his car had made her realize that, however drunk she was in future, hopping into a random bloke's car without checking, really checking, that he was a taxi first was beyond idiotic. She'd given herself a proper fright, had been certain, when he'd turned into that dark, tree-hemmed lane, that he'd pull over, rape her – rape and then kill her. The image from yesterday's front page that had so caught her dad's eye rose in her mind: the Fullers. They had looked so ordinary, as much as posh Sussex could be called ordinary. Ordinary and *so* alive.

From where she was sheltering, she could see the upstairs over the tall privet hedge that bordered their drive, see that the lights were off. She was on half-term, but her parents both had work tomorrow. She'd told them that she and Lucy were spending the evening at Julia, a new girlfriend from school's house, and the false sense of security her lie provided them with – images of an evening spent painting nails, braiding hair and discussing boys – had presumably worked its magic and nodded them into a deep sleep.

It was still raining, more heavily now than when she'd been in that weirdo's taxi, and a wind was gusting off Chichester Harbour, a few streets away. She could just make out the rhythmic sound of the yachts' metal halyards pinging against their masts. It was a sound that reminded her of midsummer, of her fifteenth birthday in August, when her dad had sailed her, Lucy and her other two best friends over to Seaview on the Isle of Wight on his Albin Vega 27, to swim off the boat and barbeque on the beach.

Shivering, the memory evaporating with the cold, she hauled her coat tight around her neck with one hand, slipped off her heels with the other and jogged across the deserted road, the tarmac feeling white-hot against her bare soles, it was so cold. But at least she could pull off a silent approach, rather than pecking down the gravel drive on her metal-tipped stilettos. As she rounded the thick privet hedge that shielded their garden from the street, she stopped. The lights were off downstairs too, not even the hall light shining from behind the faux stained-glass panel in the door.

Strange. Her parents never switched it off when she was out for the night. Awesome news for her though, as it meant they were definitely asleep. She didn't care about the dark as she had her phone torch to guide her, and anyway, they'd lived in this modern detached house on Westlands Estate in Birdham since she was five years old and she could navigate every square inch with her eyes jammed shut.

The gravel on the drive was sharp against her soles as she padded to the front door. She wouldn't put it past her dad to be playing a trick on her, teach her a lesson for staying out too late, by jumping out at her in the dark hallway and giving her heart failure. She smiled at the thought – it wouldn't be the first time – but she could really do without it after the multiple heart attacks she'd had in weirdo Charles' taxi.

Using her mobile phone to light the keyhole, she unlocked and creaked the front door open. She stood for a second on the threshold, every sense more alert than it had been in hours, feeling sober now, elated, calm, tearful, hyper, an intense stew of emotions all mixed together. So deliriously happy just to be home *safe*.

She couldn't make out any lurking Dad-shaped shadows and, now that she held her breath and listened, really listened, she was sure that downstairs was deserted. It sounded deserted, felt deserted. And her dad had never had much patience, would have jumped out by now if he was hiding.

Shutting the door quietly behind her and latching the chain, she shucked off her leather jacket and hooked it over her father's wax Barbour. It made her laugh that he dressed like a country gent, even though they lived in a modern detached house in Birdham, cheek by jowl with their 'executive estate' neighbours. She didn't know where the 'gent' influence came from. They weren't poor, but they didn't have loads of dosh either. Her dad was only a conveyancing solicitor at a practice in town. Her parents played golf, but only at the pay-and-play in Chichester, and he had his yacht, but it was a shitty old tub that looked as if it had been salvaged from the Ark and would only be worth a couple of quid if anyone was stupid enough to buy it.

The rhythmic metallic pinging of halyards on masts was dulled now that she was inside the house, the noise replaced by the rhythmic tap-tap-tap of a branch of the silver birch in the back garden, knocking against the roof. Her mum had been meaning to get a tree surgeon in for weeks to cut it back, but it hadn't mattered over the summer, with the benign weather, and now that it was autumn, windy and cold, none of the ones she'd called could come out for at least a week. The noise irritated them all to death and a couple of roof tiles had already broken.

Laying her feet softly heel to toe, Sophie moved silently from the front door to the bottom of the stairs. She used to hate walking upstairs towards a pitch-black landing when she was younger, feeling as if she was ascending into a malignant black hole full of hidden terrors. But now that she was older and focused on maths and sciences rather than English at school, that vivid imagination she'd had as a kid was boxed up and shoved in the loft alongside her favourite childhood toys.

She could still hear the branch tapping on the roof as she started up the stairs, feeling her way in the dark, her phone tucked in her skirt pocket. Her parents would doubtless have left their bedroom door open and she didn't want to risk snapping them awake with the light. One step and another, the feel of the carpet under her bare feet so familiar, every groove and bump of the banister imprinted on her palm's memory, that incredibly annoying tapping drilling a hole in her hungover brain, like her dad's snoring did in her mum's. And then suddenly, overlaying the tapping, a different noise.

Water?

It sounded like water running, as if a tap had been left on.

She stepped onto the landing. 'What the hell?' The shock of her foot squelching, as if she had just sunk into muddy ground, made her shriek the words out loud. *Fuck* – she clamped a hand over her mouth and fumbled her mobile from her pocket. The landing carpet was wet, soaked in fact, she immediately saw, water rising up between her bare toes. 'Oh *fuck.*'

Her parents would go ballistic if there was a leak from the water tank in the loft. They'd only had the landing and hall downstairs repainted in the summer. Angling her phone, Sophie shone it at the ceiling directly above her – no dampness or water stains. No water leaking down the pristine pale grey walls either. As the weak beam of her mobile phone torch traced along the walls and found the doorway to her parents' bedroom, she yelped again.

A reflection, she realized a millisecond later, not a spotlight shining up from their bedroom floor. A reflection in the water that had flooded her parents' bedroom carpet bloomed from the doorway onto the landing.

What the fuck?

She moved gingerly forward, water swilling around her bare feet with every step. Her brain doing flips with confusion, she reached the door to her parents' bedroom, and stepped over the threshold.

'Dad? Mum?'

No answer.

Then she saw him. Dad. Sitting on the floor in the doorway

to their en-suite bathroom, wearing the pale blue pyjamas he always wore, leaning against the jamb, his back to her.

'Dad?'

What the fuck *is he doing?*

'Dad.'

Why is he just sitting there? Is he drunk?

'Dad. *Daddy.*'

She reached for his shoulder and, as she did so, her gaze found the bath beyond, brightly lit by the rows of halogen spots in the bathroom ceiling. Water running over its edge from the flowing tap, the milky white body of her mother floating naked, face up in the bath. It took a long moment for Sophie to realize that her mother was dead. As her mouth opened in an agonized scream, her hand found her father's shoulder, gripping, shaking, gripping and shaking.

'Daaaddddd.'

He slumped sideways, his head lolling back on a rubbery neck, and she saw the gaping black holes where his eyes had been, his face a mask of blood and deep animal gouges.

Stumbling out of the room, she staggered across the landing, missing the top step and falling, her mouth open in a silent, agonized wail. At the bottom of the stairs, she clawed herself to her feet, and flung herself against the front door, grappling the chain unlatched, yanking it open, charging headlong, screaming, into the street. Crying and screaming in her little black dress, until lights flicked on in the neighbouring houses.

36

In his twenty-five years of policing, Marilyn was sure he'd never been so pleased to see his front door and for once he'd been able to park within spitting distance of it. Usually, when he arrived home after seven p.m., which he'd done virtually every day of his working life – *Who the hell had these fabled nine-to-five jobs and where did he go to sign up for one?* – he was forced to circumnavigate the block at least twice before he found a parking spot. So today he was gratified to see a Z3-sized rectangle of empty tarmac, almost directly across the narrow road from his tiny Georgian terrace. Stalk-eyed with tiredness, he tucked his car into the space, inching backwards carefully to ensure that he didn't grind his wheels against the crumbling kerb, which to be fair was in better shape than his alloys.

As he crossed the narrow street, a snatch of siren cutting through the chill night air snapped his eyes towards the main road in time to see a police car zip past, heading south.

NMP, he thought, *not my problem.*

Shimmying sideways to squeeze between the bumpers of

two cars that were parked intimately close, Marilyn fished in his jacket pocket for his door key, a single, simple bronze Yale key, for the one simple Yale lock on his door. His house was cheek by jowl with its neighbours, barely a few arm's lengths across from the facing houses. Thieves knew better than to try their luck in this narrow, quiet market-town-centre street, nowhere to pull over, engine idling, ready for a quick exit.

A chime. Just one from the cathedral clock. He tilted his head to listen. No more. *One a.m.* Not too late, all things considered.

Pushing his front door open, he stepped into the tiny hallway, his eyes finding the steep cream-carpeted stairway, almost wishing he'd kept the Stannah stairlift the previous owner had installed, so that he could flop into it and glide effortlessly upstairs to bed. As the door clicked shut behind him, his mobile rang. *For fuck's sake.* He was tempted to ignore the call. It would doubtless be Dr Ghoshal, still in the autopsy suite, dotting the 'i's, crossing and double crossing the 't's, aligning each letter until they were sentry-smart on parade, re-dotting, re-crossing with the anal attention to detail that made him the supremely talented pathologist he was. Precisely the anal details Marilyn didn't want or need to be kept abreast of at one a.m., after two all-nighters.

Fishing his mobile from his inside jacket pocket, he glanced at the name flashing on its face: DC Cara. Much as Marilyn liked the kid and rated him, he had a tendency to overshare.

'There needs to be a significantly better than good reason for this call.' His tone left no room for misunderstanding. If he was expecting a nervous stutter in response, he was disappointed.

'There's been another one, sir.'

His dulled brain took a moment. He was about to ask, *Another what?*

'Fuck,' he said with feeling. The police car. *NMP. Not my problem.* Fate was a comedian. 'What's the address?'

He memorized it near enough, an estate of mid-range Stepford-Wife-type houses in Birdham. His idea of dying and being transported straight to hell without passing 'Go'. The wash of blue from the marked cars and the ambulance would guide him to the exact street.

'I'll be there in ten. Hold them off until I get there. Call Flynn.'

He contemplated, for a brief millisecond, dashing upstairs and changing his shirt and suit. *Hold them off until I get there.* He didn't have time to change. Cara was in a tense stand-off with the paramedics regarding a potential witness – *the daughter*, he'd said. Marilyn hoped the girl was of coherent speaking age.

As he stepped back into the street and pulled the door closed, an unsavoury whiff filled his nostrils. The drains – they'd had problems with them in the summer. Something to do with people pouring the hot fat from their frying pans down the sink, causing a clogging 'fatberg'. The mind boggled.

Another step, another whiff. Wave, actually a wave. A whiffy wave.

Not the drains. Him. *Me.* The smell of sweat, of stress leaking from his pores, of an autopsy suite, the smell of death and viscera hanging in every molecule of oxygen in the air. The only consolation, that everyone else on the job would smell in varying degrees of the same.

37

'Sorry, mate, you're too late.'

'My detective constable told me that he asked you to wait,' Marilyn snapped.

The paramedic shrugged, Marilyn's barely contained fury water off a duck's back to him. He was of a similar age to Marilyn, late forties, skinny and rangy, with the same no-nonsense air of 'seen it all, done it all' that Marilyn wore like a second skin. He also looked as if he'd had a long night – nights – and had as few reserves of patience left as his detective inspector alter ego.

'You wouldn't have got any sense out of the poor kid anyway. She was jabbering, and who could blame her? She got back from a fun night on the town to find her parents butchered.'

'My job is to stop that happening to anyone else,' Marilyn said. 'Which is why I needed to speak with her urgently.'

'And my job is to look after my patient. Tomorrow . . . today,' the paramedic corrected, glancing at his watch. 'Mid-morning. You should be able to speak with her then.'

Stretching out two wiry arms, he clasped an ambulance door in each hand and slammed them in Marilyn's face.

As the ambulance pulled away, bathing them in electric blue, Marilyn swung around to Cara. 'Get to St Richard's and stick to that girl like glue. Call me the second, and I mean the absolute millisecond, she wakes up.' He turned back to Jessie. 'You got here quickly.'

She lifted her shoulders. 'There wasn't any traffic.'

Marilyn nodded. 'You look as well dressed as I do, though hopefully you smell better.'

'I hope I smell better too.'

'Is it that obv—'

Her smile cut him off.

'Can you not tell that I'm not in the mood for jokes?'

Jessie raised an eyebrow and smiled again, the smile as much effort as the first. 'Do two negatives make a positive?'

Why was she bothering to try to lighten the atmosphere? Neither of them were in the mood for lame banter, though she had some vague idea that joking might lessen the negative impact of what they were about to see behind the bland facade of this modern house. *Wishful thinking*. Her gaze moved past Marilyn, to the neighbours lined along the 'Police! Do Not Cross!' tape, some in nightclothes – pastel-coloured nighties or striped pyjamas in various shades of blue under thrown-over-the-shoulder coats – others hastily dressed; everyone, irrespective of their state of attire, saucer-eyed and flap-eared. She knew that Marilyn's gaze, focused thirty metres beyond her left shoulder, was taking in an identical line of neighbours manning the tape barring the other end of the street. A press van was there too, she knew. It had pulled into the road as she'd climbed out of her Mini.

'This second murder is going to create a shit storm,' Marilyn murmured.

'Yes.'

One couple's murder was an isolated incident. Shocking, gruesome, fuel for dinner-party chat for weeks, but still an isolated incident. Two was a crazed serial killer, the stuff of nightmares. Of bogeymen hiding in every cupboard.

'We need to find him, solve this, urgently. Pronto. Post-haste.'

Jessie nodded. 'Yes,' she repeated.

There was nothing else to say.

38

The house, white-painted, with battleship-grey window frames and a steeply pitched, grey-slate-tiled roof was stylish, minimalist, coastal. A yachtsman's residence, it would probably be described, if it were being marketed by an estate agent.

Soon, Jessie thought, grimly.

Not that, despite its enviable position, a couple of streets back from the foreshore of Chichester Harbour, on a quiet executive estate of similar, three- to four-bedroom detached houses, it would be an easy one to sell. She'd happily bet they'd get a host of viewings though.

'Gravel.' Marilyn's voice cut through her thoughts.

'Loud gravel,' she concurred.

Even muffled by the horrified hum from the mirrored lines of neighbours and dulled by their forensic overshoes, her and Marilyn's footsteps crunched audibly on the wide drive as they walked from the road to the front doorstep, their gazes sweeping from side to side, up and down, taking everything in.

'And no way to get to the front door or any of the front windows without walking on the gravel,' Marilyn continued.

The gravel drive, shielded from the road and the neighbours on either side by a three-metre-high privet hedge, widened halfway down to span the whole width of the house to allow, Jessie presumed, in estate agent parlance, ample parking. At night, in silence – and it was silent out here, only the ping of metal yacht lanyards against masts, out in Birdham Pool and Chichester Yacht Basin, to mar it – anyone approaching the house from the front would have been audible.

Would their man take that risk? Yes, if he'd known that the daughter was out, that the parents would most probably be in bed on a Wednesday night and perhaps they'd watched TV, had a few drinks at home, crashed out early and that anyone approaching the house would be assumed to be their daughter, Sophie. Perhaps they even left a spare key hidden somewhere. It would be typical, wouldn't it, on a quiet, out-of-the-way executive estate like this to feel secure enough to hide a spare key. The door hadn't been forced, so their man had either found a key, picked the lock, or perhaps he had been brazen enough just to walk up to the front door and knock, knowing that any knock would be assumed to be Sophie's forgotten key.

How much had he known? Enough, certainly.

The grey and white theme was echoed inside the house: grey wood-veneer floors throughout, white walls, simple, elegant, too modern and soulless for Jessie's taste. From the entrance hallway, they could see straight through to a vast lounge, the back wall, floor-to-ceiling glass bifold doors, the end one open. Tony Burrows and one of his CSI team were moving around in the garden, ghoulish in their white forensic overalls, under an arc light.

Even inside the house, the front and back doors ajar, Jessie could hear those pinging lanyards and, overlaid, the rhythmic tap-tap-tapping of a tree branch on the roof. Away from built-up areas, sound carried. She knew that from her own cottage, from the bleat of new-born lambs in spring – she could hear them even with the doors and windows closed.

They checked the downstairs quickly, knowing that Burrows' forensics team would crawl over it with a fine-tooth comb, that the only thing they were really doing, despite their overalls, was adding to the forensic footprint, making his job more difficult. By tacit, silent agreement, they moved to the bottom of the stairs, upwards, a thick carpet, the same slate grey as the flooring downstairs, silencing their twin footfalls. The upstairs of the house was lit only by the arc lights set up in the drive and the back garden, shining through the windows; Marilyn had demanded that the crime scene be left as it had been found, until he and Jessie had had a chance to see it.

Their feet squelched as they reached the top of the stairs.

'Water,' Marilyn murmured unnecessarily.

Jessie nodded silently. The armed response unit had been in first, cleared the house. She knew, logically, that she and Marilyn were alone upstairs, that no one was going to drop silently from the loft hatch, or slide out from under a bed the moment their backs were turned, but even so she could feel the beat of her heart in her chest, like the thump of a tribal drum. She glanced over at Marilyn. Was his heart beating as hard or did twenty-five years' experience make even this horror mainstream? She was pretty sure that she never wanted to find out.

They moved further down the landing, passing two other bedrooms, the one to their right used as an office, the one to the left the daughter's room, to judge from the mess of clothes carpeting the floor and the posters of boy bands papering the walls. God, Jessie must be getting old when twenty-year-old boy band members looked prepubescent.

A sudden slam, so loud. *Jesus.* She spun around, her heart rate rocketing. Where had it come from? Upstairs, with them?

No – the back door, she realized, a millisecond later, her pulse still through the roof.

'For Christ's sake, Tony,' Marilyn yelled back over his shoulder towards the stairs.

'Sorry guys.' Burrows' voice carrying from outside. 'Will someone prop the bloody back door open and properly this time.'

The husband and wife were in their bedroom and en-suite bathroom, they'd been told, at the back of the house. Water pooled around their overshoes as they stepped into the bedroom. Walking on water, Jessie thought stupidly, like Jesus. Water. Again. What has water got to do with it?

Watching.

Water.

Too many 'w's, she thought randomly, stupidly.

Scratching.

Sniffing.

Too many 's's.

The silhouette of a figure slumped in the doorway, his back to them.

A man's figure.

Beyond him light.

The only light left on in the house. Left on or switched on deliberately to illuminate a stage setting? Theatre.

'Is his wife in the bath?' Jessie murmured.

'Yes.' Marilyn's voice was monotone, without colour.

'His eyes?'

'Yes.'

210

Jessie inched sideways. She didn't want to look. Didn't want to, had to. How the hell had she arrived here, in this place, in this exact moment in time? One slash of a knife nine months ago and she was invalided out of the army, floating, struggling to find a purpose. Marilyn had given her one, but now, on the spot, she was pretty sure that she didn't want it.

When she and Marilyn had been walking up the stairs and along the dark landing, Jessie had been desperate to switch a light on, flood the house with light, with safety, but now, here in the Whiteheads' minimalist bedroom, she was grateful for the darkness, for the cloak that it threw over Daniel Whitehead. The wild animal gouges just dark streaks down his cheeks, the blood pooled on the curve of his middle-age spread, a benign black patch, his sightless eyes, John Lennon sunglasses, small and round.

Beyond him, under the stark bathroom theatre lights, Jessie's gaze found his wife. Mrs Whitehead. Eleanor. Her long dark hair fanning out, as if her head had been caught in thick dark seaweed. Dark. Mrs Whitehead was dark, Claudine Fuller blonde. An irrelevant detail, another minor, irrelevant detail; her mind fumbling for the mundane to insulate itself from the horror.

'I've seen enough,' Marilyn said.

She nodded. 'More than.'

What she hadn't seen in real life, she would doubtless see in relentlessly unforgiving technicolour detail in the crime-scene photographs. It wouldn't matter if she didn't wallow in it now, masticate on every detail. She had most definitely 'got a sense'.

'Let's get out of here and let Burrows get on with his job.'

Jessie nodded. She couldn't remember the last time she'd agreed with Marilyn so readily.

211

39

The red eye of the dummy CCTV camera surveying the Paws for Thought car park blinked in the darkness, the camera lens unseeing as a pale figure crossed the deserted tarmac and picked the front door lock. The red eye of a second dummy CCTV camera inside the reception area reflected off the toughened glass as the door swung open and the pale visitor stepped silently through, closing and locking the door carefully behind. Moving across the tatty lino, the visitor slipped out of a second door that led into the indoor kennel compound.

The dogs, asleep in their baskets, woke and began to whine as the pale figure walked on softly padded feet, between the two lines of cages. At first, the dogs had leapt at their cage doors, barking and growling, but they were used to the visitor's scent now, a scent that was so similar to their own, used to the noises he made as he walked, almost as silently as one of them would have walked, down the concrete walkway. His scent was their scent. The noises he made, their noises.

The water in each dog's bowl was full, clean bedding and toys in each cage – the people who ran the shelter were fastidious in their attention to detail, unswerving in their love for the dogs they rescued – but he stopped by every cage to check anyway, making sure that each dog had everything he or she needed, taking care of his dog pack.

The last cage on the right-hand side of the walkway was empty. The visitor knew that the cage was almost always left empty. Sliding the lock gently sideways, he opened the cage door and stepped through, closing it, locking himself in. The bedding smelt of his scent, the toys bore his claw and teeth marks. Curling into a tight doughnut, he laid his head on the soft fleece bedding and closed his eyes. He would sleep the light sleep of a dog for a couple of hours, surrounded by his kind, absorbing the love and security of the pack, and then, well before first light, he would be gone and no one would know that he had visited.

40

'Coffee, Marilyn.'

Marilyn reached out and took the Costa cup that Workman was proffering. 'Spot on, Sarah. Thank you.'

Workman eased another cup from the cardboard four-cup holder and held it out.

'Latte, Jessie, no sugar.'

'Oh . . . thank you. That's kind of you.' Jessie smiled, genuinely, she realized for the first time in a good few hours. 'And it's just what I would have ordered myself.'

'I have a great memory for coffee orders.' Raising an eyebrow, Workman tilted her head towards Marilyn, who had already mentally moved on and was surveying the front of the Whiteheads' house, his forehead creased, thinking, imagining, running through scenarios. 'It's one of the main reasons he keeps me around,' Workman added.

'There are many and varied reasons that he keeps you around, Sarah,' Jessie said. 'Coffee being a very good one, I agree.'

She liked Workman. The first time they had met, Jessie

had taken in the shapeless navy shift dress and blunt-toed, low-heeled matching navy courts and had assumed that Workman would be as solid and uninspiring as her clothing choices; great in a crisis, but not first choice when exploring creative ways to crack a case, or when it came to having fun. She had mentally chastised herself shortly after, realizing that she had jumped to a totally false first impression based purely on looks, and that, given her profession, she should have known better. Her only defence was that she was human and therefore not immune to the cognitive biases that caused people to make snap judgements of others, shallow, baseless, first-impression conclusions. It took the average person the blink of an eye to form that first impression and only three seconds more to form a 'complete' conclusion.

Now she knew better, she could see how valuable Workman was to Marilyn, beyond her uncanny memory for coffee formulas. She was his rock, to Jessie's molten lava. His back-up to Jessie's challenge, his support to Jessie's goading. She realized also, until Workman had approached her about Robbie, that she knew nothing about her beyond the job. She took a sip of the coffee that Workman had brought. It hit the spot immediately: a hot, milky shot of adrenalin.

'I saw Robbie,' she said in a low voice, lowering the cup.

Workman glanced over and met her gaze. 'Thank you. I appreciate you taking the time. I know how busy you are.'

'We're all busy.'

Workman gave a pensive nod. 'Did you meet Allan? His father?'

'Just briefly. He let me in and we had a quick chat. He was very grateful.' *Embarrassingly grateful.*

'He's at the end of his tether.' Workman ducked her gaze.

'He thinks that Robbie will commit suicide. Do you . . .' she let the sentence tail off.

'Do I believe that he's suicidal?'

Workman nodded. Jessie shrugged, noticing the slump of Workman's shoulders in response to the lift in her own, not in any way surprised by it. Her profession was often viewed as a quick-fixer, a plaster cast for the soul. Unfortunately, damaged minds were not an easy fix.

'I don't know, is the brutally honest answer. I didn't see him for long enough to make that determination. He's obviously very disturbed by what has happened . . . by his whole life basically, from the time his mother abandoned him, through the years of bullying. He clearly blames himself for his mother's departure, for breaking up his family, and I wouldn't be surprised if he blames himself for being bullied. Life hasn't given him many good breaks.' She waved a hand in the direction of the Whiteheads' house. 'I was planning to see him again today, but the Whiteheads' murder has probably put the kibosh on that.'

Workman nodded. 'I saw his self-harm scars,' she said plainly. 'It was hard to wear long sleeves all summer, though he did try. I've seen it before, with some of the damaged kids around here, but never so bad. I was shocked.'

Jessie thought of the boy sitting motionless in the high-backed chair, the sleeves of his iron-grey sweatshirt draping each heavily scarred arm. In truth, she had been shocked too.

'Self-harming is very typical in cases of bullying,' she said. Though actually, that statement wasn't entirely true, not with boys. 'Is he aggressive towards his father?'

'I don't think so. It's not something Allan has ever mentioned, but I don't know him particularly well. I know Robbie much better as I see him every week at the lunch

216

club. Allan doesn't seem to have anyone to speak with and I think the police thing made him want to confide in me.' She sighed in a self-deprecating way. 'He probably thought I could help.'

'You are helping.'

There was something about Workman that encouraged confidences; even for Jessie, who never confided in anyone. She could see why Allan Parker had felt comfortable turning to Workman, irrespective of her job title. 'The charity work, helping old people, suggests to me that Robbie's just not the aggressive type,' she said.

'I've never seen Robbie be aggressive,' Workman said. 'And old people can be very trying at times. He just seems like a kind, caring kid. It maddens me that nice kids are targeted by bullies.'

'Robbie was targeted simply because he's an easy target. If he had a cleft palate, but was a total shit, he would have been spared, but the combination of disability and niceness is too tempting for bullies to resist.'

Workman straightened, clearly surprised at the venom in Jessie's voice. Jessie smoothed over her unprofessional lapse with a brief smile. She held the coffee cup aloft.

'Anyway, I'd do anything for a latte and it is my job, after all. My proper job.'

'Not this . . . not for free. And you took Lupo in too.'

She had taken in Lupo. She wasn't sure why, wasn't sure of much these days; it was becoming a nasty habit. 'Is that another of your charities? Dogs?'

Workman shook her head. 'I'm confining myself to people at the moment.'

Jessie laughed. 'Perhaps Lupo is my first step in trying to get away from people.'

41

Jessie's cottage was silent, but lights blared from the sitting room downstairs – five a.m. and she had been expecting the first. But the second? When she opened the front door, she found Callan asleep on the sofa again, an arm thrown over his eyes, legs bent at an angle that looked hideously uncomfortable, though clearly not enough to have prevented him from crashing out. At his feet was a large dent in the sofa cushion, peppered with snow-white hairs that caught the ceiling light and cast it back at her in spangles. *Lupo*. Callan had let him up on her spotless, cream sofa. Staring at the patch, Jessie tensed against the tingle of the electric suit – her OCD raising its demanding head – but it didn't come. The only sensation was the dull ache of regret: that she hadn't been here to see her two men chillaxing together on the sofa.

Grabbing her trusty argyle throw, she draped it over Callan. His skin was pasty, his eye sockets pronounced dark hollows in the paleness of his face, and underneath their lids his eyes were as agitated as they had been a few nights ago. Nothing in his mind resolved, then. She needed to make time to speak with him about the letter.

Despite leaving his hair all over her sofa, Lupo wasn't in evidence, so she padded in socked feet through to the kitchen, where she found him lying on the back doormat, head resting on his paws, as silent and motionless as Callan. Awake though, his coal-black nose pressed to the coal-black glass of the door, eyes focused intently on the night outside, as if he could see into the curtain of darkness. *Perhaps he can.* It was only when she lowered herself down next to him on the cold tiles that she realized he was whining, low-pitched, forlorn.

'Lupo,' she called his name softly.

One ear twitched – a blink-and-you'd-miss-it twitch – but apart from that, he didn't move, not a muscle, didn't look over to acknowledge her presence. He had been curled up with Callan, but he ignored her. Was this what it was like being a parent? Competing against your partner for the attention and love of your child, feeling the pain of losing out?

'What's going on inside that head of yours, boy?'

She laid her hand gently between the peaked, snow-capped mountaintops of his ears. His fur was silky soft, his skin warm. Did he experience the same feelings as humans? Did he know hope, anxiety, fear, happiness, depression, regret, longing? She had spent her whole life focusing on humans and this creature was a total mystery to her. Though she was sure, from his statue-still body to that soft, barely there whine, that he was pining for Claudine Fuller, for the life he had lost. The love that he had lost.

'Who took you, Lupo? Who took you and tied you up to that lamp post?'

If she could just reach her fingers inside his skull, pull out the images stored there, this case would be over, a killer would be caught and she could return to her clinical patients, to her mundane day-to-day existence – an existence that she would kill for right now – until Marilyn came calling the next time.

'We'll love you, Lupo,' she said softly, sliding her hand down his neck, stroking along his back. 'I promise that we will love you as much as Claudine did. It may take a while, but you'll be happy with us, I promise.'

42

Sitting as anonymously as she could in the far corner of the incident room, facing the backs of a row of heads, Jessie tried to ignore the bloodthirsty hum emanating from the crowd of journalists occupying the station's car park two storeys below, the Venetian blinds that had been lowered over the windows behind her doing little to muffle the noise.

This second murder is going to create a shit storm.

It hadn't taken long for Marilyn's prophesy to be proven correct. He'd be furious, Jessie knew. He hated having to pander to the press vultures, as he called them, at the best of times, had hoped that his carefully curated press conference had fed them enough titbits to keep them happy. And he might have been right, but for this second murder which had thrown big-cat fresh kill among the vultures. And as the investigation had, as yet, made no appreciable progress, Marilyn would also be humming with defensiveness.

Her gaze flicked from the back of the crew cut in front of her to the walls, where the Whiteheads' crime-scene photographs had joined those of the Fullers', and were even more determinedly brutal, if that was possible, illuminated in unforgiving detail as they were by the yachtsman's residence's aluminium ceiling spots and aided by the CSI photographer's flash. Perhaps because the Fullers' murders had been the first – the only, they'd assumed at the time – the team had spent hours at the crime scene absorbing every gut-churning nuance, and the details had played back in Jessie's head ever since, seeping through her brain's defences in quiet moments: Hugo Fuller's blank, eyeless sockets; the treacle of blood coating his bloated stomach; the halo of Claudine Fuller's blonde hair in the pool, making her look like a prone angel; the bloody damage to the back of her head. Jessie had seen it all, and so the photographs had been less impactful. The Whiteheads' crime scene had been almost shadow puppet in comparison: Daniel Whitehead's injuries masked by the darkness of the bedroom, his wife, Eleanor, floating on her back in the bath beyond, drowned, but with no other visible injuries. Jessie had taken it all in, visual snatch by visual snatch, seeing just what she had needed to form an impression – get a sense – determinedly refusing to engage with more than that.

Marilyn had texted her this morning to say that Dr Ghoshal's autopsy findings refuted her hypothesis that Claudine Fuller had died first and that the murderer had forced Hugo to watch. Hugo Fuller had died first – Claudine second. *That casts significant doubt on your watching theory.*

Jessie hadn't bothered to reply. Despite the undermining of her theory, she was still sure that watching featured heavily in these murders, she just didn't know why. *Watching* . . . and . . . Her mind filled with an image of Lupo. Who had died first at the Whiteheads' house? She was sure, from the theatre of the display in the bathroom, that it would have been Eleanor, and was waiting for the results of the second autopsy to confirm or refute.

Her gaze snapped from the final photograph in the series, Eleanor Whitehead's water-bloated body, to the door. Marilyn was striding into the incident room, wearing a crumpled black suit and looking, despite the steaming mug of coffee that Jessie assumed Workman had thrust into his hand a moment ago, as if he hadn't slept for six months. She knew how he felt. There was no need for him to call for silence this time, as he had needed to with the Fullers' murders. The room was graveyard-hushed, eight months pregnant with expectation.

'Welcome back, everyone, and thank you for coming,' Marilyn said, projecting his voice over the hum rising up from the vultures below, now magnified by the room's suspenseful hush. 'I'm going to keep this brief, because myself and Dr Flynn are heading to St Richard's Hospital as soon as we get the nod from DC Cara that Eleanor and Daniel Whitehead's daughter, Sophie, is well enough to be interviewed, which I hope will be imminent.'

A brief pause while he took a sip of coffee. 'I was planning to say that it's critical we keep a lid on the details of the Whiteheads' murders for as long as we can, so that the press doesn't make the link between them and the Fullers, but it appears as if that particular horse has already bolted.' He jammed his index finger towards the window. 'Though I would be very interested to know how they made the link so quickly.'

His eyes grazed around the assembled faces. When it met Jessie's she held it calmly. Who had told? Someone must have done. Someone in this room or one of Burrows' team? Or perhaps one of the Whiteheads' neighbours had put two and two together and, unfortunately for Surrey and Sussex Major Crimes, arrived at four.

'I am not accusing anyone in this room of talking out of turn, but I'm also sure that I do not need to remind you that we are not in this job to court fame and if you don't share that view please feel free to hand me your P45 and skip off down the road to Chichester Festival Theatre.'

A ripple of polite laughter. The team were clearly feeling the strain; usually no one bothered with 'polite'. If it wasn't funny, they didn't laugh. From her observation post at the back of the room, Jessie noticed a few heads turn as their owners cast surreptitious glances at colleagues, wondering which, if any, had secured their fifteen minutes of fame as a journalist's source.

'The more attention we get from them—' Marilyn continued, jabbing an index finger towards the window. 'The harder our jobs will be, and I think everyone in this room will agree that we're under enough pressure as it is, without our every move being forensically examined by Deidre from the *Daily Mail* or Tarquin from the *Telegraph*.'

His gaze skipped from face to face, finally alighting, again, on Jessie, remaining there this time.

'Our number one priority now is to identify if there is a connection between the Fullers and the Whiteheads, to determine whether we have a random nut job on our hands, or if there is a tiny bit of method to his madness. Are these murders personal or are they not? That is the question.'

43

Jessie caught up with Marilyn in the corridor. 'Dr Ghoshal will find out that Eleanor Whitehead died first and that her husband . . .' She paused, mentally fumbling for his name.

'Mr Whitehead,' Marilyn said, with a humourless half-smile, half-grimace.

'Daniel,' Workman said, skirting around them. 'I've spoken to the doctor treating Sophie Whitehead, Anita Murawska, and you can go and interview Sophie now – briefly, she said. She sounds like a no-nonsense lady though, so watch your Ps and Qs when you're there. DC Cara is still at the hospital and will wait there until you arrive.'

'Thank you, Sarah. For both of those things.' Marilyn turned back to Jessie.

'And that Daniel Whitehead was made to watch,' Jessie finished.

'That's what you said about the Fullers.'

'I know, and I was wrong, but I'm sure there's a reason that I was wrong.'

'What if it's not personal and not about watching, Jessie?

What if it's just some loony who has binge-watched *Robin Hood: Prince of Thieves* and fancies himself as some kind of medieval torturer?' He spread his hands, the movement frustrated. 'Some . . . Christ if I can't remember Pa bloody Whitehead's name, I've got fuck-all chance of dredging the name of a famous medieval torturer from the annals of my memory. We've got a lot to do, Jessie. Sophie Whitehead to interview for starters, and then I have a second autopsy to attend. You're most welcome to join me—'

Jessie grimaced. 'Once was enough, thanks—'

'—And another press conference this evening.' He started walking, waving her along with him.

'I know. But—'

'But – what?'

But I'm still sure it's about watching, despite Claudine Fuller.

And I'm also still sure that it's personal.

And I think that you'll find dogs are involved somewhere, but I have absolutely no idea why.

She didn't say any of it. Much as Marilyn liked her – rated her, she'd venture to say – even he had his limits and he'd clearly lost faith in her theories.

'Fräulein Backastowe isn't letting you off the press conference, then,' she said, as lightly as she could manage. 'Wanting to steal the limelight?'

'Unfortunately, she does not appear to be motivated by fame. Though she did inform me, by curt text, that she is very motivated to keep a lid on that shit-show burgeoning in the car park and doubtless she will be at the press conference in spirit, daring me to fuck up.'

He stopped just inside the external door to the car park. 'Are you ready?'

Jessie raised an eyebrow and smiled. 'I don't need to be. They don't have a cat in hell's idea of who I am.' She laid a hand on his arm. 'Good luck, though. I'll see you at the hospital in an hour or two, when you've managed to extricate yourself! I'll be the one in the corner of the coffee shop reading what Deidre and Tarquin have to say on the subject of murder.'

44

Marilyn was in a stinking mood when he arrived at St Richard's Hospital, fifteen minutes after Jessie.

'That was quick,' she said, meeting him in the main reception and handing him a black coffee.

'Quick and very painful. Like an injection in the backside with a horse needle,' he muttered unsmilingly. 'Thank you for the coffee.'

'Pleasure. I thought you might need it.'

'A bottle of whisky would have been even more appreciated.'

'I'm sure, but unfortunately neither Costa Coffee nor the Friends of St Richard's charitable corner shop run to alcoholic beverages.'

'They know all the gory details,' Marilyn said, as they walked towards the lifts and the stairs. 'The torture, the eyes, the drowning.'

'How the hell?'

'I have no idea, yet, though clearly my murder investigation would make a teabag look watertight.'

'What about the personal and the watching?'

Marilyn shook his head. 'Neither of those theories were mentioned,' he said pointedly.

Theories. But he was right. However much she believed in them, they were still only theories to him, to the team.

'Are you happy to walk up the stairs instead of taking the lift?' Marilyn asked. 'The thought of being locked in a small metal box with someone in possession of a contagious disease is bringing me out in hives.'

Jessie nodded. She was delighted to oblige with a trudge up the stairs if it avoided her being locked in a small metal box with anyone at all, diseased or not.

'Jesus Christ, why do all hospitals smell the same?' Marilyn muttered, with a grimace, as they stepped from the stairwell onto the first floor.

St Richard's Hospital was a medium-sized low-rise that sprawled across countless acres of prime Chichester town centre real estate. Prinstead, the twee West Sussex village name for its adult high-dependency unit, was located along a spider's web of identical, faceless corridors, all polished to a squeak. Uniformed staff in pastel shades – blue for doctors, green for porters, salmon pink for nurses – moved past them with smooth, automaton efficiency.

Dr Anita Murawska, a beautiful black woman with a complicated plaited up-do and a huge pregnant belly, which made her look as if she'd smuggled a basketball into work under her pink-and-white-striped maternity shirt-dress, met them by Prinstead ward's reception desk. They shook hands, then she led them down the central corridor, past private rooms on both sides, each one occupied by a supine patient attached to an array of tubes and devices that flashed and beeped.

229

'Sophie Whitehead is fine physically, though obviously she is very far from fine mentally,' she cast over her shoulder. Her comfortable slip-on shoes squeaked as if there was a mouse taped under each sole, as the rubber grasped and released the lino with each step.

'We tried to put Sophie in a private room, but she wasn't having any of it,' Murawska continued. 'She screamed her head off when the night nurse tried to leave her alone. Your young colleague offered to sit with her for the night, but that just sent her even more nutty. She can't bear to be alone and she can't bear to be with anyone else, unless it's a crowd of people, which is why we ended up moving her onto the ward. Poor kid. She'll be in therapy for years.'

'We'll be compassionate,' Marilyn said, sensing the direction this conversation was heading, wanting to cut it off at the pass. He didn't want an oversensitive doctor hovering over him while he grilled his only potential witness.

'I'll give you ten minutes,' Murawska said.

'We may need longer than that.'

She held up her hand, without turning. 'Ten minutes. Take it or leave it.'

'I have a violent killer to catch.'

'And I have a patient to protect,' she countered, as uncompromising as the paramedic he had locked horns with last night. The book of intransigence was clearly required reading for all St Richard's Hospital staff.

They entered a corner ward, containing six beds, four of them occupied, windows on two sides – south-west facing, must be, Jessie thought, as she could see the spire of Chichester Cathedral from the far windows, barely visible through the drizzle. DC Darren Cara was hovering in the vicinity of a bed in the far corner of the room, clutching a saggy, half-eaten sandwich in one hand and a Costa Coffee cup in the other. He looked even more ragged around the edges than Jessie felt. It was the first time she'd seen Marilyn's keen, young DC looking anything other than immaculately turned out in his City-trader suit, crisp white shirt and snappy hairstyle, and she was sure that Marilyn would be having a sly smile at the poor kid's expense and thinking: *Welcome to a multiple murder investigation, kiddo.* Cara hurriedly tossed the remains of the sandwich in the flip-top 'Hazardous Waste Only' bin, when he clocked Marilyn steaming across the room towards him.

'Has she said anything?' Marilyn asked him, in a low voice.

He shook his head. 'She spent most of the night crying. The little time she did sleep, she thrashed around and kept calling out.' He stifled a yawn with his crumpled suit sleeve. 'She was obviously having nightmares. And this morning, she just cried some more and spent the rest of the time staring into space, totally uncommunicative.'

'Unsurprisingly. Head off home now, son, and grab forty winks. I'll see you back at the station later this evening.'

'I'm fine, Guv,' Cara protested.

'A knackered DC who can't think straight is no use to me,' Marilyn snapped. 'Grab a couple of hours' sleep and a change of clothes. You're making me look smart with that crumpled suit and the bed hair.'

Suitably cowed, Cara nodded. 'Right, Guv.' He glanced at Jessie and smiled. 'Bye Dr Flynn.'

Jessie gave him what she hoped was a confidence-giving 'don't take it personally – Marilyn's ragged too' smile back. 'See you later, Darren.'

Sophie Whitehead was hunched in the hospital bed, bent forward, shoulders sagging, as if she had just been punched hard in the stomach. She looked painfully tiny, pale and wan, a little Victorian waif in her borrowed blue-and-white-checked hospital gown, her skinny legs draped in a thin baby-blue hospital blanket. Pronounced black rings of smudged mascara underscored each eye, dark blots in the pallor of her face, making her look as if she hadn't slept for months. *She won't sleep for months*, Jessie thought grimly as Anita Murawska drew the pastel-green curtain around the bed and held up both hands in front of Marilyn's face, fingers raised.

'Ten minutes,' she mouthed. 'I'll leave you.'

Marilyn nodded meekly, also suitably cowed.

There was one chair next to the head end of Sophie Whitehead's bed, which Jessie ushered him towards.

'I'm fine standing,' he muttered.

'No, really, take the chair,' Jessie countered, in a low voice, with a firm nod of her head.

Marilyn took the hint. The last thing a vulnerable teenager who had just found her parents butchered needed was him leaning over her like some gargantuan, interrogational crow. But as always, he was driven by his core desire to get a result; the human element of policing his perennial Achilles heel.

While Jessie pulled over a second chair, Marilyn began, resisting the temptation to lean forward, plant his elbows on the edge of the bed and steeple his fingers while he spoke.

'First of all, we are very sorry about your parents, Sophie, but I assure you that we are going to find their murderer.'

At the word 'murderer', a sob burst from the girl's mouth. Dropping her head, she covered her face with her hands. She sat like this for long seconds, making muffled mewling sounds, her shoulders shaking.

'I'm sorry,' she sniffed, her hands falling back to her lap.

'Please don't worry,' Jessie said. 'Your reaction is totally understandable.' *More than understandable.* Tugging a couple of tissues from a box on the console beside the bed, she handed them to Sophie. She felt as impotent in the face of this grief as she had, aged fourteen, watching her mother grieve her dead brother, assuring her that it would all be fine, knowing that nothing would ever be fine again, that both she and her mother would forever be missing a chunk of their hearts – just as Sophie would forever be missing two chunks of hers. 'As Detective Inspector Simmons said, we're working to find the man who murdered your parents. We need to ask you a few questions . . . but you can stop the discussion at any time if you feel it's too much,' she finished, avoiding Marilyn's glare, knowing he would be more than happy to let the doctors worry about the girl's welfare. They had questions to ask; answers to get; a serial killer to find.

'Can you talk us through your movements last night, please?' Marilyn asked, cutting to the chase.

'My friend came to my house first, to collect me,' Sophie began falteringly.

'What's her name?'

'Lucy. Lucy Heath.'

'What time did she get to you?'

'About eight.' A big sniff.

'And then what did you do?'

'We'd ordered a taxi. We were excited and Lucy wanted a vape, and my parents don't like us vaping, so we went and stood outside on the pavement chatting until the taxi came.'

'What did you talk about while you were waiting outside?'

233

'Nothing much. Just about the nightclub, who we hoped would be there, that kind of thing. Lucy doesn't know anything though. She left Sheiks early, left me alone.'

'Sheiks in Bognor?' Marilyn clarified.

Sophie nodded. 'It's half-term, which is why I was allowed out late. They have half-price entry on Wednesdays and you get one free drink too.'

'Why did you stay when your friend left?' Jessie asked.

Sophie flashed Marilyn a quick glance. 'There was a boy I fancied,' she said quietly, addressing the comment to Jessie. 'But then he left too and I was tired, so I left.'

'What time?'

'About one, I think.'

'Did you talk to anyone you didn't know while you were in the club?' Marilyn asked.

'No.'

'Are you sure?'

'Yeah. I stuck with Lucy and we just chatted to the boys that we know from school, danced with them.'

'Including the boy you liked?' Jessie asked.

'Yeah.'

'And after Lucy left?'

'Just the boys . . . that boy in particular.' She lifted her thin shoulders. 'But he obviously wasn't interested in me. Not like that anyway, and then he left too.'

'What did you do then?' Marilyn cut in.

'I hung around at the edge of the dancefloor finishing my drink and then I felt really horrible, so I went to the toilets and I . . . I was sick, I think.' She nodded, almost as if to herself. 'Yeah, I was sick, and then I just wanted to be at home so badly.'

'Did you notice anyone watching you?' Marilyn asked.

'No.'

'Did you see anyone who looked odd? Out of place? Anyone who looked as if they didn't belong there?'

'No, it was full of kids from school and some other schools around here. Young people.'

'Are you sure?' he prompted.

Sophie nodded. 'Yeah.'

'OK.' Marilyn exhaled the word on a weary sigh. Jessie didn't blame him. Sophie Whitehead was their only potential witness, and so far their questioning had drawn a blank. It was a blank that they couldn't afford. 'You left the club alone at about one p.m. How did you get home?'

'In a taxi.'

'Which company did you use?'

A few moments of silence before she answered, in a quiet voice. 'I don't know.'

'Did you phone the taxi?'

She shook her head. 'It was waiting by the side of the road, down from the entrance to the club.'

'How far down?'

'I don't know. Not that far.'

'A hundred metres?' Marilyn suggested.

'Yeah, about that, I suppose.'

'Was there anyone else out there with you?' Jessie asked. 'Even people you didn't know?'

'No, just me. Sheiks doesn't close till two.'

'Do you remember the taxi's crest? The taxi company's name?' Marilyn asked. There were only three main taxi companies in Chichester and he knew their liveries like the back of his hand. Some of the taxi drivers were good customers of the police, with their sidelines in peddling illegal substances to their younger clientele.

Sophie sniffed and shook her head.

'What did the car look like?' Marilyn pressed.

'It was small and dark. Black or maybe dark blue. Metallic, I think.'

'Did you notice a make or model?'

Another sniff, another shake. 'I'm not good with cars.'

'How about the markings on the outside of the car, the taxi? Can you remember anything specific about them?'

Another sniff, this one longer, wetter; she was close to tears again. 'There weren't any,' she managed.

'OK.' Marilyn kept his voice measured, though Jessie could sense frustration bubbling up from his insides, like acid rising from a post-curry gut. 'So what made you think it was a taxi?'

Tears welled up in Sophie's eyes and a barely audible voice came from somewhere at the back of her throat. 'I don't know. I was just so tired and, I . . . I . . . just wanted to get home.' She broke off, her glitter-pink nails picking at the tissue in her hand, tears trickling down her face.

'Did it have any stickers outside, or perhaps inside, on the windscreen or dashboard?' Jessie asked gently. 'Anything at all to indicate that it was a taxi?'

A mute, teary shake of her head. Marilyn sat back with a frustrated sigh. Jessie caught his gaze and gave a minute shake of her head. He had to keep a lid on the impatience, or they'd risk losing her altogether. Sophie had clearly been drunk, big surprise. Jessie could also remember being so drunk as a teenager that she couldn't work out left from right, and would have accepted a lift home from Lucifer himself if he'd promised her safe passage to her bed in double-quick time. She doubted, if Marilyn could cast his mind back that far, that he'd have been any different – worse probably – despite his new-found attachment to clean living.

'It's OK,' Jessie cut in. 'We know that you were at a nightclub, so we're pretty sure that you'd been drinking and we really don't care. You don't need to be embarrassed to tell us anything.'

'I just wanted to get home,' Sophie sobbed. 'I was drunk even though I know it's illegal to drink at my age.'

'We're not worried about that,' Marilyn assured her. 'Right, so you found a car outside – a car that may or may not have been a taxi?'

Sophie nodded and gulped back another sob. 'Like I said, my friend left and I stayed, but the boy I fancied obviously didn't fancy me at all and I was drunk by then and there was no one left I knew and I really really wanted to get home and then I saw the taxi, saw Charles.'

Marilyn sat forward again. 'Charles? That was his name?'

'Yeah, but he didn't really look like a Charles.'

'What does a Charles look like?'

Sophie lifted her thin shoulders. 'Well, Charles is a posh name, isn't it, like the prince, and this guy wasn't posh.'

'Where do you think he came from?'

'I don't know, but he just sounded normal. Just like any normal bloke you'd find around here, but not like a posh guy, not like one of those shooting kind of guys, but not a chav either.'

'What did Charles look like?'

'He was wearing these thick, black-rimmed glasses. I remember thinking that they were like comedy glasses, the frames were so thick.'

'What colour hair did he have?'

237

'Dark brown.' Sophie's glitter-pink nails picked at the tissues in her pale hands.

'How was it cut?'

'Short and kind of spiky, like that young policeman who was here before. I remember thinking . . .' she tailed off, shredding the ball of tissue, spreading confetti across her lap.

'Thinking what?' Jessie pressed.

'That it all didn't fit.'

'What do you mean?'

'The glasses and the hair and his clothes. The glasses and clothes looked like they belonged to someone a bit shambolic, but his hair was neat.'

'How old was he?'

'About my . . . my . . . my dad's—' A sucking intake of breath as she tried desperately not to break down again, tried and failed.

Jessie took hold of her hands, held them, chewing on her lip, looking past Sophie, out of the window at the skyline of Chichester, groggy in the rain, focusing on nothing and everything, until she felt the shake in the poor kid's hands subside.

'Can you remember any other details about him?' Marilyn asked, when Sophie had calmed down enough to speak.

'Yeah,' she sniffed. 'Yeah, I can.' Unwrapping her left hand from Jessie's, she held it out. 'He had scratches across the back of his hand. Deep scratches that looked like they came from wood, maybe.'

'Wood?'

'Yeah, like the kind of scratches you'd get if you ran through woods. Like Little Red Riding Hood kind of running away from the big bad wolf, or a horror film, when someone

238

runs and gets scratches all over them from the branches and twigs. Or from, like, from fingernails.'

'Did you ask him about them?'

'Yeah and he said they were from DIY. He didn't really say much else, and by then I was getting a bit scared.'

'Scared – why?' Jessie asked.

'Well, because he locked the doors. I was leaning against the window and he said he didn't want me to fall out, but that's a bit odd, isn't it, and he also took a strange route down some really narrow, quiet lanes. I started to sober up and then I realized that I hadn't seen any taxi markings and then I got really scared.' Her face crumpled and she began to cry, great, heaving sobs that shook her shoulders and caved in her chest. 'But . . . but I suppose there was nothing wrong with him, because he just dropped me home, safe. And it wasn't me that was in danger at all . . . it was Mum and Dad.'

'That's enough,' an efficient voice chimed. Dr Anita Murawska was standing at the end of the bed. 'No more questions, I'm afraid.'

'One more,' Marilyn said.

'No.'

'It's vital. I wouldn't ask if it wasn't.'

'It's fine.' A choked voice came from the bed. 'I want to help.' Sophie dropped her hands and her bloodshot eyes moved from Marilyn to Dr Murawska and back. 'I want to help catch him.'

Murawska sighed and held up one finger. 'One.'

'Thank you,' Marilyn said. 'Sophie, have you ever heard of a man called Hugo Fuller or a woman called Claudine Fuller? They were a married couple.'

Sophie's eyes widened. 'They were those people who were murdered a couple of days ago.'

'Yes, they were.'

She bit her lip, struggling not to break down again. 'Dad kept reading newspaper articles about them, watching the news,' she managed. 'Mum got angry with him because he kept going on about them and she didn't understand why he was so interested in people we didn't even know.'

'And how did he explain his interest?'

'He . . . he said that he was trying to find out details to keep us safe.'

'And neither he nor your mum had ever mentioned Hugo or Claudine Fuller before?'

She shook her head.

'Perhaps Hugo was a childhood friend of your dad's?'

Another firm shake. 'No,' she murmured, her voice thick with suppressed tears. 'Dad said he didn't know them and Mum definitely didn't because she couldn't understand why Dad was so interested in them getting murdered.'

At the word 'murdered', Sophie's shoulders heaved and the tears she had been struggling to hold back spilled over her eyelids and tracked down her cheeks again.

'That's enough,' Anita Murawska snapped. 'You have to leave. Right now, I'm afraid.'

Marilyn nodded. He and Jessie stood.

'Thank you, Sophie, you've been very helpful,' he said, touching his hand to her shoulder. 'We'll find the man who killed your parents and we'll send him to prison for a very long time. I promise you that.'

45

Workman was back on Valerie Fuller's doorstep, feeling as if she had been teleported to the Arctic once again, though at least she had worn a scarf this time, which was wrapped tight around her neck underneath the raised collar of her favourite navy belted overcoat. She was surprised when the door opened barely seconds after her knock, and a sliver of Valerie's face appeared behind it, followed by a blue-veined hand which beckoned her inside, easing the door open just enough for her to slide through the gap sideways, her belt buckle catching on the door as she did so. Valerie shut it firmly behind her.

'Were you followed?' she snapped.

Workman bit down on a sudden, intense desire to laugh. It was doubtless the fault of exhausted hysteria that made her find the fact that Valerie Fuller was worried she'd been followed by a horde of press highly entertaining.

'No.'

Valerie gave a relieved sigh. 'I've been doorstepped virtually non-stop since Hugo and Claudine were murdered. I was polite to the first few, but then there were more and more, and *then* I read a couple of decidedly catty things about me, so I now refuse to have anything to do with any of them.'

Workman knew how she felt. Since the Whiteheads' murder last night, Surrey and Sussex Major Crimes had been under siege. They could have done with a moat and drawbridge, archers guarding the turrets.

'Yes, I'm sorry. This case is attracting a huge amount of press attention.'

'Predictably,' Valerie replied, with an arch lift of one eyebrow. 'Particularly after the latest murders.'

Workman didn't rise. She had listened to LBC on the drive over and Daniel and Eleanor Whitehead's murders had been the main topic of conversation, of speculation, of repeated morbidly horrified phone calls from listeners.

'I have a few more questions about Hugo, about his friends from childhood and his adult social and work connections,' Workman said.

Valerie smirked. 'You don't have any good leads yet then?'

'We do, but I'm afraid that I can't discuss them with you.'

Valerie's gaze narrowed, unconvinced, unsurprisingly; the lack of conviction in Workman's voice had been an easy read.

'Well, you might as well come and sit down,' she said. Her front door had opened straight into a double-height kitchen-cum-dining-cum-sitting room, decorated in various shades of off-white, simple and stylish, big floor-to-ceiling windows – the barn's previous doors – looking out over a small fenced garden and fields beyond. She led Workman to an oak kitchen table, taking a seat herself at one end. 'I made a pot of tea actually, as you'd called ahead to say that you were coming.'

Workman pulled out a chair next to her, so that they were sitting at an elliptical angle to each other. She'd learnt a few things from Jessie Flynn – not to sit end to end, so as not to make the discussion combative. Crossing her legs, she mirrored Valerie's movements.

'So – yet more questions,' Valerie said, passing Workman a cup of tea and a jug of milk.

Workman nodded. 'Let's start with Hugo's childhood.'

'I may be of little help. As I said before, Hugo was very self-sufficient. Godfrey and I only got involved when there was trouble.'

'Was there trouble?'

'His prep school called us a few times to complain about his behaviour.'

'What kind of behaviour?'

'Cheating in tests, a bit of argy-bargy in the playground, telling a teacher to fuck off once, smashing his violin against the wall in the middle of a music lesson when he decided that he couldn't be bothered with it any more.' Valerie plucked at her pearl necklace. 'And he was caught tormenting the school's rabbit. It was kept in a hutch outside and Hugo was found one lunchtime, stabbing it with a compass.'

Workman's widened eyes were met with a nonchalant shrug from Valerie.

'I did tell you that he was a little shit.'

'The school didn't throw him out?'

'No, he was suspended for a couple of days for the rabbit incident and then we agreed to send him to boarding school two years early. Westbourne House Prep School finishes at thirteen and we sent Hugo to Fettes College at eleven.'

'Do you remember the names of any of his friends from his prep-school days?'

243

'He had two good friends from Westbourne.' She twisted her pearls around her index finger, her gaze finding the ceiling. 'Martin something . . . something common.'

'Common?'

'Yes, Smith, Brown, Jones . . . something like that. And another boy, James Stoddard. Godfrey and I became reasonably good friends with his parents, though they moved up to the Cotswolds a couple of years after James left Westbourne and we lost touch.'

Workman made a note. 'Martin something and James Stodd—'

'Taylor,' Valerie interrupted suddenly. 'Martin Taylor. That was it. I did tell you it was common.'

Workman suppressed a smile. Valerie Fuller had clearly worked hard to discard the lower-middle-class tag that she had brought with her into her marriage.

'Did Hugo keep in touch with them once he went to Fettes College?'

'For a couple of years, but then they finished at Westbourne and went to boarding school too – not Fettes College – and the Stoddards moved, as I said, and they gradually lost touch.'

'Who did Hugo spend time with during the holidays when he was at Fettes College?'

'He either stayed at the house of his best friend from Fettes College, Angus Chisnall, or he came home. He'd usually spend half-terms and a couple of weeks during the summer holidays with Angus and the rest of the time with us.'

'Where did Angus live?'

'In the Scottish Borders. Dumfries and Galloway if I remember correctly.'

'And when he was here, who did he spend time with?'

'To be quite frank, I'm not entirely sure. As I said before, we had a house in East Wittering then, overlooking the beach. It was all very safe and he would just roam. I had my daughters and they were very young. Hugo made his own entertainment and didn't appear to need monitoring. He was a leader, always has been, and he was hugely attractive to other boys because of that, so he never seemed to be short of people to spend time with. I didn't like Hugo bringing boys home as they were so noisy and disruptive, so we came to an understanding pretty quickly that he could do what he wanted as long as we never had cause to worry and never had the police around.'

'Did you ever have the police around?' Workman asked.

Valerie gave a dismissive wave of her hand. 'Once. Hugo had been caught tormenting some sheep in a field with some other boys, trying to ride them evidently, and the police brought him home. But it was just the once and they only gave him a warning.'

'What about university friendships or adult friendships?'

Valerie shook her head. 'Hugo went to university in London and, once he was there, he stayed. Godfrey used to see him for lunch sometimes when he had work in London, but I had virtually nothing to do with Hugo once he went to university and I have no idea who his friends were. Godfrey never mentioned anyone specific.'

Workman nodded. 'One last question. Do the names Daniel or Eleanor Whitehead mean anything to you, Mrs Fuller?'

'Absolutely. I've heard about them virtually every hour on the hour on the radio news since early this morning. I switched on the television at lunchtime and there they were on BBC1, poor sods. They were murdered by the same lunatic who murdered Hugo and Claudine, weren't they?'

'I'm sorry, but I can't comment on that.'

Valerie gave a nasty little smile. 'You don't need to. The press are commenting on your behalf and it all sounds incredibly grim and as if you lot have made no progress at all.'

Workman swallowed back a biting retort. 'Do either of those names mean anything to you beyond what you've heard about them in today's news?' she asked, keeping her tone measured, professional.

'No.'

'Are you sure? You haven't heard of either of them, before today, in relation to Hugo?'

Valerie shook her head firmly. 'I'm absolutely sure. I had never heard of either Daniel or Eleanor Whitehead before this morning.'

46

'Sophie Whitehead confirmed that her parents left a key to the back door under the cast-iron hedgehog boot cleaner next to the back door, but only when she was out,' Jessie said, when she and Marilyn had settled themselves at as quiet a table as it was possible to find in a busy hospital coffee shop. 'Sophie said that she was absentminded and often forgot to take her door key. She's a teenager. It goes with the territory.'

Marilyn rolled his eyes. 'Why the bloody hell didn't the Whiteheads leave a note pinned to the door with an arrow pointing to the hedgehog for good measure.'

'It's not that dumb to leave a key.'

'How do you arrive at that dubious conclusion?'

'They live on a quiet, leafy, out-of-the-way estate, in the middle of the street of very similar houses. They must have felt as safe as houses, to use a lame pun.'

'It's a burglar and murderer's dream that estate, with all the shrubbery. A whole army of serial killers could hide for days and no one would be any the wiser.'

It was Jessie's turn to roll her eyes. 'There's nothing to pick out their house from anyone else's. They probably know . . . knew all their neighbours and their neighbours knew them. They'd have monthly neighbourhood committee meetings, rotating working parties to trim the grass verges, you name it, they'd have it all.'

'My idea of hell.'

Hers too.

Marilyn sighed. 'I know where you're going with this, Jessie.'

She gave a tired smile. 'And where would that be?'

'It's personal.'

'It *is* personal.'

'Sophie said that her parents often went to sleep before she got home, particularly when they thought she was spending the evening at a friend's house watching films and painting nails, or whatever the hell teenage girls do when they're hanging out with their mates.'

'Add discussing boys and posting selfies onto Instagram and that about covers it.'

'It's entirely possible they were asleep when our man let himself into the house. Sophie was on half-term, but it was Wednesday night, a work night for the Whiteheads. There was no damage to the front or back door locks or the doors themselves, so he either picked one of the locks, used the key that was left under the hedgehog or entered via an open door or window – the third option being the most unlikely given that it was a cold autumn night. Burrows should have a definitive answer to that question by now.' Tugging his reading glasses from his top pocket, he slid them, self-consciously, onto his nose and pinged off a quick text. An answering ping a moment later. 'He used the key and let himself in through the back door.'

'He's been watching them, as he watched the Fullers.'

'Or he just got lucky. As you said yourself, lots of people leave keys hidden.'

'That's not his mentality. It's all planned meticulously. Also, the timing is too perfect, while Sophie Whitehead was out. If my "personal" theory is correct, the timing would have been deliberate.'

'If—'

'It is correct,' she said, with an assuredness that she didn't feel. 'Sophie is like Lupo – an innocent. He spared Lupo and he spared Sophie, so as not to create collateral damage.'

Marilyn took a slug of his double espresso.

'How can you drink that stuff?' Jessie asked, reaching for her latte.

'How can you drink *that* stuff? It's a milky drink in the general direction of which a coffee bean may or may not have been waved.' He drained the espresso.

'Sophie and her friend, Lucy Heath, stood outside the Whiteheads' house on the pavement vaping and chatting while they waited for the taxi they'd booked to take them to Sheiks nightclub.'

'And we know how well sound carries out there, from the noise of our footsteps on the gravel. The murderer could have been hiding in the Whiteheads' or a neighbour's front garden, watching and listening, and heard Sophie and Lucy discussing their night out at Sheiks. Serial killers often revisit the scenes of the crime so that they can enjoy their kills multiple times. If . . . and only *if* your watching theory is correct, our man could have known that Sophie was going to Sheiks, murdered Daniel and Eleanor, then collected Sophie, pretending to be a taxi, and driven her home to her dead parents.'

Jessie nodded. 'We need to find Charles.'

'We do. I'll put a call in to Chichester's three main taxi firms, ask them to get their drivers to keep an urgent eye out for a rogue operator in a small dark hatchback. They hate moonlighters illegally plying for hire on their patch so if he's a legit moonlighter and not our man, they'll find him far more quickly than we can.'

'If he is still out there illegally plying for hire, he's certain not to be the killer. And if he's not out there plying for hire, he either doesn't need to any more for whatever reason, or he just picked up Sophie.'

'And the taxi drivers won't find him. So we need to – urgently – to eliminate him or arrest him.'

'Where is Sheiks?'

'In Bognor, down a side road off the main strip.'

'It sounds as if it would be busy.'

'In summer, certainly, and in the autumn and winter there are people around at pub and club closing time, but she left after pub closing time, but before club closing time, alone. And the street is shops and offices, not residential houses.' Marilyn pinged off another, longer, text. 'DC Cara,' he said, looking up. 'I've asked him to go to Sheiks, check out their CCTV, and interview any of the staff who might have seen Sophie Whitehead at the club or when she left.'

Jessie smiled. 'So much for his forty winks.'

Marilyn raised his coffee cup. 'This is a murder investigation's forty winks.' He lowered the cup. 'We can add Charles to our list of suspects, which will number one once he's added.' He gave a wry smile. 'At least I will have something to say at the press conference later to give the illusion of progress, in the absence of actual progress.'

250

47

One Year Ago

Dropping his gaze to the bleached slats of the jetty, between them to the waves, Robbie saw the image of a boy fighting against the current. It was the middle of winter, colder even than now, and the water was ice. The boy's face was blue and his eyes were saucer-wide with fear.

A dog.

There was a dog in there too. A little black and white dog. Its head was black, but its front legs were white, and Robbie could see them churning through the dark water in frantic terror. The waves were crashing over their heads, over the head of the boy and his dog, disappearing them from view, surfacing them again, coughing and spluttering, blue and enervated from cold.

Robbie looked down the lifeboat jetty towards the beach. Both the jetty and beach were deserted now. The others had gone. They had stood and watched for a while, watched and laughed. Then the laughing had shuddered and died as they realized that, this time, they had gone too far.

Only the drowning boy and his dog remained.

Robbie held his breath, willing them to survive. But he knew that all his willing was pointless. He already knew how their story ended.

'Robbie. Robbie!'

Robbie looked up. His father was staring hard at him. Robbie hadn't noticed him reappear from the lifeboat shed. He had been too caught up watching the boy and his dog. His father's face was pale, anxiety straining his expression at the look on Robbie's.

'Are you all right, Rob?'

Robbie didn't nod.

His father frowned. 'Are you all right?'

It was a question his father asked often. Ten times a day at least – had done for years. From the plaintive tone of his question, Robbie knew that he was still waiting and hoping, desperately hoping for the answer, finally, to be *Yes*. Not just *Fine*. A *Fine* that his dad knew was a lie, a feeble construction that wouldn't withstand a stiff breeze.

Robbie shook his head. He couldn't see the boy any more. The boy was gone, swallowed by the heaving sea. Only the little dog remained, its white legs pumping the waves like pistons, as it fought with raw animal desperation for its life.

Fine?

No, he wasn't even fine. Not now that he had come here, to this place.

48

Dr Ghoshal looked up from the flayed body on his dissecting table, no translatable expression in his cool, dark gaze. He'd make an ace poker player. An ace criminal. An as-cool-as-a-grocer's-shop-full-of-cucumbers murderer. Marilyn hoped that their man wasn't as sub-zero as Dr Ghoshal, or they wouldn't have a cat in hell's chance of catching him.

'As you know, Dr Flynn's theory is that these murders are about watching,' Marilyn said. 'She believed before I . . . before you proved that theory not to be correct, that Claudine Fuller was murdered first and Hugo Fuller second, after being made to watch his wife's death. But Claudine was killed after her husband. What about the Whiteheads?'

Dr Ghoshal dipped his gaze back to Daniel Whitehead's pale, slack, splayed body.

'Dr Flynn is right in the Whiteheads' case.' His habitually desiccated monotone was made more colourless than usual by the muffling effect of his clinical face mask. 'Eleanor Whitehead was killed first and her husband, Daniel, half an hour or so later. I would suggest that Daniel Whitehead was made to watch his wife's murder. Watch it and then spend some time absorbing it; or perhaps, during that time, the killer talked to him.' Dr Ghoshal paused theatrically. 'Explained.'

Marilyn nodded. *Jesus Christ*, he thought. 'What's the evidence to back up that theory, beyond the timing?'

'The timing firstly, as you point out, and secondly the location of where they were found. She was drowned in the bath and he was chained to the bathroom towel rail. He couldn't not have watched.'

'Sure, but doesn't that speak to expedience, given that we know it's a lone killer? He needed to incapacitate one of them to kill the other. He couldn't tackle both at the same time. It doesn't necessarily concur with Dr Flynn's watching theory.'

Dr Ghoshal nodded: not a nod of agreement but more the kind of patient nod that a parent would give a child to indicate that they have listened to their opinion, but have most certainly not agreed.

'The pattern and depth of the contusions around Daniel Whitehead's wrists, caused by the handcuffs cutting into his skin, suggest that he was restrained for a considerable amount of time, and that he struggled actively against those bonds, for a sustained period, before he was killed.'

'I would struggle if someone was scratching my eyes out. Intense fear does that to a person, and Whitehead would have felt intense fear, whether he was made to watch his wife or not.'

'Indeed, DI Simmons. Though he would not have struggled for so long or in such an industrious way.'

'Industrious?'

Raising his hand, Dr Ghoshal beckoned Marilyn towards

254

the dissecting table. As he stepped forward, an image of Jodie Trigg, of that dreadful autopsy he'd walked out of, rose in his mind. Though they had made scant progress so far on this case, he had scorched the earth in terms of effort and, though he felt a human level of horror looking at the injuries inflicted on Daniel Whitehead, he knew that, as with the Fullers' autopsy, he could comfortably see this one through. He looked, as dispassionately as he could, where Dr Ghoshal was indicating.

'I would suggest, from the pattern of bruising and contusions around his wrists that extend from the basal carpometacarpal joint of the thumb to halfway up his forearm, that he struggled for an extended period of time before he himself was attacked and that he tried a number of different ways to free himself. That is not the action of someone who is in extreme pain. They will fight against their bonds, but not in a calculated, thoughtful way.'

'So he was twisting and fighting against the bonds, moving them up and down his arms, trying to squeeze them over his thumb in an attempt to escape?'

'Indeed. And apart from the differences, which all come down to timing – the length of time Daniel Whitehead was tied up and the fact that he died after his wife – the modus operandi was very similar in both double murders. The drowning of the wives, the gouging out of the husbands' eyes whilst they were still alive. Their killing, finally, via multiple stab wounds, through the eyes to the brain.'

'I'd suggest that the order of the husband and wife's murders is a critical difference—' Marilyn's interruption was cut off by a raised finger. Even DCI Janet Backastowe would fail to silence him with the movement of a single digit, any digits actually. Dr Ghoshal, however, was a different kettle

255

of fish entirely. Marilyn found him as condescending to work with as did the other senior detectives at Surrey and Sussex Major Crimes, but for Marilyn, the evidence he gained was worth the humiliation he was forced to endure to secure it.

'It is my job to provide you with the clinical evidence, not to come up with theories. However, if I were to set aside that parameter for a moment, I would concur with Dr Flynn and say that your killer's motivation – or one of his motivations at least – is to do with watching. The taking out of the eyes while a person is living is a truly heinous thing to do. Unless your killer is Hannibal Lecter, there must be a very strong motivation for him to do that.'

'So why was Eleanor Whitehead killed first and Claudine Fuller second?'

Dr Ghoshal lifted his shoulders. 'There is a reason, DI Simmons. A reason that will doubtless prove critical to the case. And I would suggest, when you understand that reason, you understand much more about the killer and you stand a much greater chance of catching him.'

49

Fine grey needles of rain swirled from the oily sky and the wind bore a chill that made Jessie dread winter's approach. The hospital car park had been virtually full when she and Marilyn had arrived and she'd had to drive to the far end, squeeze her Mini into a space between a gargantuan four-by-four and the overgrown hedge that divided the car park from a public footpath. But now the car park was only smattered with cars and she felt a shiver of apprehension as she hurried, head bent, through the soupy wet twilight, the discussion with Sophie Whitehead and the thought of Marilyn at Sophie's parents' autopsy goading her imagination into overdrive.

She had hung out in the coffee shop for a couple of hours after Marilyn left, to telephone a few of her private clinical patients and write up some session notes (she was still balancing her clinical work with her police work – the former paying significantly better). Then she had sat, nursing the cold dregs of her third latte, thinking about Claudine being killed second; she was sure the opposite would be true for the Whiteheads, given the theatre of their deaths – she'd know soon. She'd thought about faceless Charles, in his dark-coloured hatchback, moonlighting as a taxi driver, and about Callan, that shifting time-bomb lodged in his brain. And, finally, about Robbie Parker. She needed to find some time to see him soon, couldn't continue to consign him to the bottom of her list, however temptingly easy that might be.

The hospital building cast a stack of repeating pale yellow rectangles onto the tarmac close to the building but, in the recesses of the car park, there was only darkness. She rarely felt apprehensive at night, loved the feeling of solitude and freedom that being outside in darkness brought, and she realized, as her heart pumped and her breath snagged in her throat with each step, how deeply the murders had burrowed under her skin.

She reached her Mini and hunched in the shelter of the four-by-four next to it, rain melting into her hair and dripping down her neck as she unzipped her puffa jacket and fished in her inside pocket for her car key. A car swished past the main road beyond the public footpath, its headlights momentarily blinding her. *Where the hell is my key?* She was sure she'd put it in her inside pocket so that she wouldn't need to fumble around her handbag, but she'd been in a rush to meet Marilyn and her slippery, chilled fingers groped in a pocket that she realized was empty.

As she swung her handbag from her shoulder, she sensed, rather than heard – what? Another car? A bike? No, neither, the road was deserted. Resisting the psychosomatic nerves that she knew were just that – psychosomatic nerves – encouraging her to twist and manically scan the dark car park, she glanced quickly over her left shoulder, her right.

Breathing out slowly, she ducked her gaze to her handbag, fingers closing around her wallet, lipstick, front door keys, then the familiar, circular fat rubber fob of her car key.

'Dr Flynn.'

'Jesus.' Her handbag hit the tarmac and she spun around.

The man – hooded, his face partially obscured, she didn't recognize him – backed away, raised hands held in front of him in a gesture clearly meant to be soothing. His face was damp and shiny with sweat.

'I'm sorry.' A familiar, soft-focus voice as irritatingly pacifying as those raised hands. 'I didn't mean to startle you.'

Jessie scooped up her handbag. 'You didn't startle me, Mr Parker. You bloody terrified me.'

'I'm so sorry. Really, I just . . .' He flapped a pale hand towards the road. 'I was just running past and I saw you. I can't apologize enough for scaring you. It really wasn't my intention—'

'It's fine. I was joking,' she lied. Anything to stop him apologizing. 'It's a miserable evening to be out running.'

Levering his long fingers into the elastic of his pale grey hood, he slid it back from his face. 'I'm training for a marathon in a month's time, so I have to put the miles in whatever the weather. I usually run in the hills, but it's blowy up there this evening, so I'm pounding around town instead.'

Jessie forced a smile, though her heart wasn't in it. The last thing she felt like doing was standing in the pissing rain exchanging pleasantries with a man she'd met once. She wished he hadn't noticed her; that even if he had, he hadn't stopped. She wouldn't have done.

'A marathon must require some commitment.'

'It does, but it's nice to have a focus, that isn't . . .' His wiry legs, tightly clad in pale grey running tights, jittered as he scuffed his trainers against the tarmac. 'That isn't Robbie.'

Jessie nodded. She wished he would just stand still. He was radiating nerves; getting on her nerves.

'I'm sure.'

'You, uh, you got on well with Robbie?'

'I did. He's a great kid,' she said simply, trying to be polite, without fully engaging.

His gaze swung away from hers; she noticed a muscle below his eye twitch. 'I often joke that when he's an adult the bullies will still be taking his lunch money, but as he loves the burgers they're serving in McDonald's he'll be happy to hand it over.' He barked a sudden, harsh laugh as forced and unpractised as his smile. 'Did he do all right in your session?'

I wasn't assessing him. 'He did great.'

His eyes travelled back and forward across her face as if he was working something around in his head. 'So what do you, uh, what do you think?'

'I don't know what you're asking.' She knew perfectly well what he was asking, but she had guaranteed Robbie confidentiality and Parker had agreed.

'Do you think he'll get over it? Move on?'

I'm not a painter-decorator, she was tempted to say. Much as she would have loved to be able to unfurl a roll of glossy, embossed wallpaper and paper over the canyon-sized fissures in Robbie's psyche, make him whole again. *Humpty Dumpty.*

'He's a smart kid,' Parker continued. 'I don't want this stupid bullying to define his future.'

As much as it has defined his past. Neither of them voiced the thought.

'He deserves more. And I don't want them to win.'

Jessie nodded. It shouldn't be about winning and losing, but they both knew that it was. Continuing to be a victim was letting the bullies win. And fuck them. Why should they win?

'I don't want them to win,' he said again.

Jessie nodded. She thought of what she had told Robbie. *You're not that child who needs to take this shit any more. Fight back.* 'I understand that, Mr Parker.'

'And . . . so.'

His tongue moved nervously around inside his mouth as he waited for her to answer. But she wasn't sure how to answer.

They won't.

It wasn't an answer she could give.

I hope not.

Better.

I pray not.

More realistic.

'I don't have an answer for you, Mr Parker, not yet.'

Why had he stopped? To be polite? To fish? Find out whether she had been able to peer, keen-eyed, straight into that hard-to-read brain of his son's? But she didn't want to talk about Robbie, couldn't. In fact, she didn't want to stand here, in the pissing rain, talking at all.

'I'm late to meet my boyfriend for dinner, Mr Parker. Is there anything you wanted?'

He tilted towards her. 'Can you see Robbie now? He's home. I'll be running for another hour and a half. You'll have the place to yourself.'

'I'm sorry, but I'm meeting my boyfriend for dinner,' she repeated.

261

He shuffled closer. 'Ten, fifteen minutes.'

Jessie leant back, felt the four-by-four's wing mirror dig into her spine. 'It's not a ten- or fifteen-minute job, Mr Parker.'

'Just to show him that you're interested. That you care.'

A low, cheap shot. Her hackles rose. 'I *am* interested and I *do* care, or I wouldn't have agreed to help him. But dashing in for ten minutes will be more destructive than not seeing him at all and I'm already late for dinner.'

'It would mean a lot.' He laid a hand on her arm. 'To him and to me.'

Jessie nodded, chewing her lip. Her insides were screaming. She stepped sideways and back, forcing his hand to fall from her arm without physically wrenching it away, tempting though that was.

'I'll see him again soon, I promise. I'm sorry about this evening, but I can't. And, to be honest, I need to be on good form when I see Robbie. Even if I had longer than ten or fifteen minutes tonight, which I don't, it's not helpful if I turn up exhausted, with only half my mind on him.'

She couldn't get a handle on Allan Parker. When she'd met him at his home, he had seemed timid, submissive, cloyingly grateful, but now he was wired and aggressively on edge. He was only a few centimetres taller than her five foot six, but he was lean and fit, those pale grey running tights clinging to well-muscled legs. People who felt mentally vulnerable often worked on their physicality, drawing comfort from the feeling of strength, even if they didn't have the mental attitude to use it.

'In the next day or so then?'

'Hopefully, yes, but I'm working on a murder case, Mr Parker, so I can't be precise.'

'Of course. I'm sorry to push, but Robbie's everything to me. *Everything*.'

'I understand that and I promise that I will make time, soon. Please tell Robbie that I'll text him when I have a better idea of what I'm up to.'

Turning away pointedly, goosebumps rising on the back of her neck, she opened the driver's door. When she glanced back to say goodbye, Parker was halfway across the car park, jogging backwards on those silent trainers of his.

He raised a hand. 'Soon,' he shouted.

Jessie raised a hand in return, didn't reply.

50

Callan's red Golf was parked snug against the pub's low flintstone front wall. There were huge, muddy paw-prints peppering the front passenger seat, Jessie noticed when she peered through the window – left to his own devices, in his own domain, Callan was as messy as always. He'd bagged a prime space, had obviously been here for a while.

Though neither she or Callan were creatures of habit, this whitewashed country inn, with its scarlet front door and matching window frames, baskets of hot-red geraniums and white lobelia hanging from the eaves of the porch, had become 'their' pub. They'd first met for dinner here last November, to discuss the Sami Scott case. It wasn't best suited to Callan, who virtually had to shuffle on his knees to a table, to avoid clunking his head on the gnarled black beams that held up the three-hundred-year-old sagging ceiling. Though Jessie was only five foot six, even she had to duck to step through the front door without risking scalping herself.

The long wooden bar, studded with taps dispensing local beers and bitters – Surrey Hills, Ranmore Ale, Baldy, Sussex

Best Bitter – usually equally well studded with locals chatting on bar stools, was empty, only an elderly couple having drinks to her right and Callan and Lupo to her left, occupying a table for two by the log fire. 'Their' table. At the sound of the door, Callan glanced over and raised a hand. He was wearing navy-blue suit trousers and a white shirt, the top button undone, and he looked so damn hot. Lupo's head swivelled, his pale gaze fixing on Jessie as she approached, but apart from that single movement, his body remained rigid.

Callan half-stood, as much as he could in the low-ceilinged room, and gave her a warm, lingering kiss. If Jessie hadn't known that the barman was eyeballing them, no one else to look at, she would have wrapped her arms around his neck and snogged him for an hour.

'Sit down and I'll get you wine.'

'A bucketful, please.'

'That bad?'

'I just had an impromptu and somewhat creepy encounter with Allan Parker.'

'Who the hell is Allan Parker?'

'Robbie Parker's dad.'

Callan looked blank.

'The bullied boy. I told you about him.'

He nodded. 'I remember now.'

He was usually exceptionally switched-on, remembered everyone's names after the first telling – names, faces, heights, attire, accents, dates, times. It was required for his job as a Redcap, a military policeman, a job he loved and was made for. Jessie thought again of the letter from Frimley Park Hospital that she'd found in his coat pocket, wished that she'd read it. Integrity was overrated.

'Are you OK, Callan? You seem a bit—'

'I'm fine.' He stepped past her to the bar, returning with a pint of beer the same amber colour as his eyes and a large glass of Sauvignon. Sliding onto the bench seat next to her, he pulled her in for another kiss.

'I'm fine,' he said again.

Jessie leant back, disengaging. 'Only fine?'

'Much more than fine. I'm always more than fine when I'm with you.'

He made to kiss her again; she pulled back again.

'Not here, Callan.'

Hurt flashed in his eyes. 'Why not? Because Lupo's too young to witness overt displays of affection?'

'Because those people over there are too old to witness overt displays of affection.'

'It might inspire them.'

'Either that or they'll be telling us to get a room.'

Callan smiled. 'I intend to, later.'

Jessie rolled her eyes, playing along, though his banter felt forced, his mind elsewhere. 'You'd better be nice to me then. All night.'

'I'm always nice to you.' He reached for his pint. 'And I did fit those two security cameras in Paws for Thought and spend an hour of my life that I will never get back explaining to a technologically challenged mad dog woman how to work them.'

Jessie grinned. 'I can imagine it was a very painful hour.'

'You cannot begin to imagine how painful.' He took a swig of beer. 'So, tell me about Adam.'

'Allan.'

'Allan. Tell me about him.'

'He accosted me in St Richard's Hospital car park.'

Callan frowned. 'Accosted you?'

'Well, not actually accosted, but he did just suddenly appear out of nowhere like some creepy pale ghoul-like thing. He said he'd been running past and had seen me. He asked me to go and see Robbie again this evening.' She stifled a yawn with the back of her hand. The few sips of wine she'd had had gone straight to her head.

'And miss dinner with me and Lupo?'

Jessie smiled, genuinely for the first time all day. 'That's what I told him. That I couldn't possibly miss dinner with my lover and his dog.'

'Our dog.'

'Your dog. He doesn't engage with me at all.'

'He's the strong silent type.'

'Like his new owner,' Jessie said pointedly, thinking of the letter.

Callan shrugged. 'So what happened with Allan?'

'He was uncomfortably insistent that I see Robbie tonight, would hardly take no for an answer. He has a kind of submissive neediness combined with an aggressive demand-ingness that I found . . . find a bit disturbing.'

'When are you seeing Robbie next?'

'Tomorrow probably, as long as no one else gets murdered in the meantime. I need time to help him properly. I can't just dash in and dash out, which is what I explained to his father. He needs to be the sole focus of my attention for a minimum of an hour at a time and I also need to be mentally switched-on to see him.' Dropping her hand to Callan's leg, she traced her fingers up his thigh, almost absentmindedly. 'I can't be counselling him with eight hours' sleep over the past eighty and while my mind is on murder cases . . .' She smiled. 'And on meeting you.'

Callan covered her hand with his. 'That's not an unreasonable explanation.'

'Yes, but Allan made me feel guilty. And I feel guilty, because I know how much Robbie needs help.' She gave a brief, dispirited smile.

'He's not your problem.'

'He's got to be someone's problem and I'm the last man standing. Clinical psychology is my job, Callan, and I'm good at it. I can't just abandon him. Also, he reminds me a bit of me when I was a teenager, except that the bullying he has experienced is so much worse. And that almost makes it harder for me to see and help him, as it makes me feel as if I'm digging over my own hideous childhood experiences, not just his. It's almost too close to home, too emotionally painful.'

'You can't help him at your own expense.' He squeezed her hand. 'At the expense of your sanity.'

'I think that my sanity packed its bags and headed on out many years ago,' she said, returning his squeeze. 'Anyway, enough of the Parkers for now. There's something else that I wanted to talk to you about.'

'What?'

She took a sip of wine. 'You,' she said evenly. 'Something up, isn't there?'

He pulled his hand from hers. 'No, there's nothing "up", as you put it.' An edge to his voice.

She held his gaze coolly. 'I can tell that something's wrong.'

'For fuck's sake, Jessie, I'm your boyfriend, not one of your patients.'

'Right. You are my boyfriend and it's my job to look after you.'

He gave a wry half-smile. 'Aren't I supposed to look after you?'

'Don't be a sexist idiot.'

'I wasn't.'

'Yes, you were.' She reached for his hand again, still holding his gaze. 'I saw it. I saw the letter from Frimley Park Hospital.'

Callan frowned. 'You shouldn't have been looking through my private stuff.'

'I wasn't. You borrowed my Mini and didn't put the key back on the rack. I didn't want to wake you at three a.m. to dig them out of your coat pocket for me.'

His gaze moved from hers to fix on Lupo, the light of the flames beyond the dog dancing in his unsmiling eyes. 'Did you read it?'

'No.'

'Good.'

'Though now you're being so weird, I wish I had read it.'

His strong fingers traced patterns in the thick white fur of the big dog's back. 'My epilepsy is getting worse,' he murmured, after a moment. 'Significantly worse.'

'Why didn't you tell me?'

He stroked Lupo, without looking up. 'You've had too much on. Too much stress with the murders of those little girls, and now this . . . this dog murder thing.'

Jessie shook her head. 'You're by far the most important thing in my life.'

'Sure, but you love working with Major Crimes.'

'I do.' Tears welled in her eyes. She blinked them away. 'But I love you more. Much much more than my stupid job.'

'I'm going to resign my commission, leave the army.'

Fumbling his hand from Lupo's back, she squeezed it

269

tight. 'You can't do that. You love being a Redcap.' She forced a half-smile. 'Even more than I love chasing murderers.'

He didn't smile back. 'I don't have a choice. They'll find out any day. I'll have an epileptic fit at work—'

'Why don't you wait until that happens? It may never.'

'Because what if I'm driving? Or on a case? Chasing a suspect, or in the middle of the fucking office, for Christ's sake. How humiliating would that be?'

'There's nothing humiliating about it.'

'There is to me.' He was still looking down at Lupo, deliberately refusing to meet her gaze. A muscle twitched in his jaw. 'I may need an operation to remove the bullet.'

'Why? They said that it was safer to leave it.'

'My neurologist suspects that the bullet has shifted, that it's creating swelling in my brain and that's why my epilepsy has worsened. He suspects that it might now be too dangerous to leave.'

Jessie squeezed his hand tighter. *But what if something happens to you? What if I lose you? I can't lose you. I love you too much.* She didn't verbalize any of those thoughts. They sounded too needy, too selfish.

'When are you seeing him?'

'The day after tomorrow for some tests so that we can make a final decision one way or the other.'

'I'll come with you.'

'You don't need to.'

'I want to.'

'What about the case?'

'Fuck the case. It's not as if I feel I'm adding much value, so I'm sure they'll cope perfectly well for a few hours in my absence. And anyway, we might have found him by then,' she finished, though she knew how faint a hope that was.

51

Now for that glass of wine.

After the shock of that ridiculous moment of intense terror yesterday evening, with the *Scooby-Doo* monster, Denise had stayed firmly off the wine. But now, after a tedious day and with a second evening alone looming, she was so desperate for just one glass that she could almost taste the woodiness of the Chardonnay on her tongue, feel its cool sliding tantalizingly down her throat.

God, I really am an alcoholic, fantasizing about wine.

She loved Leo desperately, loved being a mum, but he *was* hard work and little children could be so terribly boring. Being alone all day with only a toddler for company was isolating, and now all she had to look forward to was another lonely evening in front of the television. At least Simon was getting back from Wiltshire late tonight. Though she'd doubtless be fast asleep when he got home, he'd be there when she woke in the morning.

Leo was sound asleep now, *thank God*, Baloo clutched in his pudgy arms, and she hummed as she jogged back down the stairs – that blasted *Scooby-Doo* theme tune, she realized with a grin. Reaching the kitchen, she went straight to the fridge. A blast of freezing air hit her full in the face as she hauled the fridge door open and she shivered. She loved this Tardis of an American-style fridge that could swallow a whole week's shopping and open its gaping mouth for more, the only downside being that she felt as if she was being dunked in an Arctic ice flow every time she opened it.

Actually, the kitchen was cold, colder than it had been when she'd taken Leo upstairs to bed, she realized as she shut the fridge, clasping the bottle of Chardonnay. And even with the fridge door shut, she felt a lingering, tingling chill – not on her face, but from behind her. She lifted a hand to the back of her neck, feeling the raised hairs, the nobbles of goosebumped flesh, refusing to turn, to give in, again, to fear. Stepping sideways, she reached to the cupboard next to the fridge to grab a wine glass. But as she lifted her arm, her gaze was caught by a loose thread on the sleeve of her jumper. It was dancing, waltzing, as if to an inaudible tune. An inaudible tune, or . . . or a breeze?

It's windy outside.

But all the doors and windows are shut and locked.

I checked them, double checked them.

And so—

Forcibly, Denise blanked her mind, shutting and locking the door on her manic, fearful thoughts before they bolted away to that *Scooby-Doo* monster, to that poor sad woman in the pastel-pink suit at the village fete. As she lowered her arm, wine glass in hand, the thread stopped dancing. But the hairs on the back of her neck, the goosebumps refused to settle. *Oh, for God's sake.* Turning, her gaze found the double doors to the garden, the lock.

The key was missing.

It's in the drawer.

But it wasn't in the drawer. Simon wouldn't allow it.

Through the dark glass, she could see the ghostly shape of the weeping willow. Like the thread on her jumper, it too was dancing, waltzing to that silent tune. And superimposed over its shimmying form, reflected in the glass: a thick strip of pale ceramic kitchen floor, the thin, dark brown ridge of the oak table top, her precious aluminium American-style fridge, huge and shiny grey, and the pale blob of her own tense face in front of it.

Something wasn't right. What was it? It took her nervy, addled brain a few moments before she knew. A square of reflection was missing, as if one of the glass panes in the door had been painted a dull black.

Or . . .

Or . . . as if it wasn't there at all.

Yes, she could see that now. One pane, to the right side of the door lock, was missing. And on the floor? Glass. Broken glass.

And now she felt it.

The fear.

Utter terror that clenched a stone-cold fist around her heart.

A scream from upstairs. *Leo. My baby.* The bottle of Chardonnay slid from Denise's hand, and she watched it fall, pitch to the kitchen floor, bounce and crack, but not the bottle – the floor, her precious ceramic tiles. *Oh God, Simon will be furious.*

Another, piercing scream.

Silence.

My baby. Oh God, my baby.

52

Marilyn and Jessie stood on the gravel drive, breath making clouds in the chill night air, listening to the crack of the steel enforcer splintering the Lewins' sage-green-painted front door. One, two, three solid smacks before the lock gave way and the door ricocheted back on its hinges, slamming against an unseen inside wall and jarring back at the firearms team, four black shadows pressed against the brick wall either side of the porch. A black-booted foot was extended to inch the door slowly back open, a raised, black-gloved hand indicated two rooms to the left, another two to the right of the hall, stairs beyond, to the left.

They had rung the front doorbell first, a ludicrously, mundane, everyday action given the tension that radiated like heat from everyone involved in the operation.

Ghostie.

Leo has an active imagination.

It's the weeping willow.

Lifting her latex-gloved hands from where they were glued to her forensic-suited thighs, Jessie pressed them together, fingers steepled, praying. Praying for the little boy and his blonde Boden mum, even though she had lost her belief in God the day she'd found Jamie hanging by his red-and-black-striped school tie from the curtain rail in his bedroom.

The firearms team had waited a full minute after ringing the bell, all eyes fixed on the blank rectangle of sage green. But there had been nothing. No answer. No audible sounds from inside the house. Just the sound of Jessie's own stressed heartbeat knocking in her ears, Marilyn's chill breath hosing the air next to her.

The bell again, longer this time, the sound, a frantic bee in a jam jar, echoing throughout the house. Another tense minute, each second stretching nanometre-thin, each second feeling like an hour in itself.

Still no answer.

The woman – Denise, she was called, Jessie reminded herself, she did have a name, wasn't just 'Boden mum' – was definitely at home. Her husband's frantic 999 call had made that clear. He had telephoned his wife first, twice, calls that had rung and rung unanswered.

Her hands still pressed together in silent prayer, trying to keep the stress she felt from leaking out into other visible tics or jitters, Jessie realized that she had never experienced anything like this in real life, had only seen it stylized on the television screen. The reality was so much grittier and yet, at the same time, much more achingly normal. The grey, graffiti-covered, run-down, drug-fuelled housing estates of television were here transplanted by a street of well-tended detached houses, fronted by paved or gravel drives, bordered by neat flowerbeds and low hedges, a car or two in every drive.

Two marked cars were parked fifty metres either side of them, blocking off the road from traffic, though Jessie doubted many people, apart from residents and their visitors, drove down this quiet, leafy village lane. Their lights cast an intermittent wash of blue across the red-brick fascia of the nearby houses and the gawping faces pressed to upstairs windows, the neighbours having been instructed to stay inside.

'Be careful where you tread and don't touch anything,' Marilyn yelled, for the umpteenth time, at the firearms team's retreating backs as they surged forward through the door and into the house. This time they didn't even lift a hand to acknowledge that he had spoken. Jessie watched them moving down the hallway, giving each other cover, ducking into one room and then the next, shouts of 'Clear' reverberating back into the still night air. She laid a hand on Marilyn's arm.

'What?' he snapped, pulling his gaze from the hallway – empty now, just the muffled sound of feet pounding up carpeted stairs – and fixing it on her.

Dropping her hand, she shook her head. 'Nothing. Just—'

'Chill?'

'Understatement of the century. I know it's beyond hard, but yes—'

'They have a child,' he said. 'He's three years old.'

'I know,' Jessie murmured. *I met him. I met them both.*

They lapsed into tense silence once again. Biting her lip, Jessie dropped her gaze to the drive, hopscotching it across the pale pebbles, a move which transported her straight back to Wittering Beach, early September, just six short weeks ago, to two dead little girls; further, to last November and Sami Scott. A deeply damaged four-year-old boy. Would

Leo, the little boy who lived inside this house, get away with being deeply damaged? *Only* being deeply damaged?

Despite what Jessie had said to Marilyn – her feeble attempt to encourage him to *chill* – Jessie sensed him jittering beside her. He'd had a heated argument with Surrey and Sussex Major Crimes DCI, Janet Backastowe, in the car on the way over here, and Jessie had heard the strain in his voice as he had tried to remain civil. He was by nature a loner – a maverick, he'd probably be called if he was an American fighter pilot – and he didn't take kindly to interference. He had wanted to go into the house first, just him and Jessie, to get a sense of the crime scene and its perpetrator before every Tom, Dick and Harry tramped it to smithereens. But DCI Backastowe wouldn't hear of it.

This situation could potentially be a red herring: a woman who had taken a pill to help her sleep in her husband's absence, bolting upright in her bed in terror at the sight of a masked man, clad fully in black and toting a Heckler & Koch MP5 carbine, in her bedroom, though that scenario, the one they were still all secretly hoping for, was looking increasingly unlikely. Or it could be a crime in progress – *White Fang*, Jessie's name for him, though she hadn't shared it, aware of Marilyn's abhorrence for any tags that glamorized criminals – still in the house, hence DCI Backastowe's insistence that the firearms team went in first to secure the scene. Or it could be a scenario that had already played out its grisly reality, too late to stop another murder. *Two* more murders.

They've got a three-year-old boy.
Leo. He's called Leo.
Denise and Leo.

Whatever happened inside that house this evening, Jessie

277

and Marilyn would be interviewing the husband. His terrified insistence that his wife and son could be the third victims of the killer, of *White Fang*, hadn't escaped either her or Marilyn's attention. What had made him so certain?

It's personal.

Did Denise's husband know what that personal connection was?

And it's about watching.

Watching what – or who? What could possibly have been watched, seen, that had led to this calculated, controlled barbarity?

The murders of the Fullers had made the front page of all the local and regional press, had featured in small articles in the nationals and been discussed at length on local radio and TV news programmes. The second, the Whiteheads', just a few nights later, had propelled the case fully national, newspaper journalists and radio and TV reporters descending on this sleepy corner of Sussex in their droves. And now this, the third – if indeed there was a third – would send it stratospheric. Global. Intergalactic. The pressure was on all of them, and the last thing Marilyn wanted was for the firearms team to stamp all over his forensic evidence with their size twelves before Tony Burrows had had a chance to preserve every stray hair and skin cell of it. But he'd lost. Janet Backastowe was fierce. Jessie could see exactly how she had ended up heading Major Crimes; she wouldn't like to mess with her.

Boots crunching on gravel yanked her back to the present. She looked up into a shocked pale face. The firearms officer was early forties; he'd have been on the job for twenty-plus years, would have seen it all. Almost all.

'The house is clear.'

'Are they dead?' Marilyn asked. No point sugar-coating.

He nodded. 'She. One woman.' He pointed skywards. 'In the bathroom. Door to your right at the top of the stairs. We left it closed.'

'Was that how you found it?' Marilyn snapped.

'Exactly how we found it. The only thing we left is footprints on the carpet, DI Simmons.' A pause. 'We're just doing our job.'

Marilyn nodded curtly. 'Where is the child?'

'There is no child.'

'Are you sure?'

'We've searched the whole place, house and garden. There is no child on the property.'

'Fuck,' Marilyn said, with feeling, though Jessie wasn't sure that she agreed with that sentiment. A missing child still had hope; a dead child had none.

Without meeting her gaze, Marilyn clapped a hand on her shoulder. 'Let's go,' he called back over his shoulder to Tony Burrows, who along with his CSI team was suiting and booting in the road. 'Give us ten minutes, Tony.'

Jessie glanced across at him as they started together down the gravel drive. Marilyn's gaze was still fixed on the rectangle of light-filled hallway visible through the front door. He didn't – *wouldn't*, she sensed – meet her gaze. Not that she blamed him. Her own heart rate was through the roof and she felt as if a cannon ball had been wedged down her throat, a ball that wouldn't go up or down however much she swallowed. She bit her lip, her teeth finding the well-worn groove they'd worked on creating since the moment she'd received Marilyn's call as she and Callan were getting ready for bed, tasting copper this time, blood.

'Ready?' Marilyn asked, pausing on the porch.

No. Jessie nodded.

Marilyn smiled grimly. 'You can think "No", but you can't say it.'

'Was it that obvious?'

'Don't give up your day job to join the World Poker Series.'

Jessie's smile was stressed and fleeting. 'And there I was labouring under the mistaken impression that I had the perfect unreadable psychologist's expression.'

Marilyn matched her smile with a barely there one of his own. 'Sorry to disappoint you, Doctor.'

Side by side, they stepped into the hallway and immediately the sounds of outside dimmed, as if someone had twisted the volume switch to low. Despite the swell of cold air from the open front door chilling the back of Jessie's neck, it was warm inside the house, cosy, the heating turned up in response to the cold autumn night, the dark mahogany wooden floor muffling their footsteps after the crunch of the gravel outside, a relaxing soft beige – there was doubtless an interior designers' name for the colour – on the walls. A dark wooden wall-mounted coat rack to her right, half-hidden behind the open front door, was bunched with adults' coats in muted colours, the central hook topped by a bright red kid's puffa jacket. The sight of the jacket tightened something sharply in Jessie's chest. She hadn't noticed it when she and Cara had come knocking.

Immediately to their left, opposite the coat rack, was the door to the sitting room. The lights were off, the room illuminated only by the pale yellow wash from the street lights outside, intermittently broken by a streak of blue as the lights of the marked cars parked outside in the road swung to flood over the house's facade. She hadn't been in here either – Denise had led them straight to the kitchen.

From where she now stood, in the centre of the room, Jessie could see the black shadowy shapes of the firearms team packing up out on the drive. Burrows' CSI team were beyond them, ghostly white shapes pacing out on the street, reminding her of people she used to see when she was in the military, lit at night through thermal imaging cameras. Out of the patio doors that opened from the opposite end of the room, out into what Jessie assumed must be the garden, she could see only blackness.

Her eyes snapped shut, an automatic defence response to the flood of bright white as Marilyn switched on the overhead light; they opened slowly, squinting and blinking, mole-like, until her irises had contracted sufficiently to cope with the illumination. The windows facing the street were now black mirrors, blotting out the activity outside, locking her and Marilyn alone together in this eerily silent, empty-feeling house, reflecting Marilyn's scarecrow frame and pallid, creased face. Jessie was mirrored back to herself next to him – shorter, her face significantly less creased, but no less pale.

The room was carpeted in earth brown, the sofas upholstered in the same relaxing beige as the walls: safe, easy clean, family friendly colours. The only pop of colour came from a mess of teal-blue scatter cushions, a couple spilled on the floor. Jessie resisted the OCD tug she felt to snatch them up, return them to the sofa, order them all neatly while she was at it. A stack of opaque plastic storage boxes to the left of the fireplace were crammed with kids' toys, a freestanding mahogany bookshelf to the right, with books and DVDs. No other storage space: nowhere else to hide a spare envelope, let alone a child.

Despite having sat in the kitchen of this home a few days

ago, drinking tea and chatting, knowing that Boden mum had chosen the decor, Jessie was still surprised how comfortable the room felt, how homely. *Well, what were you expecting?* The room of a family with more important pulls on their time than to fuss about tidiness – unlike her. The home of a brutally murdered woman and a kidnapped little boy and there were scatter cushions on the sofa, plastic boxes of toys in the corner and a stack of well-thumbed women's magazines on the coffee table. It didn't feel real somehow.

None of this felt real.

While Marilyn searched the study, opposite the sitting room, Jessie opened a door further down the hallway and stepped into a downstairs toilet. It was tiny, the navy-painted walls shrinking the space to telephone-box proportions. Photographs in white frames, scores of them, studded the walls, almost all lovingly charting Leo's journey from babyhood, tiny, hours old, to summer shots of a grinning, blond-haired little boy on a beach, his bare torso spangled with sand, to the same boy zipped into that red puffa jacket, his breath making clouds in chill air. Backing out of the door, Jessie pulled it closed behind her. She would have plenty of time later to study those photographs in painful detail, to get a sense of the family, of how they had lived rather than how they – or *she* at least – had died. Jessie didn't need to disappear down that emotional black hole now. Would the bathroom upstairs be painted in this same navy blue, contrasting stunningly with its shiny white porcelain furniture and the bloodless woman floating in the bath? Not long and she would find out; she wasn't sure that her stomach or her mind were up to it.

'Jessie.'

Marilyn was beckoning her into the kitchen. He was standing by the huge aluminium American-style fridge. The fridge door was hanging open – *The only thing we left is footprints on the carpet, DI Simmons* – the light inside illuminating a two-litre carton of full-fat milk in the door. The blue label was facing outwards, exactly as Jessie arranged her own fridge – hers was deliberate, a function of her OCD, but this one was probably accidental, given the messy scatter of possessions throughout the house and the stack of dirty crockery she could see in the sink. And, just to the left of the fridge, a shatter of green glass in a puddle of liquid on the floor, the ceramic-floor tile in the centre of the shatter, shattered also by the impact of it falling.

Looking up, Jessie surveyed the rest of the kitchen. It was just as she remembered it, comfortable and homely, a chair at the far end of the oak farmhouse table where she and Cara had sat drinking tea pulled out, Lego spilled on the table top in front of it. Beyond the table, the multiple rectangles of glass in the French doors that led to the garden were pitch-black, no houses backing on to this one to cast light, no street lights throwing their illuminating glow either, not even that ghostly weeping willow visible. And out there in the darkness, beyond the broken garden fence, thousands of acres of fields and woodland.

Jessie's back was cold from the open door of the fridge – the feeling she got when she walked down the chilled aisles at the supermarket – but there was something else too, an airy tickle stirring the newly grown hairs around her hairline. But more than that, she had the feeling that someone, some*thing*, was standing outside looking in, outside watching. She shivered.

'Are you OK?' Marilyn's gaze was searching.

Keeping her gaze focused on the glass doors to the garden, Jessie nodded.

'Just getting a sense.'

A silent nod from him in return.

Black framed in the chequerboard of glass rectangles that made up the double doors to the garden. Nothing to see outside. No movement. The only noise the faint, rhythmic thwack-thwack-thwack of a helicopter, not a civilian one at this time of night, so the police helicopter scrambled from Lippet's Hill then. The air support team would doubtless be joined by dog teams, scores of uniforms, everything thrown at this search.

Dogs.

'Jessie?'

'There's a breeze,' she said, in answer. 'Can you feel it?'

'It's from the fridge.'

She shook her head. 'No.'

Stepping away from him, she skirted the kitchen island, the farmhouse table. Light from the back doormat caught in her eyes. But not the doormat, she realized, but a scatter of smashed glass reflecting the ceiling spots back at her in sparkles, like a tiny, broken patch of sea on a boiling hot day. A copper-coloured key lay among the shatter of sparkles.

'The rectangular pane next to the door lock is smashed out,' she said, calling back to Marilyn.

But he was right behind her, had already seen it. The pane was twenty centimetres tall, fifteen wide, plenty big enough to put an arm through, twist the key in the lock.

'It would have made a noise,' Jessie said. 'The glass smashing must have startled her just after she'd got the

284

wine from the fridge—' she broke off, her mind fumbling for an image. 'No, I don't think that works. If the pane had smashed while she'd been at the fridge she would have had a decent head start, while he smashed out the rest of the glass, fumbled for the key, unlocked it – it's not that quick a process. She could have dashed upstairs, grabbed Leo and the phone, locked herself in a bedroom or the bathroom, called the police. We need to check to see if Denise or Leo's bedroom or the bathroom have locks on the doors.' She broke off again, held up a finger. 'So perhaps . . . perhaps he smashed it earlier, while she was upstairs putting Leo to bed, smashed the pane and unlocked the door, but left it closed. It took us a while to see that the pane was missing. You need to look to see, don't you?'

Marilyn nodded.

'If Leo was already in bed when the kitchen door suddenly swung open, Denise would have bolted upstairs, not to the front door and escape, and if she hadn't had much of a head start, she would hardly have made it up the stairs before he—' *before White Fang . . .* she didn't say it '—got to her. She wouldn't have had time to grab Leo and lock them in there. Or perhaps he let himself in earlier, hid somewhere and then Leo woke up and saw a stranger in his bedroom. Maybe Denise heard Leo screaming, dropped the wine and bolted upstairs to try to save him. However, it happened, it's instant power, the presence of a child confers instant, unassailable power to the perpetrator. She would have done anything for the child. It's human nature – mother nature.'

Marilyn nodded. 'When I was a sergeant in Brighton, I worked on a case, a ring of Eastern European men, mugging women with children for their jewellery and money. They'd watch the family house, work out what time the women came home from the school run with the kids and pounce on them. The women would hand over everything they had, wouldn't put up a fight. Like taking sweets off a baby, because of the presence of their children.'

Jessie nodded. Her mind filled with an image, that pale figure from her sleepwalking nightmare. She shivered again. It was so intensely dark outside, it was as if the house had sunk into a lake of black oil. If the killer had been standing outside in the dark garden, looking in, he could have been only a few metres away and Denise wouldn't have been able to see him, not with the kitchen lights on. He could have been out there for hours before he smashed the glass. He could have watched her and Leo, watched their every move, and she would have been oblivious.

The image made Jessie deeply uneasy. How easy it was to voyeur. To stalk. Anyone.

'It's about watching, Marilyn. I'm not sure how or why, but if . . . if he opened the door earlier, he may have stood in the garden watching her while she was feeding Leo, tidying up, helping herself to a glass of wine, knowing, *knowing* that she had only minutes to live and enjoying that knowledge.' Jessie raised her hands, let them fall back to her sides. 'It speaks to the motivation for all this. Watching.' She shivered, but not because of the cold from the open fridge or from the missing pane in the patio door. 'Did the firearms officers say anything about her eyes?'

Marilyn shook his head, his expression grim. 'No,' he muttered, turning towards the door. 'But I think that it's time we found out.'

As they reached the top of the stairs, they heard the regular, persistent drip-drip-drip of a tap.

286

Watching.

And water.

Why always water?

There was a huge, damp swell on the landing carpet that had ballooned out from under a closed door to her and Marilyn's right. The bathroom – must be.

Footsteps squelching in unison, Jessie followed Marilyn across the soaked carpet.

As they paused outside the door, the sound of the dripping tap was swallowed by the rush of Jessie's own pulse in her ears. She glanced at Marilyn. Was he hearing the same? Had his pulse rocketed as hers had done? His expression was inscrutable, his face a mask of professionalism. He had learnt well over his twenty-plus years in Major Crimes to look convincing, at least.

As he raised a latex-gloved hand to push the door open, he glanced behind and met her gaze.

'I'll go in first.' A grim smile. 'I'm used to it.'

'Used to this?'

'You never get used to children. But she's not a child.'

'No . . . but still,' Jessie murmured, thinking, *Shit, shit, shit, get this over with.*

As Marilyn cracked the door open, the smell hit them, dense as liquid, a visceral smell of hell. Of blood and pain and terror and opened human bowels. Jessie pressed her sleeve to her nostrils.

Jesus, this can't be happening.

Another push from Marilyn's latex-gloved hand and the door swung open in one smooth movement.

The first thing Jessie saw was the navy-blue walls, matching the colour of the toilet downstairs sporting its jigsaw of photographs charting Leo Lewin's happy, carefree life. Her

287

gaze fell to the shiny white tiles below the blue, the contrast making them seem almost three-dimensional – or was that the product of the condensation, the pink condensation that peppered the tiles and pooled and ran in rivulets down them? Her gaze slid further down to the white porcelain roll-top of the bath, to an arm. A woman's pale, slender arm dangling over the roll-top. Jessie's overshoes squelched as she took another step forward, focusing on nothing but the arm, relatively benign in its alabaster immobility.

Another step forward and she saw Denise. Her body. Her face.

Ghost-white.

Slack-skinned.

One blue eye wide open, frozen and unseeing. The other socket, sightless.

Spinning around, Jessie ducked out of the bathroom and vomited her pub dinner all over the landing carpet.

53

Five-thirty a.m. and the sky over the red-tiled roofs to the east was lightening, only Venus visible, a bright dot puncturing the royal-blue sky. Jessie sat in the passenger seat of Marilyn's ancient Z3, head tilted back against the headrest, half-comatose with tiredness and shock. Jamming her eyes shut, she stared hard into the insides of her eyelids, trying to rid herself of the image of that bloodless, slack-skinned body, floating in that bathtub of pink soup, that one blank eye socket. To rid her ears of the screams of Denise's husband as he was wrestled to the ground outside his own home, as he lay on the drive sobbing and begging for news about his wife and son, as he was ushered away, limp with shock, by DS Workman.

Jessie had seen Hugo Fuller too, tied to that lounge chair beside his swimming pool, his eyes put out like some medieval torture victim. But for some reason, Denise's body, the reality of her torture and murder, had been a thousand times worse.

Was it because she was a woman? A mother? A mother

who had tried valiantly, to judge from the smashed bedside lamp in Leo's bedroom, the top drawer of his bedside table ripped out and upside down – thrown, towards the door – to defend herself and her son with . . . with nothing. A woman who had sought to escape from the open bedroom window but, with only a stone patio twenty feet below, the drop too far a fall for either her or Leo to survive. Trapped between a literal rock and a metaphorical hard place. Impossible to save herself or her child. Or was it just because Jessie could put herself in that position, could so viscerally emote with Denise, feel her fear and desperation as she'd tried to save herself and her son, in a way that Jessie hadn't been able to emote with Hugo Fuller? Because she had done the same herself, barely a year ago, in Sami Scott's bedroom, trying to save herself and him?

Despite emptying her guts upstairs – *The only thing we left is footprints on the carpet, DI Simmons*; to her shame, she couldn't claim the same – she still felt sick and headachy. She had barely slept in forty-eight hours, she realized, as she fought a strong drag downward into peaceful, uncomplicated unconsciousness. But she couldn't sleep now. *They* couldn't sleep. They had a little boy to find and a murderer to catch.

A sudden burst of cold air chilled her right cheek and her eyes snapped open.

'I'm sorry, Marilyn.'

'For what?' he asked, as he slid into the driver's seat beside her.

'The puke. I don't think Tony Burrows will find it very helpful.'

'He's seen worse.'

Jessie lifted her shoulders. *Not from me.* 'It won't happen again.'

'Never say never,' Marilyn muttered, with a grim smile. 'I have a feeling that our man is only just getting started. Go home and snatch a few hours' sleep and I'll see you in the incident room at ten a.m.'

Jessie shook her head. 'I'm fine. I don't need any sleep.'

Marilyn angled the rear-view mirror towards her. If she had looked up, she would have seen a slim, cracked rectangle of her own pallid face, looking as if she'd aged a hundred years in the last five hours.

'Have you seen yourself recently?'

But she didn't look up. Instead, she turned her head and met Marilyn's appraising, mismatched gaze, focusing on his right eye, the brown one easier to hold somehow than that azure-blue, searching left eye that seemed to have the ability to cut through her, cut through the bullshit.

'We need to find Leo Lewin, Marilyn, and then we need to solve this. We don't have time to rest.'

'The helicopter is out searching. The dog teams are out searching. We've got uniforms going house to house throughout the neighbourhood. We've got a team of volunteers, friends and neighbours getting briefed now, out in the back garden, ready to start as soon as it's light enough, which by my reckoning will be in about two hours. There is nothing you can do.'

'But if—' she broke off. 'If I can get into his mind, work out how he thinks—'

'You won't be able to get into your own mind, to work out how you think, if you don't get some sleep. And I need some shut-eye even if you don't,' Marilyn said, silencing her. 'Eight o'clock. You've got three and a half hours, three by the time we get home. It's a quick and dirty, not a luxury mini-break.'

'Fine.' She reached for the door handle and cranked the elderly car door open. 'Eight o'clock it is. I'll see you at eight.'

'You will indeed. Now go.'

54

Oh God. There was something moving in the dog's basket in the end cage on the right. The empty cage. Cherry could see from where she had stopped, halfway down the walkway between the dogs' cages.

Her heart wedged in her throat, she took a couple of steps closer, stopped again. She still couldn't see what it was, only knew that it was alien, shouldn't be there, that it hadn't been there when she'd checked the dogs' cages and locked up last night. She liked to get in early, grab herself a coffee and spend that first hour with the dogs, alone, absorbing their individual moods, assessing how each was feeling, before her employee, Anne, arrived at eight-thirty and the working day began. But at this precise moment, with her heart jammed in her throat and knocking now like the pendulum on a grandfather clock, she wished that she had dropped that routine the moment she'd realized that someone or some*thing* was letting themselves into Paws for Thought at night.

Stepping sideways, she glanced behind her to the door to

reception, which she knew to be unlocked, the reception area empty; she had just walked through it, looked sideways to the feed-room – a small space, but so many places to hide – then straight ahead to the door to the outside exercise field, which was definitely locked, wasn't it? But as that thought entered her head, another pushed it straight out. The realization that she couldn't rely on any doors being locked, if this nocturnal visitor who seemed to be able to walk straight through walls like a ghost had come last night. And – as her swollen, knocking pendulum of a heart reminded her – could still be here, inside, with her.

The hot military policeman had told her to be careful.

Do you think I'm at risk?

Someone has been accessing your facility, for reasons that you don't understand. They haven't yet done any harm, but I'd suggest that you take care. Until you understand their motivation, what they want, you don't know how they might react if you disturb them.

So why hadn't she listened to him and timed her arrival to coincide with that of her employee's? Because she'd always been impetuous. Impetuous and stupid – or just plain stupid?

55

A knock.

'Come,' Marilyn said.

The door swung open and DC Cara stepped into the room, gaze downcast, shoulders slumped somewhere around his knees, as if someone had tossed a hundred-kilo sack of coal onto his back.

Marilyn raised an eyebrow. 'That good, eh?'

'Leo Lewin hasn't been found, Guv.'

'Yet.'

Cara nodded dispiritedly. '*Yet*.'

'Update me.' Marilyn indicated the chair directly across the table. Jessie, positioned at an elliptical angle, felt a twinge of pity for Darren Cara. Tension, driven by an overwhelming desire not to make any mistakes, show himself up in front of the boss, radiated from him like heat. Having to sit opposite Marilyn, pinned to the chair by that unremitting mismatched gaze, would do nothing for Cara's confidence, particularly as he was clearly the bearer of bad news.

'The, uh, the helicopter found someone out in the woods

at six-thirty a.m., but it . . . it, sorry, *he*, turned out to be a dog walker,' Cara began.

'At half-six on a cold, drizzly autumn morning. For Christ's sake, why can't people stay in bed like I do, drinking coffee and bingeing on box-sets?'

Cara smiled and shrugged. 'The poor old geezer got the shock of his life when he was surrounded by armed officers and told to hit the deck, so he'll probably ditch the morning walk for a few days at least.'

'Old?' Marilyn wryly raised one eyebrow.

Cara shrugged again. 'Mid-forties, he was at least.'

'Stop digging, Darren,' Workman, who had just stepped into the room, said with a smile.

'What about the dogs?' Jessie cut in. She wasn't in the mood for humour: even the graveyard kind that she knew sustained investigations such as this, kept them from burying themselves too far underneath everyone's skin. She still felt exhausted, physically and mentally, and at sea with this case. The thought that a little boy was out there somewhere, that they hadn't yet found him, had no clues, no leads, no idea where to look, made her sick to her stomach and furious with herself – furious that she couldn't see their perpetrator better, that the only image she held of him was of Lupo, of a dog, a huge, white, wolf-like dog.

'They lost the trail,' Cara replied.

'Why? Because of the rain?' Jessie asked.

Cara shook his head. 'Evidently light rain helps dogs track. It freshens the scent, the dog teams told me, releases it.'

Marilyn grimaced.

'So what happened?' Jessie continued. 'Why did they lose the trail?'

'It took them a while to pick up the scent to start with. They were circling.'

'In the garden?'

'Yes.'

'Do you remember, Cara, when we talked to Denise a few days ago, that she said her son had woken up screaming, that he said he'd seen something in the back garden?'

Cara nodded. 'A ghostie.'

'Yes.' *White. Like Lupo.*

Marilyn sat forward, looking from Jessie, to Cara and back. 'What did Denise say?'

Jessie gave Cara an almost imperceptible nod, encouraging him to take over.

'She said that her husband had left Leo's curtains open,' Cara said. 'There's a weeping willow in the middle of the back garden. It's pale silver, there was a bright, gibbous moon that night and a breeze that was moving the willow's fronds.'

'So she dismissed the ghostie as the tree?'

'Not entirely. Simon Lewin went out to check the garden, to make the little boy feel safe. When he came back in he told her he'd seen footprints in front of the tree.'

'A man's footprints,' Jessie cut in.

Marilyn arched an eyebrow. 'Watching?'

Jessie didn't respond to his question.

'The back fence is broken and beyond their garden is woods and fields,' she said instead. 'Dogs sometimes run into their garden from the public footpath that cuts along outside their back fence. Lewin persuaded Denise that the footprints were from a dog walker who had come in to fetch their errant dog, but I'm not sure she was convinced. I think that she wanted to believe, rather than *did* believe.'

Marilyn nodded. 'We need to ask the husband and neighbours whether they saw anyone hanging around the woods near the back fence or even out front, in the street, in the days preceding the murder, or if he noticed anything else strange, anything out of the ordinary. Something that he might have dismissed before, like those footprints, which now seem more sinister given what has happened.'

Workman had flipped open her black notebook and was scribbling.

'And the back fence,' Marilyn asked. 'When was it broken and how? Was it wear and tear, lack of maintenance, or did someone break a hole in it, an action that they might have dismissed as accidental? These are standard questions in any investigation, but given the footprints, the fact that Jessie is convinced our man watches his victims for a period of time before the murders, it's even more important in this case.' He turned to Cara. 'Finish telling us about the search dogs, Cara.'

Cara nodded, taking a moment to mentally re-find his place in the telling. 'Yes, uh, as I said, the dogs circled in the garden for a while, then one of the handlers took his dog to the gap in the fence, physically led it to the gap, and the dog picked up a scent that led out into the woods. But it got confused again quickly, as if there were lots of trails.'

'There were lots of trails, in the garden and in the woods,' Jessie said.

'Because of the watching?'

She lifted her shoulders, avoiding Marilyn's searching gaze.

'How do dogs follow scent?' she directed the question back to Cara. 'What specifically do they scent? Which, uh, which part of the human?'

'Footprints,' Cara said. 'The scent laid by footprints is evidently the strongest, but people also continually shed skin cells, strands of hair, that kind of thing, and the dogs track the scent from those. And anything dropped, by the perpetrator or a child. The dogs can smell and see those well before humans can.'

'That makes sense,' Jessie said.

'The scent was weak, anyway, the dog teams said.'

'Whose trail were they following? Leo's or the perpetrator's?'

'Both. They tried both. But Leo's was too weak to follow.'

'He must have been carrying Leo,' Marilyn cut in.

'Yes, but shouldn't there be a trail from the child, even if he wasn't walking?' Jessie asked. 'Because of the skin cells?' *Unless . . . unless he was wrapped in something. Dead, was he dead when he left the house?* She voiced her thoughts. 'Unless he was wrapped in something.'

Marilyn swung around in his chair to face her. 'Are you saying that you think Leo Lewin was dead when he left the house?'

She shook her head firmly. 'No, that's not what I'm saying. Leo was . . . is just three. It wouldn't have been hard to carry a terrified three-year-old in a bag such as a rucksack, shove him in and tell him to be quiet or he's dead too. Or . . . or pretend that it was a game.'

She met Marilyn's gaze, recognized the flash of understanding in his eyes.

She turned her attention back to Cara again. 'So there were multiple trails to start with and the scent from the child was very weak?'

Cara nodded. 'And there's a stream, cutting through the woods a few hundred metres from the back of the Lewins' house. The dog handlers said that the dogs got confused when they reached the stream, couldn't work out which direction they were supposed to go in.'

'I thought dogs could track people through water? They do in Louisiana, in the swamps,' Marilyn said.

'In films,' Jessie countered, with the ghost of a smile.

'Like I said, nothing better than a box-set on a cold autumn morning.'

'Stagnant water is fine,' Cara continued, clearly not wanting to be knocked off his stride by banter. 'The dogs just circle the water until they find the scent again. The issue with running water is that the water carries the scent with it. So if the perpetrator enters the stream and runs in the opposite direction to the flow of water, his or her scent is masked and the dogs follow the scent in the opposite direction.'

'It can't be that easy,' Marilyn said.

Cara shrugged.

'They're dogs, not super-humans,' Jessie cut in. 'Or super-dogs, even if you've watched *Bolt* during one of your box-set binges.'

'*Bolt* isn't a box-set. It's a film,' Marilyn said with a theatrical roll of his eyes. 'We can assume, then, that our man walked in the opposite direction to the flow of the water?'

'Yes, which is what the dog teams concluded. They retraced their steps and followed the water upstream.'

'And?'

'Half a kilometre or so up, they reached a road that bridged the stream.'

Marilyn sat back and crossed his arms over his chest. 'Jesus Christ, and don't tell me, it's a quiet, secluded country lane that no bugger ever uses, or certainly not in the middle of the bloody night in late October, when it's brass monkeys outside.'

Cara shrugged. 'The dogs are much more useful when chasing a fleeing perpetrator, evidently, than if the perpetrator has already fled, if they had a decent head start.'

Marilyn nodded. 'Dr Ghoshal estimates that Denise Lewin had been dead for ninety minutes to three hours by the time we found her in that bath, so our man was long gone by the time the dogs started looking for him.' He ground his fingers through his hair. 'And that would put the time of the murder between nine-thirty and eleven p.m.' He looked from one to the other. 'We need to find witnesses. Anyone who saw a car, motorbike or bike – though clearly car is the most likely. That quiet country lane must join to a busier one. There weren't any tyre prints, perchance, were there?'

He didn't even need to wait for Cara to shake his head to know the answer to that question. 'The dogs were never going to be able to track him, not with a stream out there, a stream that led to a deserted bloody road. The bastard was lucky.'

'He wasn't lucky. The dogs were never going to be able to track him, not in any conditions,' Jessie murmured.

'What do you mean?'

She didn't answer. *What do I mean?* She had an image of a dog, a wolf-like dog, fixed in her mind. She thought of Lupo, how she had seen him early this morning, when she'd arrived home from the Lewins' house, for her snatched kip. He had been lying on the doormat in the kitchen, gazing out of the glass doors into the back garden, the sun a strip of yellow-orange fire on the horizon. She had sat down on the cold floor next to him and looked into his ice-blue eyes, so similar to her own, and she had thought that she would be able to understand him, communicate with him. But there had been nothing – no connection. He had continued to lie on the doormat, his head resting on his paws, whining softly, unreadable and unreachable. For some reason, Jessie had an image of their killer as the same. Did she just have that image because of basic psychology – the weirdo loner – or was it more than that? She didn't know. *Yet. I don't know yet.*

'At least he's left footprints all over the place.' Marilyn's voice pulled her back. 'Burrows confirmed that the footprints are the same as those from both the Fuller and the Whitehead murder scenes. We have something.'

Jessie gave a distracted half-nod, more to herself than to Marilyn.

'I detect cynicism in that barely there, hugely unconvincing nod, Dr Flynn,' he said.

Jessie shrugged. 'He's clever, well organised and careful and footprints are so obvious.'

'They're also unavoidable in muddy ground. He either had to come in the front way, on tarmac and gravel, which would have been fine at the Fullers' isolated house, but significantly riskier at the Whiteheads' and yesterday at the Lewins'.'

'For what it's worth, I think that Leo will be found alive,' Jessie murmured.

Marilyn's head swivelled in her direction. 'Why?'

'Because he could have killed Lupo, but he didn't. He made a big effort to ensure that Lupo was found quickly, and in doing so he alerted the police – us – to the fact that he had murdered the Fullers. They were murdered on Saturday night. Workman has spoken to their friends who

302

confirmed that, as far as they knew, the Fullers had no plans that weekend. They probably wouldn't have been found until Monday or Tuesday when Hugo Fuller's secretary started wondering where the hell her boss was and gone around to his house to find him or called the police. The perp set us on his trail days early, purely to baby a dog.'

'Sure, but Lupo is not a child,' Marilyn countered.

'Lupo *is* a dependent, domesticated, kept as a pet, dependent on people in the same way that a child is. Sparing Lupo shows that he has humanity. And he also murdered the Whiteheads when Sophie was out. Again, I think that was deliberate, so as not to cause collateral damage among dependents.'

Marilyn rolled his eyes. 'You're telling me that we're dealing with a gentleman killer, despite the fact that he gouges people's eyes out?'

'I'm telling you that we're dealing with someone who has some humanity, yes.' Jessie suppressed a smile. 'Humanity and doganity. The teenager and the dog were spared and I'm sure that Leo will also be spared. Despite what he's done, I believe that our killer isn't a monster. He has a reason for what he's doing – a reason that makes total sense to him.'

'I think you've officially lost it, Dr Flynn, but I would love you to be right. I would dearly love you to be right.'

56

When Cara had left, Marilyn tilted back in his seat and let out a heavy sigh.

'Coffee?' Workman asked, sliding her chair back and pushing herself to her feet. She looked as weary as Jessie felt. In fact, the three of them would be shoo-ins for bit-parts as zombies in *Night of the Living Dead*.

'Please, Sarah, and toss three spoonfuls of sugar in it, will you. Despite the two coffees I've already had this morning, my brain refuses to engage, and I need to be vaguely awake when we interview Mr Simon Lewin. Perhaps a sugar hit will do the trick.' He glanced at his watch. It was nine-thirty, sunny outside now, and though the breeze from the window that Marilyn had cracked open was chilly, it was not cold enough to shock any of them out of their sleep-deprived stupor.

'Coffee, Jessie?' Workman asked.

'Yes, please, Sarah. Milk, no sugar.'

'What are you thinking, Dr Flynn?' Marilyn asked, when Workman had left the room. He smothered a yawn with the back of his hand.

'I'm thinking the same as you're thinking, Marilyn.' She smiled an exhausted, ragged smile. 'Or at least, I think I'm thinking what you're thinking.'

'I'm wondering why murder scene three, Denise Lewin, was so different from the previous two, despite the footprints indicating that she was murdered by the same perpetrator. The only consistency is that Denise, as with the other wives, was drowned.'

Jessie nodded. 'I'm wondering the same. Why was Denise killed and Simon Lewin spared? I'm pretty sure that our perp has a reason for killing the adults he's killing, and a reason for killing them the way that he kills them. And why did he gouge one of her eyes out and leave the other? It's as if he didn't have the stomach to take them both out.'

'Because she's a woman?' Marilyn ventured.

Jessie lifted her shoulders. 'Perhaps. I think . . . thought that the reason he gouges the men's eyes out is because they have seen something, watched something that he thinks they need to atone for. And he watches them first too – enjoys the sensation that he is watching them, while they are oblivious. Watching, waiting and planning, working himself up to . . . to the task.'

Marilyn raised an eyebrow. 'The task?'

'Yes. I—' she broke off. She was about to say – *Task is as good a word as any* – but she realized that wasn't true. She was used to choosing her words carefully; it was critical when she was dealing with people, patients, who were paranoid, severely anxious, obsessive, suicidal, the whole gamut of mental illness. Her subconscious had supplied her with the word 'task' for a reason.

The door opened and Workman came into the room, balancing three chipped mugs full of steaming, murky liquid on a large black notebook. Setting the notebook on the table, she handed Marilyn a yellow mug and Jessie a white mug adorned with a blue sausage dog in a natty pink jumper. Taking the third cup, she sat down.

'Sarah, have you got anywhere with finding similar crimes from previous years, any with similar modus operandi, either in Surrey and Sussex, or from other forces?' Jessie asked.

'Nothing even faintly similar. And I also haven't yet found any connection between the three sets of victims.'

Jessie looked back to Marilyn. 'You said, back when we were sitting in your car outside the Lewins' house this morning, that he was just getting started.'

Marilyn raised an eyebrow and nodded. 'I didn't think that you were in any state to remember what I said.'

'I was and I don't agree. Despite what Sarah just said about not yet being able to find a connection between the victims, I'm sure that there is one, and I think that these murders are a task. A job to be ticked off and that may soon be done . . . may already be done. That perhaps Denise Lewin was the last.'

'Why?'

'Because I'm certain that the motivation is personal and how wide can personal be?'

'Perhaps Simon Lewin was spared because the personal relates to Denise and not her husband, and Simon, like Leo, would have been collateral damage?' Workman suggested.

Jessie shook her head. 'Both partners were killed in the other murders and, from the level of violence inflicted on the men versus the women and the whole theatre of each murder scene, I'm pretty sure that the primary victims were the men.' She glanced at Marilyn. 'And we did agree that

Denise's murder scene felt . . . odd . . . different to the other two. We don't know why though.'

'Didn't Simon Lewin say, last night, that he was on a last-minute business trip?' Marilyn cut in, directing the question to Workman.

Workman nodded. 'He told me, when we stopped him outside his house last night, that he'd been on a last-minute business trip to Wiltshire filling in for a sick colleague. Perhaps the murderer thought that Lewin was at home and found out, too late, that he was away. Lewin's 999 call was panicked, so he clearly knew that Denise was in danger.'

'Though that does beg the question why he left her alone in the first place if he thought she might be in danger,' Jessie said.

'Unless it was the Whiteheads' murder that made him realize that he – they – would also be targeted,' Marilyn said. 'Lewin might have dismissed the Fullers' murders as a one-off, related to Hugo Fuller's business, but when the Whiteheads were murdered, he realized that he and Denise were next.' He met Jessie's gaze. 'Which concurs with your personal theory.'

Jessie looked from Marilyn to Workman and back. She voiced what they must all, surely, be thinking. 'Or the other option, of course, is that Simon Lewin is our murderer.'

Marilyn nodded sagely. 'That is, indeed, a possibility.'

'Lord,' Workman said, inhaling deeply. 'We've certainly got our work cut out.'

57

Taking another step sideways, Cherry Goodwin slid the belt from around her waist and unlatched the cage immediately to her left. It housed a Rottweiler, as old as Methuselah and deaf as a bedpost, but he was huge and anyone who had watched *The Omen* – which had to be most people, hadn't it? – would be terrified of him. Swinging his door open, gritting herself against the intermittent squeaks, wishing she'd oiled the hinges, mentally adding that to her arm's length 'to-do' list, she stepped inside. The Rottweiler – Damien, she'd called him, for obvious reasons – stood there, gentle as a lamb, while she slid her belt through his collar and hauled him out of his cage and into the walkway.

'Come,' she said quietly.

Clutching the belt tight in one hand, pulling Damien to her hip, she moved forward, catching her ghostly advancing reflection in the glass door that led to the outside exercise field; her pale face, floating, disembodied, above her navy jumper and the whites of Damien's eyes, visible as two huge orbs punctured by the jet black of his irises and pupils.

As they neared the end of the walkway and the empty cage, the dog began to growl.

Was he sensing her fear? Or reacting to his own?

She laid a hand on his head, as much to reassure herself as him, felt the timbre of his growl, low and fierce, vibrating against her palm.

Oh God.

Lifting the hand from his head, white, so white – *Why is my hand so drained of colour?* – she slid the latch back on the cage. The back of the cage, the basket, was in half-darkness. She still couldn't see. *What is it?* She stepped into the cage, towing Damien, growling, resisting, behind her. *What* is *it? Just a bundle of clothes?* No – a blanket – a blanket thrown over something.

As she took a step forward, there was a piercing cry. Her own, she realized, a millisecond later as Damien ripped the belt from her hand and shot out of the cage. She leapt back, slamming into the wall of the cage.

Moving. It was moving.

God help me.

And then she saw a face. As ghostly white as her own.

A thing? A doll? A horror, demon doll?

She felt a warm trickle down her legs.

No, not a doll, a dog. A white dog's face. But the dog's face wasn't attached to a dog's body.

What the fuck?

It was attached to that of a human. A human child. Cherry watched, rooted to the spot, as the little body in the basket twisted and writhed, its tiny hand pawing at the mask covering its face, pawing, grasping, tearing it off.

A little boy stared up at her, as shocked and terrified as she was.

A balloon of pent-up air burst from her lungs.

Oh God, you poor little thing. Your poor poor little thing.

58

Marilyn sighed. 'Perhaps there are no links between the victims and our man is just a sociopath or a psychopath, killing serially for pleasure.'

Jessie shook her head. 'That's too easy.'

'Complex isn't always the answer, Jessie.'

'No, not always, but . . .' she tailed off. The snatched three hours' sleep had just seemed to exacerbate her exhaustion and dull her brain. She felt as if her head was wrapped in thick mulch, as if her whole body was sinking into a vat of it, no mental or physical energy to resist.

'But what?'

'The Psychopathy Checklist Revised, which is the most common checklist used to assess someone as a sociopath or a psychopath, states that a sociopath tends to be nervous and easily agitated and that they are volatile and prone to emotional outbursts, including fits of rage. They're likely to be uneducated and live on the fringes of society, unable to hold down a steady job or stay in one place for very long. We know that our killer's not a sociopath because crimes committed by sociopaths, including murder, will tend to be haphazard, disorganized and spontaneous rather than planned. These murders were meticulously well planned and very efficiently executed.'

Marilyn winced at the word 'executed'.

'Sorry,' Jessie said. 'Carried out. Is that better for your sensitivities?'

'Much better, Doctor.'

'As we know, he was watching the Fullers and Whiteheads before their murders, possibly for an extended period of time. Watching and planning. He brought a lead to the Fullers', for Christ's sake, to take Lupo away with him. He may have collected Sophie from Sheiks and driven her home, just to draw out the pleasure of his kill. He left multiple trails to confuse the search dogs at the Lewins'.'

'Unless Simon Lewin is our man; there would already be multiple trails from him in his own garden.'

'But not out in the woods behind his house, unless he laid them there deliberately because he's our man, which again concurs with an extended period of planning.'

'I concede both those points,' Marilyn said with a wry smile. 'Psychopaths are highly intelligent and their crimes, whether violent or non-violent, will be highly organized and generally offer few clues for authorities to pursue. QED. I've read the Psychopathy Checklist Revised too. At six o'clock this morning actually. Homework.'

It was Jessie's turn to roll her eyes. 'If I had a gold star, I'd give it to you, but you'll have to settle for finishing your cold coffee instead. Psychopaths *are* usually highly intelligent and can be very charming and disarming, but they are basically playacting because they are unable to feel real empathy with others or to feel remorse. They learn to mimic emotions, despite their inability to actually feel them, so they'll appear normal to unsuspecting people. Some are so good at manipulation and mimicry that they have families and other long-term relationships without those around them ever suspecting their true nature. And, as you pointed out, when committing crimes, psychopaths carefully plan out every detail in advance and often have contingency plans in place.'

Marilyn raised a hand and mimed making a tick in the air with his index finger. Ignoring him, Jessie ploughed on.

'But, for me the key is that whole "playacting" thing. A psychopath feels no empathy and no remorse, not towards people or animals. They have no empathy for other living creatures – full stop. One of the key traits that bind psychopaths is the torturing and killing of animals, before they move on to the torturing and killing of people. In my opinion, there is no way that our man is a psychopath, because not only did he spare Lupo, he went out of his way to ensure that Lupo was found.'

Marilyn sighed.

'I hate to sound like a broken record, but I'm sure it's personal, Marilyn, and I'm also sure that our killer is very disturbed, but not sociopathic or psychopathic.' Jessie sat back, crossing her arms over her chest. 'When we find out what the personal connection is, we find him.'

With another, more theatrical sigh, Marilyn laid his hands flat on the table top and pushed himself to his feet. 'OK, Doctor, I believe you. Now shall we go and have that chat with Mr Lewin and see if he can enlighten us?'

Jessie held up a hand. 'Yes, but before we go to talk to Lewin, we need to agree a strategy.'

Marilyn didn't have time to formulate a reply before the door was flung open and DC Cara burst into the room.

59

'It is customary to knock, DC Car—'

'Leo Lewin has been found, Guv.' The words rushed out of Cara in an unbroken, barely intelligible stream.

Marilyn slumped back down in his chair with such a thump that it was as if someone had hacked him off at the knees. Lifting his arms above his head, he raised his eyes to the ceiling. 'Thank you, God, for finally giving us a break, in every sense of the word.'

After his last case, Jessie knew that he had been beyond stressed about the disappearance of the little boy.

'Where was he found?' she asked Cara.

'You're not going to believe this.'

She wasn't so sure that he was right. 'Was he left, safe and well at Paws for Thought, the dog-rehoming charity in Forestside?'

Cara swung around to face her. The expression on his face resembled that of a five-year-old whose mind has just been boggled by seeing a magician pull a live rabbit from a top hat for the first time.

'Left there some time during the night, while the charity was closed? Put into the cage at the far end of the kennel room on the right-hand side?'

'How did you know?' stammered Cara.

Jessie flashed him a guilty half-smile, before turning to meet Marilyn's laser-sighted, mismatched gaze.

'Am I missing something or are you in the wrong job?' he snapped. 'Shouldn't you be dressing in a black headscarf and calling yourself Baba Vanga?'

At times like this, she found it far easier to hold the gaze of his milder-mannered brown eye than risk connecting with that piercing azure-blue one that could cut through steel.

'Someone has been letting themselves into Paws for Thought at night,' she said.

It took Marilyn a moment to reply. 'Sorry – what did you say?'

'Someone has been letting themselves into Paws for Thought at night. Not every night, just some nights.'

'There must be police reports if someone has been breaking in.'

'They haven't been breaking in. They've been letting themselves in. They either have a key or can pick locks.'

'What are they doing when they're there? Stealing things? Hurting the dogs?'

She shook her head. 'Hanging out.'

'You're not making any sense, Dr Flynn,' Marilyn snapped, rubbing a hand over his eyes. 'Not to me, at any rate.'

Jessie sighed. She appreciated that what she was about to say sounded mad – madder even than everything else she had told Marilyn to date.

When she had finished filling him in on Cherry Goodwin's

night visitor, he barked out an incredulous half-laugh. 'I assume you're joking.'

'Unfortunately, I'm not. Cherry told me a couple of days ago, when I went to adopt Lupo.'

Fishing around in her handbag, she withdrew the rubber bone that she had taken from the charity in a plastic freezer bag and laid it on Marilyn's desk. Marilyn looked as if she had just dropped a steaming dog turd in front of him.

'I took the bone. It has teeth marks in it, human teeth marks.'

Picking up the freezer bag, he turned the bone around in his hands. 'Why didn't you tell me about this before?' he asked finally, looking up.

'Because I didn't think it was relevant to the case.' She shrugged. 'I didn't know how it could possibly be relevant, but as soon as DC Cara came in, it just seemed obvious. It's circular and it all comes back to dogs. To dogs and to watching and to being personal.'

'Of course, there will be no witnesses to Leo Lewin being left because our man is far too clever for that.'

Jessie met his gaze and raised an eyebrow.

'What?' Marilyn asked, suspicion in his tone.

'I asked Callan to give Cherry some advice about security. He installed a couple of CCTV cameras.'

Marilyn lifted his hands to the ceiling again. 'Hallelujah. Though I'm sure that I don't need to point out to you that the local dog-rehoming charity is not military police jurisdiction.'

'He didn't do any policing. Cherry was worried, unsurprisingly. The CCTV cameras she had up were dummies as deterrents, which made no sense when you can buy a great nanny cam off the Internet for fifty quid.'

'So, last night should have been recorded on a CCTV camera hidden inside a teddy bear?'

'A Border Collie.'

Marilyn rolled his eyes. 'A what?'

Jessie grinned. 'Actually, I have no idea, though I do absolve myself entirely of responsibility. However, being a good military man, I'm sure that camouflage would have been at the top of Callan's mind.'

'God help me. Though at least there's a decent chance that our perp didn't spot the cameras, if Captain Callan installed them.' He swung around to Cara. 'Get Tony Burrows over there five minutes ago with his CSI cavalry.'

'Already done. Burrows has locked the whole place down. He and his team took Leo's clothes, nail scrapings, the works, and they're now going through the place with a fine-tooth comb.'

Marilyn leant back in his seat and ground his fingers through his hair. 'And there I was thinking that you were barking up the wrong tree with your dogs, Baba Vanga. But you may have something, though God knows what, let alone how it all fits together. Now shall we go and see what Simon Lewin has to say about all this?'

Jessie nodded. 'Sure, but as I said before, first we need to agree a strategy.'

60

'Am I under arrest?'

Simon Lewin was a tall man with dark hair cut short, a strong, square-jawed face and deep brown eyes. He should have been handsome, but there was something about him, an edge, an undercurrent, that twisted his good looks and made them unattractive. What was it exactly? Jumping to conclusions about people was entirely against the ethos of Jessie's profession – *Keep an open mind, peel away the layers, look for the cause behind the effect* – but for some reason she didn't feel unfair taking a leap in relation to Lewin. She realized suddenly that her thoughts had subconsciously driven her to lean back in the chair, fold her arms across her chest, body language that radiated doubt, said 'I'm closed for arguments', before the man had even opened his mouth. It was schoolboy-error psychology. Subtly, she tilted forward, unlocking her arms and resting one forearm lightly on the table edge, deliberately relaxing her facial muscles, curving the corners of her mouth into an enquiring smile that she hoped didn't look as false as it felt.

She and Marilyn had agreed on a strategy: Marilyn's job was to elicit the words; hers to decode the nuances of Lewin's behaviour, what his subconscious was telling them in the minute changes of facial expression that people found it hard to actively control, in the tone of his voice, in the subtle movements of his body. They had also agreed not to tell Lewin that Leo had been found. They wanted him fearful, on edge, and feeling as if he needed to keep them on side to ensure they put the maximum effort into finding his son. They would have done so anyway, irrespective of how his father behaved, but parental love was a strong motivator.

Marilyn raised an eyebrow. 'Should you be under arrest, Mr Lewin?' he said, in response to Lewin's question.

Lewin shook his head jerkily. The movement reminded Jessie of Callan, of the unconscious movement he made when he thought of Iraq, of the piece of shrapnel lodged inside his brain. What was inside Lewin's? No physical foreign body, surely? A psychological one then? An uncomfortable truth? Or a pack of lies and deceit?

'No, of course I shouldn't be under arrest.' His tone unnecessarily aggressive. 'Have you found my son?'

Jessie sensed Marilyn pause for a fraction of a second. It didn't come naturally to a policeman to lie. She held her breath.

'Leo was found safe and well half an hour ago,' Marilyn said.

Fuck. She resisted the urge to whip her head around, give Marilyn an evil stare for blowing a core part of their agreed strategy out of the water within the first minute. In her opinion, he had just made their job significantly harder, pulled the rug from under the one advantage that they had – unless Lewin already knew that Leo would be found safe, because he'd left his son at Paws for Thought in the first place.

Lewin froze for a few seconds, his eyes fixed on Marilyn's, and then his head fell to his hands. Jessie and Marilyn sat in silence, watching his shoulders shake. After a minute or so, he straightened and massaged the heels of his hands into his eyes.

'I need to see Leo.'

'He's been taken to St Richard's Hospital in Chichester for a check-up. He is being looked after by specially trained family liaison officers and he's fine.'

Lewin rocketed from his chair. 'I need to see him now.'

'Sit down please, Mr Lewin.'

'I want to see my son.'

'Sit down, Mr Lewin.' No 'please' this time.

'For Christ's sake, I'm the victim here and I want to see my son *now*.'

Marilyn stayed sitting, though Jessie could tell he was fighting the urge not to rocket from his chair as well. 'Your wife is the victim, Mr Lewin,' he snapped. 'Not you. Now sit down *now*. I won't ask you again.'

Simon Lewin remained standing, glaring contemptuously at Marilyn. The tension in the room was palpable, two stags squaring off for a fight, the reason not a female, but a child. Or more accurately, dominance, always the reason for males' rutting fights.

'This had better be quick,' Lewin said, sitting finally. The sentence a consolation prize to salvage his ego, Jessie recognized.

'It will take as long as it takes,' Marilyn replied, not giving Lewin's ego an inch.

Jessie glanced quickly across. Marilyn's thin face was set

into an intractable rectangle. He wasn't treating Lewin as the innocent husband of a murdered woman, the frightened father of a recently missing child, despite refusing to lie about Leo being found.

'Firstly, I'm sorry for your loss,' Marilyn said, resetting the tone of the discussion.

Lewin gave a curt nod in response.

'But before I let you visit your son, I need to ask you a few questions.'

'I don't know who killed my wife.'

Marilyn raised a hand.

'I was on a business trip to Wiltshire,' Lewin continued. 'I left home at five a.m. on Tuesday morning and returned last night, as you know.'

'What do you do?'

'I'm a travel agent. I was checking out some new hotels to list. We're trying hard to promote UK tourism.'

'We'll need the names and contact details of everyone you met with.'

Lewin's eyes widened. 'Why do you need those details?'

'It's purely routine.'

Frowning, he shook his head. 'Routine isn't good enough. They're business contacts. I don't want the police calling them. It wouldn't look right.'

Marilyn eyeballed Lewin across the table. 'Your wife has been murdered and your son kidnapped, thankfully now returned safe, Mr Lewin. I'm sure that your clients would feel nothing but sympathy for you. My detective constable, Darren Cara, will sit down with you once this meeting is over and get a list of names and contact details.'

The frown lines between Lewin's eyes deepened. 'I'm sorry, but I'm not comfortable with the police calling our clients.

They won't be able to tell you anything that I can't. I'm an employee, for God's sake, not the business owner. I can't be made responsible for any damage to my employer's business that your . . . your . . . your . . .'

Jessie tensed in fascinated horror, expecting Lewin to spit out the word *plods*. Or worse, *pigs* . . . *filth*, even.

'Staff,' he spluttered eventually, 'might cause by poorly handled interviews.'

'My staff are exceptionally well trained and I can assure you that they will be sensitive,' Marilyn replied, entirely unruffled. 'The matter is not up for discussion.' He looked pointedly down at the black notebook open on the table in front of him, cutting eye contact.

Throughout his discussion with Marilyn, Lewin's hands had been knotted together, as if he needed to tie them down to stop his agitation – his agitation and his lies – from transferring themselves into body language tics. Jessie resisted the urge to broadcast her conclusion. Marilyn had many years' experience in interviewing suspects and she had none, zip, zilch. But what she did have was experience of counselling disturbed patients, the depressed, pathological liars, sociopaths, psychopaths, and from that experience a keen sense of people. She mentally bagged the information to divulge to Marilyn later.

'You finished your last meeting at what time?' Marilyn asked.

'Seven-thirty p.m. or thereabouts. It was over drinks in a pub.' A pause, before he quickly added, 'I only had a small glass of red.'

'And you then drove home?'

'I sat in my car in the pub car park and ate a sandwich I'd bought earlier in the day and then I drove home.'

Marilyn nodded. 'And you left the car park at what time?'

'Shortly after eight.'

'Did anyone see you sitting in your car?'

He shook his head.

'Unsurprisingly,' Marilyn muttered. 'What was the name of the pub?'

'The, uh, the Fox . . . something with foxes.' Lewin paused. 'The Fox Goes Free – that was it.'

'Where in Wiltshire were you?'

'All over.'

'Where was your last meeting? Where is the Fox Goes Free?'

'Chippenham.'

'So you took the M4, A34, M3, M27 back to Chichester?'

Lewin's eyes widened.

'My sister lives in Calne,' Marilyn said, by way of explanation.

Though Jessie knew that Marilyn had once been married, had two children, she struggled to envisage him as anything beyond the stereotypical maverick policeman, the self-contained loner. She couldn't imagine a sister, a female Marilyn. The mind boggled.

'No, I didn't take that route.'

'Why not? It's the obvious one. The only one that makes sense, I'd venture to say.'

Lewin shrugged. 'I drove across country.'

Marilyn raised an eyebrow. 'It gets dark at five p.m., so it couldn't have been for the views.'

'I drove there via the A34 and M4 on Tuesday morning. There are roadworks on the A34 and what should have been a two-and-a-half hour journey took me four and a half. My satnav said that the A34 was clogged on the way

323

back, and I didn't fancy spending the evening stuck in traffic.'

Marilyn nodded. He wasn't giving much away in terms of words, expression or tone of voice. But neither now was Lewin, who appeared to have settled into his narrative. Poker faces all round.

'Mr Lewin, you telephoned 999 from your mobile at eleven thirty-four p.m. last night. Where were you when you made that call?'

Lewin's gaze broke from Marilyn's and moved upwards, to survey the right-hand corner of the room. Jessie's gaze followed and alighted on a fat black spider motionless in the centre of a gossamer web that laced the corner. A fly was struggling in its silken threads. Many psychologists would conclude, from that eye movement, that Lewin was lying – when she was younger, less experienced, Jessie would have done the same. But she'd spent much of the time during the months since she was invalided from the army reading, learning, and eyes moving upwards and to the right as an indication of lying was old hat. Lying was more in the voice – tone, minute hesitations – in hand movements – exuberant – in body language – over-animation. Now Lewin was just visualizing where he had been when he'd made the 999 call and she'd bet good money that he was going to tell the truth.

'Near East Meon. I filled my car up at a petrol station and then pulled across the road to call Denise, tell her that I'd be home in half an hour. I phoned twice, let the phone ring and ring both times, but she didn't answer. I knew that she and Leo were home, so I panicked and called 999. I was tired, overwrought. I'd had a very long day.'

'It is tiring driving across country,' Marilyn agreed, a facetious tone in his voice. 'To avoid traffic.'

The frown lines between Lewin's eyes contracted minutely; he had picked up on Marilyn's tone, was making a conscious effort not to respond negatively to it in body language.

'Yes, driving at night is tiring,' he said, his voice measured.

'What car do you drive, Mr Lewin?'

'An Audi A3.'

'Saloon or hatchback?'

'Hatchback.'

'In . . .?' Marilyn let the question hang.

'In, uh . . . oh, right, sorry, I didn't quite get what you were asking. It's "Cosmos Blue",' Lewin responded, chancing a brief, chummy smile.

'And what shade of blue is Cosmos?'

'Dark blue, metallic.'

'What's the registration number?'

'MK 16 UWA.'

Marilyn scribbled the registration number in his notebook, looked back up. 'You told the operator that you feared for your wife and son's lives and that you wanted police to go to your house urgently to check on them.'

'The woman . . . the operator, wouldn't believe me. She thought it was a hoax call.'

'But you insisted,' Marilyn recapped. 'You told her that you had called your wife twice and that she hadn't answered, despite the fact that she was definitely at home and always answered the phone. You told her that you were worried that someone might have broken in and harmed them.'

'Yes.'

'The operator asked you why you thought your wife and son's lives might be in danger, didn't she?'

Lewin nodded.

'What did you say in response?'

'I said that my wife had been receiving death threats from an ex-boyfriend.' Lewin unlocked and spread his hands in a 'can you believe that?' gesture. 'The boyfriend used to beat her up when they were together. She left him and he never forgave her.'

'Is that true? The death threats?' Marilyn asked.

No, it's a lie – those hands.

Lewin nodded. 'It's true.'

'OK,' Marilyn said, making a deliberately unhurried note in his black book. 'What is the name of your wife's ex-boyfriend?'

Lewin shrugged and spread his hands again.

'Mark, Martin, something like that. I'm not great with names and Denise didn't like to talk about him. He terrified her and she'd moved on.'

'But he hadn't?' Marilyn asked.

'Evidently not.'

Jessie leant forward. 'Why did you leave your wife at home alone if you were worried about a dangerous ex-boyfriend?'

Lewin's eyes bored into hers, challenge in his gaze. Challenge and overconfidence. He clearly felt his narrative was a winner. Perhaps he was right. She wanted to hear his story play out; maybe he had a smart move palmed in those recently animated hands of his.

'Who are you?' Lewin asked.

'I'm a psychologist working with the police.'

'What the hell?' Something else flickering in his eyes now. Apprehension? Fear? 'I'm not going to speak to a bloody psychologist.'

'Dr Flynn is employed by Surrey and Sussex Major Crimes,' Marilyn said.

'I don't care,' he snapped. 'I didn't agree to speak to a bloody psychologist.'

'Dr Flynn is here to help us find your wife's killer, Mr Lewin. She is here to *help* you, not to catch you out. I'm very surprised that you don't want to speak with her. If you have nothing to hide, you have nothing to fear.'

Lewin's gaze met Jessie's again, held it, but the overconfidence was gone. 'I have nothing to hide,' he muttered.

'I'm relieved to hear that, Mr Lewin. Please answer Dr Flynn's question.'

'I have a job, Dr Flynn. I need to earn money. I had to go. And I didn't think . . . didn't think he'd . . .' His voice wavered. A swallow, his Adam's apple bobbing in his throat, bobbing and sticking. 'I didn't think he'd kill her.'

'Did your wife ever report her ex-boyfriend to the police?' Marilyn asked.

'No.'

'Why not?'

'Because the police have a terrible record when it comes to protecting women from domestic violence and she felt that reporting him would aggravate him and she'd be more at risk.'

'How about her medical records?' Jessie asked. 'Did she go to her GP or to the hospital with injuries?'

He shook his head. 'Not that either.'

'Why?' Jessie pressed.

'Why what?'

'Why did she never go to hospital? If her ex-boyfriend is violent enough to have killed her, he surely must have given her some very serious injuries when they were together.'

Lewin nodded. 'She was frightened when she lived with him. Too frightened to go. And he never broke anything, she

327

told me. Well, just her nose and doctors can't do anything about noses, can they? He was careful not to break any other bones, specifically because he didn't want her to go to hospital.'

'How long have you been married, Mr Lewin?' Marilyn asked.

'Nearly five years.'

'And how long did you date before you got married?'

'Two and a half years.'

'So why now?' Jessie asked, anticipating Marilyn's next question.

They were making a good tag-team, and both of them randomly firing questions was forcing Lewin to look constantly from one to the other, unsettling him.

'Why now what?'

'Why did her ex-boyfriend start threatening her now?' Marilyn said.

'I don't know . . . maybe, he, uh . . . Oh yeah, she said that he had just broken up with his latest girlfriend, wanted to get back with Denise. He really loved Denise.' His gaze locked with Jessie's and she felt the pulsing resentment, that undercurrent of aggression. 'Despite what he did to her,' he finished.

Jessie nodded. 'Many abusive men are violent because they love, or believe that they love their partner beyond anything and can't bear to lose them. Violence is a way of controlling their partners, ensuring that they are too frightened to leave.' She smiled collegially, playing the psychology. 'It's very typical, that intense, undying love.'

Lewin clearly hadn't expected her validation: he shifted uncomfortably in his seat, destabilized by the change in her.

'What is her ex-boyfriend's name?' Marilyn asked.

'I, uh, I already said.'

'Remind me,' Marilyn pressed.

'Martin.'

'Definitely Martin?'

'Yes.'

'And his surname?'

'She wouldn't tell me.'

'And when the threats started?'

'Even then, she wouldn't tell me.'

'Why not?' Jessie prompted.

'Because she knows that I can get angry. She didn't want any conflict, didn't want him getting hurt.'

'Or you.'

'What?'

'Or you,' Jessie repeated, with another smile. 'Getting hurt. I can understand that. She clearly loves you and was very happy in your marriage.'

Lewin nodded. 'Yes, she was happy. I made her happy.'

'Great,' Jessie said. 'That's great. It's lovely that she found happiness after being in such an abusive relationship.'

The overconfident light was back in Lewin's eyes. He was lying through his teeth, though Jessie didn't need to be a psychologist to see that.

'What did you say to the emergency operator after telling her about Denise's abusive boyfriend?' Marilyn asked, resting his elbows on the table and steepling his fingers, eyeballing Lewin over their tips.

'I didn't say anything else. I'd got the message across. She agreed to send a patrol car around to check on Denise and Leo.'

Marilyn was leading him slowly, playing out lengths of rope. Would Lewin end up hanging himself?

'Are you sure?'

Lewin leant back in his chair and nodded. Emboldened by Marilyn's dishevelled appearance, confusing lack of deportment with absence of mental acuity, as many suspects had before him. 'As I said, it had done the job.'

'Shall we listen to the call?'

Though Lewin's eyes remained on Marilyn's, his expression intractable, Jessie noticed his jaw tighten.

'We tape all 999 calls.' Marilyn smiled. *So that we can cover our arses in case of complaints.* He didn't say it. 'In case we need to use them in court.'

'I know that you do.' An edge now to Lewin's voice. 'But we don't need to listen to the call. I made it. I remember what I said and I've just told you what I said. Why is it important, anyway? I was driving back from Wiltshire while some psycho was murdering my wife and you're wasting your bloody time listening to me speak, when you should be out there looking for him and I should be seeing my son.'

'We'll need to establish that.'

Lewin frowned irritably. 'Establish what?'

'That you were driving back from Wiltshire when you said you were.'

Lewin shot to his feet, the chair clattering to the floor again. 'What the fuck? How dare you—'

'Sit down please, Mr Lewin.'

Lewin remained standing, legs jittering, his complexion raspberry. '*I want to see my son.*'

Marilyn slammed both hands flat on the table top, the sound like a shotgun report in the silence. '*Sit down now, Mr Lewin. Right now. I will not ask you again. I will just charge you with obstructing justice.*'

330

'Jesus Christ, no wonder the crime rate's through the fucking roof in this shitty country with people like you in the driving seat,' Lewin shouted back, but he righted his chair and lowered himself into it. Crossing his arms and legs, he eyeballed Marilyn, unblinking.

Jessie had seen, studied, many people under stress, had read about countless more. Some people remained calm, in control, others folded, collapsed like a house of cards. Still others became angry. Simon Lewin was of the latter breed. She didn't doubt that he would be perfectly charming when everything was going his way, but as soon as he felt under stress, he'd become aggressive, nasty.

There was static for a few moments after Marilyn pressed play on the digital recording device, white noise between radio stations, then the voice of the 999 operator sounding bored, as if she was answering a call to report a broken boiler or a complaint about an electricity bill.

'*Hello, emergency service operator, which service do you require? Fire, police or ambulance?*'

Silence, a burst of noise, a panicked male voice – Lewin's, must be – fading in and out, the words unintelligible.

'*Please repeat. Which service do you require? Fire, police or ambulance?*'

'*Pol—*' Static – fade. '*Police.*'

More static, and background noise, a car driving past? '*I need the police.*'

A click, then another woman's voice, this one clipped, businesslike.

'*Police emergency. Hello caller, what's the emergency?*'
'*Police.*'

Another crackle of white noise, the sound Jessie heard when Callan was out running in the hills and had stopped

331

to call her – no phone masts up there to spoil the beauty. The downside, terrible mobile reception.

'*I need the police.*'

'*This is the police, sir. How can I help you?*'

The same man's garbled voice, interspersed with more crackle.

'*Please slow down, sir.*'

'*You're not listening to me. Just send the police.*' Clearer now, and unequivocally Lewin's voice.

'*Slow down, sir. Your mobile reception is poor and I can't understand what you're saying.*'

'*—In the countryside . . . I'm in the countryside. I'm not at home.*' Shouting now, down a line that was clearer, each word enunciated, as if speaking to an intellectually challenged toddler. '*You need to send the police around to my house. My wife and son are in danger.*'

'*Why do you believe that your wife and son might be in danger, sir?*'

'*Are in. Are in danger. Not might be.*'

'*Why do you believe that your wife and son are in danger, sir?*'

'*We've, uh, uh, we've been receiving death threats. From, uh, from an ex-boyfriend of my wife's. He has a history of violence.*'

'*What makes you think that he is a risk to your wife now?*'

'*He used to beat her up when they were together.*' His tone rising, voice breaking with tension. '*And I've just told you that we've been receiving death threats.*' Lewin's personality creeping into the call. '*Can you send a marked car around to my address? Now. It's urgent.*'

'*I'm sorry, sir, but unless we have—*'

332

'*Please—*'

'*Sir—*'

'*For Christ's sake, listen to me. I've called Denise twice and she's not answering. She's definitely at home and she always answers.*'

'*I'm sorry, sir, but—*'

'*For Christ's sake.*' Verging on hysterical now. '*It's connected to the murders of the Fullers and the Whiteheads. My wife and son are at risk from the same killer. They might already be dead. You need to send the police to my house now.*'

'*What is your address, sir?*'

Marilyn cut off the recording and looked up.

'I was desperate,' Lewin snapped. 'The operator wouldn't believe me and she was doing nothing.'

'Mr Lewin, I am arresting you for perverting the course of justice—'

'What the fuck?'

'Anything you say, may be used—'

'What the fuck are you doing? You can't fucking *arrest* me.'

Marilyn continued in a dry unemotional monotone that would have made Jessie want to punch him in the face had she been on the receiving end.

'In evidence—'

'I'm the victim here,' Lewin yelled. 'We're the fucking *victims* here.'

'—against you. You have the right to remain—'

'OK, OK, stop.' Lewin held up his hands, visibly deflating in his seat. 'Just *fucking* stop.'

'These murders were personal, weren't they, Mr Lewin?' Marilyn said. 'The Fullers', the Whiteheads', your wife's. Can you tell me why?'

Lewin shook his head. 'I don't know anything about the Fullers' and the Whiteheads' murders.'

'You said something entirely different to the police emergency operator.'

His eyes slid from Marilyn's, alighted briefly on Jessie's, before flitting away again.

'Mr Lewin.'

'That's because she wouldn't listen to me.'

'The police emergency operator?' Marilyn clarified.

'Yes. She wouldn't listen to me. I told her the truth, about Denise's ex-boyfriend, and it wasn't enough. I'd just refuelled at a petrol station and I'd seen the newspaper headlines, pictures of the Fullers and the Whiteheads on the front pages. It suddenly occurred to me that the way to get the emergency operator to take me seriously was to tell her that my wife and son were in danger from the same man.'

'It sounded a lot more than that to me, Mr Lewin,' Marilyn said. 'It sounded like genuine fear.'

Lewin shook his head. 'No, it wasn't.' He paused. 'Well, yes, it was, but not from that killer, from Denise's ex-boyfriend.'

Lewin's hands were in his lap, so Jessie couldn't see them, but from the stiffness in his arms, the contraction of his muscles, she suspected that they were knotted tightly. Knocking her pen off the table with a flick of her finger, she rolled her eyes at her own ineptitude, then tilted sideways to pick it up, glancing under the table as she did so. Lewin's hands were balled into fists, his fingers white with the pressure of his grip, but churning nonetheless.

'I think you're telling us a pack of lies, Mr Lewin,' she heard Marilyn say as she righted herself.

Lewin swallowed again, his Adam's apple bobbing in his

334

throat as if it was a constriction that wouldn't go up or down.

'Did you murder your wife, Mr Lewin?' Marilyn said, in a low voice.

'*What? How dare you,*' Lewin snapped, leaping up. 'I've had enough of this *fucking bullshit*. I want to see my son.'

'We can't help you if you lie to us, Mr Lewin.'

'I'm not lying. I want to see my son, now. *I want to see him now.*'

Marilyn planted his hands on the table and stood. 'Fine, Mr Lewin,' he said with a weary sigh. 'You can see your son, but first, I have two more very simple questions.'

Lewin gave a mulish half-nod.

'What is your shoe size?'

'Ten.'

'And do you like dogs, Mr Lewin?'

'What?' Lewin looked incredulous. 'Are you seriously asking me about dogs when my wife has been murdered and my son kidnapped?'

'Answer the question.'

'No, I don't particularly like dogs,' he muttered. 'I didn't grow up with pets. Leo loves dogs, but don't most kids? We had no intention of getting him one.'

'Do you know of a charity called Paws for Thought?' Jessie asked.

Lewin's incredulous gaze moved to meet hers and he gave an exaggerated sigh. 'No, I—' He broke off. 'Actually yes, I do know Paws for Thought, now that I think about it. We took Leo there once, earlier this year. They had an open day, and we popped in so that Leo could pat some dogs. It was Denise's idea and she ended up chatting to that mad woman who runs it for an age. The whole thing bored me

335

rigid, to be quite frank.' His gaze snapped back to Marilyn. 'Is that all now?'

'Thank you, Mr Lewin, that is indeed all.' Marilyn paused. 'For the moment, at least.'

61

Once Marilyn had deposited Simon Lewin into DC Cara's hands with strict instructions to obtain a full list of Lewin's Wiltshire tourism clients before dropping him off at St Richard's Hospital to see his son, he and Jessie headed straight to Paws for Thought. Jessie drove while Marilyn fired poor Cara a list, via text, detailing other jobs that needed to be completed quicker than immediately. It included impounding Lewin's Audi A3 so that the CSIs could crawl all over it; asking the members of Burrows' team still at Lewin's house whether any of Lewin's shoes matched the prints found at the three crime scenes; identifying the location of the mobile telephone mast that had picked up Lewin's 999 call; finding the garage where he had claimed to have filled up his car and interviewing the person who had been on duty that night; telephone interviewing all those Wiltshire clients, starting with the one Lewin claimed to have been with until seven p.m. last night; mapping roadworks and identifying traffic congestion on the M4 and A34 last night. *And pronto*, Marilyn had added, again. *Delegate.* If iPhone texts allowed bold and underlining, he doubtless would have made full use of those too.

'Shit, sorry – I didn't expect it to be quite so sharp,' Jessie said, as she navigated a right turn too fast, sending Marilyn snatching for the door handle.

'Where the hell is this place?' he snapped.

'Forestside.'

'Jesus, doesn't anyone around here appreciate being able to get their hands on a bottle of milk without having to drive five miles?'

'It's a converted pigsty. The land and buildings were cheap.'

Marilyn raised a cynical eyebrow. 'Really? In the middle of bloody nowhere. You surprise me.'

She raised a matching eyebrow. 'Paws for Thought doesn't have quite the celebrity backing or access to fat wallets that Battersea Dogs Home has. It's spit and sawdust.'

'If you'd have told me that we were going to a pigsty, I wouldn't have worn my best suit.'

When Jessie had first met Marilyn, he had dressed in black drainpipe jeans and a battered black leather biker jacket. Since then, DCI Janet Backastowe had pressured him into wearing clothes more befitting a senior officer in Surrey and Sussex Major Crimes, and he had ditched the biker jacket for a black suit, though the trousers were still drainpipes. It was a standing joke that with the number of identical black suits he must have hanging in his wardrobe, Marilyn could kit out an undertaker's workforce and still have spare.

'What do you think?' Marilyn asked.

'About your best suit or Lewin?'

'I won't dignify that facetious question with an answer.'

'Lewin pretty much lied his way through our whole interview,' Jessie said.

'He was definitely lying about the abusive boyfriend.'

'I think he was also lying about his Wiltshire tourism clients. He was far too keen that you didn't contact them.'

'Perhaps he's worried for his job. Tourism is a tricky industry, very subject to downturns in the economy.'

'Perhaps,' Jessie said, unconvinced, unconvincingly. 'But he was also gripping onto his hands for all he was worth, I think to stop them from being overactive. Animation in someone who is not normally so suggests lying—' Her Mini bounced over a pothole, catching air and landing with a groan. 'Bloody hell, my poor suspension. This road is shite.'

Marilyn snatched for the ceiling grab handle. 'The joys of the countryside,' he muttered. 'At a minimum, Lewin knows something about the murders, is hiding something. He said that his trip to Wiltshire was last minute, that he was standing in for a colleague who had to cancel, so perhaps our perp thought Lewin was at home and found out, too late, that he wasn't. '

'But that doesn't concur with a murderer who watches his victims carefully, because he would have known that Denise Lewin was alone with Leo, that Simon Lewin was away. He would have waited until he was home. And there was the anomaly of Denise Lewin's eye.'

Marilyn nodded. 'The driving across country was fishy. Conveniently, there are no APNR cameras on the route he claimed to have taken back from Wiltshire.'

'Depending on where he made the 999 call, he could have murdered his wife, dropped his son off at Paws for Thought knowing that he'd be safe for one night, locked on his own in a cage, and then driven back out in the direction of

Wiltshire. If he was telling the truth about calling from East Meon, it isn't far. Twenty minutes from Forestside, if that, driving fast.'

'On country roads, on a weeknight, no traffic, no witnesses.'

'And he has a small dark hatchback like Charles.'

'Which I hope is being impounded as we speak. His shoe size, ten, is the same as that of our perp, but that also applies to a large chunk of the male population.' Marilyn looked across. 'He knew of Paws for Thought.'

'Yes, he did.'

'It makes sense to assume that whoever dropped Leo Lewin off at Paws for Thought is also your friend Cherry Goodwin's night visitor. And if Captain Callan is half the military policeman I believe him to be, we should have that man on CCTV.' He rubbed his hands across his face. 'Jesus Christ, I thought I'd seen it all in my twenty-five years, but the knockout blows just keep on coming.'

They had reached the village of Forestside, such as it was. Paws for Thought was on the left, set in a clump of trees and surrounded by fields, the only dwelling visible, a clay-tiled roof three or four hundred metres away, around a bend in the road. The entrance to the car park was barred with yellow 'Police! Do Not Cross!' crime-scene tape. Burrows' forensics van was parked beyond, jammed against the hedge that bordered the narrow lane, barely room for a car to squeeze past if, by some remote chance, one wanted to. Two marked cars were top-and-tailing it, also bumped up onto the grassy kerb, and DS Workman's navy-blue Ford Fiesta was tucked in beyond the far one. Jessie tagged her Mini onto the end of the line.

'I didn't like him,' Jessie said, cutting the engine.

'What?'

'Lewin. I didn't like him.' Jessie glanced over with a brief smile. 'Though obviously my personal opinions are entirely irrelevant. Most of the people I don't like haven't butchered five people.'

'Do you not like many people?'

'I suppose my job encourages me to look for the negative, seek out the dysfunction.'

Marilyn nodded thoughtfully. 'Your opinion is duly noted, Baba Vanga. I didn't like him either, for what it's worth.' Theatrically pinching his nose between pincer fingers, he swung the passenger door open. 'Now are you ready to face the pigsty?'

Cherry Goodwin's battered white Corsa, fenced in by the tape, was the only car in the tiny, potholed car park. Four numbered yellow cones were dotted in an approximate line from the car park entrance to the front doorway. One of Burrows' team met them by the roadside and handed them forensic overalls, overshoes, hairnets and latex gloves. As he pulled the forensic suit over his crumpled black one, Marilyn quizzed her.

'What have you found?'

'A cigarette butt, gum, chewed and spat out, a two-pence piece and one silver stud earring in the car park.'

'Anything else of note?'

The woman nodded. 'The toughened glass in the top half of the door was smashed.'

'The door lock wasn't picked?' Jessie cut in.

'No. As I said, the door glass was smashed. The perp then unlocked the door from the inside, by reaching through the broken pane.'

Jessie and Marilyn exchanged glances.

341

'That's not how he usually gets in,' Jessie said. 'He has a key or picks the lock.'

'Perhaps he forgot the key this time,' the CSI said. 'If he was in a rush.'

Jessie lifted her shoulders. 'Perhaps.'

The CSI's gaze moved back to Marilyn. 'Tony Burrows asked me to send you through to the kennel compound at the back of the facility.'

Marilyn nodded. 'What about CCTV?'

'We've viewed it.'

'What does it show?'

'You'd better see it yourself, sir. I think it would lose something in the translation, if I described it to you.'

'Why is that?'

'Just, uh, just watch it, sir.'

Marilyn pulled a face. 'That weird, eh?'

'Weirder, I'd say. Weirder than weirdy weird.' The woman arched a plucked eyebrow. 'I can quite safely say that I've never seen anything like it.'

62

Inside the reception area at Paws for Thought, Marilyn and Jessie found Cherry Goodwin sitting with DS Workman, both clutching chipped mugs of steaming tea, the tremor in Cherry's hands rippling the surface of hers. Jessie laid a hand on her shoulder, felt her muscles snap to stressed attention underneath her touch.

'Are you OK, Cherry?'

Looking up, she nodded. 'Thank God for your boyfriend. He wasn't only ridiculously hot, he was also useful. Hang onto him. Men like that are rare as hen's teeth.' She clamped a hand over her mouth. 'Sorry, that was totally inappropriate. The man – the forensics man. I can't remember his name.' Dropping her hand, she mimed a rounded stomach.

'Tony Burrows,' Workman said.

'Yes, Tony Burrows. Sorry, that . . . that miming thing was totally inappropriate too.

'I don't know what the hell has got into me. I just feel as if I've lost my mind, like that thing, whoever or whatever

343

it is, has burrowed right in here.' She pressed an index finger to her temple.

'I'm sure Burrows won't mind,' Workman said, with a placating smile. 'He's used to being insulted on a daily basis by his colleagues about his resemblance to certain Teletubbies.'

'He said that they've caught the intruder on CCTV, but they haven't told me what he looks like. They probably should. I might know him or have seen him around. That's likely, isn't it?'

'I'm sure we'll want you to see the video, but let's just let the forensics team do their job for the moment,' Workman said, in what Jessie would describe as a perfect bedside manner. It was an art that she had failed, in her thirty years of life, in her six years as a clinical psychologist, to ever perfect.

Cherry gave a distracted half-nod. 'How's the little boy?' she asked, addressing the question to Jessie.

Jessie had no idea how Leo Lewin was psychologically, though she did know that he was physically unharmed. 'He's fine,' she said. 'His father is at the hospital with him now.'

Was he? She didn't know whether Simon Lewin would have reached the hospital yet, didn't know and didn't care. She didn't trust the man as far as she could kick him.

'That's good,' Cherry said. She took a fidgety sip of her tea. 'Will the dogs be all right? They're all still in their cages and the forensics guy . . . Burrows . . . Mr Burrows wouldn't let me feed them or anything.'

'We want to minimize traffic through that room,' Workman said. 'So that we can preserve as much evidence as we possibly can. This might give us the breakthrough that we need, Cherry.'

Workman seemed to be in control and she was more in tune with Cherry than Jessie was. Despite her job, tea and sympathy wasn't Jessie's forte. Moving over to the door that led to the indoor kennel compound, she stepped through to join Marilyn who was waiting outside the cage at the end of the walkway – *the empty cage* – watching Burrows crouched inside, studying something in his hands. A few dogs were standing by their doors, observing the forensics circus with tilted heads; others had retreated to their baskets, Burrows and his team already old news. A few tails thumped in baskets as Jessie passed, but most of the dogs seemed to be over visitors.

Hooking latex-gloved fingers through the wire wall of the cage an arm's length above his head, Burrows hauled himself to his feet as she joined them. The effort required seemed much like the effort that would be required to raise the *Titanic* from the ocean floor.

'Good morning, Jessie.'

'Morning, Tony.'

'What have you found?' Marilyn asked.

'Morning to you too, Marilyn,' Burrows replied, with a pointedly cheery smile, opening the cage door and stepping into the corridor. 'We've found a couple of items of significance. Firstly, the CCTV video – you really *do* need to watch that.'

'What the hell does it show?'

He rolled his eyes. 'I have no intention of ruining your viewing pleasure, DI Simmons, by giving away spoilers.'

'It had better be good after everything I've heard.'

'Oh, it's better than good. It nails a five-star rating, no question. It's the strangest thing I have ever seen.'

Marilyn raised an eyebrow. 'So we have five-star video evidence and we have . . .?'

345

'This . . .' Burrows said, twisting the evidence bag three-sixty so that Marilyn and Jessie could study the object contained inside. A mask of thick flexible rubber, white, covered in jet-black dots. There were two elliptical holes for eyes and two small round holes, punched into the oil-black nose, for breathing. It should have been fine, fun even, at a stretch, but in the context of where it was found, encased as it was in the plastic evidence bag and knowing that it had significance – *God knows what yet* – in the grisly murders of five people, it was just plain creepy.

'It's for dressing up, I presume. A dog,' Burrows said unnecessarily, before adding, equally unnecessarily: 'A Dalmatian.'

'Did the perpetrator drop it or leave it behind?' Marilyn asked.

'Neither. Leo Lewin was wearing the mask when Cherry Goodwin found him. She said that he wasn't moving when she first went into the room, so unless he was drugged, which toxicology will tell us, we can assume that he was asleep and that the dogs barking at Cherry woke him.'

'Any forensics on the mask?'

'No fingerprints unsurprisingly, but we have a hair caught here . . .' He raised the evidence bag to Marilyn's eye level, and pointed. 'Where the elastic headband is attached to the mask itself.'

'Leo's?'

Burrows shook his head. 'An adult's, I would say. Children's hair is finer. I took a sample from Leo, obviously, before he was taken to hospital. And I have his clothes, fingernail scrapings, clippings, the works. The poor little bugger screamed his head off while I was doing it all, but needs must and all that. Sarah did a good job of playing nanny, until the paramedics carted him away.'

'Expedite it, Burrows,' Marilyn said, jabbing his finger at the hair. 'Expedite the lot. I don't care how much it costs.' He turned to Jessie. 'Shall we look at the CCTV now, Dr Flynn? Find out what everyone is getting so hot under the collar about.'

63

When Jessie arrived home at half-past midnight, she found Callan, still awake, stretched out on the sofa reading, Lupo lying on the floor next to him. There was another dense patch of silvery-white hairs on her not-so-spotless cream sofa, which Callan was attempting to hide with his feet. Jessie put her hands on her hips.

'Callan?'

Tossing his book on the coffee table, he smiled up at her, a relaxed, easy smile that lit his amber eyes the colour of warm honey. 'He heard you coming and jumped off. He already knows not to mess with the boss.'

'Have you been dissing me to the new boy in my absence?'

'No dissing required. He's a perceptive chap, is young Lupo.'

Jessie smiled. 'My OCD is old news anyway. I am reborn and I am perfectly fine with having a thousand snow-white needles covering my sofa. I may yet become Cherry Goodwin and ship in a whole load of mangy mutts.'

Kicking her shoes off on the doormat and leaving them

in a heap, ignoring the tiny fizz from the electric suit she felt as she walked away, she tossed her handbag on the coffee table next to Callan's book and watched it sag, spilling her diary and keys onto the spotless gnarled oak surface – another fizz, also ignored. She then lay down on top of him and kissed him hard. 'I've missed you.'

'I've missed you too, gorgeous.'

Wriggling sideways, Jessie wedged herself between the back of the sofa and his warm, solid bulk and laid her head on his shoulder.

'I saw on the news that Leo Lewin was left at Paws for Thought,' Callan said.

'Yes, thank God. It would have tipped all of us over the edge if that little boy had come to any harm. We're telling the press that he was handed into reception.'

He raised an eyebrow. 'Wasn't he?'

'Er, no. That would be far too easy and far far too normal for this case.'

'So where?'

'He was left in *that* cage.'

'*That* cage? The imprint cage?'

She nodded; he was interested now. Swinging his legs off the sofa, he sat up.

'Did Cherry Goodwin switch on the nanny cams when she left for the night?'

'She did.'

'Thank God for that. The woman gave me no faith at all that she'd be able to operate them. Teaching my mum how to work her bloody mobile phone was a less painful process.'

'Goes with the territory of mad dog woman, I'm afraid.'

A look of amusement in those watchful amber eyes. 'Just don't ask me to go around there again. I trained one camera on the front door and hid the other camera above a wall light in the kennel room, so that it focused down the central walkway. There is no way in or out of those cages without going down the walkway. What did the cameras record?'

'The camera in reception recorded the perp breaking the toughened glass in the top half of the front door.'

'With what?'

'Something small, a nail maybe. The image wasn't clear enough to see.'

'You can shatter toughened glass with pretty much anything sharp.'

Jessie nodded. 'The camera then recorded Leo Lewin being carried past the reception desk and out of view. The second camera picked up the perp walking down the central walkway, still carrying Leo in his arms, entering that end cage and laying Leo in the basket. Leo was leaning against his shoulder and appeared to be asleep the whole time, even though some of the dogs were barking. The perp left the way he'd come.'

'Was he recognizable?'

Jessie didn't speak for a moment. 'You're not going to believe this,' she said finally. *God, I sound like DC Cara now.* But even she was still struggling to believe what she had seen on the screen.

'Try me,' he said.

Just what I said to DC Cara.

'Leo Lewin was dropped off at Paws for Thought by someone dressed as a dog.'

'A dog? What the hell? You mean someone in a dog onesie, a fancy dress outfit?'

'Sort of.' She paused. 'Actually, no not really.'

'Sort of, actually, no not really, is a nothing answer, Jessie.'

Callan's tone one of barely suppressed irritation. He had his policeman's head on now.

'It was someone dressed as a dog, but a proper dog, a big pale grey dog, like a husky, like Lupo. The full works.' She moved her hand to cover her face. 'A full rubber head mask with pointed ears like a husky, eye holes and a black nose. An all-in-one pale bodysuit.' She balled her fists. 'Paws for hands.'

'Paws?'

'Yes, like gloves, but in fists. Grey fist gloves with paws printed on the bottom, and claws.'

'Claws made of what?'

She shrugged. 'You couldn't tell on the CCTV, but they were dark. Metal, maybe.'

'Jesus. That's so fucking weird that it's almost funny.'

'No, it wasn't. Seeing it really wasn't funny. It was mad and *very* disturbing. Knowing that the man in that suit, in that husky suit, has murdered five people. Murdered them horribly, Callan.' She met his gaze; not warm now, just enquiring. 'That dog is our man, as it were, and we need to find him.' She grimaced. 'What the hell is going on in that man's head?'

'That's your department, Doctor.'

'Sure, and I've seen many things, but I've never seen anything like that.'

'Look, you have two choices. Firstly, it's just a fetish, which to my mind is the most likely option. Fetish goes with the brutal murders, the drowning, the gouging out of the victims' eyes. It's scene setting. Like setting up a play. Theatre.'

Jessie shook her head. 'I don't buy that. Fetishes are usually sexual, aren't they?'

'They don't have to be. And sexuality manifests itself in many different ways, not just in kinky sex. Lots of people get off on dressing up and not actually having sex.'

'OK, I'll take your word for that, but I still don't think it's a fetish. I think that's too easy.'

'You told me that's what you said to Marilyn, about the perpetrator being a psychopath. That it was too easy an option. Though from what you've said you saw on the video, psychopath doesn't sound that far from the truth.'

Jessie shook her head. 'A psychopath wouldn't need to dress up. Most psychopaths hide in plain sight and they enjoy hiding in plain sight, enjoy pulling the wool over people's eyes by pretending that they're normal. They don't go around in black cloaks with red devil horns pinned to their heads.' She paused. 'And actually, I'm not sure the dressing up is the most interesting thing in this case.'

'Isn't it?'

'No. I think—' she broke off again, banged the heels of her hands against her temples. 'God, my brain is just so slow.'

'That'd be the eighteen-hour days and no sleep.'

She laid a hand on his chest and smiled. 'You should have told me that police work was such a nightmare and I never would have signed up.'

'Too late now, Doctor.' He entwined his fingers with hers. 'What were you saying about the dressing up?'

'It's the visiting Paws for Thought, staying there, sleeping in the basket, playing with the toys. I think the dressing up is almost incidental. Actually, not incidental, but necessary.'

'Necessary, how?'

'Necessary to become who he wants to become, which is a dog. I don't think he's dressing up as a dog, I think that he wants to *be* a dog.' She chewed her lip. 'And the oddest thing is—'

'One of the oddest things,' Callan interrupted. 'Everything is fucking odd about this case.'

'OK, yes, *one* of the oddest things is that none of the dogs in the cages reacted to the dog-man at all on that video, even though he was carrying Leo. Most just lifted their heads to listen, but stayed in their baskets. A couple came to the front of their cages and wagged their tails in greeting, but that was it. When I went in there with Cherry the first time, they leapt around, barking.'

'They knew him.'

She nodded. 'And not just knew him, but were very familiar with him. So familiar that, even when he was carrying some-thing foreign to them – Leo – they still didn't react. Their lack of reaction was the human equivalent of not batting an eye.' Reaching over, she stroked her fingers across the stubble of his cheek, sandpaper against her fingertips. 'Why would someone want to be a dog, Callan?' She drooped her hand to his chest. 'Talk to me about dogs, lovely boyfriend.'

Callan wrapped one arm around her shoulders, dropped the other to where Lupo was lying on the floor, a living statue, feeling the warmth of his skin through the soft, white hair. 'They're loyal, faithful. Dogs in a pack have each other's backs and support each other unfailingly against outside aggressors. There's a hierarchy in a dog pack, as there is in a wolf pack. Everyone has a place in the hierarchy and everyone is accepted for who they are. They only challenge each other for a reason, such as to achieve elevation in the pack hierarchy, not just because they can.'

Jessie nodded. 'They're not judgemental. There's no nasti-ness, no bitchiness.'

353

'Modern dogs, pets, get everything done for them. They get given food, water, walks, and they can play with toys. It's a no-pressure job. I could do with one of those myself.'

'Me too. Would you still love me if I started dressing as a poodle?'

'No, I can't stand poodles.'

'Why not? They're very intelligent and they have cute pom-poms in all sorts of cool places.'

Callan suppressed a grin. 'I'd be exceptionally supportive if you got into playing with balls and boners.'

'For fuck's sake, Callan.' She elbowed him hard in the ribs. 'You have a filthy mind and I'm trying to be serious here.'

'I only have a filthy mind where you're concerned, Patch.'

'Patch? Where the hell did you get Patch from? I really don't see myself as a Patch. It's far too mundane.'

'There was a Patch on the radio years ago. I can't remember which station, but the DJ used to joke about a black and white Jack Russell called Patch.' The ghost of a smile crossed his face. 'Black hair, white skin, feisty, persistent, irritating, never lets anything go. You're a dead ringer.'

Another sharp jab in the ribs. 'Remember when I called you lovely boyfriend at the beginning of this conversation? Well you can scratch that description for starters.'

64

Jessie felt as if she was fighting upwards through thick layers of cotton wool, coating her body, wrapped tight around her head, pressing into her ears and eyes, insulating her brain. It was a feeling she'd been waking with for days now – the feeling of forcing her exhausted brain and body to face the day – a day she would give much not to have to deal with. Not just the case to think about, but Callan's appointment with his neurologist at the Ministry of Defence Hospital Unit, Frimley Park Hospital, at two this afternoon. Decision day. D-Day. *Fuck*.

Sitting up, she ground her knuckles into her eye sockets, trying to galvanize her eyes into action. Callan stirred beside her, clamped strong fingers around her wrist.

'Where do you think you're going?'

Jessie ducked down and planted a kiss in the soft, warm concave space between his neck and collar bone. 'Coffee or me?'

'Both?'

A clang, the letter box, which they ignored.

'Nope. You have to learn to prioritize.'

He smiled a lazy smile. 'It's a no-brainer. You first then coffee.'

The letter box kept clanging.

'Who the fuck is that?' he muttered.

'Clive probably. I'll be back, with coffee.' Throwing on her white towelling dressing gown, she padded down to the front door where she found Lupo sitting quietly on the front doormat watching the letter box as it flipped up and down, clanging tinnily against its surround.

'Your doorbell is broken and you don't have a knocker,' the postman, Clive, said. He was shielding a parcel under one side of his navy waterproof jacket over his uniform, which was being peppered with raindrops. He saw Lupo, and took a step back. 'Woah, he's a big boy. Is he a new addition?'

'Yes, a rescue.'

'I didn't know you were thinking of getting a dog.'

'We weren't.'

He nodded sagely, as if he understood exactly what she was talking about. 'Well he's certainly a handsome chap. He's not a great guard dog, though, is he? Didn't bark once when I was making that racket with the letter box.'

'No, he's not a great guard dog.' She laid a hand on Lupo's head. 'He looks as if he should be, and then it all goes horribly wrong when it comes to execution.'

'They're sled dogs, aren't they?'

Jessie nodded, indicating the small parcel in his hand. 'The next parcel you deliver here may be twenty times the size of that one and have runners.'

'Well, there are a ton of red berries on the holly trees already which is supposed to mean that we're in for a cold winter, so you might be in luck if it's snow you're after.' He handed her the parcel, hopefully the dog-training treats Callan had ordered.

'And here's another one. A letter.'

The proffered letter was addressed to Captain Ben Callan, and bore the insignia of the Ministry of Defence Hospital Unit, Frimley Park Hospital, in its top left-hand corner, the sight of it as painful as a punch in the stomach from a pro-boxer.

'I'd better be getting on with my round, love.'

Jessie looked up. 'Sorry, Clive, bit distracted.'

'Bad news?'

She shook her head. 'Oh God no, just another bill.'

Though she exchanged pleasantries with Clive on those days she was late to work, she had never shared private confidences and she wasn't about to start now.

He grinned. 'Bills are the only post I get these days too. I'll soon be as popular as a traffic warden if I just deliver bills.'

Jessie held up the parcel. 'You saved me a trip to the shops and you can always redeem yourself on birthdays and at Christmas.' She smiled, a smile that she felt nowhere but in the stretch of her lips. 'Take care and I'll see you soon.'

Shutting the door, she dropped her hand to ruffle Lupo's head. He looked up at her and for the first time ever – for her at least – wagged his tail. She almost felt like falling to her knees and flinging her arms around his neck, she was so ridiculously delighted. This was probably what a parent experienced when their child took their first steps.

'Let's get that lazy arse Captain Callan and me coffee and you breakfast, hey?'

Padding into the kitchen, Lupo at her heels, Jessie flicked the kettle on and heaped four large teaspoons of coffee into the cafetière. She needed a strong one to even begin to get her brain into gear. Then she needed to duck to the office – her proper office – for two private client sessions, before driving up to Frimley Park with Callan. Marilyn had given her the day off, though not with much grace.

Brilliant timing, Dr Flynn, he had said, his voice dripping with sarcasm.

I don't think the bullet in Callan's brain consulted the resident psychic as to who was going to be out and about on a murder spree in Sussex before it decided to shift, Marilyn. Very remiss of it, I know – equally sarcastically and with a big dose of suppressed fury.

To his credit, Marilyn had looked suitably contrite. *Sorry, sorry, Jessie. I was out of order. This case* . . . He'd tailed off, raised his hands in surrender, then added, *Please make sure you're contactable at all times. And send my best wishes to Callan.*

She rated Marilyn hugely, enjoyed working with him, but even his trademark calm-in-the-face-of-a-nuclear-storm had taken a battering on this case. *Unsurprisingly.* The whole team were ragged with exhaustion. She didn't need to be physically present to contribute to the case anyway, could think just as well driving with Callan or pacing the reception area at Frimley Park Hospital.

While the kettle boiled, she grabbed Lupo's bowl, tossed a couple of handfuls of dry dog food in it and added some mince that Callan had cooked for him.

'How come he never cooks for me?' she said, as she put it on the floor by the door, catching their twin reflections in the dark glass of the oven door as she did so. In reflection, they looked almost interchangeable, Lupo in his white pelt and her in her fluffy white dressing gown. Doppelgängers.

He's not a great guard dog, though, is he?

Clive was right. Jessie had never heard Lupo bark, not once, for anything. Callan had let him out a couple of nights ago and he'd disappeared over the back fence into the farmer's field, so Callan had shut the door and crashed out on the sofa, obviously feeling shit again. When Jessie got home, at some hideous time approaching dawn, she had thrown a blanket over the sleeping Callan, ducked into the kitchen to grab herself a snack and jumped out of her skin at the sight of Lupo's pale face staring silently through the glass doors. The poor dog had been outside for hours, they'd worked out later, though he hadn't seemed the worse for wear for his ordeal and, to be fair, he was very well adapted to cope with a forced sojourn in the cold.

Back upstairs, two coffees in her hand, she crawled back into bed.

'Have you ever heard Lupo bark?'

'No.'

Jessie frowned. 'Never?'

'Never. Huskies aren't supposed to be great guard dogs. Why?'

'The old lady who found Lupo tied to the lamp post outside her cottage said that she was woken by the sound of a dog barking in the street, by Lupo barking. But he never barks.'

'Do you think she's lying?'

'No, she's an old person.'

Callan laughed. 'You don't get a dose of the truth drug just because you've hit seventy.'

359

Jessie smiled reluctantly. 'Yes, all right, but why the hell would she have lied? She had no reason to, did she?'

'You're asking the wrong person, Jessie. My experience of old people is limited to my mother and Ahmose.'

Jessie nodded, thinking. She was the wrong person too. The oldest person she knew was Ahmose, but he was ludicrously switched-on and self-sufficient for his age. Her mind fumbled for more information and landed in a tiny flat in Farnham, a year ago now, grime coating the windows from the busy road outside, washing-up piled in the sink from a lack of motivation to do anything but mourn the missing and the dead. An old lady who had lost her son and grandson.

Old age is not for the faint-hearted. There's nothing glamorous about us.

'Maybe she was embarrassed,' she said.

'About what?'

'About being old.'

'Why would she be embarrassed about being old?'

Jessie didn't answer. Something Cara had said was niggling her. Laying her coffee cup on the bedside table, she picked up her mobile.

65

'Nice to see you again so soon, Mr Lewin,' Marilyn said, with blatant sarcasm.

Gazing at a point somewhere on the wall between Marilyn's left shoulder and Workman's right, Lewin squirmed in the hard plastic chair, his discomfort nothing to do with the unyieldingness of his seat. He looked wretched: red-eyed and dishevelled.

'Can I have a coffee, please?'

'No,' Marilyn said. Picking up his own cup, he took a sip. Workman glanced over, suppressing a smile; she had almost expected her boss to enhance the pantomime with an appreciative 'Mmmm.' Though Lewin's mouth had thinned to a tense, angry line, he remained silent, seeming to sense that he had run out of road. Road and fight.

'Yesterday, you told me and my colleague, Dr Jessica Flynn, that you had been on a last-minute work trip to Wiltshire while your wife, Denise, was being murdered,' Marilyn began.

'I was on a last-minute work trip to Wiltshire,' Lewin muttered, his voice strangled.

'Mr James Carter, the CEO of Classic Collection, was most disconcerted to be dragged from a dinner party yesterday evening by my detective constable to answer questions on his *former* employee.'

Lewin's eyes widened, but he didn't respond. The silence stretched.

'Mr Carter informed my DC that you were made redundant four weeks ago and that your last day working with Classic Collection was the day you were given notice. He stated that you were an effective sales and marketing manager and that the reasons for letting you go were purely economic. He did, however, feel that you seemed excessively aggrieved at your dismissal and so he decided that it would be better to pay you to stay at home, rather than to let you work out your notice period.' Marilyn took another sip of coffee, eyeballing Lewin over the rim of the cup as he lowered it. 'Would you care to enlighten me as to why you claimed to have been visiting tourism clients in Wiltshire the two days before and the day of your wife's murder?'

He had more information up his sleeve, from other telephone conversations that DC Cara had conducted with Lewin's so-called 'Wiltshire tourism clients', but he had given Lewin enough rope. Would he hang himself or use it to haul himself to safety?

66

It was raining. DC Cara drove to a steady beat on the car roof and the tinny tunes of Heart FM fading in and out as the radio suffered at the mercy of the South Downs' patchy reception. He was so exhausted that his eyes felt as if they were on stalks, and that thought brought to his mind, in full horrific technicolour, an image of Hugo Fuller's ravaged eye sockets. Then another image, this one imaginary, but feeling just as gut-churningly real: an eyeball pierced and stretched from its socket by a razor-sharp claw until its optic nerve thinned and snapped like over-stressed elastic. *Shit.* He needed to get control, needed some sleep, couldn't remember the last time he had wanted to crawl into bed this badly. *Welcome to a multiple murder investigation, kiddo.*

The night before last, he had been closing his eyes after a sleepless twenty-four hours at the hospital, when Marilyn had called with an instruction to get over to Sheiks in Bognor and interview the staff, see if anyone had seen Sophie Whitehead getting into a small dark hatchback that might or might not have been an official or unofficial 'moon-lighting' taxi. Though the visit had brought back fond memories of his own teenaged drunken nights in seedy clubs, downing Jägerbombs with his mates and fumbling with girls in dark corners, it had been fruitless from a policing point of view. The only CCTV was directed at the strip of road directly outside their front door and none of the doormen had bothered to stand outside in the cold at one a.m. when they could hang around in the club's foyer, chatting.

Cara had spent most of last night working through Marilyn's texted list, though that had been fruitful, at least, and now he was on his way to East Meon, Google having been unable to find the petrol station that Lewin claimed to have filled up at.

The petrol station, which he finally found on Workhouse Lane, a quiet road in the back of beyond, on the outskirts of East Meon, was tiny – just a couple of pumps that looked as if they had been lifted from the set of a 1960s film, and a kiosk so small and ramshackle it could have doubled as an elderly couple's potting shed. Pulling to the side of the road, Cara pressed stop on his mobile's stopwatch function. *Twenty-six minutes* – during the day, without breaking the speed limit and with five minutes of circling East Meon to find the petrol station. At Marilyn's request, he had driven here via Paws for Thought, pressing start as he'd passed the gate. He texted Marilyn – *27 min* – then, leaving his hazard lights flashing so that he wasn't back-ended by some elderly, hard-of-sight country dweller while he was in the petrol station, he cut his engine and climbed out, just as his mobile rang.

At the sight of the name flashing on its screen – *Dr Jessie Flynn* – Cara's heart did a flip. He had enjoyed the time they'd spent together on the knock earlier this week, even if they had ended up interviewing poor bloody Denise Lewin. If he were five years older, he'd have tried his luck with Jessie. Christ, even if he weren't five years older, and she didn't have a boyfriend, he'd have tried his luck. She was beautiful, intelligent, fun, his perfect woman, just out of reach. His practised thumb found the answer symbol.

67

'Jessie,' DC Cara said in his most professional tone. 'How can I help you?'

'Hi Darren. Sorry to bother you, but I have a quick question about the case.'

'I didn't realize you were working today.'

'I'm not. But I still have a question.'

'OK. Ask away.'

'The old lady who found Lupo tied up outside her house. Remind me exactly what she said to the dog team who attended, please.'

'She said that she had been woken by barking. That she'd gone to her bedroom window, looked out and seen Lupo.'

'She definitely said that she was woken by barking?'

'Yes.'

'And did the dog team believe her?'

'Yes.'

'OK. You went to her cottage and interviewed her, didn't you, Darren?'

'Yes. Later on Sunday.'

'What did she say to you?'

'She said that—' he broke off. Jessie could hear the knock of his mobile against his ear; he must be walking. 'She said that she'd been reading by her bedroom window, opened the curtains and seen him.'

'Which isn't what she told the dog team.'

A moment of silence. Jessie waited, chewing her lip.

'No.'

'Didn't you think about the inconsistency?'

Another long moment before he answered. 'She just found the dog, Jessie. I was only there for five minutes, getting a brief statement for the files.' His tone was defensive. 'Does it really matter?'

'Can I go and have a chat with her? Can you give me her address?'

Cara sighed heavily. 'Look, it's probably a moot point anyway.' *Just as my hike to East Meon is probably a moot point.* 'That hair Burrows found trapped in the mask that Leo Lewin was wearing is being DNA-tested, expedited as we speak. If we're lucky the results will be back today.'

'It definitely wasn't Leo's hair then?'

'No. Hopefully it's one from the perp.'

'Hopefully—'

'Probably—'

'Give me her address anyway, please, if you don't mind.'

'Sure. I'll text it to you.'

'Thank you. Send my—' she broke off. She was about to say – *Send my love to Marilyn* – but that would have sounded ridiculous. He was her work colleague, nominally her boss. 'Say hello to Marilyn for me,' she finished. 'And tell him that I'll have my mobile with me all day if he needs to speak to me.'

For some ridiculous reason she felt bereft that the day they had what might prove to be a real break in the case she was off-games. Since this case had begun, all she had wanted was for it to end. But now, with it gathering pace in her absence, she realized how emotionally invested she was, how deeply she wanted to see it through. And how she could do with burying herself in work, today of all days, to take her mind off Callan's appointment. *D-Day.*

The phone clicked off. Silence. Just the beating of her heart, hard in her ears, and an unsettling sense that something was wrong. Something more than the everything she already knew was wrong.

68

Eyes fixed on the table, Lewin nodded slowly. He seemed to have shrunk to a half his previous size and aged ten years in the fourteen hours since Marilyn had last seen him.

'I was made redundant four weeks ago.'

'What were you doing in Wiltshire? Or were you not in Wiltshire at all?' Marilyn already knew the answer to both these questions, but he wanted to see if Simon Lewin had a truthful bone in his body.

'I was interviewing for a new job.'

'With whom?'

'Kids-Go-Too.'

'Which is?'

'A travel company specializing in holidays for families with young children. I feel that I have, uh, I have expertise in that area.'

Marilyn resisted the temptation to roll his eyes. He had no interest in Lewin's fitness or not to take up a role with *Kids-Go-Too*. 'And the interviews took the best part of three days?'

Lewin nodded. 'I was sales and marketing manager at Classic Collection, so I'm going for a senior job – director of sales and marketing. I had a dinner on the first evening, six interviews and a load of psychometric tests. The assessment finished with an informal drink in the Fox Goes Free with the CEO, as I said yesterday.'

Marilyn nodded. 'As you said yesterday,' he echoed, his voice dripping with sarcasm.

'Why did you tell your wife – and us – that you were meeting with Classic Collection's Wiltshire tourism clients?'

Lewin rolled his gaze up from the table to meet Marilyn's. 'I *was* meeting with a tourism company based in Wiltshire.'

Marilyn didn't credit his response with a comment. Lewin squirmed in his seat as the silence ballooned awkwardly, filling the room.

'Denise didn't know that I'd been made redundant,' Lewin said finally.

'Why?'

'What I told you yesterday – about the abusive boyfriend – that was true.'

Marilyn raised a cynical eyebrow.

'Denise *did* have an abusive boyfriend . . .' A whine in his tone.

'Mr Lewin, may I remind you that everything you say can and will be used against you in a court of law. DS Workman read you your rights before I entered the room, did she not?'

'Yes, but—'

'And as we currently stand, you are, at an absolute minimum, responsible for perverting the course of justice.'

'What the *fuck*?' It was the first time Lewin had seemed truly animated since Workman had collected him from his

370

son's bedside at St Richard's Hospital at seven a.m. and brought him in to be interviewed. 'You can't fucking charge me with—'

Marilyn slapped a flat hand hard on the table, cutting him off.

'I strongly advise you that you have told enough lies and I suggest that you play it straight with us from now on, *for your own good.*'

Lewin scrubbed agitated fingers through his hair. 'She did have an abusive boyfriend. She *did.*'

'But she wasn't frightened of him now, was she?' Workman asked in a gentle tone.

'She trusts me . . .' He raised his hands to shield his face. Workman slid a plastic-wrapped packet of pocket handkerchiefs across the table and she and Marilyn sat in silence while Lewin sniffed and pressed a tissue to his red-rimmed eyes.

'She trusted me completely, with everything,' he said, after a few minutes, his voice thick with emotion. 'To look after her, to provide for her and Leo, to keep them safe. She gave up her secretarial job the day she found out that she was pregnant and I knew that she'd never work again. It was all down to me and I didn't want to worry her.' A pause, while he sucked back a sob. 'We overextended ourselves with the mortgage on the house and we're in debt. I couldn't tell her that I'd lost my job. I *couldn't.*'

Marilyn sighed wearily. 'Have you been moonlighting as a taxi driver since you lost your job, by any chance, Mr Lewin?'

'What? What the hell are you talking about?'

Marilyn spelled it out. 'Have you been giving people lifts to make a bit of extra money on the side? Cash in hand, easy money.'

371

'No, I haven't. I've been applying for jobs and travelling around the country going to interviews. Endless interviews.' The expression on his face was stricken.

Marilyn nodded. Despite Lewin's losses – of his job and his wife – he had no patience with or sympathy for this man. 'Did you murder your wife, Mr Lewin?'

'*What?* No. *No.* I loved Denise. *I loved her.*'

His knotted hands were clasped tightly together on the table top. Marilyn wondered what Jessie Flynn would make of them. Were they an indication of angst, or of more lies?

He felt the weight of his iPhone in his suit pocket, still maddeningly silent. DC Cara was due to telephone imminently with information as to whether Lewin had at least told the truth about his visit to a small garage in East Meon. Crossing his arms over his chest, he settled back to wait for Cara's call, eyeballing Lewin across the table, enjoying watching him squirm.

69

A man in a black turban sat on a high stool behind the cash till, reading *The Times* newspaper. On the chest of his navy V-neck jumper was pinned a yellow button badge that read: 'Don't freak, I'm a Sikh'. He grinned when he noticed Cara's eyes flash down to the badge.

'Some of my customers are a bit, how would one say? Stick-in-the-mud? Old-school? They see this face and the only name that pops into their heads is Osama Bin Laden. The badge is to reassure, and it's a conversation starter. It's boring here on my own, sixteen hours a day.'

Cara nodded. He wasn't interested in engaging with anyone's conversation starter. He was here to gather information as expediently as possible, then leave, perhaps grab a quick twenty minutes' kip in a layby on the way back to the office. He held up his warrant card.

'Darren Cara, Surrey and Sussex Major Crimes.'

The man extended his hand. 'Gurpreet Sidhu. Nice to meet you, Officer Cara.'

'Detective,' Cara said, taking Sidhu's hand, tiredness lending his tone more edge than he'd meant.

Sidhu's smile was without edge. 'Pardon me for the mistake, Detective. Now how can I help you?'

'Were you working on Thursday night?'

Sidhu nodded. 'I own the garage. I work all day and every night apart from Wednesday afternoon and Sundays when I pay my cousin to run the garage.'

'What time do you close?'

'Midnight.'

'I'm interested in the period between around ten p.m. and closing time.'

'It was quiet on Thursday night.'

Cara wondered if it was ever anything but quiet. 'I'm interested in a man who would have been driving a small dark blue hatchback, an Audi A3. He said that he filled up here at around eleven-thirty p.m.'

'He did.'

'At that time?'

Sidhu shrugged. 'I'm not sure as to the exact time, but it was definitely during the home run.'

'The home run?'

'The last hour. I restock the shelves, clean the shop floor, tot up the takings for the day, that kind of thing. I was probably halfway through the home run when he came in. Big, square jaw, dark spiky hair, late thirties or early forties.'

'You have a good memory.'

Sidhu smiled. 'I do have a good memory. And I also remember because he came in directly after another customer, a lady, one of my regulars. And because he stopped on the way out.'

'Stopped?'

'Yes, halfway to the door.' Sliding off his high chair, Sidhu leant over the counter and pointed at a spot on the worn blue vinyl floor. 'About there, level with the crisps. He froze.'

'For how long?'

'Twenty seconds or so.'

'It's not long. Odd that you noticed it.'

Sidhu tilted his head sagely. 'Ah, yes, but he dropped his car keys also.'

'While he was standing there?'

'Yes. They fell from his hand when he froze and he didn't bend to pick them up. He was staring at the rack of newspapers. Just standing, totally motionless, and staring.'

Turning, Cara surveyed the cramped petrol station shop. There was a rack of newspapers on the wall, four metres away, which would be shielded by the door when it was opened. He certainly hadn't noticed the newspapers when he'd entered.

'I asked him if he was OK,' Sidhu said.

'And?'

'He didn't answer and so I flipped up my counter and picked up his car keys, held them out to him. But he didn't notice that I was even there. He was staring at the newspapers and he was in shock, I would say, very much in shock.'

'What happened next?'

'I touched his shoulder and he leapt right out of his skin. It was only then that he seemed to realize I had been standing next to him.'

'Did he say anything to you?'

'He said "There's been an . . . another murder." Just like that, in a stuttering sort of a way.'

'Was that all he said?'

Sidhu nodded. 'I replied with something like, "Yes, they're terrible, aren't they?" but he didn't respond. He seemed suddenly very agitated. He snatched his car keys from my outstretched hand, yanked the door open, ran to his car and drove off.'

'Quickly?'

'Across the road.'

'Excuse me?'

'He screeched out of the forecourt, but then I saw him stop, just down the road, twenty metres.'

'How long was he stopped for?'

'Five minutes or so. He was talking on his mobile phone.'

'How could you tell?'

'It's pitch-black out there at night. I saw the glow from his mobile through his back windscreen.'

Cara nodded. 'And then what did he do?'

Sidhu lifted his shoulders. 'He screeched off again, very fast.'

Cara waved his hand towards the window. 'East?'

'Yes, east.'

70

Marilyn lowered his mobile from his ear and re-entered the interview room. Workman and Lewin were sitting in silence, the latter shock-faced and red-eyed.

'It seems as if you are unlikely to be guilty of murder, Mr Lewin.'

A balloon of pent-up tension exhaled from Lewin's lungs. He unclasped his knotted fingers. 'I told you. I *did* tell you.'

Marilyn raised one of his hands, cutting Lewin off. 'And if you had told the truth in the first place, you would have saved yourself and us a lot of trouble.'

'Can I go now?' He half-rose from his seat. 'I want to get back to the hospital.'

Marilyn waited a beat, eyeballing him across the table, before shaking his head. 'No, you cannot go. I used the term "unlikely" for a good reason. You are still, by no means, off the hook and when you do finally leave this interview room and return to the hospital, it will be in the company of a police officer who will stick with you like a pungent smell until this case is solved. Now, please sit back down, Mr Lewin, I have more questions.'

Lewin hesitated, hovering.

'Sit,' Marilyn snapped. 'Who killed your wife, Mr Lewin?' he asked, when Lewin was seated, his hands once again locked tightly together on the table top in front of him.

'I don't know.'

'I think you do.'

'I don't. I really don't.'

Marilyn leant forward, planting his elbows on the table, steepling his fingers.

'Dr Jessie Flynn, the clinical psychologist you met yesterday, is sure that these murders are personal – driven by some personal connection between the victims.'

'My wife had no connection to either of the couples who were murdered.'

'Dr Flynn also believes that the personal connection relates to the men and not to the women, as the men appear to be the primary victims.'

Lewin shook his head firmly. 'I don't know anything.'

'But you know them. Hugo Fuller and Daniel Whitehead.'

'What? No. *No.*'

'Are you interested in helping us find the man who murdered your wife?'

He slumped back in the chair like a sulky teenager. 'Of course I am, but I told you that I don't know who murdered Denise.'

'I stepped outside a moment ago to speak with my DC. He confirmed that you were at the petrol station in East Meon, filling up your car when you said you were, and that you made the emergency telephone call from the roadside outside the petrol station.'

'I told you that I was. You should have believed me.'

Marilyn raised an eyebrow. 'It is gratifying to know that not everything you told us yesterday was a lie. Though, at a stretch, you could still have finished your Wiltshire meeting at seven-thirty p.m., driven back to Chichester, murdered your wife, kidnapped your son and been at that petrol station in East Meon at around half-past eleven.' He raised his hand again, cutting off Lewin's burgeoning protest. 'However, the garage owner did say that you stopped in the middle of the store – dropped your car keys and froze, was the way he described it. Can you tell me what you saw that made you freeze?'

'I didn't freeze.'

'Did you drop your car keys?'

'Not that I recall.'

Marilyn sighed wearily. 'I'm reaching the end of my tether with you, Mr Lewin.'

Workman leant forward. *Good cop, bad cop.* Marilyn was more than happy to leave her to it. He was too tired to play word games with a lying little toerag like Lewin and he was one stretched-taut thread away from snapping, lunging across the table, grabbing Lewin by the collar and shaking the truth out of him.

'You saw the newspaper headlines, didn't you, Mr Lewin?' Workman asked, in a soft voice.

Lewin shook his head mulishly.

'You saw the headlines alerting you to the fact that Daniel and Eleanor Whitehead had been tortured and murdered and you realized then that whoever had killed them would, most likely, come after you and your wife. Perhaps you had dismissed the Fullers' murders as a one-off, related to Hugo's less-than-savoury choice of business,' she pressed.

379

'But once the Whiteheads were murdered, you made the connection.'

Another shake, but with significantly less conviction that the first. Perhaps what Marilyn had said was getting through to Lewin: that if he admitted he'd seen the headlines, realized that Denise was in danger, he would be off the hook for her murder – and the murders of the Fullers and Whiteheads – himself.

'You do realize that you are busy hanging yourself, don't you, Mr Lewin?' Marilyn cut in. 'The only reason that I suspect you didn't murder the Fullers, the Whiteheads and your wife is because the garage owner—' He glanced down at his notes. 'A Mr Sidhu, testified that you were genuinely shocked and disturbed when you saw the newspaper headlines.'

Lewin stared hard at the table top, in silence.

'What are you hiding, Mr Lewin?' Marilyn shouted, slamming both hands flat on the table top.

'Nothing.' A strangled denial.

'I don't bloody believe you.'

71

Callan bounced two wheels of his Golf up on the kerb, cut the engine and looked across, unsmiling. 'I can't be late for this appointment.'

Pulling his hand from the steering wheel, Jessie pressed it to her lips. 'I know and I'll be quick.'

Except for its position, in the middle of a village, over-looking the A24 and cricket green beyond, rather than buried in the midst of a dense, dark forest, Eunice Hargreaves' cottage was straight out of Hansel and Gretel with its steeply pitched, hand-moulded clay-tiled roof, lead-latticed windows and flintstone walls. Picture postcard, but when Jessie stepped through the wrought-iron gate, she saw that the beds in the narrow front garden were a disorder of rotting plants, weeds pushing up through the cracks between the path's paving stones, and the windows were opaque with dirt. There was a lamp post directly outside the gate – the post that Lupo had been tied to, she presumed.

Her knock was answered after a couple of minutes by a very elderly lady, bent as a wind-blown shrub, sparse clumps of goslings-fluff grey hair the first glimpse Jessie had of her. A grey jumper and skirt that matched her hair and her feet were jammed into sheepskin house slippers.

'My name is Dr Jessica Flynn,' Jessie said, ducking a little so that Eunice Hargreaves could see her face. 'I work with Surrey and Sussex Major Crimes.' Fishing out one of DI Simmons' business cards, which she had purloined from the stack on his desk a couple of days earlier, in case she needed to prove her legitimacy at any point (hers were still at the printer's) she proffered it, hoping the card would be sufficient to gain her an audience. Eunice's cloudy blue eyes studied the five-millimetre-tall embossed black letters that Jessie was sure she couldn't read. 'I have a few questions about the Siberian husky you found tied to the lamp post on Sunday morning.'

Eunice tilted her head, so that she could eyeball Jessie directly, and her brows knitted together in irritation. 'Sunday morning?' she snapped. 'It was the middle of the night.'

'Yes. I'm sorry about that.'

'Well, it's not your fault, is it? You'd better come in, if you have some questions.'

Leaning heavily on her stick, Eunice led Jessie down the hallway, into a kitchen-diner at the back of the cottage. Dark oak kitchen units lined two walls, a small round wooden table and four wooden spindle chairs occupied one corner, and a reclining reading chair was set in front of the window, so that its occupier could look out over the back garden. It reminded Jessie of Ahmose's reading chair by the fire, and that thought goaded her with the realization that she hadn't seen him since this case had greedily absorbed all her waking hours, apart from briefly this morning when

382

she and Callan had dropped Lupo off to be babysat for the day. She needed to spend some quality time with him soon; she couldn't neglect him, her adopted family, just because of work.

'Would you like a cup of tea, dear?'

Jessie didn't want a cup of tea and Callan had his appointment to make, but seeing Eunice Hargreaves' hopeful expression, remembering the weeds on the path and the grime on the windows, reminded her of how isolated Ahmose would be if she didn't live next door, and of a bleak memory from a year ago, the pin-sharp old lady locked in that soulless flat above the shops, nothing to live for but her hope. They still had three hours until Callan's appointment and Frimley Park Hospital was, at most, two hours' drive from here. *Plenty of time.*

'I'd love a cup of tea, thank you. Can I make it?'

'If you wouldn't mind, dear, that would be lovely. The teapot, cups and teabags are in the cupboard above the sink and the milk is in the fridge. I like mine strong, but milky. I'm very particular, I'm afraid.' She hobbled over to the reading chair and lowered herself into it stage by painful stage, one diaphanous hand gripping the arm of the chair like an eagle's claw, the other her stick.

'Pull up one of the kitchen chairs, dear,' Eunice said, when Jessie had made two cups of tea and set them on the side table next to the reading chair. 'You had some questions, about that husky I saw tied up outside.'

Jessie nodded. 'He's called Lupo.'

Eunice pressed her hands together. 'Lupo – wolf in Latin. What a perfect name. They brought him to the door when they'd untied him, those two lovely police-dog men, so that I could give him a pat. He was huge and magnificent looking,

383

but ever so gentle. I watched a documentary filmed in Canada a few weeks ago and he reminded me of a timber wolf, took me right back there when I first saw him . . .'

Jessie sipped her tea while Eunice talked, resisting the urge to glance at her watch.

'You told the police-dog team that you were woken by Lupo barking in the street, that you then got out of bed and saw him from your bedroom window,' she asked, when Eunice had finished.

Eunice nodded. 'I did see him from my bedroom window.'

'Because you'd been woken by his barking?'

'Huskies rarely bark, dear. They're not bred as guard dogs.'

'Perhaps he was barking because he was cold and trying to get attention?' Jessie pressed. She needed a definitive answer.

Eunice regarded her with a look pitched between pity and disdain. 'Huskies can withstand temperatures of minus sixty degrees centigrade, Dr Flynn.'

'So, he wasn't barking?'

'I suppose that you don't get much time to watch television, do you, dear, not with your demanding job?'

'No, I don't.' Jessie mentally added 'TV' and 'slob' to her 'to-do' list' for when this case was solved, before Marilyn came knocking again – if he ever did come knocking again after the spectacular lack of contribution she felt she'd made.

'Well, I spend most of my time watching television, animal documentaries especially. David Attenborough's voice really is quite sublime, don't you think?'

Jessie smiled. 'Yes, I do.'

'I watched a documentary about an extreme dog sled race

across the Yukon Peninsula in Canada and that documentary on wolves I mentioned. The camera crew spent two years living in the Canadian Rockies with the wolves, can you imagine, and their footage was quite spectacular.'

Jessie spun her wrist and glanced surreptitiously at her watch. It was twenty-five minutes since she'd lifted her hand to knock on Eunice's front door. Callan was stressed enough about his appointment without her keeping him waiting. Unconsciously, she raised a hand, heard Eunice's flow falter.

'I'm ever so sorry. It's living on my own, you see—'

'It's fine,' Jessie said, heat infusing her face, angry at herself for that unconscious physical display of her impatience. The lack of sleep was catching up with her. 'I'd love to listen, but my boyfriend drove me here and he has a hospital appointment soon.'

'Oh, I'm so sorry. Whenever I get a chance to talk I just talk and talk. Ask your questions, dear.'

'Thank you.' Jessie smiled, mentally fumbling to re-find her place. 'So you told the police-dog teams that Lupo's barking had woken you up.'

'I was already awake, Dr Flynn. I don't sleep so well since my husband died. I have a reading chair by the window and I get up and read instead of lying in bed tossing and turning. I open the curtains so that I can see the stars.' She met Jessie's gaze with a melancholy smile. 'Two young policemen are not interested in the loss and heartaches associated with old age, Dr Flynn, and so it just felt easier to say that the dog's barking had woken me. Does it really matter what I said, dear?'

Jessie wanted to say, *Yes, it does matter.* She was sure that it mattered, even if she couldn't yet work out how or why.

'No, not really. We just need to make sure that all witness statements are accurate so that when we catch him, there are no loopholes for his legal team to squeeze through.'

'The law is an ass. My darling Derek used to say that. He absolutely hated legalese.'

Jessie nodded. 'Can you just quickly confirm exactly what happened on the night you saw Lupo?'

Eunice nodded. 'I woke at just past one, got out of bed, opened the curtains and that's when I saw Lupo standing on the pavement right outside my cottage, like a magnificent Canadian timber wolf.'

72

Marilyn fetched himself an uninspiring cup of strong black coffee, tossed three sugars into it, and retreated to his office, shutting the door behind him, wishing not for the first time that whoever had fitted out Surrey and Sussex Major Crimes offices had appreciated that senior detectives required locks on their doors. A blind to pull down over the glass spy-panel wouldn't go amiss, either. He had an overwhelming desire to barricade himself in, pull down that imaginary blind and sleep for a week. Either that or drown in whisky. This clean-living malarkey was barely bearable when life ran smoothly, but nothing hit the spot during times of stress like a bottle of Jack Daniel's.

Whatever Simon Lewin was concealing – and Marilyn was sure that he was concealing something major, that Jessie Flynn's 'personal' theory was, in fact, correct – he clearly felt silence was worth more to him than any contribution disclosure might make to the hunt for his wife's murderer. And it was also highly unlikely that he was the elusive taxi driver, Charles, in his small dark hatchback, so Marilyn couldn't even nail him with illegally plying for hire. Lewin was bloody Teflon.

Marilyn took a few quiet minutes to finish his coffee, knowing that he'd not get many more moments of peace until this case was over, then reached for his mobile. His practised thumb scrolled through the list of recent calls he'd made until he found Chichester's three main taxi firm numbers, listed one after the other. He pressed the first and his call was answered almost immediately.

'DI Simmons,' a rough male voice answered. 'Back so soon.'

'I knew that you'd be on to this in a heartbeat, Gary, given how protective you are of your income stream.'

A deep, sonorous laugh. 'You know me too well, DI Simmons. I was about to call you actually, but you've saved me the trouble. I've got a make, model and licence plate for you. Black Skoda Scala, LD57 JKF.'

'Are you sure that's the one?'

'Yup. He's been around for a couple of weeks. One of my guys spotted him and challenged him this morning, told him that he needed a licence from Her Majesty to practise as a taxi driver. He said he'd lost his job a month back and that he was trying to earn money to tide him over until he got a new one. Seemed genuine and he had those cuts on the back of his left hand, like you said. He introduced himself as Charles Morris.'

'I'll get my detective constable to pay him a visit to check that his identity is genuine.'

'And if you could also ask your DC to warn him off doing it again, I'd be most grateful, DI Simmons. I'd hate anyone to think that they can moonlight as a taxi driver on my patch and get away with it. Good luck by the way, catching that looney-tune out there.'

'Thanks for your help, Gary.'

'Pleasure. And remember to give us a call when you need a lift somewhere.' Another deep laugh. 'I'd hate to see you giving business to those charlatans over at South Coast Cars or Sussex Radio Taxis.'

Marilyn cut off the call. Charles Morris: so the man had told Sophie Whitehead his real name. Not the hallmark of a ruthless serial killer. And neither was continuing to illegally ply for hire, despite having butchered five people. Nevertheless, he fired off a text to DC Cara with the name and number plate, asking him to source Charles Morris' details off the APNR database and swing by on his way back from East Meon, check that he was, indeed, cast-iron benign.

Tilting back in his chair, he stretched his arms above his head and yawned. Another blind avenue, though at least he hadn't wasted too long on it. And he didn't blame Mr Morris for moonlighting as a taxi driver; it was easy money, cash in hand. He just wished the man had stayed the hell off his suspect list.

Now, his only remaining lead was the hair that Burrows had found in the Dalmatian mask Leo Lewin had been wearing. He resisted the urge to glance at his watch. Resisted the urge to snatch up his mobile and call Burrows, ask him to plant his boot firmly up the lab's backside, tell them to get a bloody move on. Resisted the urge to call Jessie Flynn and ask her whether her Baba Vanga crystal ball had thrown up any killer insights. Instead, he crossed his arms over his chest and closed his eyes to grab a quick forty winks, hoping that his frazzled brain would seize the opportunity of rest to provide him with some startling insights of its own.

73

'Was it useful?' Callan asked, starting the engine and pulling away from the kerb outside Eunice Hargreaves' cottage.

'I don't know, to be honest. I just felt that I needed to get Eunice Hargreaves' story straight.'

'What are you thinking?'

'I was wondering why the perpetrator tied Lupo up outside her cottage.' Jessie gave a wry smile. 'Apart from the fact that there's a handy lamp post outside the gate. Something's niggling, but I can't pin it down.'

'It could be no more complex than the lamp post. Most villages aren't lit.'

'No, but there are plenty of handy trees.'

Callan smiled. 'I'll concede that point, Doctor. But you also told me that Walderton is the closest village to the Fullers' house.'

'Not by much. And it's mainly woods between the Fullers' house and Walderton, not easy walking, particularly not at night.'

'But it's guaranteed cover,' Callan said. *Ever the military man.*

'Is cover really an issue at – what? – midnight, in the middle of the Sussex countryside. You can drive for miles around these country lanes at night and not see anyone.'

She touched her thumb and forefinger to Callan's satnav, shrinking the map, scrolling left until she found Walderton, left again until the Fullers' extensive house and grounds were centred in the screen.

'The Fullers' house is here.'

Callan took in the map briefly before snapping his gaze back to the road. They were winding through the South Downs area of outstanding natural beauty, hills rising on either side, the thin strip of tarmac curling ahead of them between thick hedges. Jessie expanded the satnav map again, until an area of a couple of kilometres around the Fullers' house was featured.

'Walderton *is* the closest village, about a kilometre away, mainly through woods, as I said. But there's also Stoughton, Lordington, Adsdean, East Marden, all within two kilometres, and to get to the latter three he'd have been able to cross fields or . . . Look, for Adsdean and Lordington, he could have moseyed down the drive and walked two kilometres along country lanes, so the going is far easier, particularly in the dark.'

'He was dressed as a dog.'

'Sure, but wouldn't he take the mask off? Shove it in his pocket? And he could have left a coat in the Fullers' woods, picked it up after the murders and thrown it over the dog suit. Even if he wasn't wearing a coat, it could pass as a pale tracksuit.'

'At a stretch.'

'Running tights then. A tight running outfit or cycling garb. The murders are meticulously planned and cleverly executed, so we know that he's organized and clever, and so I doubt he's going to be walking around the countryside in full regalia, mask and all.'

Callan didn't answer immediately. They were cresting Harting Hill, a stunning vista of West Sussex and Surrey unfurling beneath them.

'Doesn't that go back to psychology though?' Callan said, changing down to third, the gearbox groaning as it controlled the car's descent. 'What dressing up as a dog means to him, and that's your department, Doctor.'

Jessie sighed. He was right. It did come down to psychology. *Talk to me about dogs, lovely boyfriend.* Was the murderer dressing up as a dog or did he want to *be* a dog? She suspected the latter, which would mean that when he was in character he would stay in character until the role – his work – was done. Until the murders, and all the actions associated with them, were complete.

'You're right,' she said. 'But even if he was dressed as a dog, wearing the full works, what would happen if someone drove past a man dressed as a dog, leading a huge, white Siberian husky, on a dark country lane, at past midnight on Saturday night/Sunday morning? They'd probably just think "Man coming back from a fancy dress party" or, failing that, they might think, "What the actual fuck, total weirdo, can't wait to tell my mates about this" and keep on driving. They might slow down and gawp, stare in the rear-view mirror as they drove away, but they wouldn't stop – would they? – in the dark to confront a man dressed as a dog, leading a dog the size of Lupo, to ask him why he's dressed as a dog? And they wouldn't recognize him because of the

392

mask. So whichever way you cut it, I don't think that handy lamp post outside Eunice Hargreaves' cottage makes as much sense as everyone seems to think it does.' Tipping her head back against the headrest, Jessie sighed. 'Sorry, that was a bit of a mad rant.'

'You've had a mad few days.'

She smothered a yawn. She was so utterly exhausted that she felt as if her brain had been doused in a vat of high-strength paracetamol. 'I told Marilyn that I thought our perp taking Lupo somewhere that he would be found quickly, and alerting the police to the Fullers' murders by doing so, showed that he has humanity.'

'Did Marilyn agree with you?'

Jessie gave a wry smile. 'No. He was of the opinion that our perp is a psychopath, plain and simple.'

'Are you sure that he's so wrong about that?'

'Yes, actually, that's about the only thing I *am* sure about.' She sighed. 'Because psychopaths have no empathy, for anyone or anything. Lupo could happily survive all night outside in the UK, many nights in fact, but perhaps the perp didn't know that.'

Callan frowned. 'Virtually everyone must know what Siberian huskies are bred for, where they come from. The name sort of gives it away.'

'Right. But that's just the point, isn't it?'

'You're being opaque, Jessie.'

'No, you're being thick, Callan. Lupo *could* have quite happily survived until morning. If the perp hadn't cared, he could have tied Lupo up in the woods or left him running free and at some point he would have been found. But instead he tramped a kilometre through woods, in the middle of the night, to Eunice Hargreaves' cottage.'

393

'To a lamp post outside a cottage in the nearest village. We've been through this.'

'I know, I know. Like I said, something's niggling, but I don't know exactly what and I can't think straight.' Reaching over, Jessie took Callan's left hand from the steering wheel and pulled it into her lap, entwined her fingers with his. He was used to high-speed driving as a military policeman, could easily navigate this winding B-road at fifty with only one hand. 'Let's just forget the stupid investigation for the rest of today. They're waiting for DNA results on the hair they found in Leo Lewin's mask, anyway, so the case may be solved by this evening. We've got more important things to . . .' *worry about* '. . . think about.'

Tilting her head against the window, she closed her eyes, cradling his strong, safe hand in her lap. Callan was more important than the investigation. More important than anything. She'd pace the reception area at Frimley Park Hospital while he was in his appointment and then they'd drive back into the country and find a nice pub for dinner, a proper locals' pub, low-ceilinged and dingy, more dogs than people. Then they'd drive back home, collect Lupo from Ahmose's cottage next door and head to bed and she'd wake up in the morning to find that the case had been solved – or not. Either way, she'd deal with tomorrow, tomorrow.

Woods were flashing past the passenger window when Jessie opened her eyes sometime later. She wasn't sure if she'd dozed or actually slept, though she did feel stiff and uncomfortable, as if she'd been sitting in this car seat for hours. She would have thought they were closer by now, in Frimley, not still in the countryside. She heard the sudden tick-tock of the indicator as Callan slowed and the seatbelt tightened against her chest.

394

'Where are we?' she asked, sleepily.

'Here,' Callan said.

'Huh? Where?'

'At the hospital.'

'What? Oh God, I thought—' A yawn truncated her sentence.

'Thought what?' he asked, pulling into the hospital car park.

'I thought we were still in the countryside.' *Stuck. Stuck in Sussex . . . at the Fullers' . . . in Walderton with Eunice Hargreaves.* But they were in Frimley, Camberley, at the hospital. *D-Day. D-Hour. D-Minute – finally here.*

Finding a parking space, Callan cut the engine. 'Ready?'

Jessie squeezed his hand hard. 'Are you?'

He pulled a face. 'As I'll ever be.'

Raising his hand to her lips she kissed it hard. 'I love you, Callan.'

'I love you too, Jessie Flynn.'

74

The sliver of toughened glass in Marilyn's office door filled with the doughy moon of Tony Burrows' face. Even from a distance and through the none-too-clean pane, Marilyn could tell that Burrows was ragged, his pale blue eyes sunken and ringed with shadows, the combination of bald pate and six days' worth of stubble curling now into a beard, making him look as if he'd accidentally put his head on upside down.

'Come on in,' Marilyn called out, trying to keep a lid on the eagerness in his tone. The fact that he probably looked like a teenager eyeing up his first date – far too keen for his own good – didn't escape him, but he was in desperate need of a lifeline, a rubber ring, a ragged piece of driftwood, anything that he could grab onto to save the case, and himself, his beleaguered, battered reputation, from sinking.

Burrows stepped into his office, holding the door open behind him for Sarah Workman, who followed him in. He was wearing a tomato-red jumper atop a marginally darker shade of red corduroy trousers, bagging at the knees, and he looked like a particularly low-end, jobbing Santa Claus.

'Is your wife away, Burrows?' Marilyn asked.

Burrows raised an eyebrow in surprise. 'On a girlfriend's fiftieth birthday trip to Majorca. Nine menopausal women loose on a small island. God help the locals. How did you know?'

'I've been spending a lot of time with Baba Vanga.'

Marilyn's gaze moved from Burrows to Workman, lowered to fix on the A4 sheet of printed paper clasped tightly in her hand, though he didn't have a cat in hell's of reading it at this distance. His gaze rose again to take in the grave expression on her face, on Burrows'.

'Don't tell me that the bastards at the lab are still messing around with the hair from Leo Lewin's dog mask? I paid them half my annual CSI budget to expedite it.'

Burrows shook his head.

A balloon of air emptied from Marilyn's lungs with an audible 'pouf', the human equivalent of a punctured tyre, as he pictured his only piece of hard evidence slipping through his fingers, swiftly followed by the case and his blood-sweat-and-tears, hard-earned reputation. 'We didn't get a match on NDNAD?'

Another shake. 'The lab came back with a DNA profile from the hair half an hour ago and we did get a match on the database.'

It took Marilyn a moment to comprehend what he had said.

'So why the long faces, people?'

Burrows didn't answer. He looked across to Workman, who lifted her shoulders dispiritedly.

'For Christ's sake, spit it out, Sarah,' Marilyn snapped.

75

One Year Ago

Robbie shook his head. He couldn't see the boy any more. The boy was gone, swallowed by the waves. Only the little dog was visible, its white legs pumping the waves like pistons, as it fought with utter animal desperation for its life.

Fine?

No, he wasn't even fine. Not now that he had come here, to this place.

'What was it like?' he murmured.

His dad looked confused.

'Shall we go to the pub and get some dinner?' Allan said, shivering. 'It's freezing out here. Perhaps we shouldn't have come, but I thought some bracing air would whet our appetites for dinner.'

The wisps of mouse-coloured hair that he combed across his bald pate had caught the wind and were standing on end, waving like the tendrils of seaweed that Robbie could see in his mind's eye, clinging to the boy's bones. His dad looked ridiculous. Pale-faced and scared.

Robbie knew scared. He had been scared every day of his life. Just as the boy and his little black and white dog knew scared.

'What was it like?' he repeated, louder.

'Robbie?'

'What was it like, Dad?' he shouted. 'What was it fucking like?'

'What was what like?'

'Watching? What was it like watching him die?'

76

Over his quarter century in Surrey and Sussex Major Crimes, Marilyn had arrested more people than he could count without resorting to an abacus. He used to rehearse each arrest in his mind multiple times before enacting it for real, like a professional footballer visualizing the perfect goal before his foot connected with the ball. Arrests could be unpredictable beasts, particularly when the arrestee was at the mercy of a substance – alcohol, drugs – or had an extreme mental disorder, and it paid dividends to be prepared for every eventuality. But Marilyn realized, as he stood in Allan Parker's hallway, the splintered mess the steel enforcer had made of the front door hanging off its hinges behind him, that he hadn't done that for a long time, that arresting criminals was as natural to him now as stepping off a kerb.

Allan Parker's hands were cuffed behind his back, a brick of a uniform clutching his arm. One firearms officer stood to Marilyn's left, guarding the entrance to the kitchen, with eyes up the stairs; another to his right, covering the entrance to the lounge, eyes on the patio doors beyond; and two more firearms officers outside in the front garden, two in the back – Marilyn wasn't taking any chances. DC Cara hovering by the front door, taking it all in, learning, doubtless committing every detail of this arrest to memory as Marilyn had done in his rookie days. He met Allan Parker's insipid blue gaze with his own, mismatched one, directly, with challenge.

'Allan Parker, I am arresting you for the murders of Hugo Fuller, Claudine Fuller, Daniel Whitehead, Eleanor Whitehead and Denise Lewin and for the kidnap of Leo Lewin—'

Silent and ghoul-pale, Allan nodded.

'You do not have to say anything, but it may harm your defence if you do not mention when questioned something that you later rely on in court. Anything you do say may be given in evidence against you.'

Despite what Jessie Flynn said – that the label of psychopath was too easy – despite her logical reasoning, he couldn't agree with her. Observing Allan now, the blankness of his expression, the cold emptiness of his gaze, Marilyn was convinced that Flynn was wrong.

Stepping back, he addressed himself to the uniformed brick-shithouse clutching Parker's arms.

'Take him away, please.'

A sudden movement on the stairs caught Marilyn's eye, the armed officer standing beside him responding at the exact same moment. He dodged as the business end of a Heckler & Koch MP5 clipped his ear.

'Jesus Christ, put that fucking thing away,' he snapped.

'Sorry, sir.'

A boy, Robbie Parker Marilyn presumed, was standing at the top of the stairs, pale, diminutive, appearing so much younger than the fifteen years Marilyn knew him to be. At the sight of his son, the expression on Allan Parker's face flashed to one of intense vulnerability and for a brief moment he looked almost as young as Robbie, boy-like, brittle and pregnable.

'Let me go,' he shouted, springing to life, struggling and kicking out, as if some invisible finger had found his on switch. 'For God's sake, let me go.'

The brick-shithouse must have given him a swift jab in the side with his elbow as Marilyn heard a 'pouf' and Parker bent double.

'Enough,' Marilyn snapped, warning in his tone to both of them. He addressed himself to Robbie. 'I'm sorry, son, but I'm going to have to ask you to show me your hands.'

One pale hand and then the other slid from where they had been buried deep in the pockets of his baggy jeans. The ragged, chewed sleeves of his iron-grey sweatshirt gathered around his elbows as he raised his arms above his head. Even Marilyn had to take a breath to stop himself from reacting with horror at the sight of the kid's arms, the self-inflicted gashes carving up his skin like crazy paving.

'Come down the stairs slowly, please,' Marilyn's voice croaked from a parchment-dry throat.

Arms raised, Robbie stopped a few steps from the bottom. Looking at him now, at the devastation of his arms, the ravaged expression on his face, Marilyn regretted his rush to arrest Allan Parker. He should have put a watch on their house, front and back, then called Jessie, waited for her to drive back from Frimley Park Hospital before charging in mob-handed. What would another couple of hours have cost him?

'I'm sorry, Robbie,' Marilyn said.

The boy's shoulders lifted in a tiny shrug.

'*I'm* sorry,' Allan wailed. 'For *everything*.'

Robbie ignored his father. From under the concealing darkness of his fringe, his deep green eyes remained fixed on Marilyn.

'I'm afraid that I must ask you to leave the house, so that we can search it,' Marilyn said. 'But Detective Sergeant Workman, Sarah, has said that you can stay at her house for tonight until we can sort out a foster family placement or find space in a children's home. Go back upstairs and grab a few things for the night.'

A barely there nod, but Robbie didn't move.

'Detective Constable Johns will go with you.' Marilyn gave a nod to the firearms officer to his left.

'Let me speak to him,' Allan Parker pleaded. 'Please, just let me speak to my son for one second, like a human being.'

There was nowhere for Parker to run: Marilyn had the place in lockdown.

'Go ahead, Mr Parker,' he said.

Christ, where had that sliver of humanity come from? He never used to have a heart, not for scum like this.

'I never meant it to happen, Robbie. I was weak and self-centred,' Allan implored, his voice breaking. 'And I've had to live with the truth of what I did for my whole life.'

What the hell is he talking about? Marilyn's gaze moved from Parker to his son. Robbie was standing motionless on the stairs, his face an unreadable mask. He had lowered his arms and his hands were clenched into fists, the right larger than the left, fingers moving, kneading . . . a ball, Marilyn realized. Marilyn had one himself, on his desk, filled with sand. A stress ball.

But Robbie didn't looked stressed.

Despite the ravages of his arms and the paleness of his

face, he looked calm, serene almost. Then the corners of his mouth twisted into a tiny smile. Slowly, very slowly and deliberately, he began to shake his head.

'No, *I've* had to live with the truth of what you did for *my* whole life.'

He opened his fist and the ball fell. Five pairs of eyes watched it bounce down the stairs, stream across the hallway and out through the open front door, Marilyn stepping aside to let it pass, as if it was a bomb.

77

The policeman, that block of wood in the uniform clutching onto his dad for all he was worth, began to fade from Robbie's vision. And the two firearms officers, and the young, handsome multi-racial chap who Robbie bet had never been bullied in his life, and the scarecrow in the black suit. They melted away, along with the characterless beige walls and the shit-brown carpet that Robbie had always thought summed up his life way too fucking perfectly.

The only person who remained in their dingy hallway was his father. But instead of carpet, Robbie saw, in his mind's eye, pale, weather-beaten wooden slats under his father's feet, a yawning crevasse between each, and ten metres beneath, a chill, grey-black churning, swallowing sea. His father wasn't a middle-aged man, but a boy of about the same age as Robbie was now. But he and his boyhood father looked nothing alike. Where Robbie had spent his life creeping through the shadows, making himself invisible, apologizing by every means he knew how for his existence, his father was the opposite. He stood tall, feet planted wide apart, hands jammed into the pockets of his army-green parka, which he wore casually, slouchily, the same way he wore the second skin of arrogance that Robbie had never known, would never know or wear.

But something wasn't right. His father's face was pale – not from cold, Robbie realized, but from shock.

It was too late now, though.

Too late to have regrets.

Too late to save the boy.

'What was it like, Dad?' he asked quietly. 'What was it like, watching him die?'

78

Jessie could hear the persistent miaow-miaow of the siren cutting down the phone line, could picture the blue lights washing across the front of Allan and Robbie Parker's chalet-style house, the black-clad figures of the firearms teams in the front garden, slapping each other's backs, packing up their kit, Allan Parker handcuffed and secure, another job well done. The elderly neighbours in their small, out-of-the-way cul-de-sac would be watching the unfolding drama with the glee of hyenas eyeing fresh kill – much as Parker's victims' neighbours had watched from their windows as the black-bagged bodies were shunted from the sanctity of their homes to the morgue's van – nothing sacred in this media age, nothing too personal, too base, not to be classed as entertainment. Perhaps there would be a couple of press vans there too, the team's leaky teabag, whoever that was, doubtless keen to cash in on the final triumph with highly paid tip-offs.

'Jessie.' Marilyn sounded distracted, unsurprisingly. Jessie didn't care. She was practically combusting from fury.

'You should have told me that you were going to arrest Allan Parker. I should have been there, *be* there now.'

'I'm sorry, Jessie. DCI Janet Backastowe stepped in as soon as an arrest was imminent and I'm now just a highly overqualified sidekick. Thank you for all your help on this case, but we can take it from here. Your work is done.'

'No, it isn't. Robbie needs me.' *Someone. He needs someone who understands him, at least, and I'm the best he's going to get.*

'Workman is looking after him.'

'Sarah—' Jessie broke off. Should she tell Marilyn that she'd just got off the phone to Sarah Workman who had pleaded with her to sprint back down to Chichester, that she was terrified for Robbie's mental health? No, she couldn't break Workman's confidence.

'Workman isn't a psychologist, which is why she asked me to help Robbie in the first place.'

'Workman is a very capable—'

'Detective sergeant,' Jessie cut in.

'Woman, I was going to say,' Marilyn cut back. 'And Robbie knows her.'

Jessie sighed, exasperated. Why the hell was Callan taking so long in his neurologist's office, she wondered, a moment later chastising herself for being so . . . so selfish? But it wasn't selfishness driving her. It was a desperate need to be in two places at once, to support two people who needed her. The electric suit hissed and crackled across her skin at the feeling of being trapped between a gargantuan rock and a limitless hard place.

'I'm sorry, Jessie. I feel for the kid, really I do, but this is way bigger than Robbie. We couldn't risk Allan Parker absconding while we waited for you to finish holding Callan's hand.'

Jessie didn't rise, not that she wasn't tempted, but she knew how stressed Marilyn must be to have made that comment in the first place. And her attention had been caught by the door to Callan's neurologist's office opening, further down the hallway, Callan emerging, walking towards her, the expression on his face – what? She couldn't tell. He was wearing his military policeman's poker face. Was that good or bad? Phone clamped to her ear, she raised her hand, forced a stressed smile.

'Robbie's spending tonight at Workman's cottage as, surprise surprise, given the funding cuts, there were no emergency foster care spaces,' she heard Marilyn say. 'And we'll hand him over to Children's Services tomorrow.'

'He's been through way too much to be dumped in a children's home or in a foster home with people he doesn't know, Marilyn.'

'I can't have this discussion now, Jessie. I have a quintuple murderer in custody and I need to question him.'

'He'll end up committing suicide.'

'I can't have this discussion now.'

'And his blood will be on our hands. Marilyn. *Marilyn*.'

Silence.

'*Fuck*.'

79

Allan Parker closed his eyes and tuned into the sound of the car's tyres swishing on the wet road, trying to sink into the unchallengingly repetitive noise in the same way he tried, vainly, every night, to sink into the state of blissful relaxation his guided sleep meditation tapes promised. But there was one repetitive sound that he could never listen to, that snapped him back to relentless wakefulness, lodged a choking lump in his throat: the sound of breaking ocean waves.

Now, his mind's eye found Robbie standing gazing down at him from the stairs, found his ruined face, the look on it. He had spent the past fifteen years loving Robbie with every molecule of his being, fighting fiercely to protect him, to ease his path through life, and he had recognized in that one look that his efforts had been in vain. Though, in truth, he had known long before. He had known the second his son was born, terribly disfigured, that karma had caught up with him. Had known, when he had collected Robbie from prep school on that first afternoon, when he saw his son's scarred face bruised and tear-stained from the first incidence of the bullying that would come to define his life.

Because of what Allan had done twenty-five years ago.

Because of who he had been.

What was it like, Dad? What was it like, watching him die?

He had expected the boy to struggle, to fight to the death for his life. They all had. But as soon as Hugo had thrown his little dog into the freezing sea, he had diminished, physically diminished in front of their eyes. He was small and thin and pale, always had been, but when he saw his little dog disappear under the slate-grey surface of the water, it was as if every bone inside his body dissolved, leaving only a baggy carcass of skin. He had been standing on the edge of the lifeboat station jetty, pleading with Hugo to let his dog go.

Fine, Hugo said, in retort. *I'll let him go.*

But Allan caught the look on Hugo's face, the sly smile. It was a smile that Allan knew well.

What happened next played out as if in slow motion, the little black and white body flailing as it fell, feet pedalling for purchase, finding nothing but air. The boy had turned to face them, standing in a row as they were, all of them laughing. But even then, Allan remembered their laughter had had a hollow timbre as if, in that moment, they had all realized that Hugo had gone too far – that they had all gone too far. They knew what the little dog meant to the boy. They knew the home the boy came from, the grim life he led, no light, no colour in it, no kindness and no love, except for his dog. But still they had tormented him for years purely because they could. And because it was so much fun.

80

Jessie sped away from the bend, pressing the accelerator to the floor, wrenching the gearstick from third to fourth, finding second accidentally – her scarred hand still its own master when she most needed it not to be – wincing as the engine screeched in protest.

Thank God Callan wasn't here to witness the sacrilege she was inflicting on his gearbox. Quick change to fourth, concentrating hard on the movement of her hand, then fifth. The country road wound ahead of her through dense woods, the solid trunks of the trees only faintly darker than the spaces between, into the open again, the hills that she knew rose on either side hard to distinguish from the black sky above, the twin cones of the headlights picking out the thin strip of tarmac, guiding her towards Chichester. Nightfall at barely five p.m.

Callan was spending the night in hospital, undergoing an MRI scan and a plethora of other tests, and Jessie would collect him in the morning. *So much for that romantic dinner in a poster-child country pub.* Allan Parker was safely in custody, doubtless now sweating under the unrelenting questioning of DCI Janet Backastowe, Marilyn resenting his relegation to 'bit-part' status. Robbie was at Sarah Workman's cottage, secure and comfortable – for tonight at least. **Marilyn's on my case. I'm needed back at the office pronto.** Workman had signed off with: **Robbie seemed OK. He surprised me** ☺. And Jessie would be there soon to make sure that he really was OK.

So why the hell did she feel as if the electric suit was wrapped claustrophobically tight around her, hissing and snapping, its wires constricting with each kilometre she drove?

81

The bleached wooden planks creaked and groaned beneath teenage Allan Parker's feet. Goosebumps rose on his exposed skin from the chill wind and his eyes stung from the salt spray thrown up by the waves slamming against the jetty's pilings. None of them had expected Hugo to actually do it: to toss that struggling little bundle of fur into the freezing sea. The boy's eyes found each one of them in turn, a world of impotent pain and horror in his look, and then he turned, climbed calmly over the jetty's rusted railing and dropped from view.

One of them had leapt forward, trying, too late, to grab him, save him. Who? Simon? Daniel? Allan couldn't remember. He only knew that it hadn't been Hugo and it hadn't been him. He had been a coward back then and he was a coward now. All he had wanted to do throughout the many years they had tormented the boy was to ensure that he wasn't a victim and he had been prepared to do anything to secure his own safety.

Now, he saw the image of a boy, his face blue with cold,

as he was tossed and slammed by the waves. But it was the boy's little black and white dog that held Allan's attention more. Allan could see its white front legs churning through the dark water as it fought with utter determination for its life, driven by a survival instinct no one could break. They had burnt it with cigarettes and lighters, sliced its skin, kicked it between them like a football until its ribs cracked, stamped on its two front feet so that it hobbled on clubs, until finally Hugo had tossed it off the jetty into the freezing sea and still the little dog wanted, so badly, to live.

The boy, though, was different. For the first time in the eight years that Allan had known him, tormented him, he looked at peace. He had lost. He had been losing his whole life and now he looked as if he had made peace with that reality. As if he knew that whatever he survived in life, it would never be enough, that he was born to lose, would always lose. That someone up there – God, fate, whatever – didn't want him to live a good life.

Allan looked towards the beach. It was deserted, no one there to witness what they had done, no one to save the boy or his dog. They would need to save themselves – or die.

Even Hugo realized that they had gone too far this time. Flinging himself onto his front, he reached over the edge of the jetty.

'You can make it. Swim, you fucker,' he yelled.

But they were ten metres above the freezing waves and even if the boy had stretched his arms up, tried to save himself, there was no way that Hugo could have reached him.

The boy didn't stretch up. His face – so starkly pale against the jet-black heaving swell of sea – bobbed, once, twice and was gone.

'Swim, you stupid fucker,' Hugo screamed at the empty sea.

Darkness pressing in around them, they waited, watching, four sets of eyes glued to where they had last seen him. Allan, his lips moving in silent prayer, remembered the nervous laughter, Hugo's assurance that he was just *dicking them around*, that he'd *fucking kill the little shit when he made it to shore*. They had turned then, as one, and scanned the shoreline for a dark break in the pale froth of breaking waves, for the boy's skinny, beaten body dragging itself from the sea.

But there was nothing. Only the white line of foam advancing, retreating, advancing again, unbroken.

Hugo swung back around to face them, awareness and fear in his eyes. 'Let's get out of here,' he snapped.

A voice in Allan's head chanted: *We killed him . . . we're murderers . . . we killed him . . .*

'Hugo,' Allan managed.

'What, Allan?'

'Shouldn't we—' *Shouldn't we – what? Turn back time? Have been nicer – for years?* It had been going on for years and years by then, the bullying. And Allan had enjoyed it. He *had* enjoyed tormenting the boy, torturing his little dog.

We killed him . . . we're murderers . . . we killed him . . .

Hugo rounded on him savagely. 'What the fuck do you want, Allan? Do you want me to dive in, do you?'

'We can't leave him.'

Hugo lunged at him then, grabbing him by the shoulders, propelling him backwards towards the edge of the jetty. 'Why don't you fucking dive in, see if you can save the little shit.'

Allan's terrified gaze flicked from Hugo, to Daniel, to Simon. Neither of the other two would meet his eye.

416

'You've always been a fucking coward, Allan,' Hugo sneered. 'A follower and a coward.' He gave Allan a shove that sent him reeling. 'He's not dead, anyway. He's just dicking us around.' Sauntering to the middle of the jetty, Hugo stamped hard on one gnarled plank. 'Come out, come out, wherever you are.' He jumped up and down, the jetty shivering beneath them. 'I know that you're under here somewhere, you little fucker, clinging to a piling, waiting for us to leave.' He jumped from one plank to the next, threw his arms out wide and raised his face to the black sky. 'Well, I don't care,' he yelled. 'I hope you're dead. You were a pathetic excuse for a human being and I hope you're fucking dead.'

And still the voice in Allan's head chanted: *We killed him . . . we're murderers . . . we killed him . . .*

'Enough, Hugo,' Simon stammered.

Dropping his arms, Hugo spun around.

'Enough, Hugo,' he whined. Turning away, he swaggered down the jetty towards the beach, stamping every few steps, jumping up and down every few more, yelling at the top of his voice. 'I hope you're dead, you stupid little cunt. You and your miserable fucking rat-dog.'

Allan, Simon and Daniel straggled down the jetty after Hugo. Half an hour ago, they had marched in the opposite direction – dragging the struggling boy, Hugo dangling his little dog by the collar, its body jerking and snapping as it fought for air – their footsteps pounding the gnarled wooden planks in unison, an army marching to war. Now they moved in silence, a routed gaggle, heads hanging, avoiding each other's gazes. The chant in Allan's brain, constant as the breaking waves: *We killed him . . . we're murderers . . . we killed him . . .*

At the end of the jetty, Hugo turned and held up his hand. 'Stop.' His hooded, dark gaze drilled into each of them in turn. 'What goes on tour stays on tour, right, boys?' His tone a warning.

Speechless nods from dumb beasts.

Hugo raised his voice. 'Right?'

'Right,' Daniel Whitehead muttered.

'Simon?'

Simon Lewin nodded.

'Say it,' Hugo demanded.

'Right,' Simon muttered.

'Allan?'

'Yes, of course.' He was as complicit as any of them. What choice did he have – to confess their crime or to conceal? There was no choice.

'Where were you, Allan?' Hugo demanded.

'What do you mean?' he stammered.

'Where were you, if we get asked? For the last hour – where have you been?'

'Uh, at . . . at home?'

'No, you weren't home,' Hugo snapped, with derision. 'Because your mum is there, isn't she, so she'll know that you're not.'

'My mum and dad are working late in the restaurant. You were at mine, Allan, weren't you?' Simon Lewin muttered.

Allan nodded. 'Right. I was at Simon's.' His mouth was parched and his throat had closed up.

'What were you doing? Watching TV, playing the PlayStation, kicking a football around in the garden, toying with your dicks?'

'PlayStation,' Simon managed.

'Which game?'

'Come on, Hugo.'

'*Which game?*'

'Air Combat,' Simon stumbled over the words.

Hugo nodded. 'Stick to it. You too, Allan.'

A silent, bovine nod.

'Daniel?'

'I was out running. I'm training for cross-country.'

Hugo looked down at Daniel's feet. He was wearing the trainers he habitually wore when they saw him down here during the holidays, when he was staying with his grandparents. 'Fine, that works.'

No one questioned Hugo as to where he had been.

'No one squeals or they'll have me to answer to.' He laughed, the sound a harsh, animalistic bark that cut through the chill air and the pressing darkness. 'Me and the police. Because we're all in this together.' He mimed slicing his hand across his neck. 'Bonded by blood now. *Forever*, bonded by blood.'

A sudden movement caught Allan's eye, a break in the pale line of frothing waves. The boy's little black and white dog had made it to the beach.

'What the fuck are you looking at, Allan?'

Allan snapped his gaze back to Hugo's. 'A seagull,' he muttered. 'Caught my eye. It's gone now.'

Hugo's eyes narrowed. Allan could tell that he didn't believe him. Suspicion was cracking them wide open already. They had killed and now fear and blame would fracture their merry band, blow it wide apart.

He crossed his fingers behind his back, silently praying for the little dog. Hugo would kill it if he saw it; Allan knew he would. Was its survival instinct so acute that it would know to hide?

* * *

419

Allan's eyes snapped open. Trees hugging either side of the road now, lit by the squad car's headlights. *Brandy Hole Lane*, he recognized it. He used to take Robbie here when he was a toddler, before the bullying started, walk him through the woods foraging for wild mushrooms, peeling bark from fallen trees to send woodlice and red ants scuttling, Robbie, head thrown back, laughing gleefully, unselfconscious of his ruined face at that age. Would he ever walk in these woods again or would he die in prison? *Whatever.* He didn't care. The only thing he cared about was Robbie and now he would be safe.

What was it like, Dad?

He had known, the moment Robbie was born, when he saw the ravaged mess that was his baby boy's face, that it was his fault, his punishment, karma. Had known, every time that Robbie came home with tears staining his scars, that he was being punished for his father's boyhood cruelty. And however hard Allan fought, he had been unable to save his son from the bullies' torment. Just as the boy had been unable to save himself and his little dog from them.

What was it like, watching him die?

'I murdered them,' he said, testing the feel of the words in his mouth. 'I murdered them.' Louder. 'All of them. I murdered them all.'

82

Sarah Workman's three-hundred-year-old cottage reminded Jessie of her and Callan's favourite pub, with its thatched roof and whitewashed walls. But where the pub's woodwork was scarlet, with matching red lobelia clustered in the hanging baskets, Workman's cottage was muted with greys and blues. Jessie imagined that in summer the cottage garden would be filled with white roses, soft blue delphiniums, larkspur and hollyhocks. But now it was bare, the wind cutting across the surrounding fields, bearing the chill of approaching winter. Warm lights pulsed from behind translucent linen curtains in the downstairs windows, though she could see no movement, hear no sound.

Allan and Robbie Parker's house was now in lockdown, she knew, Tony Burrows' CSI team crawling all over it, DCI Backastowe and Marilyn grilling Allan Parker, evidence being expedited, a party atmosphere among the team. A job well done.

Except.

Except for Robbie.

Pushing the gate open with a creak that sounded like branches rubbing against each other deep in a forest, Jessie walked up the front path, the heels of her boots clacking on the uneven slabs, the 'Welcome' doormat muffling the last of her footsteps. The grey-blue-painted front door was unlocked, resting against the jamb, and it swung open with barely a touch. She hadn't expected that, though in truth she hadn't given much thought to anything beyond getting here as quickly as she could. Odd though.

A shiver ran down her spine, someone walking over her grave, as she stepped into the dimly lit hallway. A face right in front of her and she leapt back, her heart rocketing to her throat. But it was only her own over-stressed, ghostly pale face looking back at her from a wall-mounted mirror.

Where to now? Only two options, left or right. Turning left, she stepped into a narrow, low-ceilinged kitchen that ran from front to back, spots casting mellow light onto pale grey units, a navy-blue Aga pumping a blanket of cosy heat that Jessie would have given a lot to be able to sink into, blotting out the real world, if only for a few moments. No time for that, though. Backing out of the empty kitchen, she stepped quietly across the hallway into a sitting room, which again ran from front to back. Signs of Sarah Workman were everywhere: in the navy-blue cushions carefully ordered on the pale grey sofa and matching armchairs; in the navy-swimsuited beach photographs; in the framed letters from various charities – Age UK, The Salvation Army, Dogs Trust – thanking Workman for volunteering. Navy blue featured heavily in Workman's life, much as black featured in Marilyn's: in the prim skirt suits and the sensible low-heeled courts and in the navy accents everywhere in this warm, homely cottage.

Jessie stopped in the middle of the room. 'Robbie,' she called.

No answer. No sound at all that she could hear inside the cottage. Only the faint rustle of trees in the garden and something loose knocking out in the street. Moving towards the stairs that rose upwards from the far corner of the sitting room, she called out again.

'Robbie, it's Dr Jessie Flynn.'

Silence still.

Was she too late? Had he gone? Run? He'd know that his only option was a foster family or children's home, so why wouldn't he have run? He'd be stupid not to. She would run, if she was him. *Fuck, I'll kill Marilyn.*

This is bigger than Robbie.

No – he could have held DCI Backastowe off, waited for her to get back from Frimley Park. He could have, *should* have.

Tossing her coat onto the chair, she climbed the stairs. Three doors at the top, one either side of her, both in darkness, block shapes of beds and wardrobes in each. And straight ahead of her, a door ajar to the only room that was lit: a white-tiled bathroom, fluffy white towels neatly folded on a towel rail to the right, a toilet straight ahead, the seat down. Nothing here to goad her OCD and the electric suit into life – but still the suit hissed and snapped, searing her skin.

Water. It's about water. Watching and water.

Images strobed through her mind: Hugo Fuller, strapped to a steamer chair, his face a mask of bloody gashes; the halo of Claudine Fuller's blonde hair around her broken, bloodied head; the gaping black pits of Daniel Whitehead's sightless sockets; Eleanor, beyond, bathing in a pool of her

423

own blood; the pale, slack-skinned form of Denise Lewin; hot acid bile in her mouth, the taste real or imagined, she couldn't tell. She ran her tongue around her palate, knowing that it was fear, adrenalin that had parched her. But it was a phantom fear, nothing to be frightened of. *It's only a bathroom. There's no water, no running water, no blood.* But still the electric suit burned.

A sudden noise – quiet, but there all the same.

'Robbie? Is that you?'

83

While Allan Parker was being processed downstairs, Marilyn made himself a quick cup of coffee, strong, tar black, three sugars, tossed in another sugar for good measure and retreated to his office for five minutes of respite before the interviewing circus began. Even with the windows closed, he could hear the clamour of the press out front in the public car park. If the volume was anything to go by, their numbers were swelling by the second, and the noise gave him a slight, sick feeling in the pit of his stomach. In his opinion, the press was rarely useful and unfailingly brutally judgemental, and they had proven that theory to be correct many times over on this case. He had garnered more column inches in the past few days than in the past twenty-five years of policing, ten per cent of those inches, at best, flattering. Though, to be fair, he was never going to cut it as the media's perfect poster-child cop.

His coffee cup had barely touched his lips when there was a knock at his door and DC Cara stepped into his office.

'What have I told you about the etiquette of knocking and waiting to be invited in before entering?' Marilyn said in a weary voice.

Pressing the back of his hand to his mouth, he suppressed a yawn, hoping Cara hadn't clocked the unbefitting lapse. The finish line for this horrendous case was a mere stumbling length away. All he had to do was to hold it together for a few more hours and then he could sleep the sleep of the dead at his leisure. Or at least secure that elusive Holy Grail of eight solid hours.

'There's a woman, with her teenage son, at the front desk asking to see you, sir,' Cara said.

Marilyn's eyes hung closed for a moment. 'Cara, I was under the impression that you were working with us on the Allan Parker case, that you appreciate we have a serial killer in custody who we need to interview post-haste.' He indicated his mobile, a silent, black rectangle in the midst of the sea of white papers flooding his desk. 'I am awaiting an imminent summons from DCI Janet Backastowe and I cannot go AWOL to have a tête-à-tête with some lady and her son hot off the street with a beef about God knows what.'

Cara nodded. The kid looked as wrung-out as Marilyn felt. Wrung-out, but not put off, his expression depressingly determined.

'They say that they need to speak to you about the Parkers, sir. Urgently, the woman said.'

'Interview them on my behalf, DC Cara.'

'They won't speak to me, sir. The woman, Mrs Scuffil, she's called, said that she wants to speak with the organ grinder.'

Marilyn's jaw tightened. *The organ grinder.* Surely no one

426

in their right mind, in this day and age, would have inferred that a multi-racial detective was the monkey in that particular scenario.

'She's not the most pleasant,' Cara said, with a sardonic half-smile. 'And the son looks as if he's gone ten rounds with Tyson Fury. I think you need to speak with them yourself, sir. I got the impression that it was important to the case.'

Planting his hands flat on the desktop, Marilyn hefted himself to his feet. 'Fine.' He dropped his mobile into his suit jacket pocket. 'Remind me of their names, Cara.'

'Mrs Sharon Scuffil and her son, Niall.'

'Niall . . . Niall Scuffil. Why does that name ring a bell?'

'I don't know, sir.'

'No, sadly neither do I.'

The woman in reception was late forties, blonde hair dyed to a shade of platinum that reflected the unforgiving strip lights above her head with eye-wincing brightness. She was whippet-thin, wearing tight, distressed denim jeans and a sleek black leather biker jacket, glamorous in a mutton-esque kind of way, but with an air of dishevelment, as if she'd slept in her clothes. At significantly taller than six foot, her son towered over both her and Marilyn. He was broad-shouldered, square-jawed, blond and handsome, and Marilyn could imagine teenage girls melting for a piece of him, but for the purple-black bruises ringing each bloodshot eye, the puffy right cheek, and swollen, bloodied lip. His right arm was encased in a plaster cast to the elbow, and he was bent slightly at the waist, as if it hurt him to stand straight.

'Mrs Scuffil. I'm Detective Inspector Bobby Simmons. What can I do for you?'

Mrs Scuffil made no move to take Marilyn's outstretched hand. Spinning, she reached for the hem of her son's shirt.

'You need to arrest Parker for assault, right now.'

Her son stood, meek as an oversized baby, while she hauled his shirt up around his shoulder blades to show two burn spots on his chest. *Taser marks.* After this case, Marilyn could recognize them at a hundred paces. His gaze moved down the expanse of skin from the boy's breastbone to his waist, mottled with huge black and purple bruises.

'Tell me what happened.'

84

Robbie was standing in front of the bathroom mirror holding something up to his face. From where Jessie stood in the doorway, at an elliptical angle, she couldn't see what it was, couldn't see its reflection in the mirror either. She knew only that it was pale. One of Workman's white towels?

'Robbie.'

He spun around. And she saw.

Jesus Christ.

Lowering the mask from his face, he met her gaze. His eyes were bright.

'Robbie? What the . . .' *What the fuck?*

He glanced down at the dog mask clasped in his marble-pale hands.

'I found it in a box under my dad's bed.' His robotic voice barely there, the rise and fall of his shoulders exaggerated as if he was having difficulty catching his breath. 'There was other stuff too. A whole costume.' He balled a fist. 'And gloves, paw gloves with sharp steel claws embedded in them. I left everything, except for this.'

Jessie nodded, trying to maintain her composure, the image of that pale figure from the security camera at Paws for Thought rising in her mind, the images of the dead rising there also. The electric suit hissed hot across her skin and clenched cloyingly tight around her throat. She took a breath, trying to steady the crazed beating of her heart. She had to be calm, for him – for herself.

'When did you find them?'

'This afternoon. My dad went out for a run and I went through his things.'

'Why?'

Robbie lifted his shoulders. 'He's been acting odd for weeks. It's only the two of us, so I know. He's out running all the time in the evenings and I'm often asleep before he gets home. I'm prescribed melatonin. It knocks me out.'

'He's innocent until proven guilty, Robbie, and police make mistakes. It's early days in the process.'

Robbie nodded. 'Yes, I suppose . . .' he murmured.

There was something in his voice, an odd tone, an unsettling intonation that Jessie couldn't put her finger on.

'You need to give the mask to DI Simmons,' she said gently. 'It's very important evidence.'

'I shouldn't have taken it, should I?'

'No, you shouldn't have.'

'Will it be contaminated now? Will I have ruined the case against my father?'

Jessie shook her head. 'They have the stuff you left, the dog suit, and other evidence, DNA evidence.'

Robbie was looking at her oddly, his head tilted, green eyes shining.

'Do you want to ruin the case?' she asked softly.

He lifted his shoulders, the shrug strangely nonchalant. 'Not if he did what they said he did.'

'As I said, he's innocent until proven guilty.' Pulling a towel off the rail, she spread and held it out to him. 'Drop the mask in the towel, Robbie, and I'll call DI Simmons to say that we have it.'

Though Robbie nodded, he didn't move. His fingers were clasped tight around the mask as if he didn't want to let it go.

'Robbie. The mask.'

He still didn't move. It was as if the mask, everything it represented, had rooted him to the spot. The silence became a tangible shape, stretching between them. Jessie closed her towel-wrapped hand around the mask and, as she did so, images of the dogs at Paws for Thought rose in her mind.

They're loyal, faithful. Everyone has a place in the hierarchy and everyone is accepted for who they are.

I don't think he's dressing up as a dog – I think he wants to be a dog.

She thought of Eunice Hargreaves.

Huskies can withstand temperatures of minus sixty degrees centigrade, Dr Flynn.

So why had the perp tramped a kilometre through woods, in the middle of the night, to Eunice Hargreaves' cottage, to ensure that Lupo would be found?

Because he had humanity.

Her hands froze on the mask.

Because he was young and naive, and because he loved dogs . . . and was accepted and loved by them in return, far more than he had ever been accepted or loved by people.

431

She looked up into Robbie's pale face. Met that bright gaze.

'I'm sorry,' he said.

85

Sharon Scuffil dropped her son's shirt and spun back to face Marilyn.

'Late last night. It happened late last night. I was out . . . on a date. Niall called me to say that he'd been attacked. Parker came to our house and, when Niall opened the door, he hit him with one of those electric cattle prod things and beat him up.'

'Crazy,' Niall lisped, through his swollen, bloodied lip. 'He's fucking crazy.'

You'd be right there, son, Marilyn concurred silently.

'I told them outside,' Mrs Scuffil said. She flapped a midnight-blue-lacquered hand over her shoulder. 'I told them all.'

'The press?' Marilyn asked incredulously.

'Of course. Everyone needs to know.'

'We have Mr Parker in custody, Mrs Scuffil. Involving the press—' *any more than they already are* '—is very unhelpful.'

'I'm not interested in being helpful to the police. It's your job to help us—' She broke off. 'How did you know?'

'What? How did we know what?'

'To arrest Parker. We've only just come in. We've been at St Richard's Hospital all night and most of today getting Niall's injuries treated.'

'We have Parker in custody on a different charge, Mrs Scuffil, though I would like to take a formal statement from you and Niall.'

There was a blast of cold air and a sudden wall of clamouring voices as the station door opened, the noise muffled again as DS Workman stepped through, shutting it quickly and firmly behind her. She was breathing hard and looked shock-faced, as if she'd just run a modern-day gauntlet, which doubtless she had, courtesy of their friends from the media.

'They're everywhere,' she muttered, undoing the top button of her belted navy-blue overcoat, moving to skirt around them. Marilyn caught her eye and held up a finger, asking her to wait. He turned back to Sharon Scuffil.

'Detective Sergeant Workman here will take your statement. Just give her a moment to take off her coat and get settled.'

Marilyn saw Workman's eyes snap from Sharon Scuffil to her son, linger, a look of pure disgust overtaking her face. Light suddenly illuminated the dark corners of his mind, where previously there had been none. He narrowed his gaze.

'I remember why I recognize your name, son.' He addressed himself to Niall. 'You're the schoolboy who bullied Robbie Parker, the boy who broke his leg.'

'That was a bad tackle on the football pitch,' Sharon Scuffil snapped. 'My son isn't a bully.'

'You also broke his arm,' Workman said, stepping forward. 'I took the statement from Allan Parker myself.'

Marilyn was watching Niall Scuffil. His feet appeared suddenly to fascinate him, given the intensity with which he was studying them.

'I don't care what report you have. If my son has ever had cause to raise a hand to Robbie Parker it would entirely have been in self-defence. That boy is totally mad. For Christ's sake, look what he did.' She jabbed her son in the small of his back. 'Stop staring at your feet like some hopeless bloody wet blanket, Niall, and tell the detective what Robbie Parker did to you.'

Marilyn's head was aching. A night spent interviewing Allan Parker under the judgemental gaze of DCS Janet Backastowe was starting to look appealing. 'What Allan Parker did?' he corrected wearily.

'What?' Sharon Scuffil snapped. 'What on earth are you talking about?'

'You've come in to make a complaint about Allan Parker. I thought you said that Allan Parker did this to you?'

'Niall, look at the detective and tell him what happened. You said it was Robbie who did this to you.'

Niall nodded. 'Robbie.'

'It wasn't his father?' Marilyn pressed.

The boy, still refusing to meet his eye, shook his head. 'Robbie,' he lisped. 'I opened the door and he jammed this thing, this electric prod, in my chest. I collapsed and he went batshit fucking crazy. Kicking me, punching me, stamping on me. He's fucking mad, man. He's totally fucking mad.'

Jesus, Marilyn thought. *The bloody Parkers.* The kid must have found his dad's Taser, thought he'd take the opportunity to even up some scores. Had he sensed – been influenced by – his father's dysfunction? Had his father encouraged

435

him to finally stand up for himself? Embark on his own, more minor, rampage of revenge?

'As I said, DS Workman will take a statement from you,' Marilyn reiterated, waving Workman over.

He took the stairs back up to his office two at a time, pulling his mobile from his pocket as he jogged, jamming his finger on Jessie Flynn's number. A ringtone, on and on, unanswered, then a flip to voicemail.

'Call me urgently,' Marilyn snapped. 'I've got some information for you about Robbie Parker.'

86

Panting and shaking, her head throbbing as if it had been cleaved in two with an axe, Jessie came to, lying on Workman's bathroom floor. An explosion of pain as her exploratory fingers found a fleshy section at the back of her skull, came away coated in scarlet. Rolling onto her stomach, she felt for the edge of the bath and hauled herself gingerly to sitting, the room spinning at the movement, her mouth filling with vomit which she gulped back down. The bathroom door was shut, locked from the outside, she realized, when she crawled over and reached for the handle. Was Robbie outside, waiting, listening? Or had he gone, run?

'Robbie? Robbie, are you there?'

No reply. Only the throb of her own manic pulse in her ears. Then a voice, barely a murmur.

'I'm going to tell you a story about a boy called Sam and his dog, Buddy.'

'Karma?' she murmured, when he had finished.

'Yes, karma.'

'How did you find out about them . . . about Sam and Buddy?'

'My dad keeps a diary, in a locked box, hidden under his bed. A confession, I suppose it is. He keeps photographs of my mother in the same box. And some of me when I was tiny, back when I used to smile. I found it a year ago.'

'And you unlocked the box?'

'I taught myself to pick locks when I was ten, simple ones at first, like my dad's box. Then more complex ones. I have a lot of time on my hands and the Internet is a great teacher.'

'So the murders, framing your dad, was karma? For Sam and Buddy?'

'For them . . . but for me too. I was born as I was, a deformed loser who was always going to be bullied to punish him for what he had done. To punish him for being a bully and driving a boy to his death. And I am now his karma . . . their karma. They deserved it, Hugo Fuller, Daniel Whitehead, Simon Lewin. Bullies deserve it – all of it. You told me that, too, didn't you? Take the head off the snake and the body dies.'

'I didn't mean murder—'

'What did you mean?'

What had she meant? Violence? Yes, she felt so strongly about bullies that violence was exactly what she'd meant.

A soft laugh. 'Don't worry, Dr Flynn, it's not your fault. I decided to inflict karma on those men long before I met you. I decided it the day I found my dad's diary and I've been planning and preparing ever since.'

He's been watching them . . . Watching and waiting. Planning.

'And the women?'

'I didn't want to kill Claudine. I knocked her out, but she came to and surprised me, pulled my mask off, so I had no choice. I met her at Age UK. She was a good person, kind. I didn't want to take the same risk with Eleanor Whitehead, and she did choose to marry a murderer.'

'You didn't kill Denise Lewin, did you?' Jessie said, clarity flooding the places in her mind where there had been none. 'Your father did. He found out what you were doing, dressed in your dog outfit, murdered Denise and left Leo at Paws for Thought, with the clue – the hair – in the mask Leo was wearing so that the police would catch him, blame him for all the murders.'

'He realized that I'd read his diary, that I knew everything. He's been able to track my mobile via the Find My iPhone app for years. Given my history of being bullied, he likes to know where I am.'

'And you knew that he could track you?'

'Sure. I often go out at night, walk through the countryside. I like the solitude. He knows that I've been visiting Paws for Thought for months, letting myself in, spending time with the dogs. He didn't like it, didn't like me breaking in, but he never tried to stop me. He knows that I love animals and he was pleased that I had finally found somewhere I enjoyed being, where I was safe. He wasn't suspicious until the night the Whiteheads died. He must have tracked me, found out where I was.' Another soft laugh. 'Too late though.'

'And Denise?'

'He drugged me with my melatonin that night, put it in a bottle of beer he gave me as a treat, I think, so that he could kill her and frame himself for the murders, save me. The ultimate sacrifice. He didn't know that I was wearing his trainers when I murdered the Fullers and Whiteheads, that I was going to frame him anyway. He's always been a fool. A weak, cowardly fool – and guilty. I have no sympathy for him and I have no sympathy for them.' Silence for a moment. 'I paid Niall Scuffil a visit last night too.'

'Niall Scuffil? The boy who led the bullying against you?'

'Yes. The head of the snake.'

'You didn't—' she broke off. Jesus, had Robbie killed Niall too? Killed a fifteen-year-old boy?

'No, I didn't kill him, if that's what you're asking, though only because I couldn't frame my father for the other murders if I had.' Another soft laugh. 'I wanted to, though. I really fucking wanted to.'

'I'm glad that you didn't kill him, Robbie.' God, what an insane understatement.

'I'm not.'

Silence again, then, 'Thank you for helping me, Dr Flynn.'

Thank you for helping me. And she *had* helped him, but not in the way that she had intended. They had all helped him. Her. Workman. Even Marilyn. *Jesus.* What should she say? It's a pleasure? *Fuck.* Why hadn't she sensed that he wasn't all he seemed to be?

'Robbie, please unlock the door so that we can talk properly.'

'Goodbye, Dr Flynn.'

'Robbie.'

Silence.

'*Robbie.*'

Silence still.

Twisting onto her back, Jessie slammed the sole of her boot hard against the wood, close to the lock. Pain ricocheted up her leg, jarring through her body, slopping her aching brain around inside her damaged skull. Taking a breath, she pulled her leg back again, slammed harder. Slammed again and again until the wood around the lock splintered.

87

Every light in Workman's thatched cottage burned now, and Jessie could see figures moving around inside, the ceiling lights throwing huge, malevolent-looking shapes of their shadows on the opaque linen curtains.

'Fuck,' Marilyn said, with feeling. 'How the hell did we not see it?' He glanced across; Jessie studiously ignored his gaze. 'You talked to him, for God's sake.'

Jessie bit down on the shrug that was threatening to lift her shoulders, knowing that the movement would be a red rag to Marilyn's stamping, bellowing bull.

Hindsight's a wonderful thing. She didn't say that either, but now that she looked back, should she have been able to recognize that Robbie had murdered the Fullers and the Whiteheads? That Robbie had been the pale figure at one with the dogs?

Dogs in a pack have each other's backs and support each other unfailingly against outside aggressors.

Everything that Robbie didn't have in his human life. Everything that he wanted, that anyone wanted: only to be accepted for who they were, to fit in, to belong – somewhere.

Should she have known?

Jessie had met many disturbed people over the course of her working life – was disturbed herself, she knew, however hard she had tried to paper over her own psychological cracks. But Robbie, how he'd survived the abandonment by his mother and the ferocious bullying that had defined his childhood, what he had done to avenge a child who had been bullied as ruthlessly as he had, to punish his father for his involvement, was a level apart, far beyond any psychological dysfunction she had experienced. But having said that, it also all made sense. A hideous, warped, sick, logical kind of sense. Sense for a boy whose life had been destroyed by abandonment and bullying.

His finally taking revenge on Niall Scuffil also made perfect sense and, as he'd said, letting Niall live still allowed him to frame his father for the murders. He could doubtless have told the police, her, Marilyn, that Allan had goaded him into taking revenge, and that Allan's coercion, in addition to the atmosphere of dysfunction in his home, and finding his father's Taser, had finally propelled him to do so.

A blinding wash of light as the police helicopter flew overhead, the thwack-thwack of its rotor blades muffling the barks of the police dogs as they fanned out over the fields behind Workman's cottage. The helicopter was now searching the woods a few hundred metres to their right, Jessie saw, lighting up the swaying canopy of leaves with the gargantuan spotlight hanging from its belly that had robbed her of her night vision.

Would they find him? The dogs? The helicopter? The

uniforms being yanked off other duties and given hurried instructions no more complex than, *Find him?* Whatever it takes, *Find him.* If the investigation into the deaths of those two little girls had been a shit-show for Marilyn's career, this threatened to blow it wide open, no chance of reprieve ever, if Robbie escaped.

Unless. Unless, Jessie took the blame.

'I should have known,' she said, swinging around to face him. 'I'm sorry. It was my fault that Robbie got away. I let you and the investigation down and I'll take the blame.'

'I don't need you to do that, Jessie. I'm the SIO on this case. The buck stops with me.'

'I want to.'

'This isn't about blame, Jessie. It's about both of us trying to do our jobs to the best of our abilities, in very difficult circumstances. We're both human, we both make mistakes and this—' His hand curved an arc through the dark, cold air. 'None of this was textbook. There were no records about that boy Sam Garry's death, so we never could have found the cause of all this. And there were no obvious connections between the four men, apart from them being approximately the same ages. They met at West Sands Funfair in Selsey one summer, started hanging out, Allan Parker told us.' His hand found her shoulder. 'However good a psychologist you are, and you are a great psychologist by the way, one talk with Robbie Parker could never give you an idea of what lay beneath.'

'I know. But even so, if heads roll, if a head needs to roll, it should be mine.'

'We'll see.' He gave her a slightly sick-looking smile. 'We have Allan Parker in custody, so we have Denise Lewin's murderer, at least.'

He had too much pride, Jessie knew, to pass the buck on to anyone else, even if she was happy to bear it. It was one of the things – one of the many things – that she admired about him.

'It's a moot point anyway. He won't get away.' Fumbling in his suit pocket, he extracted a packet of cigarettes and a lighter. 'Clean living is overrated,' he muttered, catching her look. The lighter's flame leapt behind his hand, the stream of smoke that replaced its firefly glow swirling into the night sky. 'Remember that discussion we had about sociopaths and psychopaths?' he continued, after a moment.

'Yes.'

'Robbie Parker is a sociopath.'

'He's not a sociopath.'

'Isn't he? The bullying — he didn't fit in.'

'You'd be bullied if you looked like he does. If you were as kind and gentle as he is.'

Marilyn almost choked on his next drag. 'Kind and gentle. Are you insane?'

Probably. She shook her head. 'This isn't a chicken-and-egg question, Marilyn. The bullying made Robbie who he was, made him dysfunctional. First off, he was abandoned by the *one person* in his life who is supposed to love him unconditionally, his mother, and then he was ferociously bullied for the whole of his childhood. Bullying is never the victim's fault, Marilyn, and there is no excuse for it.'

She stared hard at the shadow puppet show playing out across Workman's pale linen curtains, knowing that Marilyn would be eyeballing her, an incredulous expression on his face. But she had no intention of letting him see the hurt and anger in her eyes, the deep-down, long-since-buried self-hatred that meeting Robbie had caused to resurface.

444

The electric suit hummed, searing her skin, despite the chill wind cutting across the surrounding fields.

'He murdered four people in the most gruesome way possible and two of the people he murdered – the women, the wives – were innocent. His father murdered a third woman, poor bloody Denise Lewin, to frame himself for the murders his son had committed because he had no idea that Robbie was already framing him by stamping all over every crime scene in his trainers. The women's only crime was to marry wankers and if every woman who married a wanker was murdered, we'd be tripping over dead bodies with every step.' He took a long drag, huffed out a cloud of smoke. 'Have I missed anything out?'

'No, I think you've pretty much nailed it,' Jessie said, without enthusiasm. Her rational mind concurred with everything that Marilyn was saying. But her unconscious mind? Her emotional mind? She would never admit it out loud, but a maverick part of her wanted Robbie to escape. To win. 'Allan Parker is still saying that he's guilty for all five murders, isn't he?' she murmured. 'Claiming responsibility.'

'He clearly blames himself for Robbie's actions and is still trying to protect him.'

'Is he? Or is he trying to find redemption?'

'Revenge isn't worthy, Jessie. It might be very human, but it's not worthy.'

Jessie shook her head. 'It wasn't about revenge. For Robbie it was about karma – delivering karma. He believed that he was born disfigured and had to endure a childhood defined by bullying as karma for his father's role in bullying and ultimately killing that boy . . . Sam . . . twenty-five years ago, and that it was also his responsibility to deliver that karma to the others involved.'

445

Cut the head off the snake. Bullies are snakes. Take off the head and the body dies.

Sam hadn't been able to do that for himself. Hadn't had the strength, the opportunity. And because of that, he had been driven to his death. How many other children had died or had their lives destroyed by bullying since Sam? Tens of thousands? Hundreds of thousands? A million? A million lost souls?

'Bullying is never OK.' She wasn't sure, until she sensed Marilyn look across again, whether she'd said it out loud or only thought it. 'There is never an excuse. Never. Not *ever.*'

'Did you not see them?' His voice was incredulous. 'Were you not there? Hugo and Claudine Fuller? Daniel and Eleanor Whitehead?'

'You know I was there.'

'And?'

Had what she had seen been so gruesome, so much – too much – that it had blunted her emotions? A baptism of fire so unreal that, deep down, she still couldn't believe it had been real?

'Those men and Allan Parker killed. They tortured another child and his dog for many many years and then drove him to his death.'

'It's not classified as murder. It's manslaughter at the most, if that.'

She spun around to face him. 'Well it should have been, should be, classified as murder. Because when children drive another child to suicide due to bullying, they are wholly responsible for that death.'

'People get away with heinous crimes every day, Jessie, and the law is an ass. But the fact remains that Robbie

446

Parker is a mass murderer and it is my job – our jobs, given that you are working for Surrey and Sussex Major Crimes – to bring him to justice.'

Jessie didn't answer for a few long moments. 'I'm sorry,' she murmured eventually. 'For the outburst. It was unprofessional.' But even as she said it, that maverick part of her was still with Robbie, wherever he was now, hoping, slightly hoping, that he got to win just this one time.

88

There was a pale shape at the end of the jetty by the lifeboat shed, an immobile disc that glowed luminously in the moonlight. Jessie approached slowly, her arms wrapped tightly across her chest, as much from apprehension as to stave off the biting wind that tore down the hood of her puffa jacket and whipped her hair around her head. The gnarled wooden planks creaked beneath her feet with each step, and with the weight of water swelling against the jetty's pilings.

Should she have told Marilyn that she was coming here? Probably. But at the moment, she felt as if she owed Surrey and Sussex Major Crimes nothing. They had cut her out of the final part of the investigation – *Your work is done* – so it felt like quid pro quo. And her intuition might be wrong anyway. Robbie might be taking cover in an outhouse somewhere up on the Downs, be concealing himself in thick woods, or he might have returned to Paws for Thought to live out the final few moments of freedom with his pack. She was no Baba Vanga, after all.

She had left Marilyn outside Workman's house, using the

after-effects of Robbie's stun-gun attack, which lingered in the burns on her chest and in the thumping headache that refused to subside, as an excuse for leaving. There had been no need for her to stay anyway, watching impotently as the police search played out.

'I'll let you know when we catch him,' Marilyn had said. *When* not *if*.

She had nodded. 'Please do.' Hadn't been able to bring herself to add, 'Good luck.'

Also, she'd had a strong sense that Robbie would have planned every detail of these murders from beginning to end, that he would never allow himself to be caught.

The pale, luminous disc was a mask, Jessie realized, when she reached it. A dog's mask. Robbie's mask. And underneath, she saw, when she slid the sleeve of her puffa jacket over her hand, ducked down and moved the mask to one side, an iPhone. She pressed her index finger on the home button and the screen lit up. Not Robbie's face staring back at her, but a picture she recognized: a little black and white Jack-Russell-type dog hiding underneath an upturned fishing boat. Hiding from Hugo Fuller. From Simon Lewin. From Daniel Whitehead. And from Allan Parker.

Slipping the mobile into her pocket, she stood and leant over the worn metal railing, looking out to sea. Only a relentless procession of black waves rolling towards her, their tops whipped into a milky froth by the wind. And further out, scattered pinpricks of red, green and white lights, the navigation lights of fishing boats and of the container ships that ploughed through the Solent day and night.

Was Robbie out there too? All the way out there on the horizon, his body dragged that far by the current? Or had he duped them all again? As much as she believed that he would never allow himself to be caught, she had an equally strong, disquieting sense that nothing he had experienced in the first fifteen years of his life would make him think that the next sixty-five were worth sticking around for.

'I'm sorry,' she murmured, not quite knowing who she was saying it to.

Robbie, certainly. But them too. The people he had killed – the women at least. Perhaps if Workman had asked her a few months ago, she would have been able to save him. Save him, and save them.

Or perhaps not.

Perhaps, he was already too far gone by then. Too damaged. Too broken.

Bullying is never OK. There is never an excuse.

Leaning over the railing, she opened her hand and let the mask fall.

'Goodbye, Robbie,' she murmured. 'Wherever you're going, go safely.'

Pulling her mobile from her pocket, she dialled Marilyn's number.

89

By tacit agreement they spoke about nothing substantial on the drive from Frimley Park Hospital to the pub. In lieu of the dinner they had missed out on last night, Jessie had booked lunch, dithering about where to go, not knowing what the MRI and other tests had revealed, what mood Callan would be in, or if he would yet have made a decision about his future. She had finally plumped for the safe option and booked their favourite table by the fire, in their favourite pub, close to home in the Surrey Hills.

In truth, she felt beyond exhausted herself, heavy and sluggish in mind and body, as if she was hefting a sack of rocks around in her brain and on each shoulder. She'd had no sleep last night – another night of no sleep – and had spent half the night at the lifeboat station in Selsey with Marilyn. Half an hour after she'd called him, he'd arrived with the cavalry – two vanloads of uniforms to comb the beach, a police helicopter and two RNLI B-class rigid inflatable lifeboats to comb the water. She had waited for them on the beach, crouching in the shelter of an upturned fishing boat, staring out to sea, her body deadening with immobility and cold. Paying her quiet respects to Robbie before all hell broke loose. He deserved that, at least, for how he had lived the first fourteen years of his life, if not for the last year.

She had debated coming up with some bullshit excuse to explain why she'd driven out to Selsey on her own, why she'd lied to Marilyn about heading home nursing her cracked skull. But, in the end, she decided that she didn't care enough to lie, that her duplicity was fair payback for him cutting her out of Allan Parker's arrest, whatever the hell DCI Janet bloody Backastowe had thought, said or commanded.

The day was dull and cold, ponderous grey clouds hanging so low in the sky that she felt as if she stood on tiptoes and reached up, her fingertips would be swallowed in dense grey candyfloss. By the time she reached Frimley Park, it was raining, fat globs splattering the windscreen. She parked Callan's car as close as she could get to the hospital, then she and Lupo dashed through the rain to the entrance where they found Callan skulking under the awning outside like some degenerate teenager. He grinned when he saw them, ducked down and hugged Lupo.

'He looks good,' he said, straightening and wrapping his arms around her. 'You look good too.'

Jessie rolled her eyes. 'Is this what I'm going to have to get used to? Playing second fiddle to a huge, hairy lump of a creature?'

'Less of that – I shaved this morning.'

'Ha bloody ha.' She grinned. He seemed happier than when she had left him yesterday evening, as if a weight had been lifted. Was it too much to hope that he'd had good news? She didn't want to ask yet, risk breaking the heady spell of the moment. They sprinted back to the car, holding hands, towing Lupo behind them.

'No need to ask why you brought my car and not yours,' Callan said, catching sight of the forest of white hairs on his back seat.

'He's blowing his coat.' Jessie suppressed a smile. 'Anyway, the hairs just add to the general ambience created by the crisp packets, chocolate bar wrappers and empty Coke cans.'

'So . . . how are you?' they both asked, in unison, when they were settled in the pub next to the fire.

Jessie shook her head. 'You first.'

'No – you.' Callan reached for her hand. 'Marilyn phoned me a while ago.'

She frowned. 'At the hospital? Why?'

'He's worried about you. He thought you might need some . . . how did he put it . . . emotional support.'

'What the fuck? He quite happily cut me out of the arrest and interviews with Allan Parker and then he decides that I need emotional support.'

'Don't be too harsh on Marilyn. He genuinely cares about you. And the case was a fait accompli anyway, or at least they thought it was, until you showed them otherwise.'

'Found out otherwise is a more accurate way of putting it.' The fingers of her free hand unconsciously found the two burns on her chest from Robbie Parker's stun gun. 'I don't actually care now, anyway. Last night, it seemed so important to be involved every step of the way and I was furious with Marilyn. And then I found out the truth and none of the small stuff mattered any more.' She paused. 'You know that Robbie Parker killed himself, then, obviously. One of the lifeboats found his body.'

Callan nodded. 'Marilyn told me.'

'I'm so angry with myself that I didn't work it out.'

'It wasn't obvious.'

'No, but I should have been able to work out why Lupo was left outside Eunice Hargreaves' cottage. Robbie knew her from Age UK's lunch club, must have heard her talking about her insomnia. That was why he chose her cottage, because he knew she'd see Lupo almost immediately.' She gave a wry smile. 'It was nothing to do with the handy lamp post outside her gate. Taking Lupo to safety, risking getting caught because of it, showed a naivety that didn't gel with the murderer being a ruthless adult . . . anyone ruthless in fact.'

'I'm not sure Marilyn, or the people Robbie Parker murdered, would agree with your diagnosis that he was lacking in ruthlessness.'

Jessie lifted her shoulders. 'Bullying destroys lives, Callan, and Robbie is . . . was an example of that. If he hadn't been so severely mentally damaged by bullying, he wouldn't have killed. It may be a harsh truth, but it's still a truth.'

'You liked him, didn't you?'

'I'm not excusing what he did, but, yes, I did like him and I did sympathize with him. Sympathize and empathize with him.' She held Callan's hand, looking off over his shoulder, feeling too vulnerable suddenly to meet his eye. 'Anyway, enough of Robbie Parker. It's your turn to talk.'

Callan ruffled Lupo's head with his free hand.

'And given that you're patting your living comfort blanket, I assume that the news isn't great,' Jessie said, chewing her lip.

Callan shook his head. 'Actually, it's not as bad as I expected. The bullet has moved and created swelling in my brain, which is why my epilepsy has worsened. But it hasn't moved as much as my neurologist thought it might have done. On balance, he decided that it's better to wait, see how it goes, rather than operating now.'

Jessie's eyes hung closed for a brief moment. *Thank God.*

'But I am going to resign my commission.'

'When?'

'Tomorrow.'

'Why so soon?'

'Because there's no point in delaying. I've made up my mind and, to be fair, I don't have a choice. I've been living on borrowed time since I came back from Afghanistan. I can't keep lying to people I've worked with for years, people who trust me, because at some point I'll have an epileptic fit at work and I can't control when that happens. I might put my colleagues in danger and it's not fair to do that.'

'Can't you stay in the military police and get a—' She was about to say, *an admin job*, but she knew that he never would. Asking Callan to be happy with an admin job would be like sending Lupo to live in the Sahara Desert. 'What are you going to do then?'

He ruffled Lupo's head again. 'Hang out with my main man and think about what to do next.'

'Well hopefully Marilyn won't come knocking for a while and I can just see my private clinical patients and hang out with both my main men too.'

Callan rolled his eyes. 'I wouldn't bet on that, if I were you.'

Jessie smiled back sweetly. 'Lucky I'm not a betting woman then, isn't it?'

Acknowledgements

It is always hard to know where to start with acknowledgements as the list of people who have helped me, both with this novel and with my entire writing career, is long and humbling.

Thanks to my amazing agent, Will Francis, who is incredibly and enduringly supportive, and to the rest of the wonderful team at Janklow and Nesbit (UK).

I am indebted to Julia Wisdom, my Publisher at HarperCollins, for being such a great champion for the Dr Jessie Flynn crime thriller series and for her patience, enthusiasm and insight. I thoroughly enjoyed working with Finn Cotton, my original Assistant Editor, who has moved on to pastures new within HarperCollins, though I am delighted to have the opportunity to work with Sophie Churcher, his exceptionally capable and enthusiastic replacement. Massive thanks also to publicity guru Felicity Denham, Rhian McKay who has an unrivalled eye for detail, and the rest of the fabulous team at HarperCollins. It is a privilege to work with you all and a dream that I never thought would become reality.

I am lucky to be part of the Killer Women group of female crime writers who are a hugely encouraging and fun writing community.

Thank you to all my friends who have been so supportive throughout life's journey, writing and otherwise – it has been lovely having you all along for the ride. Thanks also to my great friends Daniel and Eleanor Whitehead for being kind enough to lend me your names and for not being horrified at your brutal and untimely demise!

Love always to my family, Pamela, Maggie, Daan, Charlie, William, Jo, Isabel, Anna, Alexander and my late father, Derek, who appeared in this novel as Eunice Hargreaves' beloved husband. I miss you even more than Eunice misses your fictional counterpart. Lots of love and massive thanks to my own beloved husband, Anthony. I am very lucky to have you.

Most of all, thank you to the readers who pick up *The Watcher* – enjoy. I would not be able to continue doing what I love without you. And please do track me down via social media. I love hearing from readers and am always up for a chat.